The Legacy
of the Lost Rider

TOKENS OF RYNAR SERIES,
BOOK 1

Amanda L. Henry

Copyright © 2022 Amanda L. Henry.

All rights reserved. No part of this book may be used or reproduced by any means, graphic, electronic, or mechanical, including photocopying, recording, taping or by any information storage retrieval system without the written permission of the author except in the case of brief quotations embodied in critical articles and reviews.

This is a work of fiction. All of the characters, names, incidents, organizations, and dialogue in this novel are either the products of the author's imagination or are used fictitiously.

WestBow Press books may be ordered through booksellers or by contacting:

WestBow Press
A Division of Thomas Nelson & Zondervan
1663 Liberty Drive
Bloomington, IN 47403
www.westbowpress.com
844-714-3454

Because of the dynamic nature of the Internet, any web addresses or links contained in this book may have changed since publication and may no longer be valid. The views expressed in this work are solely those of the author and do not necessarily reflect the views of the publisher, and the publisher hereby disclaims any responsibility for them.

Any people depicted in stock imagery provided by Getty Images are models, and such images are being used for illustrative purposes only.
Certain stock imagery © Getty Images.

Interior Image Credit: Casi Erin Gray

ISBN: 978-1-6642-7380-1 (sc)
ISBN: 978-1-6642-7382-5 (hc)
ISBN: 978-1-6642-7381-8 (e)

Library of Congress Control Number: 2022914028

Print information available on the last page.

WestBow Press rev. date: 08/15/2022

Dedicated to my grandparents
Emil and Annabel Henry, and
Vincel and Anita Allee
for their love and support
and Christ-honoring examples.

In special memory of Anita Allee,
who shared her love of writing with me.

Acknowledgments

I would like to thank my dear friend, Casi Erin Gray, for her assistance with the cover art and for several of the interior images. Although I created the map, I valued her work with the text and the banners for the different realms.

I also want to thank family members and colleagues who supported me in this endeavor. They provided precious encouragement and feedback during my writing.

Will and Gabriella,

Thank you for your support!

[signature]

10/26/22

Booster Gala — 11/12/22

Farcost
Lord Atregar

Trineth
Lord Edgerr

Ettidor
Lord Beristo

Sassot
Lord Felond

Monterr
Lord Tolem

Fortur
Lord Salistom

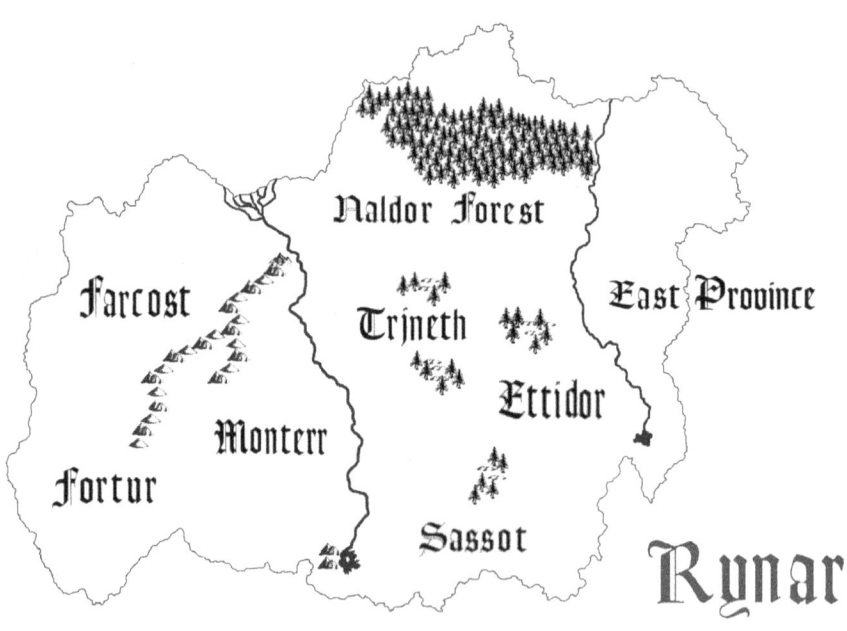

Prologue

From a window opening to the radiant surface of Miritor Lake, Sir Oreloc gazed out upon the small ship sailing toward the castle of Valmontes. The wind stirred the blue banner waving from the mast. Flashing in the sunlight, a golden gull stretched its wings across the ship's bow.

Sir Oreloc faced the approaching vessel with a set jaw and a narrowed gaze as his hand reached down, clasping the hilt of his sword. A long, jagged scar ran from the left side of his face down his cheek and over his jaw. A fitting remembrance of the costly victory that ended twelve years of war for Rynar or so its bearer thought whenever he caught sight of his disfigurement.

He turned his gaze away from the ship long enough to observe the sun as it shone above the western mountains. The water of the Miritor gleamed under these formidable giants as it flowed around the island. On the northernmost edge of the lake, the water swept down into the Septamar River, which traversed many hundreds of miles until the mouth of the river poured out into the Selgoa Ocean.

But here on the island in the Miritor, protected by the mountains and deep water, the castle of the king of Rynar remained secure. No enemy had ever crossed the lake. No marauder had set foot on this stretch of land. *Not until today*, Sir Oreloc thought.

Blue standards marked by a golden lion waved from the towers of Valmontes, and Sir Oreloc surveyed them with a grim expression. The approaching ship reached the dock below the castle, and the men stepping off that ship strode forward under a different banner.

Sensing the presence of another person, he turned and then bowed. King Eisron walked into the corridor and joined him near the window. Sunlight illuminated the weariness in the king's face produced by age and recent hardships.

"Their arrival came sooner than I expected. It seems that they did not waste any time after receiving an invitation," he said, looking out at the ship.

"This journey has been a part of their plans for over a year, your majesty. The Evaliscan princes are as arrogant as they are ambitious. If they had not felt it necessary to wait for your consent, they would have been at our doors months ago."

"Sir Oreloc, reconcile yourself to their presence in Rynar. For the sake of our people, we cannot refuse their help … not after the devastation that has followed the war with Petrigor."

"My concern is for the people and for you, sire. Must we defeat one invader to welcome another?" Sir Oreloc asked as he turned to the king. "I would rather face another army from Petrigor than honor these Evaliscans."

He gestured toward the six figures disembarking from the ship with guards and attendants following them. Each one of the princes was a young man between the ages of seventeen and thirty, and even from a distance, their ornaments and fine clothes were apparent.

"They seek to claim what they have neither earned nor deserved," Sir Oreloc continued. "And if I have said more than I should against your decision to grant them an audience, it is only because I cannot be silent when thieves are invited into your hall."

"I understood their ambitions after reading the first of many letters sent to this castle," King Eisron assured him. "And for a time, I cast their letters in the fire, despising them as you do. But then I saw our people struggling in poverty, the fields remaining burnt and bare, and the houses of the nobles standing empty. The war destroyed so much of Rynar that we cannot recover from it alone. And if we choose to turn these Evaliscans away, they may go to Petrigor and help our enemies rise again to crush Rynar."

Sir Oreloc said nothing, raising no argument with the king's concerns.

"I hope that I may continue to trust one of my few remaining knights to aid me in the coming years," King Eisron said. "Even when he disapproves of my decisions."

"You have my loyalty, your majesty. Give me a command, and I will serve you faithfully as I have in the past."

"While I live, I would have you at my side here in Valmontes," the king said. "I need someone I can trust near at hand. But when I die, you must disappear. A time of change will come for Rynar with these Evaliscans, and I shall rely on you to carry our hopes beyond their reach."

As he watched the king with a questioning gaze, Sir Oreloc started to speak, but the king held up his hand and directed his attention to the Evaliscans approaching the entrance to the castle.

"We will speak more of this later. Go down and see to it that they find their way to the great hall."

Sir Oreloc bowed and strode toward the steps leading to the base of the tower. After his descent, he followed a long corridor and reached two massive wooden doors. The guards opened them upon his command, and he saw the

Evaliscan princes walking up the steps with their attendants. At the front of the procession walked a prince with long dark hair and a well-trimmed beard. He seemed older than the others, and his amber eyes scrutinized the people around him with a gleam of interest.

A sense of revulsion filled Sir Oreloc as he watched this prince and the others enjoy the stares of the people outside the castle. Many of the Rynarians bowed after catching sight of the bright clothes, the gold rings, and the silver crests worn by the princes, but when the strangers reached Sir Oreloc, he remained standing and greeted them with a cold gaze.

"His Majesty King Eisron is ready to speak with you."

"Our voyage demanded that we travel many days and through rough seas. Then we had to cross miles of your land in the south before we reached the edge of the lake," one of the younger of the six answered. "You should first take us to our rooms so that we may rest and refresh ourselves before meeting with the king."

"Were you not offered refreshment and rest upon our ship that carried you across the lake? Have your horses not received attention from our men?"

"Perhaps the messengers you receive here are accustomed to having demands made upon their time, but we are the sons of the King of Evalisca. Show us to our rooms."

Sir Oreloc shot the speaker a glare and gestured for them to continue inside the great hall.

"Your meeting with the king will determine whether you will be staying or whether you will be back on that ship before the day has ended. If the latter, you will have no rooms here."

With a resentful glint in his eyes, the young guest closed his mouth and followed the others into a furnished hall of stone with windows casting warm light onto the floor. His older brother with dark hair and beard said nothing, having watched the exchange in silence.

At the end of the hall, a set of stairs rose up to a dais, and there King Eisron of Rynar sat upon his throne. In his right hand, he held his gold scepter with a tight grip. It had been passed down from his ancestors, eventually becoming a sign for the royal house of Rynar. It was shaped more like a spear than a scepter, and its tip was crafted from a rare, white gem called a zalist.

When the Evaliscan princes had drawn near enough to the stairs, they bowed, and the dark-haired man at the front spoke,

"Congratulations on your victory over the armies of Petrigor, Your Majesty, and may the standard of Rynar always fly above your land with pride. I am

Prince Mastren of Evalisca. My brothers and I are pleased to be welcomed into your kingdom to help you celebrate the end of a difficult war for your people."

The king raised a well-worn roll of parchment in his left hand as his gaze rested on Prince Mastren.

"Such was the message I received in one of your many letters requesting an invitation to my court. But why do you wish to celebrate a victory which you had no part of? Your father, King Teyres of Evalisca, refused to offer aid to my people during the war, and now you present yourselves as my allies?"

"We asked our father to send you supplies and men, but he would not hear our requests," the prince answered. "Yet now that the war is over, he no longer forbids us from visiting your court and seeking to help you. We know that twelve years of war have diminished the splendor and glory of your kingdom. It is our desire to return Rynar to its former greatness."

King Eisron turned his gaze from them to glance at his guards and attendants standing along the edge of the hall. All of them were women and men beyond their prime, and he appeared the oldest of them all with his gray hair and beard surrounding a careworn face lined with wrinkles.

"I cannot deny that we have spent all of our wealth to attain victory against those who first attacked our coasts. And the strength of my people died with our young men in battle. Even my own son and heir has been lost."

Prince Mastren stepped closer with a sympathetic gaze.

"If only your troubles were those of our father, who has many heirs but only one kingdom. Here you see all of his sons except for the eldest who remains in Evalisca. We have each been promised an inheritance of great wealth, but only the eldest will be granted the throne."

"And what can I offer you?" the king asked with a furrowed brow. "A chance to fight among yourselves for my lands and bring further destruction upon my people?"

"Your lands are vast, your majesty, exceeding even Evalisca in size. There may be six of us, but we could still divide your kingdom among ourselves and be content."

An abrupt and scornful laugh escaped the king's lips.

"Content? I have never known young princes to be content. Nor am I such a fool as to imagine that six kings could live peacefully so near to each other. Yet, even if I gave you the land, would you not also take my people? Dividing them among yourselves when they should remain unified?"

Prince Mastren's expression darkened.

"We sailed to Rynar seeking to help you because you are our father's uncle.

But if you have no use for our inheritance, then we shall leave you and your kingdom to sink into further decline and ruin."

Raising his hand, King Eisron spoke again,

"Peace, there is a place for you here, and I am willing to grant you land and authority. But not the highest authority."

"Your people will need a king when you are gone," one of the other six brothers said pushing his way forward.

Prince Mastren seized his arm to silence him.

"And that is why you came here, isn't it?" the king said. "To take the throne of your aging kinsman? But I shall not relinquish it so easily. Perhaps I am old, but I am not on the threshold of death yet."

"Then what would you have us be?" Prince Mastren asked. "We will not use our inheritances to help Rynar without something in return."

"You shall be lords … six lords, each with his own lands and estate, but all serving the same kingdom, so that Rynar may live on, and my people may have peace."

"You intend to reduce princes to mere lords?"

"In Evalisca, you are princes, but in my land, you are nothing unless I raise you to distinction. And if you seek to challenge my authority, you will find that defending my rule is an army, battered though it has been by war."

"We did not come here to challenge your rule, but is it wrong for us to wish to be more than lowly thanes in your kingdom?" Prince Mastren said, and with a smile, he added, "Are we not family?"

A corner of King Eisron's mouth turned up in amusement as he met the prince's gaze, but when he spoke, his tone remained firm.

"Nothing causes a king more trouble than his own family. Many years of dealing with your father, my own sister's son, has taught me that."

The prince's smile faded. King Eisron rose from his throne and held his scepter over the brothers.

"Be lords with estates and land in my country or sail back to Evalisca where you are princes living under your eldest brother's shadow without any land at all."

Each of the six brothers turned to the other in silent consideration, and after a moment, Prince Mastren bowed and said,

"We will accept the offer, Your Majesty."

"Then I will accept your help and will not fail to reward faithful service. But on the day that one of you dares to claim more than what has been given to you, beware, for my judgment shall live on even after I am dead."

Chapter 1

Over Two Hundred Years Later

The shadow of a gnarled tree stretched across the edge of an overgrown field. Weeds snapped under the mud-stained boots of a young woman as she walked slowly toward the wide trunk before her. Tracing a rune carved deep into one of the tree's knots, her tan fingers moved carefully over the bark. With a searching gaze, her eyes turned to the tall grass concealing the tree's roots, and amid the weeds, she found a pile of stones shrouded in moss.

The girl's long, dark hair fell over her shoulders in loose waves as she knelt to dismantle the crude marker. As her hands pulled the rocks aside, her fingernails scratched the top of a sealed wooden barrel.

Withdrawing her hand at the sudden touch of a strange object, Inesca studied the barrel for a moment and then pulled her wild hair back behind her head. She tied it there with a loose piece of cloth that she tore from her sleeve. Between the frayed hem of her tunic and the worn patches stitched across her skirt, one torn sleeve was barely noticeable.

Inesca wedged her hunting knife between the lid and the barrel and managed to jar it open. A beetle scurried out just as she started to reach her hand into the barrel. In the dim evening light, it was impossible to see what else might wait inside.

Behind her, Nycor, her father's dapple-gray stallion with a black mane and tail, snorted and stamped his hoof in the dirt. Inesca paused long enough to hear other horses in the distance. They were nearing the house, and her thoughts rushed to her father, Koldoth, but it was too late for anyone or anything to change what had happened. Her father's words came back to her as she sat motionless under the old tree's branches.

"I once had another life," he had told her. "Too long, I've kept it from you. And now you must leave our home, since I cannot protect you anymore. Go to the old tree on the western border of our land, and you will find pieces of my past buried under the stones. May God use them to help you find your way when I am gone.

"Seek out Sir Coltar from the realm of Monterr in Rynar. Tell him that you *are a part of the oath he swore twenty years ago. He will provide shelter for you. He promised to do so, though he knows it not."*

Her father's strange assurance left her little comfort, but Inesca reached into the dark mouth of the barrel and seized the object she found. She withdrew her hand, grasping a leather pouch, and noticed a faded insignia upon its side. The strap of the pouch fell over her hand as Inesca stood to open it, but Nycor suddenly stomped the ground again with one of his hooves. She noticed how he had his ears pricked forward before he shook his head and snorted.

Inesca turned around and caught sight of smoke rising from the direction of her home. She climbed onto Nycor's back, placing the pouch's strap over her shoulder, and urging him into a gallop. Once past a grove of trees, Inesca drew him to a halt. From her position, she could see that flames licked the charcoal walls of what had been her home. A tear slipped down her face. There would be no burial now, no time to lay her father to rest under the protection of the forest that he loved.

The sounds of horses reached her ears again, and this time, they were much closer. Inesca guided Nycor toward the western field, but at that moment, a group of riders burst through the trees and blocked her path.

"I knew you would try to steal the best for yourself," one of them, a gangly rider, said.

Inesca backed Nycor away as she watched the man warily. He wore a fur trim around the collar of his tunic, and a silver pendant hung on a cord around his neck. Six swords appeared on the pendant in a fanlike shape as a symbol of the authority granted to him.

This was the mark of a Rynarian sheriff and far from a welcome sight to Inesca's eyes. Here in the East Province, a largely forgotten land on the border of Rynar, the sheriffs ruled the Easterners according to their pride and selfish whims. And this particular sheriff, Roegur, had given Inesca many reasons to despise him.

"Don't be a fool. Surrender the horse, and we'll leave you to mourn your father's ashes," he said with an edge of cruel mockery in his tone.

"You couldn't even wait until after I'd buried him to burn our home and steal his horses?"

"Why should I have allowed your wretched father's remains to be buried on this land? It might have become as cursed as he was."

"His only curse was parasites like you, Roegur."

"Hold your tongue. I owned this land before your father, and now I'm taking it back."

"Take it, then, along with the other horses, but you cannot have this stallion. He was given to me with my father's dying breath."

Roegur laughed. "And what would you do with him?' he asked. "You can't even afford to feed yourself, and they will have no room for him at the mill."

Inesca reached down and touched the satchel at her side.

"I had a different plan in mind."

"Well, I don't care where you go, but you'll be walking there. The horse is mine."

"Only if you can take him from me."

Inesca directed Nycor's head toward the northern gate and spurred him into motion. The stallion burst across the field as his hooves rushed into a gallop. A loud protest broke out from Roegur, and his men raced after the horse and its rider.

* * *

Less than a mile from the burning house, two men rode uphill with a small band of armed companions. A green standard, bearing the symbol of a golden hound, flapped in the breeze. It was a strange sight in the East Province, since the individual standards of the lords of Rynar rarely appeared outside the Six Realms.

Within the company of travelers, one of the men sighed and drew his hand over his brow to block the light of the evening sun. "I still say this journey to buy horses is a fool's errand. You were quick to take that man at his word about the animals owned by a vagabond in exile."

"Sirryn, I've always valued your honesty, but that sounded dangerously close to an insult."

"Perhaps it was, my lord, but you won't listen to flattery. And what good am I as a member of your council if I can't get your attention?" Sirryn said.

Lord Beristo's broad shoulders shook as he laughed. The ruddy color of his face grew more noticeable as it always did when he was in good humor, but it could also turn a deep red when he grew angry. His hair and beard had grown predominantly gray over the years, but they still retained some of the reddish-brown hue of his youth.

The councilman at his side was thinner with darker hair, though much of it was also gray, and his features were far less round than those of his lord. His brown eyes were often brightened, as they were now, by a sharp and clever light.

"Tell me, Sirryn. My other council members do not speak to me as you do. What inspires your audacity?"

"Simply the need for someone to speak sense to you, my lord. The other members encouraged you to buy as many horses as you wish, but who will ride them? You have no one capable enough for the Great Races."

"Well, nothing will deter me from seeing these horses. The merchant Anarond said they were the best horses in—"

A shout interrupted Lord Beristo, and the two men rode to the top of the nearest hill with Lord Beristo's guards following behind. When they reached the crest of the hill, they saw smoke rising into the air, but more interesting were the strangers on horses below them.

"We seem to have interrupted a theft, my lord," Sirryn said as he pointed to the lone figure riding in their direction. Four more riders chased it while waving ropes and swords.

Lord Beristo observed the scene for a few seconds before he said, "The thief won't get far. The gate he's riding toward is closed."

"And yet he's not slowing down."

As they watched, the horse began to gallop even faster as it approached the gate. Just moments before reaching it, the rider urged the horse into a jump. Lord Beristo held his breath as he watched, but the horse's hooves cleared the top of the gate. It was a magnificent leap, and the horse landed without missing a single stride as it raced on.

The other riders were now nearing the gate. Two of them slowed and turned aside. The third swerved, and the rider guided his horse toward a section of crumbled wall that was shorter than the rest. It was a longer detour, but the horse made it over the barrier. The fourth directed his mount toward the gate, but it stopped abruptly in front of it, and the man was thrown over the wall, landing roughly upon the ground. Meanwhile, the third rider tried to pursue the runaway horse and rider, but the thief and its prize were still moving at an incredible speed.

"Come," Lord Beristo said as he tightened his grip on the reins of his horse. "If we go now, we may be able to catch up with that rider."

"I think the thief has earned the right to keep that horse. Let's go on and see the rest," Sirryn said, turning his horse to the right, but Lord Beristo did not move to follow him.

"By the Six Realms, I will not give up so easily on such a horse—or such a rider."

He spurred his mount down the hill to intercept the thief, but his intent was quickly recognized, and the thief tried to pull away. He succeeded in drawing closer to the rider and horse, but the thief still managed to stay ahead of him. Lord Beristo looked behind him and saw Sirryn and his men trying to keep up, but they were not fast enough to help him. It seemed that the stolen horse would surely tire soon, but minutes passed, and the stallion still remained several feet ahead of him.

When he felt his own horse starting to tire, Lord Beristo pulled out his horn and attempted to signal the rider ahead of him with the blast of a high note. He saw the rider's head turn toward him, and he held up an empty bridle embroidered with silver threads that gleamed in the light of the setting sun.

The rider slowed and turned the horse but remained tense, as if ready to ride again at a moment's notice.

"Stay where you are," the rider demanded when Beristo attempted to move closer.

The voice startled Beristo as he realized the thief was a young woman. Now that he was closer, he could also see that her hair was bound behind her head.

"Do you know what this is?" Beristo called to her as he held up the bridle.

"I have heard that a patron will display an ornate bridle when choosing a rider. But who are you, and why do you signal me?"

"I am Lord Beristo of the realm of Ettidor, one of the Six Realms of Rynar. I came to buy horses from Koldoth, but I am also in need of a new rider for the Great Races of Rynar."

"Koldoth was my father."

"Was?"

"He died only hours ago. This horse was his gift to me. And I'll defy anyone who tries to take him from me."

"The horse is magnificent, but I held up this bridle because I wanted you."

Her expression reflected a moment of surprised hesitation before her gaze swept over his face and then turned to the bridle in his hand.

"I will ride for you, but only if this stallion remains my horse—and mine alone."

Lord Beristo let his eyes drift to the beast shifting restlessly beneath her. There was a wild look in his eyes, and his black mane lay tousled over his neck by the wind. The muscular, yet long legs of the stallion were of good size and build, as if he had been bred for racing.

"You ask a high price. How do I know that you are worth it?"

He looked back to the girl, and her lips tightened into a thin line as her eyes narrowed.

"You'll see how good of a rider I am if I take off again, but you will lose your chance to bargain with me."

He opened his mouth to speak, but shouting and the sound of horses' hooves caught up with them.

"Don't let her go! She's a thief!"

The girl pulled the horse's reins taunt as another group of men rode closer.

"Hold. I will settle this matter," Lord Beristo said.

"You there. Seize that horse before she tries to escape again!"

"And who are you to order a lord of the Six Realms to do anything?"

The approaching sheriff fell silent as he drew close enough to recognize the crest of Lord Beristo on the bridle of his horse.

"I ask your pardon, your lordship. I did not expect to find one such as you roaming through this lowly country, but you should know that due to an old debt, this horse belongs to me."

The young woman drew a hunting knife and held it ready.

"In the eyes of a rat, the whole world is his feast," she said bitterly.

The sheriff grabbed a whip from one of his men and moved to fling it toward her, but Lord Beristo drew his sword and thrust the blade at the sheriff's neck. The whip fell limp as the man froze.

"Do you own the girl as well?"

The sheriff stiffened as the blade pricked his skin, but he continued to scowl.

"If I did, her tongue would already have been cut out. But consider your situation carefully, my lord. Traveling alone in the East Province can be dangerous. My men and I could offer you protection. If you're still interested in the horse, I might be willing to sell it to you for the right offer."

The armed men who had been riding with the sheriff started to surround Lord Beristo with their hands hovering near their weapons. The sound of galloping hooves broke the stillness as Lord Beristo's guards appeared with Sirryn and surrounded the sheriff and his men.

"Traveling alone, am I? Your thoughtful concern for my safety is unnecessary, Sheriff … ?" Lord Beristo said as he lowered his sword and waited for the man's name.

The sheriff's face had grown pale, and his voice wavered when he answered. "Roegur, my lord."

"Then I have an offer ready for you, Roegur. I'm taking the horse and the rider with me since they're too much trouble for you. And in exchange for helping you return to your other duties, you may offer a gift to me as a token of your gratitude for my assistance."

Lord Beristo pointed the tip of his sword at the money pouch tied to Roegur's belt. One of his guards rode forward and cut it loose. Then he tossed it to Lord Beristo, who weighed it in his hand for a few seconds.

"It will suffice. Now ride out before I decide to include your name in a report when I return to the Six Realms."

Roegur rubbed his neck as he started to turn his horse away. "Do as you wish, your lordship," he said. "But you'll regret taking the girl with you. She's not worth the trouble she'll cause."

"Trouble or not, she rides better than any of your men."

"You plan to send her to the races?" Roegur asked with a smile. "In that case, I'll start celebrating her funeral. You should have agreed to go to the mill, girl."

With that, he and his men rode away as Lord Beristo's guards moved to let them pass. The girl tensed again as Lord Beristo's men surrounded her.

"Will you honor my father's decision?" she asked.

Lord Beristo raised his hand to stop his men from riding too close.

"The stallion is yours as long as you ride for me. After all, I need both a rider and a horse, and I doubt there are many who could ride this stallion as well as you do."

Her shoulders relaxed as a sudden weariness filled her eyes.

"Then I will come with you, my lord," she said. "And as long as you honor your part of the bargain, I will honor mine."

Lord Beristo nodded. "See that you do. You won't escape so easily if you try to run from me."

Chapter 2

Over two hundred miles west of the East Province, Lord Edgerr's estate rested under a clouded night sky. Across from the lord's manor, a grand stable built from ebony-colored stones dwarfed a long wooden house with a thatched roof.

The house had few windows, but most were covered only by a thin layer of cloth. A gust of wind burst through one, waking twenty-four-year-old Kestorn from a muddled dream. Without opening his eyes, he stretched his hand to his older brother's bed and yanked the blanket from the mattress. Pulling the blanket over his own, he grasped them both tightly and waited for the inevitable. But seconds passed without retribution, and finally, Kestorn opened one eye.

"Derreth?"

Rising from his bed, Kestorn first searched the empty mattress and next the dark room with half-opened eyes. He rubbed his neck as he sat down again and started to pull the blankets back over his legs.

All at once, the window lit up, and shadows were thrown upon the wall. Shouts broke the silence from the other end of the house. Leaving his boots behind, Kestorn stumbled toward the door wearing only his tunic and breeches. He reached the door that led to the courtyard, and as he pushed it open, he saw flames surrounding the stable.

Kestorn urged his feet into a run as several men rode around the stable to the other side. They wore the black hoods of the Raegond, men who fought in rebellion against the lords of the Six Realms of Rynar. But he didn't have time to focus on them, because the flames in and around the stable rose higher each minute.

Diving over the burning and broken stable door, Kestorn landed on the ground and rolled a couple of feet. He pushed himself up and darted toward two stalls on the right. Horses reared in terror behind every gate, but Kestorn stopped just in front of a golden stallion with a pale mane and a red stallion with a white stripe down his face. He tied sashes around their eyes and ropes around their necks before unlocking the gates and leading them from their stalls.

Smoke filled the air, making it difficult for him to find an exit. Feeling trapped, Kestorn turned and opened the gate for two of the other horses. They panicked, nearly trampling him, but then suddenly turned and raced toward an open end of the stable. Kestorn led the two stallions behind him in that same direction. He saw a few other riders stumble inside to find their horses, and he realized that they must have opened the doors on the far end.

"Come on, just like in the races, Halon," he said, climbing onto the red stallion's back.

Urging the horse into a lope, Kestorn kept a firm grasp on the other stallion's lead as they broke from the stable, leaving the smoke behind them. Two of the hooded riders chased after him with swords drawn. Pulling the sash from his mount's eyes, Kestorn had to release his hold on the golden stallion to avoid losing his right arm as one of the riders swung his sword to divide them.

The Raegond circled the riderless stallion as it shook its head and managed to free itself of its own blindfold.

"Go, Celestro!" Kestorn shouted as he watched his brother's horse rear and strike at the intruders with his hooves.

The second Raegond rode up on Kestorn's left side, and a rush of air swept past Kestorn's ear as his enemy's blade narrowly missed him. Leaning his head forward, Kestorn balanced himself in such a way to urge Halon into a faster gallop, but his pursuer was already too close to outrun.

The sword cut through the air again. Kestorn managed to move Halon farther away, but the tip of the sword still sliced his arm. Gritting his teeth, Kestorn guided Halon toward the riders' house as Halon's speed finally forced the Raegond's horse to fall behind. A sharp turn took him around the corner of the house where a post jutted out from the roof. Kestorn seized it and held on as Halon kept running.

The Raegond rode around the corner a second later, and Kestorn jumped onto his horse behind him. He grabbed the man's hand that held the sword and wrapped his left arm around the man's neck.

"Lord Edgerr and all those in his service will die tonight," the stranger insisted.

"Wait and gloat after we're dead," Kestorn said.

As he tightened his grip around the man's throat, the Raegond finally dropped his blade, which Kestorn quickly seized and used to strike him on the head. But before he could ride after the red stallion, a firm grip seized Kestorn from behind and pulled him from the horse.

Pain shot up his spine and through his head as he landed on the ground. Dark figures rode up and surrounded him.

"You riders are all the same," one said as he spat at Kestorn. "So proud of your reputation as if the races were all there was to life. When the only purpose you serve is that of a distraction."

Another of the Raegond leaned closer and said, "But soon, the mockery of skill and strength will end. No more riders. No more races."

As if on cue, one of the Raegond jumped down and raised his sword over Kestorn. Shouts broke out behind them, and they all turned their heads toward the noise.

"Kill him. We're running out of time," one of them ordered impatiently as most of the others rode toward the shouting.

The one with his sword drawn remained behind, and Kestorn imagined him grinning behind his hood. A flash of red appeared behind the executioner, and Halon reared, striking with his hooves. As his attacker was forced to back away, Kestorn pulled himself up far enough to grab Halon's mane and swing his leg over the stallion's back.

Halon quickly turned and raced off. Kestorn slumped forward as he felt his vision growing blurry and finally dark.

Fifty miles east of the Etta River, the boundary between the Six Realms of Rynar and the East Province, Lord Beristo ordered that a camp be set up to allow the horses some rest. His men raised a large tent for him, but everyone else would sleep under the canopy of the stars.

Inesca found a stream at the edge of their camp where her horse could drink as she lay in the soft grass. Exhaustion had finally begun to overtake her as the pain of her father's loss settled in her heart, striking her with a growing sense of loneliness and fresh grief. A cool night breeze brushed over her face, and Inesca turned her gaze toward the sky.

At the sound of approaching footsteps, she sat up quickly and saw a man with dark gray hair and a beard walking toward her with a torch in one hand and a bundle in the other. He wore fine clothes, but not as fine or ornate as those of Lord Beristo. She started to rise, but he held up his hand.

"There's no need. I am Sirryn, one of Lord Beristo's council members. Here, you may need this tonight."

He held out a blanket to her, and Inesca stood as she accepted it.

"Thank you. This will help," she said.

Instead of the disinterest or pride Inesca knew from most Rynarians, she noted with surprise that this one watched her with a mixture of sympathy and concern.

"Have you ever been to the Six Realms before?"

"No, but I have heard some about them, particularly Ettidor because it is the closest to the East Province."

"Yes, it is the realm that Lord Beristo governs. The others are Monterr, Sassot, Trineth, Fortur, and Farcost."

Inesca listened and tried to think of anything she could remember about the five other realms, but only one of them sounded familiar. Her father had instructed her to find the man called Coltar from Monterr.

"Lord Beristo heard news of your father from a merchant. I was surprised when he insisted on making this journey himself, but he grows tired of being on his estate for too long. He is eager for the racing season to begin so that he can travel to the other realms."

As Sirryn's gaze turned to her again, his speech slowed, and he stared harder at her face. His hand lifted the torch higher, and Inesca stepped back, suddenly uncomfortable with his attention.

"Forgive me," he said, realizing that he was staring. "It's just that I noticed you have blue eyes. Strange for an Easterner to have that color, isn't it?"

"My father was from the Six Realms, like you. My mother was an Easterner. I am what many call a half-breed. It's not a kind name, but I suppose it means that neither the east nor the west will claim me."

"Yes, I have heard the term used before," he said, sounding regretful. "I fear there are some who will hold your mixed parentage against you. But it may comfort you to know that Lord Beristo cares very little about blood. I believe that he noticed only your riding skills."

Inesca nodded.

"It is strange to me that Lord Beristo sought out my father to buy horses," she said. "He had a reputation among many people as being cursed because of his misfortunes."

"The news we had of him indicated nothing of the kind. What sort of troubles plagued him?"

"Mostly those that come with shaping a new life in a different land. He was not the first to come from the Six Realms. Others have shared his struggles, but Roegur and his thugs always made things difficult for him. Even his death was hastened by their brutality. They attacked him while he was in a nearby village trading for some supplies. He managed to return to our home, but …"

Her voice trailed off as she remembered the pain he suffered from his wounds. When he had first returned, he insisted he needed only rest to recover, but he grew worse despite Inesca's attempts to aid him. Then he sent her from his room, although Inesca still heard some of his prayers and distress.

"Have you no mother?" Sirryn's voice drew her back from such grim recollections.

"She died when I was a child. An accident in the village market with a wagon. My father had to raise me on his own after that."

Sirryn listened quietly for a moment. He appeared reluctant to press her for more information, but he finally said, "You have known your share of difficulties, but you are mistaken if you believe your circumstances will improve by coming with us. Lord Beristo's offer may have appeared to be a chance for you to escape, but it is not uncommon for young and inexperienced riders to die in the races before they have finished their first year."

"And the experienced riders? Where do they come from?"

"They're the ones you have to watch out for because they survived the first year."

Inesca considered his words before she glanced up at his face. "Thank you for warning me," she said. "I doubt Lord Beristo would be pleased."

"He knows I speak my mind, but I fear it's not as though you could escape. He has guards posted on all sides of this camp, and they're not just there to watch for rebels or bandits."

"I never doubted that my bargain with Lord Beristo was binding, but why would you warn me about the races if you knew I couldn't leave?"

"Because you should know what's ahead of you, and if you get a chance to get out, you should take it. There is some hope that if you offer your horse to Lord Beristo, he might release you from his service."

Inesca's expression hardened. "I didn't accept his offer for safety or comfort … or protection. I accepted it because he agreed that I could keep my father's horse. The laws of Rynar do not permit women to have any claim on their horses. This is the only way that I can keep what is mine," she explained.

"That animal will be yours only as long as you can ride it. If you become seriously injured or die in the races, you'll lose him."

Inesca walked back to the stallion and scratched Nycor's neck.

"I know it's not much, but it's the best deal anyone's offered me so far."

Sirryn studied her. "Are you so certain this horse is worth your life?"

Turning to face him, Inesca forced a smile as she stood beside the stallion's flank. "He's worth a chance at a new life, and I'm willing to take some risks to get there."

The Legacy of the Lost Rider

Sirryn acknowledged her decision with a nod.

"Bold words. I hope that you don't come to regret your choice, but if you do, don't forget what I told you."

He began to walk back toward the tent of Lord Beristo, but Inesca suddenly started after him.

"Why did you bother trying to help me?" she asked.

Sirryn paused and glanced back at her over his shoulder.

"How old are you?"

"Eighteen."

"I had a daughter that age once. She also sought a new and exciting life. After one rash decision, she married a favored councilman of a lord, a young man with a surplus of ambition, but little discretion. He and my daughter were targeted by the Raegond and killed in a vicious attack. Her life was taken because of a man she barely knew and one she loved only because he offered her something different and thrilling. She was not unlike you in some ways."

As he spoke, Inesca dropped her gaze until he turned away from her again.

"For your sake, I hope your choice turns out to be the right one. But if not, then surrender the horse and leave before it's too late."

When she remained silent, Sirryn held out the torch to her.

"Here. You may wish to have a fire on such a cold night."

Inesca accepted it, and Sirryn climbed the hill to return to Lord Beristo's tent. His words had done little to lighten her spirit after such a long day. Could it have been only hours ago since she saw her father take his last breaths and then followed his instructions to dig up his possessions near the old tree?

Remembering the pouch, Inesca retrieved it from her saddle and sat down in the grass again. She searched for the edge of the flap that was caked under a layer of dirt. Bits of hay clung to the leather amid the dried mud, a clear sign that her father's attempts to preserve this strange possession had not protected it from nature. Her fingers found a crease and tugged firmly. The leather cracked in her hands but finally opened.

Before reaching inside, she brushed away more of the dirt as she tried to make out the insignia on the pouch. In the light of the torch, she could see a straight line cut through black shapes, and after staring at it for a few minutes, Inesca decided that it must be a sword and that the smaller line at the top had to be part of a cross hilt. The black shapes dancing around the sword looked like flames.

The symbols led Inesca to think of a blacksmith, but why not a hammer instead of a sword? And why would her father carry the mark of a blacksmith?

He had never been able to craft anything using fire and had always bought tools and horseshoes from the blacksmith in the village.

Reaching inside the pouch, she removed the contents carefully and laid them upon the large mossy stone at her side. The first was a tarnished silver medallion hanging from a blue sash that might have been handsome once, but now appeared stained and ripped. Inesca ran her fingers over the figure of a galloping horse with its rider in the center of the medallion. Her father had always known so much about horses, but she had never asked him how. A falcon hovered above the horse with its wings outstretched, and below the horse's hooves, she noted an odd collection of circles.

Lying sprawled beside the medallion was a little wooden man that matched the length of her hand. He was in poor shape, but some black paint was still visible on his chest and arms. His feet were gone as if something or someone had cracked and broken his legs, but his figure still stood straight and stiff like a guard waiting for orders. And the design of his attire suggested that he was a knight of Rynar.

The sight of this wooden figure bothered Inesca as she noted how much it reminded her of a gift for a child, but it had never belonged to her. A sudden tightness seized her throat, and Inesca quickly set the knight aside with the medallion.

The final item was smaller than either of the first two objects. It was a silver ring. Tarnished just like the medallion, it appeared to be very plain except for one flower that had been cut into the ring. In the middle of the flower lay a tiny red gem. Inesca tried to slide the ring onto her finger but quickly saw that it was not designed for her hands. The woman who wore this ring must have had delicate fingers, not strong and sturdy hands like hers or her mother's.

Holding the ring between her index finger and her thumb, Inesca stared at it until her head began to ache. As she pressed a fist to her temple, the image of her father with his arm around a strange woman and a little boy playing at his feet appeared in her mind.

"Father, why couldn't you have told me?" she whispered. "After all those years together, I don't even know you."

Tears pricked her eyes, and she took a deep breath in an attempt to relieve the pressure building in her chest. She remembered her father asking God to spare his life for her sake. When he thought she had left the room to fetch him water, she heard his prayers as he seemed less afraid for himself and more concerned with leaving his daughter to be an orphan. But as he grew more delirious, he had also asked to be spared *for their sake*. Distracted with grief at that time, she hadn't considered whom he might be pleading for. Now, it felt wrong to discover these secrets when she was past all hope of receiving an explanation. Instead, she was left to suffer through her questions alone.

She closed her fist around the ring, and she rose to her feet with her arm poised to throw it into the stream. A cool night wind rushed past her, and Inesca froze as it struck her skin. Casting her father's possessions into the water wouldn't change the truth, a truth that she still wanted to understand. Her arm relaxed, but the ring seemed to grow heavier the longer she held it in her grasp.

Chapter 3

"Kes, wake up. Haven't you had enough sleep yet?"

With a loud groan, Kestorn shielded his eyes and shoved away the hand prodding his shoulder.

"Come on, little brother. Lord Edgerr says that even heroes have to get out of bed to work."

Still blinking, Kestorn peered out from behind his hand. His older brother, Derreth, sat watching him with a faint smile and a light in his brown eyes. Looking around, Kestorn realized that he was lying on a straw mattress inside a tent.

"Where were you last night?"

Derreth passed a hand over his mouth and short, brown beard. When he drew it away, his smile had disappeared.

"I was out riding as I sometimes am, but it seems it was poor timing."

"Poor timing?" Kestorn asked as he sat up. "I had to save your horse because you weren't here. And if you were out riding, why didn't you take Celestro?"

"We've been over this before, Kes. Celestro is not my horse any more than Halon is yours. They both belong to Lord Edgerr, and he allows us to ride them in the races. Last night, I took a different horse out, one that Lord Edgerr is less likely to miss. And you shouldn't have risked your own life running into a burning stable to save any of the horses."

"Don't waste your breath scolding me. You would have done it."

Derreth stood up and dipped a cloth into a bucket of water before tossing it to Kestorn.

"There's still some blood on the side of your head, but your arm's been bandaged. Do you remember what happened?"

Kestorn pressed the cool cloth to the bump on his head.

"One of the Raegond knocked me off a horse, and I think I hit the ground pretty hard. Might have even knocked my head against a rock, but I do remember them being eager to kill me. Did they get any of the other riders?"

"Benger and Illusu are dead. Trestan's wounded and won't be able to ride for at least a few weeks."

"So, it's just you and me," Kestorn said.

"For a while, I was afraid it was just me. The riders' house and the stable were both burned badly when I returned, and some of the other men were dead. It wasn't until you were found in the forest with Halon standing at your side that I was able to relax."

"How did Lord Edgerr take your return since you're not supposed to leave without his permission?"

"I think he was just glad to have one rider unharmed, but I'll probably be watched more carefully after this."

Kestorn stretched midway and then grunted in pain as his back began to ache. "Why don't you ever take me with you when you go riding? You don't even tell me when you're going to do it."

"Two riders are more noticeable than one, and I go out there to be alone."

"That excuse worked when I was twelve," Kestorn scoffed.

"Well, what excuse do you want to hear?"

"The truth. What are you really doing out there? Meeting a girl?"

Derreth laughed and ruffled his brother's flaxen hair. "Well, if I were like you, I wouldn't have to go anywhere to find a girl. They'd just flock to me. Once word gets out about the attack, the butcher's daughter will be over here crooning over your battle wounds."

Kestorn groaned at the thought of the boisterous Galda and her high-pitched voice. "Why did you wake me up again?"

"His lordship wants everyone except Trestan to help clean up the mess from the attack."

"Didn't you tell him I was wounded?"

"He didn't think a scratch and a few bumps were severe enough to keep you in bed."

"Well, we could say that I caught pneumonia out in the forest."

"Come on, Kes. Besides, I don't think you want anyone else tending to Halon this morning. He's been a handful ever since we brought him back."

"What about Celestro? What happened to him?"

"Thanks to you, he's fine. Now, let's go before you're counted missing again."

Two more days of hard riding with Lord Beristo and his men took Inesca miles beyond the small stretch of country that she had known in her life. Villages and farms disappeared once they reached the Etta River and the magnificent stone bridge that stretched over the water. Here, the land itself seemed to be carved from rock, and jagged peaks jutted up from the ground with a thin layer of vegetation covering the ground.

Inesca glanced back over her shoulder at the distant hills and fields that now lay far behind her. Once she crossed the long bridge ahead of them, she would leave the East Province and enter Ettidor, one of the Six Realms of Rynar.

As her gaze shifted away from her homeland, Inesca saw that Lord Beristo had stopped his horse in front of a small mound over which lay a tarnished helmet with a dent in one side. The image of horses and riders charging toward an army had been carved into a large stone that rose above the mound. After riding closer, Inesca noted that *The Battle of Tortesra* was inscribed on the stone.

"Have you ever been to this place before?" Lord Beristo asked after he turned and observed her staring at the stone marker before him.

"Never, my lord. I did not have a reason to come this far west until now."

"But you have heard of this battle, surely?"

"I have heard of the Tortesra Plains, but no one has ever spoken to me of this."

His eyes widened, and his mouth twisted into a frown. "So, you have not received proper instruction in history. What was the focus of your education?"

"I can read and write, my lord. Apart from that, most of my knowledge is devoted to the worship of God and the care of horses."

"Which god?"

"The only one there is, my lord," Inesca answered with a confused expression. "My father said that God was known to all in the Six Realms of Rynar, though there are some in the East Province who do not worship Him. Is this not true?"

"Well, I suppose all in Rynar know of Him. Many ask for His blessing and will swear by the God who reigns above. But only some believe."

"Do you?"

His short figure stiffened, and the Evaliscan lord hesitated while Inesca waited quietly for an answer.

"As a lord, it is my responsibility to carry on the ideals of my ancestors. And it is demanded that all lords uphold the faith, so I do."

Inesca's thoughts turned to her father, who had relied so heavily on his faith during his difficult life. And when she had questioned God in their times of trouble, he had asked her, *"Why are you surprised to find pain and injustice in this world? You will never be short of enemies in this life. Look to God and trust him. We have been called not to complain of evil, but to oppose it."*

"I am surprised you were never told of this battle," Lord Beristo continued as he turned his attention back to the stone. "If not for the knights of the Six Realms, the Raegond would have seized the East Province for their own. I trust you know of the Raegond?"

"I believe they caused some trouble for the lords in the Six Realms. But why was the battle fought here?"

"This land once served as a refuge for the Raegond. They became stronger by leaving the Six Realms, but they continued to return to attack us and then flee here to a region where they believed they were safe. So, the lords, including myself, held council and called the knights to find and destroy them. What happened here at this bridge worked to our advantage because those rebels were preparing to cross the river for an attack, and so our knights caught them out in the open and killed many. It took more time to take the rest of the East Province away from them, but due to our efforts, you have grown up here without having to fear them."

"And the sheriffs who patrol our lands, claiming authority in the name of the Evaliscan lords so there can be peace and order outside the Six Realms, were the Raegond the reason they were appointed?" she asked.

"A way was needed to keep the Raegond from regaining control, so we sent out sheriffs with men and resources to keep watch over the land, and now we can ride into the East Province without running into a Raegond stronghold."

"That man who tried to steal this horse from me and who challenged your authority was one of those sheriffs, my lord. His interests have always been centered on taking advantage of the people around him, not on keeping the peace."

Lord Beristo smiled and shook his head as if she was a child complaining about the taste of the food set before her. "You're too young to know what it was like before the East Province was under our control. Trust me, girl. Your people, these villagers, they're better off now."

He turned his horse and started across the bridge. Inesca placed her hand over her father's pouch that was rolled up in a blanket over her saddle. Sirryn rode up beside her.

"Once you cross that bridge, it will be difficult to get back. Here, you have your freedom, but inside the Six Realms, you'll be an outsider. As far as the Evaliscan lords and their men are concerned, you are no better than a slave."

"Not if I am a rider in the races," Inesca insisted. "Riders are given protection and respect if they earn it. Even in the East Province, we have heard of such things."

"When you're surrounded by five other armed riders in the middle of one of the Great Races, what good will that protection and respect be then?"

"I am grateful for your warning, but if I go back now, I will face more than five armed riders. And I would have to face them without a horse since giving Nycor to your master is my only option for leaving his service. I'll take the odds of five against one in the races."

"Then prepare yourself for another day and half of riding to Lord Beristo's estate. After that, you will no doubt be pushed into training right away."

Sirryn rode past her toward the bridge, and Inesca urged Nycor after him.

"Who trains Lord Beristo's riders?" she asked.

"A bad-tempered, one-legged man known as Omaron. He was a slave from one of the southern islands who became a rider in the Great Races, but after he was injured, Lord Beristo bought him from another lord. A few months later, our lord granted him the status of a free man in Rynar. He offered Omaron the chance to train his riders and pays him well for his services."

Inesca considered that her own position would be lower than that of a trainer. There had been no discussion of her receiving wages, and her choices, if she had any, were few and restricted.

"How did Omaron lose his leg?" she asked, turning back to Sirryn.

"During his fourth race, one of the other riders severely wounded him. An infection set in, and the leg had to be removed to save his life. He's still bitter about it, so don't expect a warm welcome when you start training. And don't ask him about his missing leg or stare at his crutch. He has enough strength to fracture bones with his fists."

"What about Lord Beristo's other riders? Don't most lords have several?"

"They do, but he is running short on riders at the moment. That's why he needed you. He has only one other, Jirro, who is still recovering from some injuries."

"From other riders in the races?"

Sirryn shook his head and tried to contain a smile.

"No, he just fell off his horse. Jirro's skills as a rider are limited, particularly when he's been drinking too much. Lord Beristo's more skilled rider, Lolker, was killed in one of the last races. Again, not because of something the other riders did, but because he lost control of his horse and fell while riding at a dangerous speed. His neck was broken. So, you see, even accidents are dangerous in the races."

"My father taught me the risks, but it's never kept me from wanting to ride,"

Inesca assured him. "But from what you've said, it sounds as though I am the only one in Lord Beristo's service who can ride."

"You are," Sirryn cautioned. "And there's only a month left before the first of the Great Races begin. You will not have much time to prepare."

"Is this Omaron a good trainer?"

"Aside from the fact that he is impatient, relentless, unpleasant, and unforgiving, he is what I would call an excellent trainer."

"Then I will learn to overlook his faults," Inesca said.

Sirryn responded with a scornful huff.

"We'll see. Also, he's not going to like you."

"It doesn't sound as though he likes anyone."

"That may be so, but you're going to learn soon enough that there are some who are strongly opposed to female riders in the races. Omaron is one of them."

Inesca frowned.

"Does he think I won't be able to compete with the other riders?"

"Not necessarily. I've heard many other reasons. Some say that female riders have an unfair advantage because they are lighter in weight. Others say that you are a distraction for the male riders. But you will not be the first female rider to enter the races, and I doubt you'll be the last. But don't assume the other riders will go easier on you because you are a girl. I've even seen female riders treat each other viciously during races if two compete in the same race."

"I'll need to learn more about the riders from other realms before I compete," Inesca said.

"Ask Omaron about that if you can catch him in a good humor, which for him means only a mildly ill-tempered mood. He watches all the races closely, and he knows the riders of the other lords better than most."

"It must be hard for him to not be able to race anymore."

Sirryn let out a scornful laugh. "You won't feel so sorry for him after you meet him," he said. "I may not have been able to convince you to quit, but if Omaron can't change your mind, then no one can."

Chapter 4

"Getting slow back there, Derreth! Are you sure it's the horse doing the running and not you?"

"You'll find out when I pass you at the finish. You always let Halon go out too fast, Kes!"

"Do we look like we're slowing down?" Kestorn shouted back at his brother as Halon raced forward with a new burst of speed.

The red stallion charged over the field like a fiery wind flying through the grass. Derreth's chosen steed, Celestro, ran just a short distance behind Kestorn's horse. As the two horses raced over a hill, a wide ditch opened up at the bottom of the slope where a stream cut through the field.

Derreth turned his horse to the left and rode toward the place where the ditch became narrower, but Kestorn continued to ride straight down the hill.

"Kes, it's too wide! Turn around!"

But Kestorn showed no signs of changing course as he allowed Halon to charge down the hill, urging him into a jump at the last possible second. Derreth stopped to watch as the ground beneath the stallion's hooves crumbled just as it leapt into the air. The horse's front hooves made it to the other side, but the back hooves hit the muddy embankment and started to slide. With a determined effort, Halon pulled himself up onto the ledge and started to run again.

Kestorn whooped triumphantly as Derreth shook his head and rode on, allowing Celestro to jump a much easier part of the divide. He urged his horse into a faster pace to catch up with his reckless younger brother. Celestro's powerful legs propelled him quickly up the field, and soon Derreth found himself almost side by side with Kestorn.

They rode up and over another knoll, making for the old tree on the outside of the distant town that was their usual marker. Suddenly, another horse darted out into their path and stopped directly in front of them. Both Derreth and Kestorn had to bring their horses to a halt to prevent a collision with him.

"What are you doing? Can't you see that we're in the middle of practice here?" Kestorn fired at the newcomer.

Derreth held out his hand in an attempt to stop his brother when he saw it was Lerom, Lord Edgerr's new captain of his guard.

"I am to escort both of you back to Lord Edgerr's estate, and you are to go and speak with him," Lerom said, directing his gaze to Derreth.

"We'll be on our way then," Derreth said. He turned his horse around and started riding in the direction of the estate and the stables as his brother reluctantly followed him.

Color flushed Kestorn's face, and he stared straight ahead with a burning gaze. Derreth glanced back at Lerom, and he couldn't help thinking about the risky jump his brother had taken with one of Lord Edgerr's prized horses. Had Lerom seen it?

The rest of the ride passed in silence until they finally reached the estate. The stable had been repaired since the attack, and Derreth dismounted, handing Celestro's reins to his brother. "Take care of him for me. I'll be back later," he said.

Kestorn nodded, but Derreth could tell he was still fuming about the interruption. Lerom rode on ahead to the manor, leaving Derreth to walk the rest of the way on his own. When he finally entered through the doors of the manor, he saw Lerom already talking to Lord Edgerr. The lord's expression was clearly marked by a frown.

"Thank you for the report, captain. You are dismissed," Lord Edgerr said as Derreth approached.

Lerom bowed his head slightly and left them alone. Lord Edgerr continued to study the papers in his hands, and it was a few moments before he spoke.

"Times have been hard for me lately," he said. "This is an account of the damage from the raid and what it will cost me. And it is no small sum."

Derreth listened in silence as he watched the gray-haired Evaliscan. Lord Edgerr's eyes were narrowed in concentration as he continued to read.

"The realm is not pouring out taxes as it should be. And now, this attack from the Raegond ... some of my horses were even killed."

"And some riders too, my lord," Derreth reminded him.

"Yes. You ought to know," Lord Edgerr said.

"My lord?"

"Never mind the attack now. Captain Lerom tells me that you were out riding beyond the estate with that brother of yours. I don't remember granting permission for you two to take my stallions anywhere today."

"We were training for the races. The fields have always been considered open to your riders—"

"Training? Why do you need to be training?"

Derreth paused and studied Lord Edgerr's face before speaking. "Tell me what I have done to displease you, Lord Edgerr. My brother and I train only to better serve you in the races."

"But you will not be racing this season. Neither will your brother."

"Then who?"

"Trestan will ride for me. He will recover from his injuries before the first race. But you and your brother will remain with the camp to tend to the horses when we travel. And that will be the only reason you're coming along."

Derreth felt his face grow warm. He and his brother could ride circles around Trestan, and Lord Edgerr knew it. His lordship was apparently willing to sacrifice winning a race for the sake of his pride and sense of control.

"May I ask why we will not be allowed to ride?" Derreth said, guarding the tone of his voice, lest it reveal what was churning inside of him.

"It should be clear to you that your brother is a liability. That red stallion is one of my best, and I paid a fortune to get him. But every time your brother rides him, he threatens to ruin the horse. I was told that he almost had another accident today."

"Kestorn takes risks, but, my lord, no one else has been able to ride your red stallion as well as my brother."

"Perhaps I haven't tried hard enough to find a new rider for it, but I assure you that I will now. As for you, Derreth, you disappear from my estate at odd times, and I've reason to question your loyalties."

"My loyalty is to you, Lord Edgerr."

"I'm not convinced. I find it strange that you happened to be missing on the night of the attack and that your brother is the only one of my riders who escaped serious injury and death at the hands of the Raegond."

"You believe that I was one of the men who attacked your estate? Who attacked my own brother?"

"If not, then where were you?"

"I wanted to visit a friend who was staying in town."

"And you had to disobey my orders about leaving the estate at night to see this person?"

Derreth said nothing in response.

"Well, you and your brother will ride for me again only when I decide that you're worth the trouble that it cost me to take you in and allow you to join my riders. But if you two continue to recklessly disregard my orders, then I'll see that you end up as slaves in the mines of Monterr. Is that clear enough?"

"Yes, my lord," Derreth acknowledged coldly.

"Then go. Make sure those horses are seen to, and you're not to ride them again unless I say otherwise."

⁓

In the realm of Ettidor, Inesca settled into her room near the servant's quarters in Lord Beristo's manor. After their arrival a short while earlier, she had been sent here to bathe and prepare to meet with her lord again before her training began. It was late in the day, and Inesca wished that sleep was the only task she had left before her. However, Lord Beristo was impatient for her to begin working with Omaron. Based upon what Sirryn had told her, Inesca doubted the trainer would feel the same.

As she ran a brush through the thick waves of her hair that lay over her shoulder, Inesca remembered her father noting how much her locks reminded him of her mother. *Hers was just as dark and as rich as yours, like the earth under the fields of wildflowers that you love to ride across.* His hair had also been nearly the same color, though not quite as dark, and it had been coarser with strands of gray woven among the brown. But his skin, like that of all Rynarians, was fair, not tan like hers.

Having received many stares from the servants, Inesca quickly understood that she would be viewed and treated as a foreigner here. People from the East Province possessed darker hair, eyes, and skin than those from the Six Realms. Together, these small variances determined whether you were part of the Evaliscan realms of Rynar or whether you were an outsider.

As her thoughts drifted back to her home, a sense of loneliness returned with the memories. *The tint of one's skin never attracted attention at home, but there, we were all outsiders. Only the sight of a sheriff's pendant would cost one unfriendly stares. Father always insisted I was a free-born daughter of Rynar and the East Province. He warned that the sheriffs or others might try to enslave me, but he never wanted such a life for me.*

As she finished braiding her hair, Inesca's gaze drifted to a book about the realm of Ettidor, which Sirryn had brought to her room after their arrival. It was strange to her that the Six Realms of Rynar used different names for its people and its lords. All those born inside the Six Realms were called Rynarians except for the lords and their heirs. These were still called Evaliscans, even though it had been many years since their ancestors had come from Evalisca to live in Rynar. Their blood was more Rynarian than Evaliscan now, but the distinction in names had been preserved. Inesca had never thought to ask her father why it remained that way, and he had never told her the reason why the Evaliscans had come to Rynar.

Looking into the mirror on the wall before her, Inesca twisted a loose strand of dark hair around her finger. The color of her hair and her skin were the remains of her inheritance from her mother, who had the features of an Easterner. Yet gazing at her reflection in the mirror were two blue eyes like her father's, not dark-brown like her mother's. Inesca closed her eyes and drew in a heavy breath as the pain of her father's loss struck her again, but her thoughts swiftly moved to another grief. *I wish I could remember more of my mother*, Inesca thought as she clasped the edges of her hair. But having lost her mother at age five, she could recall only the faintest of memories about her.

Opening her eyes again, Inesca reflected on how the only person she had ever felt closely connected to was her father. But now, with the discovery of her father's secrets, even that connection felt strained. Whenever she had questioned him about his reasons for leaving the Six Realms, he made it clear that he did not wish to discuss it. Inesca had let it go, knowing there were other Rynarians who had fled across the border after falling into disfavor with their lords. Many of them had changed their names, and Inesca suspected that Koldoth had not been her father's name when he lived in Rynar. But she had never known him by any other name.

Inesca moved her hand to the bundle of her father's possessions that lay on the table near her. In following their clues, she hoped to discover his secrets and the things that drove him to accept his difficult life in the East Province.

A knock at the door interrupted her thoughts as a servant offered to escort her to the place where Lord Beristo awaited her. Inesca rose quickly and tried not to trip over the plain green dress the servants had given her to wear. It had been designed for a girl of taller stature, but Inesca knew she was a few inches shorter than most young women her age. Her small but strong frame served as further evidence that she was her mother's daughter.

Following the servant through the large halls of Lord Beristo's home, Inesca was reminded of how short she felt in comparison to others. It was so much easier to feel comfortable and confident while riding. At least while on a horse, she didn't have to worry about people looking down at her. And they didn't have to notice that she wasn't tall and delicate like some of the other girls when her riding skills were enough to draw attention and admiration.

The servant girl in front of her paused and gestured to a door at the end of the hall. Inesca thanked her as she pulled her skirt away from her feet and continued on alone. Once she passed through the door, a large dining hall opened up before her. Four long tables formed the shape of a square in the center of the room. Long green tablecloths with gold trim covered each one.

The banners that hung from the wall were also green with figures stitched in golden thread. Each depicted a hound holding up its head in pride as it stood above a crown with six points. Inesca recognized the crown as the symbol of the Six Realms. Every Evaliscan lord displayed it on his standard.

The sound of Lord Beristo clearing his throat drew her gaze to the far table where he sat waiting for her. Inesca walked nearer and bowed as he watched her.

"Well, you will never pass for a lady, but without the mud and the rags, you no longer look like a beggar. What do you think of the dress?"

"It is a little long, my lord. I fear that I have not met someone's expectations."

Lord Beristo looked down at the hem of the dress that covered Inesca's feet and lay in a fold on the floor around her.

"Most riders possess longer legs than yours, but you'll not be the one doing the running, will you?"

"No, my lord. But if I may, I request a pair of breeches for when I ride. I fear that racing in a dress will impede my skills."

"I find that difficult to believe after seeing you evade Roegur. Were you not wearing a dress then?"

Inesca nodded.

"You rode so well that evening."

"But I can do better," she persisted.

"Better?" Lord Beristo repeated thoughtfully. "It would not be considered proper attire for a woman. Still, if you are certain it would make a difference, then I will have some made for you. But you will wear dresses when you are not training or racing."

"Thank you, my lord. I promise you will see the difference it will make."

"Indeed, I will, for you will be training with Omaron during the next three and a half weeks. He accepts nothing but constant improvement. However, at the moment, he is late."

Inesca glanced around the room and saw no sign of the intimidating trainer who Sirryn had described earlier. As she turned back to Lord Beristo, she noticed that he had a map of the Six Realms of Rynar laid out on the table before him. Her eyes were drawn to the realm of Monterr near the middle of the map.

"Lord Beristo, may I ask if you have heard of a man named Coltar of Monterr?"

"The Coltar of Monterr I know is one of the knights of the Six Realms. Why do you ask?"

"My father mentioned his name once, but I had no knowledge of who he was. I thought he might have met him."

"You believe a knight could share connections with a poor horse breeder from the East Province? Impossible. Your father may have heard of him, but it is unlikely that they ever met. Most knights never travel beyond the border of the realms, with the exception of those who fought in the Battle of Tortesra."

"Have you ever met this knight?"

"I never bother with the knights from other realms unless they are providing an escort for a guest. And you should stay away from them as well. Remember that you will be racing in a competition on my behalf against those who serve other lords. You are not to associate with any knights, servants, or riders from other realms."

The doors on the other side of the room were thrust open with a loud groan as Lord Beristo finished speaking. The shape of a huge man filled the dimly lit corridor behind the doors. The color of his skin made him seem like a shadow stepping out into the lamp light as he entered the room.

"Ah, Omaron. Come and meet my new rider," Lord Beristo stated with a tone that sounded both proud and amused.

The trainer's face was knit in a stern expression as his eyes turned toward Lord Beristo but refused to acknowledge Inesca. Lowering her gaze, Inesca saw that he was missing his right leg below the thigh. Omaron moved with the aid of a large iron rod that he plunged in front of him as his remaining foot took steady and determined steps.

He stopped alongside Inesca with only a few feet between them and bowed stiffly to Lord Beristo. When he spoke, it felt like his deep voice shook the floor under Inesca's feet.

"I see no rider."

"Oh, come, Omaron," Lord Beristo huffed. "This girl is the one I have chosen for the race in Sassot, and you will train her."

"I do not train girls."

Omaron finally turned his head to cast a look of disdain at Inesca. For a moment, she felt the heaviness of his rejection settle over her chest, but she refused to let her gaze drop in shame from his stare.

"Then I will not beg you to change your standards, though I believe I could learn much from you," she said, drawing a deep breath. "But I will ride in the next race whether you train me or not."

"If that is your choice, you are dead where you stand, little mouse."

Inesca turned toward him and felt her anxiety burn away under his insult.

"You are quick to judge someone you've never seen ride. Why not give me a challenge first, and then decide if I am a waste of your time?"

Omaron's unyielding gaze studied her.

"Brave words for a child … but foolish. Still, you will have your challenge."

"Excellent," Lord Beristo interjected with a grin. He raised his goblet. "How about tomorrow morning?"

Omaron shook his head.

"Tonight."

Lord Beristo coughed and barely managed to swallow his wine.

"It is late, Omaron …"

The thought of a weary night awaiting the chance to prove herself troubled Inesca's thoughts, and she knew that she must respond before the opportunity left her.

"I accept."

Omaron nodded and finally turned his gaze away from her.

"Meet me at the stable in an hour with your horse saddled and ready … or don't come at all."

Chapter 5

Rycor jerked his head restlessly as Inesca held his reins in her hand outside the stable. The starry midnight sky retreated behind the brightness of the full moon. Boots trampled the hay spilling out from the stable door, and Inesca turned to see Lord Beristo approach from the other side of the stable.

"This challenge had best be quick," he said, pulling a warm cloak around his shoulders. "And I trust that you understand how important it is that you do not fail. I may command Omaron to train you, but you will receive far better training if he believes you are worth his time."

In other words, his approval is essential. But I doubt it is easily gained, she thought. Inesca felt her heart beat faster as she tried to guess what this challenge might be.

"I will do my best, my lord."

Movement distracted her gaze as Omaron finally appeared from the direction of the field to the left of the stable.

"The challenge is ready. Mount your horse and ride quietly to those trees north of the field. From there you will see a Naldorr buck feeding on Lord Beristo's wheat crop as it has done for many nights now. To complete my challenge, you must herd the buck into the walled enclosure with the two gates," he said, directing her gaze to the enclosure just beyond them. "You must do this before the sand in my glass runs out."

Omaron held up an hourglass that had not yet been turned and watched her expectantly.

"You will not be given a full hour. Half should be enough for such a decent rider. It begins when you ride toward the trees."

"There is more than speed to this challenge, Omaron," Lord Beristo said as his expression deepened into a frown. "Naldorr bucks can be dangerous when startled. The horse may be injured. What then?"

Omaron crossed his arms over his chest.

"If your rider is as good as you claim, then there is nothing to fear. This is my challenge. There is no more danger to the horse in this than the danger it would face in a race."

The Legacy of the Lost Rider

Inesca pulled herself up into the saddle, hoping not to betray the uneasiness in her legs. The challenge seemed both ridiculous and impossible.

Omaron walked alongside Nycor and checked her saddle.

"You will not use any weapons. Only speed and what you find out there."

Inesca nodded.

"Let it start then," she said, urging Nycor forward into a lope.

The noise and tremors of a full gallop might startle the buck and bring about an early failure, so she kept his pace light and easy. Along the eastern edge of the field, the ground sloped down where a stream cut its way across the border. Inesca leaned forward against Nycor as she guided him toward the trees that Omaron had pointed out.

The wind was blowing from the west, so Inesca knew that the buck would not catch their scent from this side. Still, she was unable to see the animal without riding up and out onto the field, but she dared not risk that yet.

Once she reached the trees, she turned Nycor back toward the field while trying to keep him hidden in their shadows. A cloud moved away from the moon, and then she saw it.

The bold creature stood among the wheat, grazing without concern for the world around it. It was unusual for a Naldorr antelope to graze alone, but Inesca could tell from the height and shape of its horns that it was a buck, as Omaron had said. Perhaps while seeking a new herd, it had chosen Lord Beristo's field as an easy meal.

The Naldorr antelope were named for their usual home in the northern forests that stretched above the Six Realms. Sometimes they traveled south into the Six Realms, or even into the East Province, and were hunted, but more often they were known for causing trouble. Although they were not very intelligent, these beasts were still daunting pests.

Standing between four and five feet high, not including their twisted horns, they were powerfully built and often aggressive beasts, and the shape of their ugly heads seemed to resemble a goat more than the graceful outline of a stag. The horns of a Naldorr buck twisted in a spiral and then jutted forward, perfect for ramming an enemy with piercing force. Their legs could propel them up to the speed of a horse, but they were built for short bursts of speed rather than endurance.

Inesca had heard of these beasts being hunted by large groups of riders, but never herded as if they were cattle. How could a lone rider even begin to accomplish such a task?

"Any suggestions?" she asked softly while stroking Nycor's neck.

The stallion shook his head. The animal several yards in front of them was of no interest to him.

Time was being lost, and Inesca knew she had to act soon, but charging out there without a plan might send the buck running in the wrong direction. Inesca let her mind wander until she recalled a time when her father was faced with helping a neighbor get a bull back into its pen. But instead of trying to drive it inside, they had angered the stubborn creature enough that it chased them inside the fence where it was trapped.

"If that's our only option, then I hope this beast has a bad temper. I've no time to chase down a coward if it won't cooperate."

Inesca looked down and noticed some small stones just outside the field. She climbed down from Nycor and gathered them in her hands before returning to the saddle.

"Time to unleash that obnoxious spirit of yours," she said as she slowly rode Nycor closer to the field.

The buck continued grazing contentedly as they drew nearer. Inesca continued to debate the best way to approach the creature. If they charged out into the field at full speed, it might let its instinct dictate its reaction and run. But attempting to sneak up behind it was absurd, and Inesca knew that she would not be able to reach it without being heard first.

Turning Nycor to the left, Inesca urged him to enter the field on its eastern end. Perhaps if they approached slowly from the side, the buck would ignore them at first.

The moon set the field aglow, and the stalks of wheat crunched under Nycor's hooves. The buck lifted its head with its ears raised and stared at them. Inesca prayed silently as she continued to urge Nycor along at a slow walk as if they were not interested in the buck. After what seemed like an eternity, the buck lowered its head back down to the wheat and continued to eat.

She took a deep breath. *That's a good sign. He may prefer fighting to flight.*

After they passed the buck from a distance, Inesca directed Nycor toward the center of the field. It still did not move, and Inesca wondered if the beast might love the wheat too much to chase after them if she was able to anger it. But if they were to challenge it properly, they would have to approach it from the front. A predator would attack from the side or from behind. A rival would challenge it head-on to provoke a fight, and though Inesca had no interest in fighting, she would have to make the beast believe she wanted to.

As she guided Nycor within the final yards of the beast, the stallion grew restless and tossed his head more often. He did not wish to be this close to the strange animal, but he still continued on at her urging. Inesca did not doubt that he could also sense her own nervousness.

The buck raised its head again and snorted. Inesca wondered at what point her plan would fall apart as she finally drew Nycor to a halt. Would it be when the buck bolted suddenly for the trees? Or when it rushed forward to gore Nycor with its vicious horns?

For a moment, nothing happened as Inesca debated how to draw the buck into aggressive action. She fingered the stone in one of her hands but hesitated to use it.

The buck did not turn back to the wheat again. Instead, it snorted and shook its horns as a signal for them to leave. Nycor interpreted it as a threat and reared slightly before bringing both of his front hooves on the ground in front of him, sending a tremor through the dirt. The buck moved forward a bit and shook its head again.

Inesca raised her arm and let the stone fly. It struck the beast on the head, but it was not hard enough to do any real damage.

"Fight back," Inesca urged. "Come on!"

At first, nothing happened as the buck seemed to be contemplating what had hit it. Inesca raised her arm again to throw another, but then she caught sight of the movement of its legs as it poised to spring forward. With a firm kick to Nycor's side, she spurred him into a quick turn and a gallop toward the far side of the field where the walled pen lay.

At the same time, Inesca felt certain that the buck was not following them. Why should it chase them once they began running? She looked back over her shoulder, and a gasp caught in her throat.

Barely a few feet away from Nycor's hind legs, the buck charged at full speed. Its head was lowered as it tried to strike at the stallion from behind. Inesca urged Nycor into a faster gallop as she now feared that the buck was following too closely.

The two beasts cut across the field like a northern wind driven before a storm. Inesca could just make out the silhouette of the enclosure as it came into view in the moonlight. Now the test was a matter of a race between the buck and the stallion. If she could not get Nycor through both gates in time, then disaster would follow. Looking back, Inesca could see just how fast the buck was proving to be. Nycor was only just managing to keep ahead of its horns.

Finally, the first gate of the walled pen opened up before them like a mouth. Inesca feared that the buck might notice it and turn aside, so she took another stone and tossed it at the charging beast. Her aim failed her as the stone hit the ground several feet away, but her second throw hit the buck's horn.

When she saw it snort and charge even faster, Inesca turned her attention to the gate ahead of them, and she urged Nycor to increase his speed. Rushing through the first opening, Inesca heard Lord Beristo's servants push the doors shut behind them.

As she reached the second, Inesca grabbed the bar above the second gate and dropped from Nycor's back as he ran under it. She whirled around and shoved the doors closed, letting the bolt fall to seal them shut. It fell into place just as the buck's horns rammed the door.

The impact shook the panels in front of her face, and Inesca felt faint as her balance wavered. Placing her hand against the stone wall beside the doors, she turned and saw Omaron standing near Lord Beristo. His stern expression remained unchanged, and the sand in the glass beside him had run its course.

Lord Beristo looked from Inesca to Omaron and then at the hourglass. He quickly grabbed it and shook it slightly so that a little sand fell back into the first section before setting it down again.

Omaron continued to stare at Inesca, and the weight of his unyielding gaze weakened the hope that she had held for her future here. She bowed to Lord Beristo and turned to lead Nycor back to the stable. Omaron remained silent as he watched her go.

"You will not begrudge her a few seconds of time," Lord Beristo insisted once Inesca was gone. "It was not a fair challenge, but regardless, you will train her."

"I will."

Lord Beristo paused and glanced up at him.

"I did not expect her to complete the task at all," Omaron stated. "Still, it could have been done better."

"Then the next time my fields are being consumed by a Naldorr buck, I'll send you out to take care of it."

Omaron looked down at him without seeming concerned.

"Unshaken as always." Lord Beristo sighed. "But though you will not admit it, I have surprised you today. I have brought you a rider who will surpass your expectations."

"She was still at least a minute late," Omaron insisted.

"And you are always late, so the two of you have something in common. But enough of this; I am satisfied that you have agreed to train her willingly. Tell my men to have that beast killed. It has stolen enough of my wheat, and now I will get something back for my lost crop. I will have the servants send some of the meat back to you, since this was your idea. And you may keep the horns for yourself."

"What of the hide?"

"That will go to the girl as a reward for justifying my confidence in her riding abilities and for bringing the stallion back unharmed."

Omaron bowed and moved inside the stable as Lord Beristo walked off in the direction of his bed. In the dim light of the stable, Omaron found Inesca brushing her horse in silence. Her eyes widened when she saw him, and hesitantly, she stepped out of the stall.

"Be here at dawn," he said. "We start with the morning light."

Inesca's expression betrayed her surprise, but he turned away, using his iron staff to propel him back into the night air.

"I know that you do not think women should ride in the races," Inesca said, following him. "I was told that there are many reasons for such a view. What is yours?"

Omaron paused in the door frame. "I say that you should not be here. That is all the reason I will give."

"I have nowhere else to go."

"You may think differently when it is too late to change your mind."

Inesca glanced down at his missing leg. "Does that mean that you regret riding in the races?"

Omaron turned his head slightly but did not reply to her question. Before anything else could be said, he pulled himself into the darkness and left her alone in the stable once more.

Chapter 6

The crisp morning air wrapped Inesca in its bracing grip, and she shivered and quickened her pace. The sun heralded its coming with a dim light on the edge of the eastern sky. A few bright stars were still visible overhead.

Inside the stable, Nycor was resting with his head bowed as he stood, but as Inesca drew closer, he awoke and moved his head forward to greet her. She reached up and patted his neck.

"Do you think we can handle more of Omaron's challenges today?"

The gray stallion nodded his head, and she laughed. Inesca ran her fingers through his thick black mane and pulled out a few pieces of hay. Opening the stall door, she moved inside and began to brush his coat. A dapple pattern consisting of brilliant white and various tones of gray covered the stallion's flank. Inesca remembered her father telling her Nycor would draw attention wherever he went, and for that reason, he wanted her to ride the stallion only close to their home.

When she finished brushing Nycor, Inesca picked up a blanket and a saddle and walked back into the stall. She and Nycor would have to accept the rules and boundaries of a new home now.

"You will not need those today."

The sudden interruption of another voice made her jump, and she was grateful that she was hidden behind Nycor. When Inesca carried the saddle out of Nycor's stall, she saw Omaron standing there, watching her and leaning upon his rod.

"I'm not riding today?"

"You already know how to ride. Don't you?"

His tone indicated it was more of a statement than a question. Without further explanation, Omaron turned and began making his way to a table in the open area at the end of the stable. Inesca placed the saddle back on its rack. As she closed his stall door, Nycor stamped his hooves and whinnied.

Omaron seated himself on a large chair at one end of the table and motioned for her to sit down on the bench.

"Have you ever seen one of the Great Races before?"

"No."

"Can you tell me the rules of the races?"

Inesca shifted uneasily on the bench. "No, I can't."

"Have you ever met a rider from the races aside from myself?"

She sighed. "I don't think so."

Omaron crossed his arms. "Perhaps it would be better for you to start by telling me what you *do* know. And why you dare to attempt to be a rider in these races."

"I know that the races can be long and that they are dangerous. There is one rider for each lord in a race. If a rider does well, he or she may gain fame throughout the Six Realms and be remembered for his or her skills by many people."

Omaron let out a short, scornful laugh, startling her again. "Is that why you came here? For fame and glory?"

"I came because this was the only way for me to keep the horse my father gave me. And because no one appreciates riding skills at the mill where they wanted to send me."

A brief pause followed her answer.

"Are you certain that you made the right choice?"

His usual disapproving tone was absent for a change. Inesca looked up at his face and gave a confident nod.

"The mills in the East Province are well known for their ability to draw in the poor women and turn them into workers who are little better than slaves. You may have food and a bed, but service is demanded until death, and no one cares how you are treated. Had I simply given up and allowed myself to be sent to such a place, I always would have regretted not taking this chance."

"Keep that reason in your mind then," Omaron said as he leaned forward over the table. "And do not tell me later that you believe the mill would have been better than the races."

"May God curse me as an ungrateful craven if ever I say such a thing."

Omaron sat back in his chair with an amused expression. "Oh, so you are from the East Province, but you believe in the god of the Six Realms of Rynar?"

"I believe that He is God over every land."

"This god was not known on the island where I came from, but here I have seen lies and cruelty performed in his name. Perhaps you know only as much about the god of this land as you know about the Great Races."

"My father told me not to judge God based on the actions of men. He said that the only times you can see the hand of God in the acts of men are in moments of love and sacrifice."

Beneath the surface of the table, Omaron's hand drifted to the stub of his right leg as his expression grew solemn again. After a moment, he used his staff to pull himself up, and he grabbed two belts with scabbards and swords from the wall.

"Our time for your training is brief. You'll have to learn on your feet." He tossed one of the belts to her and walked out into an open area just outside the stable's walls. Inesca fastened the belt around her waist and drew the weapon from its scabbard to get a better look at it. In her right hand, she held a short sword with a cruciform hilt. The total length of the hilt and the blade could be no more than two feet.

"Have you ever used a blade before?" Omaron asked.

"Only a hunting knife."

Inesca held up the sword and waited for Omaron to draw its twin, but he smiled and called one of the young stable keepers over to them.

"You are bold but not ready to fight me yet. Tarain is not a warrior, but he knows how to use one of these."

Omaron handed his blade to the stable keeper, Tarain. "Let's see how you fare against each other."

Tarain grasped the hilt firmly as he moved toward her. Inesca instinctively backed away, but Omaron used his iron rod to shove her forward.

"Rule one," he said. "No rider is allowed to back away from the race. You may slow down or speed up, but you must always move forward. Once you start a race, you must finish it. If you turn back, you will be disgraced."

Tarain thrust his blade toward her to test her movements but stopped short of actually striking her. Inesca froze even though she knew she had made herself a perfect target.

"Learn to maneuver around him," Omaron insisted.

Tarain came at her again, but Inesca saw an opening and side-stepped his attack.

"Remember to defend yourself! Rule two is that each rider is allowed one weapon for short-range conflict. You will never pass the other riders if you do not learn to defend yourself and your horse."

When Tarain's sword turned to pierce her shoulder, Inesca used her blade to knock it aside. But Tarain regained control fast enough to strike again, and this time the edge of his sword tore through the skin of her arm.

Omaron stepped in suddenly with his staff and struck both Inesca and Tarain with it. Then he seized Tarain's sword and started to swing it down upon the boy. Inesca saw Tarain cringe, and she thrust her own sword out to intercept

Omaron. She managed to deflect his blade, but he quickly turned on her as if he had anticipated her move. With a blow to her head from his hilt, he knocked her back to the ground.

"Rule three. *Never* help another rider. It is forbidden to show mercy on your competitors. There are no *allies* in these races. Do not try to make friends with the other riders. Do not trust them."

Omaron cast a glance down at his missing leg. "You must see them as your enemies. Or be prepared to suffer the consequences."

Inesca pushed herself up from the dirt. "So, I should not expect any form of kindness or courtesy from them?"

"No, you should not. But no matter how the other riders treat you, learn to focus only on winning the race. You must always be prepared to defend yourself against the other riders or to leave them behind, even if they are being attacked."

"That is not how my father raised me," Inesca admitted. "And what happens if this rule is broken? Disgrace?"

"Any rider who breaks this rule will be seized and imprisoned. After that, you may die in a dungeon or as a slave. Most riders have no trouble keeping this rule. See to it that you are one of them."

"Why is the punishment so severe?"

"The lords will not tolerate riders who put anything before the goal of winning. If a rider focuses on defending another, the purpose of the race is cast aside. The lords want only to see competition, not compassion."

Inesca glanced back at Tarain, who had dusted himself off and was returning to his chores without giving her another look.

"Are there no exceptions to these rules?"

"No, not for a rider who hopes to be a success. The only time riders are not penalized for turning around is when they can offer proof of being threatened by other riders."

"You mean riders can turn around to escape other riders who are trying to attack them?" Inesca asked.

"No," Omaron answered curtly. "They turn around to attack the ones who threatened them to prevent them from carrying out their plans. If you are looking for an escape, you must ride forward toward the finish. Turning around to ride in the other direction will gain you nothing but pain and disgrace."

Inesca picked up the sword and held it awkwardly. "I can ride well enough, but I'm not sure about this. Could I have a bow instead? I've hunted with one many times before."

"Long-range weapons are not permitted in the races. It creates an unfair advantage. A rider in the back could shoot down all of his competition and cross the finish without truly racing anyone. Riders may carry only short swords, clubs, short-handled spears, daggers, or maces."

"Some of those can be thrown," Inesca argued. "Doesn't that make them long-range weapons?"

"It does when they are used that way, but if no one sees the attack, who will know the difference? There is a section of each race that falls after the first length and before the final stretch to the finish where only a few scouts will be watching the progress of the riders. Rules are often broken at that point, but most weapons are never used until the end of the race. The final mile is always the most dangerous."

Omaron raised his sword and gestured for her to do the same. "Practice is not over yet. Block my blade as I strike at you, and perhaps we'll strengthen that arm of yours. If you cannot defend yourself against a stable boy," he said as he looked at the shallow cut on her arm, "then you're not ready for the races."

The morning sun was still low in the sky, and Inesca drew a deep breath as she tightened her grip on the hilt of her sword and prepared for a long day.

The sounds of a stallion's protests echoed in the early morning air across Lord Edgerr's estate. Derreth found his younger brother leaning against the stable with his eyes fixed on the pasture.

"Don't force yourself to watch, Kes."

When no answer came, Derreth sighed and followed Kestorn's gaze to the sight of Halon attempting to throw Trestan from his back. Trestan's gangly limbs and lack of control reminded him of a scarecrow flailing about in the wind.

"He doesn't deserve to ride Halon. I nearly fed him my fist this morning when he walked by with a smug grin on his face and told me that I'd be responsible for his chores today."

"He's not grinning now," Derreth said with half a smile, but Kestorn only continued to stare with a furrowed brow.

Halon swished his tail and pulled at the reins as Trestan finally got him to start moving across the pasture. Once Halon began to run, he weaved from side to side as Trestan seemed unable to keep him running in a straight course.

"He's trying too hard to hold him back. He'll never be able to manage Halon in an actual race," Kestorn said.

Derreth watched as Trestan finally managed to slow Halon down, but instead of just slowing his pace by a little, Halon stopped running altogether and started fighting Trestan again. One of the men from the fence tossed Trestan something, and it wasn't until he raised it up in the air that Derreth could see what it was.

Shouting loudly, Trestan whipped Halon again and again. Kestorn's fist tightened, and Derreth grabbed his shoulder as he started to move forward. "If that stallion's half as stubborn as you, he can handle this on his own," he said.

With each blow from the whip, the red stallion only became more enraged. Halon began rearing and throwing his weight around recklessly. When Trestan finally fell, several of the men had to grab him and drag him out quickly before Halon trampled him.

"Come on, little brother. They'll stop for a while now. I'll help you with those chores." Derreth walked away and opened the door to the stable, but he waited until he saw Kestorn following him to enter.

"How can Lord Edgerr not see that it's not me who's going to get Halon injured, but his new favorite?" Kestorn asked as he flung the stable door shut.

"Trestan isn't his new favorite. He's just the only rider left, aside from us."

"But why does he hate you? Why can't you ride in the next race instead of me?"

Derreth walked to Celestro and stroked the golden stallion's neck. Celestro greeted him with a nod and a huff of air.

"He doesn't trust me," Derreth replied.

"Why? You've never said a word against him."

"It doesn't matter why. His pride was wounded by the attack, and he's decided to take it out on us since the Raegond escaped."

"And losing the race in Sassot is going to help his pride? Doesn't he see that Trestan could never win?" Kestorn asked as he shoved a pitchfork into a pile of hay.

"He's not even thinking about that, Kes. He's just angry."

Kestorn tossed the pitchfork against the wall. "He's not the only one. It's not right for him to let someone else ride my horse."

Turning back to his brother, Derreth snatched up the pitchfork to finish filling the stall with new hay.

"He's not *your* horse. Halon is the property of Lord Edgerr."

"Yes, but can he ride Halon?"

The shuffling of hay was all that answered him.

"There have been nights where I've thought about taking him and not coming back. He'd be better off away from Lord Edgerr. And so would I."

Derreth turned back to his brother. "You know what the penalty for stealing a racehorse is."

"I might get away. I'm a fast rider, and what horse could catch Halon if he had a head start?"

"It wouldn't be enough," Derreth said sternly. "They would hunt you down. And then what? Do you think I could watch you being beaten and then burned to death? And what good would it do Halon? He'd be brought back here and treated badly until some rider could break him."

Kestorn dropped his gaze, and Derreth thrust the pitchfork back into his hands. "*This* is our life. We're together here. And Lord Edgerr will change his mind and let us ride again."

Derreth's stern expression faded as he grinned and said, "After the humiliation that Trestan will cost him at the race, what choice will he have?"

A faint smile crossed Kestorn's face. Looking around them to make sure they were alone, Derreth then moved closer to his brother and put his hand on his shoulder. "Promise me that you'll put that idea of running away out of your head."

"For now," Kestorn agreed. "But I'd tell you if I was going to leave. You know I wouldn't keep secrets from you."

Gripping the pitchfork, Kestorn moved to the next stall that needed more hay. Derreth remained still as the word *secrets* echoed in his thoughts.

Chapter 7

After a week of training with the short sword, Inesca stretched her arms out and let the wind sweep past her as Nycor galloped over the fields. Omaron had finally allowed her to begin riding in preparation for the race, and each day, he sent her out farther with Nycor.

The Great Races of the Six Realms required hours of skilled riding across chosen courses that stretched across each realm for many miles. Endurance as well as speed was necessary to win. Inesca had taken Nycor on long rides within the East Province, but these races would still require more from him and from her.

Inesca prepared herself as Nycor charged through a grove of trees and toward the final field that lay between them and the stable. Five targets rose above the field on circular posts with outstretched beams like stiff limbs waiting to greet her. Each target had a wooden circle on one limb and a club with spikes on the other.

Drawing her sword, Inesca urged Nycor into a faster gallop as they charged toward the first target. If she hit the target and failed to ride away fast enough, then the wooden figure would spin and the club would swing around, striking her on the back.

Nycor raced past the first target, and Inesca just barely scratched the circle with her sword. When they reached the second, she managed a stronger blow but felt the wind rush past her as the club narrowly missed her.

The third and fourth targets were a success, but as Nycor neared the fifth, she caught sight of Omaron watching her with a stern gaze. She watched him for a second too long, and Nycor carried her out of reach of the fifth target as she tried to stretch back and hit it. But she was too late, and in another few seconds, they had reached the end of their practice route.

Inesca guided Nycor to a halt and sheathed her sword as she dismounted. Patting Nycor on the neck, she felt his body tremble with energy as though he was still ready to keep going. Omaron used his iron rod to draw closer to them, digging it into the ground as he moved.

"Never look away from the race. You must always know what is ahead of you and what is beside you. And sometimes, even what is just behind you."

"I think I'm going to need another pair of eyes for all of that," Inesca said, smiling.

Omaron's stern expression remained unchanged.

"I know. Hold my tongue and train harder," she replied as her smile faded. "What else?"

"Your time was not good enough. It's still too slow."

"But I finished within the time limit."

"Your goal cannot just be to finish the race. It must be to win. There is only one reward, and that goes to the lord whose rider finishes first."

"Right. So, I'll be faster tomorrow."

Omaron held out his arm to block her path to the stables. "We are running out of tomorrows, and time must be given for the stallion to rest before the race."

Inesca sighed as she glanced at the training field before facing him. "Couldn't I practice some jumps with Nycor instead of this? We need only a few obstacles for that."

Omaron studied her quietly, but Inesca did not lower her gaze. She had shown him that she could manage difficult jumps with Nycor before, and yet, he never admired that skill. Despite his cold silence, Inesca still loved to achieve jumps with Nycor. It reminded her of the lessons her father had given her, and she heard his praise even if others scorned her.

"It is a risk to the horse," Omaron insisted. "And speed is required, not the tricks of a fool. Go out again for a short ride across the eastern plains. I'll time you from the wall."

Inesca mounted Nycor and rode toward the open eastern gate that led to the plains just outside the walls surrounding Lord Beristo's estate. The dry and level ground was ideal for riding.

With a slight kick, she spurred him into a gallop once they were through the gate. Nycor's hooves sent a cloud of dust whirling behind them as he raced alongside the wall. Inesca didn't try to hold him back as he charged into a faster pace with his black mane and tail flying in the wind.

None of her father's horses had ever loved to run as much as Nycor. Always restless in the stable and quick to take on a challenge off the forest trails, Inesca believed the gray stallion longed for this new life as much as she did. Her father had once claimed they were a perfect pair for trouble, but still he had given her Nycor as he lay dying, not one of the other milder horses. Inesca hoped it was because he believed in her abilities and intended this opportunity for her.

The Legacy of the Lost Rider

Taking a deep breath, Inesca watched as they approached the corner of the east wall and the north. Suddenly a flash of red caught her eye, and she saw a man in a mud-stained cloak appear from around the edge of the north wall. Guiding Nycor to the right, she managed to prevent her stallion from running him over, but the man still stumbled and fell to the ground as if he had been struck.

"Are you all right, sir?" she asked as she guided Nycor to stop and wait.

With a groan, the stranger shielded his eyes until he could manage to pull himself up into a sitting position. Aside from the hand covering his eyes, his face was almost hidden by unruly brown hair and a thick beard. His white tunic, which looked like it might have been costly once, was stained and worn.

"What fool is riding across the practice field?" he protested loudly.

"One who is practicing," Inesca replied impatiently. "If you knew it was the practice field, why weren't you more careful?"

The man stumbled to his feet and took his hand away from his eyes. It seemed to take several minutes for him to see her properly. "Oh, it's you. I heard that Lord Beristo brought a woman back from the East Province, but you're not even a woman yet, are you, girl?"

Inesca could smell mead on his breath as he moved closer with an unpleasant smile.

"And you are hardly a man. Stay out of my way, or I may not be able to stop my horse next time."

But the stranger did not back away, and the ridiculous grin on his face did not fade. "Been working with Omaron, have you? Does he have you riding in circles out here? You know you don't have to do everything that brute tells you."

Inesca tried to move Nycor farther away from the man and his potent breath.

"He used to order me about, but I don't listen anymore. I'm still a rider, and he's not. No reason for me to pay attention to someone who lost his leg and his horse."

Inesca glanced back at him. "You're a rider for Lord Beristo?"

"My name is Jirro, and I'm his only rider since Lolker died. Won't be long before I'm riding this stallion. You didn't think he was actually yours, did you?"

As he finished speaking, Jirro's hand seized Nycor's bridle, and the stallion reared with his front hooves flailing and his ears flattened back against his head. Experience had taught Inesca how to hold on when someone upset Nycor, so she managed to stay in the saddle.

Jirro was struck by one of the stallion's hooves and thrown to the ground. Inesca tried to calm him and finally jumped down while still holding the reins. When the stallion saw her in front of him, he finally stood still, though he continued to toss his head. Inesca stroked his neck and spoke softly to him before turning to Jirro. He appeared dazed as Inesca bent over his limp form and checked his head for an injury.

"Drunken fool! Don't you know better than to grab the bridle of a strange horse?" she said.

Another shadow fell across them, and Inesca looked up to see Omaron approaching with his rod pounding the ground as he took each step with his remaining foot.

Jirro opened his eyes and saw Inesca leaning over him. His hand seized her wrist as if to pull her closer to him, and in a flash, Inesca's other hand grabbed her sword and sliced his arm.

"Ahh! You little wretch," he growled as he released her and put his hand around the shallow cut on his arm.

Inesca stood up and backed away from him with her sword still drawn.

"Next time you come across a rider on the ground," Omaron said, "don't stop to see if he's alive."

"Yes, I know. Show no compassion to other riders." Inesca sighed. "But he works for Lord Beristo, and I was afraid—"

"I told you to ride. If he can't stay out of the way, the fault is his."

Jirro's smile returned as he looked up at Omaron. "So, there you are, old man. Why don't you let me train her for a little while?"

Omaron continued to direct his stern gaze at Inesca, but he raised his rod and let the end of it fall on Jirro's nose. Another cry of pain shot up from the ground.

"Bring your horse back to the stable," he commanded Inesca.

She nodded and carefully led Nycor around Jirro as he lay in the dirt.

"You won't last long in the races, girl," Jirro called after her, but his voice sounded far more nasal and muffled than it had before. Then he laughed as he rose and stumbled back toward the north wall.

"What is he doing out here?" Inesca asked as she caught up to Omaron.

"Lord Beristo has forbidden any of the servants or any of his men to give Jirro wine or mead, but that does not stop him from wandering to the nearest town and drinking there. No doubt, he has just returned from such an errand."

If the land beyond the wall was Jirro's favorite place to wander after drinking, Inesca thought she might try to avoid riding alone there if she could. As they drew near to the eastern gate, Inesca suddenly remembered something she had wanted to ask Omaron.

"This morning, you told me that the lord is the one who receives the reward if his rider wins the race. Does the rider win anything?" she asked.

"The satisfaction of knowing that honor was brought to his lord."

Inesca remained silent for a moment as she considered that.

"What kind of reward were you hoping for?"

Hesitating a moment longer, Inesca finally drew out something from a bundle tied to her saddle. After a few seconds, she handed it to Omaron.

"I was wondering if a rider might ever get something like this."

Omaron studied the medallion that she had given him. It was difficult to read his expression as he lifted it and turned it around, but his deep voice possessed a solemn tone when he asked, "Where did you get this?"

Inesca tightened her grip on Nycor's reins, and he pulled at them as if sensing her agitation. "I found it in the East Province. I'm not even sure what it is."

He shot a quick but hard gaze in her direction. "Years ago, they gave out medallions to the riders who won the races. But the medallions cost money, and the lords hosting the races became reluctant to spend their wealth on prizes for riders that were often not their own. Now they allow winning riders to choose a piece of gear for their horses from their stables. And if their own riders win, then they don't have to give them anything."

"But the markings on the medallion," Inesca pressed. "What do they mean?"

"The realm of Trineth bears a falcon on its banners. Since that is the animal that appears above the horse and rider, this medallion was won there."

"And the mark at the bottom?"

Omaron ran his thumb over the raised circles and then lowered the medallion. "Each set of races had its own mark, placed here under the horse. These spheres are a reminder of the strange moon some men saw in the sky before that racing season, when it became red like blood in the night sky."

His tone grew more forbidding, and Inesca asked, "Do you remember when that was?"

"Thirty years ago. It was one of the last times that medallions were awarded in the races."

"And who won the race in Trineth that year?"

Omaron turned to look down at her, and Inesca drew back, feeling ill at ease as his gaze narrowed.

"Why do you want to know?"

"I want to learn more about the races. This medallion interests me even though I don't know the man it belonged to."

"That man died many years ago fighting in the war against the Raegond.

And this is a dangerous object to be carrying. Bury it or throw it in the river. It doesn't belong here."

He shoved the medallion into her hands.

"No! I can't just ... I mean, it may be valuable," Inesca protested as she held the medallion to her chest.

Omaron's expression deepened into anger. "You intend to sell it?"

"No, but—"

"Its only value is its worth in silver, so if you're not going to sell it, it has no value."

Even as Omaron started to move forward again, Inesca clutched the medallion tightly in her hand.

"That medallion is nothing but trouble. Get rid of it," he insisted.

As he disappeared through the gate, Inesca opened her hand and looked down at the medallion. What if the man who won this prize thirty years ago had not truly died in the war? What if he had remained in the East Province to hide from some danger that lay here in the Six Realms? *If this is my father's medallion, I must learn the name by which he was known when he won it. Without that name, I'll never know who he was or why he left*, she thought.

Chapter 8

As the final days before the race in the realm of Sassot drew near, Inesca found that her training sessions were cut off almost as quickly as they had begun. Omaron gave her specific instructions regarding the care of Nycor, but he insisted that she not take him out riding.

"We'll have a long journey to Sassot, and that is more exercise than any horse needs before the race," he told her.

After caring for Nycor each morning, Inesca felt as though she was growing just as restless as he was. Lord Beristo's servants were busy packing for the journey, and if Inesca remained inside the manor house for too long, she often felt as though she was in the way. However, taking walks outside was even more unpleasant because Jirro lurked around the edges of the estate. More than once, Inesca caught him watching her with an expression of mixed jealousy and derision. She decided that he kept away from the manor house so he could continue his drinking and avoid Lord Beristo.

Once, Inesca attempted to follow Omaron and ask him more questions about the race, but he bluntly told her to go away and let him rest, adding that she should be doing the same. Lord Beristo had no time for her, either. He was busy checking over every detail of the preparations for the journey, and at other times, he met with his council.

On the afternoon of the day before their departure, Inesca found Sirryn walking through the great hall while reading over a letter. He looked up when he heard her footsteps and smiled kindly.

"I suppose you haven't changed your mind about being a rider, have you?" he asked.

"No, but I wish we were already at the race. I can't stand all of this waiting."

"Ah, yes, the journey to the races is always my least favorite part," Sirryn admitted.

"Then you will come with us? I thought the members of Lord Beristo's council would remain behind."

"The rest of them will. After all, they will be in charge of the realm of Ettidor while Lord Beristo is away, but they never listen to me anyway, so I won't be missed," he said with a flicker of amusement in his expression. "The races are more exciting than our meetings. And I have a brother whom I mean to visit when we reach Sassot."

"Why doesn't your brother live here in Ettidor?"

"Well, he is a member of Lord Felond's council. The only times that I get the opportunity to see him are during the races in Sassot."

"How often are the races held in Sassot?"

"Once every other year. This happens because three of the lords host races one year, and then the other three host races during the next year, and so on."

"That's a long time to be separated from part of your family."

"Compared with others who have families in different realms, I am fortunate to see him so often. But these customs must seem strange to you compared to life in the East Province."

Sirryn folded the letter in his hands and started to turn away, but Inesca darted in front of him.

"You're right. I need someone to teach me."

He noted her expectant gaze but smiled as he moved past her. "What an excellent idea. I'll discuss it with Lord Beristo the next time I see him."

"Please, Sirryn, just a few questions," Inesca persisted as she followed him to the far end of the great hall. "I have reached Omaron's limit, and he refuses to answer any more."

"I'm surprised he answered any at all." He continued to walk toward the next corridor, but Inesca remained by his side.

"How are members of a lord's council chosen?"

Sirryn sighed, but his smile did not fade. "There are twelve men on each council, but only four of them are chosen by the lord himself. I am an example of one of those four. I was permitted to stay in the realm in which I was born and to serve on the council."

"Permitted? Then your brother was forced to leave?"

"In a way, I suppose he was. Although it would be more accurate to say that my parents were forced to let him go. Have you heard of the city of Valmontes?"

"The island city?"

"It was once the home of the king of Rynar. Now, that island in the center of the great Septamar River is the home of the Royal Council of Rynar."

"What is the Royal Council?"

Sirryn shot her a surprised glance. "How could you not know about them?"

"I've heard of very few councils in the East Province, and here, you have so many. I don't understand why you need councils if each realm is ruled by a lord."

"I can see that there is much you do not understand about our ways. Have you ever wondered why the Evaliscan lords are only lords?"

"That's the way things have always been, isn't it?"

"I suppose everything seems as though it has lasted forever when you're young. But the truth is that once, Rynar had a king. There were no great councils, and Rynar was not divided into six realms. The country had its nobles, but many of them died in a war that nearly devastated the kingdom. Six Evaliscan princes came to Rynar, offering to help restore the kingdom, but they wanted something in return. However, the king was unwilling to make them the absolute rulers over his people, so he made them lords, nobility subject to a higher rule. And yet, the king had no heir, so he had to find someone to take over his rule when he died and keep the lords accountable for their actions."

"So, the Royal Council was the king's replacement?"

Sirryn nodded. "King Eisron never felt comfortable choosing just one man as his successor, so he appointed men he trusted to the Royal Council to watch over his kingdom after he died. And he insisted that each lord have a council within his realm with whom he must confide. Eight of the members of each of these councils are chosen and trained by the Royal Council. Remember I told you that only four are chosen by the lord of that realm."

"I still don't understand why this means your brother had to leave Ettidor."

"All of the council members who were trained in Valmontes were once boys who were sent away from their families at age five to be raised and educated in the island city."

"Why would they take them away from their families?" Inesca asked.

"It is considered a necessary sacrifice to preserve peace between the Six Realms. In Valmontes, the boys become men who are trained not to favor one realm above another, but always to seek to maintain the balance of power between the realms and to prevent war. Have you ever considered why Evaliscan lords never go to war with each other? Or why one lord does not seek to take possession of a second realm? It is not because they have not wanted to, but because the councils are in place to prevent those desires from turning into actions."

"Doesn't each lord have his own knights and men-at-arms? How can the councils prevent war if that's what the lord commands?"

"All these men are also trained in Valmontes, and they are trained to be loyal to the council. Their duty is to protect their lord from threats like the Raegond or to arrest criminals that arise within the realms. But if a lord attempts to steal land or power that does not belong to him, they must obey the council of that realm and ultimately remove that lord from power. When this happens, another Evaliscan becomes the new lord in place of the old. It has happened before."

"Are boys also sent away from home to be trained as men-at-arms in Valmontes?" Inesca asked.

"No, those trained to be knights and men-at-arms must choose that life, and there are many who do. But they must be at least sixteen years of age when they arrive in Valmontes for their training."

"But they may also be sent to serve in a different realm and be separated from their families?"

"Yes, that is generally what happens, but they are allowed some time of their own to travel during their years of service. In some ways, they have more freedom than those of us who serve on the councils."

"It seems to be a strange way to keep the realms united."

"The last king of Rynar did not wish to see the lords divide his kingdom into separate countries to make war on each other. His measures may have been extreme, but they appear to have worked for the past two hundred years. But that's enough of a history lesson. I still have arrangements to make with the council before our departure."

"Just one more question," Inesca added quickly. "There's a rider I'm curious about, but I've given up asking Omaron any more questions."

Sirryn laughed. "And you think I'm the one to ask? There was a time when I couldn't even remember all of the names of Lord Beristo's riders. What makes you think I'll be able to help you?"

"I think there was something special about this one. Do you remember the name of the rider who won the race in Trineth thirty years ago?"

"Thirty years ago? That's a long time to remember something. Do you know anything else about this rider?"

"No." Inesca sighed.

"Well, as I tried to warn you, I'm useless when it comes to these things. But you could try the library. Lord Beristo has some records on the races. Come along and I'll help you find them before I return to the council."

Inesca followed close beside him as he led her down the hall and toward another corridor. The walls were lined with portraits of Lord Beristo's predecessors. Many of them had something in their appearances that reminded Inesca of Lord Beristo. Maybe it was the hint of reddish-brown coloring in their gray hair or the roundness of their noses. The ones closer to his portrait were large with broad shoulders, like him, and seemed to be his father and grandfathers.

He's fortunate to know where he came from and who his family was, Inesca thought as she passed by the images. Each one was set under words inscribed in gold on a wooden plaque that read: The House of Glenmir.

"Glenmir was the original lord of Ettidor," Sirryn explained as if reading her thoughts. "He was the youngest of the brothers who became the six lords of Rynar."

They continued down the hall until they reached the doors of the library. Sirryn led her inside and directly to a book that he set out on a table. "Ah, I believe this is it," he said. "Lord Beristo was looking up some information about a past race just yesterday."

Inesca eagerly leaned closer as he turned the pages until he came to the right year.

"There," she said as she pointed to the entry for the race in Trineth and followed it to a name. "Arryn of Fortur … does that name mean anything to you?"

Sirryn's brows furrowed.

"I don't know about this rider, but Sir Arryn of Fortur … that's a name I know. He was a faithful servant of the Six Realms of Rynar before his death in battle. He was considered an honorable knight and well-respected by many."

"Could the rider and the knight have been the same man?"

"Perhaps. I never knew Sir Arryn's past, but any man who rises to distinction can become a knight."

"Do you remember anything else about him?"

"Only that he died in the Battle of Tortesra."

"Omaron indicated that the rider died in the same way."

Sirryn took the book from her. "I thought you said that Omaron wasn't listening to any more of your questions. How is it that he told you that, but not the name of the man he was speaking of?"

Inesca felt her face grow warm. She had a feeling Omaron had not wanted to tell her the name of the man who won the medallion she showed to him, and she thought it would be best if Sirryn did not know her reasons.

"He was trying to teach me something about the races by using this man as an example, and he didn't believe the name was important."

"But you disagree. Why?"

"I think he might have known my father," she said hesitantly.

Sirryn studied her with a skeptical expression, but he started to put away the book without saying anything else. Inesca's gaze wandered toward the rest of the library, and a portrait of a red-haired woman on the far wall caught her attention.

"Sirryn, who is that?"

He smiled and shook his head. "And you are surprised that Omaron believes that you ask too many questions." Still, he followed her gaze until he was also looking at the portrait. "That was Lord Beristo's wife. She died suddenly after an illness. They never had any children, and he has never remarried. As a result, he will have to let the Royal Council choose an heir for him."

"Am I allowed to ask any more questions?"

"No. But I am assuming that you want to know why Lord Beristo never remarried. So, I'll ask you a question in return. You told me once that your mother died when you were young. Yet your father never remarried, did he?"

Inesca shook her head.

"Then I suspect they both had their reasons."

She glanced back at the portrait. "I'm sorry that I'm such a nuisance at times, Sirryn, but thank you for being willing to answer my questions."

"You bring a bit of bright energy to this old house, Inesca, but promise me that you'll be careful in the races."

Inesca nodded, but she felt as though *careful* would not be enough. She wanted to win the upcoming race, and from what Omaron had taught her, that would require more than a few risks.

Chapter 9

The town of Cerdost had tripled in size with the number of travelers coming to the race that would be held less than ten miles from Cerdost's walls. Aside from the lords and their riders, many had also come to watch the event. For the people of Rynar, nothing else in the Six Realms could compare to the anticipation of watching one of the Great Races. But unless they were merchants, knights, or lords, most had the opportunity to see only the races held in their own realms.

With the race due to begin in just two days, Lord Beristo entered the city accompanied by his men, Sirryn, and Inesca. Because of his handicap, Omaron had to ride in a wagon that would meet up with them later. Inesca decided that it was a good thing the wagon was traveling around the city instead of through it as they were because there was barely room for her to ride Nycor through the crowds. He moved nervously beneath her, and Inesca knew this was one of his weaknesses. He had never been comfortable in large crowds of people.

Climbing down from his back, she tied a rope to his bridle and walked beside him while holding it so he could see her better. Speaking to him gently, she noticed him relax a little more as they followed Lord Beristo and Sirryn.

Walking on foot with her lack of height made it difficult for Inesca to see where Lord Beristo was leading them. But as the crowds shifted, Inesca's eyes were drawn to a man in fine scarlet clothes riding a magnificent white stallion. His hair was dark with some visible strands of gray, but any marks of age upon him could not detract from the strength he projected. Inesca imagined he was still capable of wielding the sword at his belt with significant force.

"Is that one of the other lords over there?" she asked Sirryn.

Sirryn looked down at her from his horse and then noted whom she was watching. "No, but he is wealthy and powerful. That is one of the knights of the Six Realms, one by the name of Sir Coltar."

"Coltar of Monterr?"

The crowds pressed closer, and her question was lost among them as Sirryn disappeared from sight. Nycor snorted and pulled at the rope as people moved around him, but Inesca's eyes followed only the figure riding toward the main road leading out of Cerdost.

Is that the man my father spoke of?

Drawing the rope tight in her hand, Inesca tried to squeeze through the masses walking around her. The real difficulty was getting Nycor to turn around and move against the oncoming flood of travelers.

"Please, let me pass!" Inesca said as she tried to push through them and hold onto her stallion's lead rope.

Her gaze searched for Coltar, but he must have already ridden out of the gate. She had only a few minutes to catch up to him. In desperation, Inesca moved faster as she drew Nycor forward through the edge of the crowd, but her actions pulled them right into the path of another group of travelers and their horses.

A flash of red filled her vision as two flailing hooves struck the air in front of her face. In a clumsy attempt to escape the danger, Inesca stumbled backward and landed on the dirt road. Nycor charged forward to challenge the red stallion that was about to trample her.

The two nearly collided as they tried to bite each other, but Inesca leapt to her feet and guided Nycor to move his head and look at her with a firm hand on his rope. She had him follow her in a turn before putting her hand on his neck to calm him, and a fair-haired young man steadied the red stallion at the same time. But when this stranger turned to Inesca, his expression was far from forgiving. "Unless you and your horse wish to be injured, stay out of our way, slave."

Already flushed by the tension of the moment, Inesca felt her face grow even warmer at the words of this stranger. "Call me a slave again, and you'll be the one on the ground, stable hand. At least I can handle my horse!"

The stranger's blue eyes widened. "I'm a stable hand, am I? And I thought everyone knew the best rider in Trineth. But I suppose an Easterner like you wouldn't know anything about riders."

Inesca felt her hand tighten into a fist, but then she took a deep breath and smiled. "The *best* rider in Trineth? Well, when you think you have nearly finished the race, look ahead of you. I'll wave from my horse as we pass you on the final mile."

His surprised and outraged expression only encouraged her smile, but before he could respond, a well-dressed man with light gray hair and an angular nose rode up beside them. "Why have you stopped?" he asked. "What's going on?"

Inesca caught herself staring at the rich blue tunic that the man on horseback was wearing and the silver broach glistening from his gray cloak. His style of dress matched Lord Beristo's, and Inesca lowered her gaze as she realized that he must also be a lord.

"This girl pulled her horse directly into our road, Lord Edgerr," the young man insisted. "I had to prevent Halon from hurting himself when this stallion challenged him."

"He was only protecting me from your horse," Inesca argued.

"Silence! If you've damaged my horse, girl, I'll have you whipped. Where's your master?"

"Now, now, Edgerr," Lord Beristo said as he rode toward them with Sirryn alongside him. "What has you so excited this morning?"

"Is this your slave, Beristo?" Edgerr demanded.

"This is my new rider and my new horse. And if you damage either, then you will be the one to pay for them."

"Rider?" Edgerr scoffed. "Are things so bad that you had to start calling one of your slaves a rider? Don't you still have that drunk, or is he incapable of staying on a horse now?"

"Save your criticism until after you see her compete in the race. As for this little disruption, your horse appears uninjured, so there's no harm done. Come, Inesca. No doubt you became lost in the crowd, but you should not have wandered so far from us."

Inesca could feel the young man and Lord Edgerr glaring at her, but she turned in defeat to follow Lord Beristo and Sirryn to their original course. Coltar had vanished, and she was without hope of reaching him now. Lord Beristo's reprimand was a reminder that she had agreed to serve him. Perhaps she had less freedom than she wanted to admit. But she didn't have to let that conceited fool call her a slave.

Back among Lord Edgerr's own attendants and men, Kestorn was still patting Halon's neck as the stallion pawed the ground and shook his head uneasily. Derreth appeared with Celestro, who turned his head and blew air at Halon through his nose. The red stallion relaxed and greeted him in the same manner. Even though both were stallions, they had been together since Halon was a colt and without any mares to fight over, they had become friends. Celestro's calm temperament usually helped to soothe Halon's high-strung personality.

"What happened, Kes?" Derreth asked.

"Some girl from the East Province walked right in front of Halon with another stallion. I thought they were going to fight here on the road."

"The owner of the stallion should know better than to have a slave leading it."

Kestorn released a scornful laugh. "That's what I called her, but it seems she's a rider for Lord Beristo."

"He's in need of a new rider," Derreth said thoughtfully. "I would not have expected him to choose someone like this, though. What did the stallion look like? Have you seen it before?"

"I had other things to worry about, Derreth. Protecting Halon for example."

"And arguing from what I heard," Derreth added with a smile. "I'll see what I can find out about this rider and the horse. I like to know who our competition is among the new riders."

"Competition?" another voice laughed.

Derreth and Kestorn looked up to see Trestan appear beside them, but he was riding, while they were leading horses on foot.

"Neither of you will have any competition this season," he continued. "Or have you forgotten that you're not racing?"

Kestorn started to walk toward Trestan, but Derreth held him back. "You'll have to win this race to assure us of that, Trestan."

"Not a problem. I've seen the other riders, and in this group of amateurs, there's no way I can lose."

He rode on ahead of them with an arrogant smile.

"He could be right," Kestorn admitted grudgingly. "He's improved his riding on Halon lately. And if he wins this race, we might not get another chance to ride this season."

"Even if he has improved, that's no guarantee that he'll win, Kes. And no matter what happens in this race, we both know he's not ready for the races that come after this one."

Each lord attending the race in Sassot was provided with a plot of land upon which to set up tents for himself, his guests, his guards, his servants, and of course his riders and horses. From the edge of Lord Beristo's camp, Inesca stood and watched as a massive green and gold tent rose up from the ground at the hands of the servants.

A place had been provided for her to tie up Nycor and let him rest, but he moved around uneasily behind her as she held his reins.

"I don't like it either," Inesca said softly as she turned to pat his neck. "To wait one more day for the race seems like such a long time, and yet not long enough to prepare."

The Legacy of the Lost Rider

Leading him away from their camp, Inesca followed a dirt path up onto a ledge from which she could see the camps of the other lords. Distinct colors set apart the tents of each lord, but Inesca was surprised to see only three camps arranged below her. Where were the camps of the other two lords?

A grinding noise signaled Omaron's arrival as his rod struck the ground and pulled his body forward with each step. He stopped at the top of the ledge and surveyed the other tents. "There are not as many as I thought there would be," Inesca said as she followed his gaze.

"Some consider this race in Sassot to be unworthy of their efforts. It is shorter than most, and the smooth terrain presents little challenge to horse or rider. This race is mostly used as a means to train new or inexperienced riders."

"Then there are other riders here who have never raced before?"

Omaron nodded. "Aside from Lord Beristo, only three other lords have entered their horses in this race. I have never seen the man riding for Lord Atregar before. This race will determine his future in the races, as it will yours."

Inesca followed Omaron's gaze to Lord Atregar's camp, which was marked by vibrant greenish-blue tents. Lord Atregar's standard flew atop the largest tent. It was turquoise in color with a white fish jumping upon its cloth. The realm of Farcost covered much of the western coast, and Sirryn had told Inesca that the richest harbors in the Six Realms flourished there under Lord Atregar's rule. Lord Atregar was a tall, broad-shouldered man with light brown hair that nearly reached his shoulders and a beard and mustache that covered much of his lower face.

But nearest to the camp of Lord Atregar, Inesca noted the purple tents of Lord Felond, the youngest of the lords, and seemingly, the least impressive. Inesca assumed he was ill when she caught sight of his thin frame, pale skin, and watery eyes, but Sirryn assured her that he always appeared that way. His hair reminded Inesca of damp straw trampled on the floor of a stable. He wore it long around his face, as if trying to appear older, but a beard would have served him better. However, despite his physical shortcomings, he walked with his nose lifted in the air and a look of disdain in his eyes. His pride matched that of the white stag on his standard that reared with its front hooves trampling the air.

Omaron's warning stirred her thoughts as she looked out at the men in the camps. Even though she was Lord Beristo's only rider, with the exception of Jirro, Inesca knew that if she failed Lord Beristo in this race, she might not get a chance to prove herself in another.

"What about the others?" Inesca asked. "There are two other camps here aside from Lord Atregar's."

"Lord Felond would not hold a race in his realm without entering his own rider. But even though Destrod has raced before, he has never won. Lord Felond hopes that in time, he may become a better rider, but Destrod couldn't win if he was racing against a herd of cows."

"Then why does Lord Felond keep him?"

"He is more concerned with bloodlines and pedigree than ability. Destrod is the second son of a wealthy knight who was once a capable rider."

"What about his horse?"

"A blue roan mare, a pureblood that cost Lord Felond a fortune, and she is equally inept in the races."

"So that's one rider I don't have to worry about?"

Omaron shot her a scalding look.

"But that's not what you taught me." Inesca sighed.

"Every rider is a threat. Destrod knows the limits of his abilities, so he has sought other means to get ahead. Do not ignore him."

Inesca nodded. "And the last lord?"

"Lord Edgerr. I was not expecting him to enter a rider in this race, but he has done so."

"Yes, I met that rider this morning," Inesca said grudgingly.

"You leap to assumptions the way that horse charges obstacles," Omaron said with a grim tone. "That was not the one you met. Next time, find out who someone is before you begin an argument with a stranger. Lord Edgerr has chosen Trestan to compete in this race, but you only spoke with Kestorn, one of his other riders."

Inesca dropped her gaze. "I guess they told you what happened."

"Everything that concerns Lord Beristo's riders and their competition is my business. If you do something foolish, be assured that I will learn of it."

Under his stern gaze, Inesca shifted uncomfortably. Then she asked, "So has this Trestan raced before?"

"He has some experience, but this will be the first time that I will see him ride Lord Edgerr's red stallion in a race. Usually, it is Kestorn who rides him."

"This Kestorn said he was the best rider in the realm of Trineth. Is that true?"

"If he isn't, then only his brother could surpass him. It is difficult to determine which one is better. Riders must take risks to win races, and Kestorn is not afraid to do so. I have also seen him reach incredible speeds on the red stallion. But sometimes charging into danger is unwise. His older brother, Derreth, is more cautious, but he is just as skilled. Derreth uses his head, and if you think only speed matters in these races, he'll teach you otherwise."

The Legacy of the Lost Rider

"Then they will be my toughest competition in the races after this one?"

"No."

"But you just said …"

"They are the best riders *here*, though they are not racing this time. You are forgetting that there are still two lords not present at this race with their riders."

Inesca caught sight of the rider named Kestorn as he walked toward Lord Edgerr's camp with a heavy sack over his shoulder. The tents surrounding him were a deep blue with silver markings. On Lord Edgerr's standard, a silver falcon with outstretched talons flew over a crown with six points.

"So, Lord Edgerr has two riders who are brothers. Was their father also a rider?"

Omaron crossed his arms and continued to stare down at the gathering below them as he leaned against his staff.

Inesca turned away with a sigh. *I asked one question too many, but I can never quite figure out where I've crossed a line*, she thought.

As she returned to Nycor and started to mount, her foot kicked a bundle tied to her saddle. Inesca heard something tumble out onto the rocks, and her breath caught as the medallion landed near the edge of the cliff. Omaron's rod struck it in the blink of an eye, pinning it to the ground before it could fall. His gaze turned on her, and Inesca felt as if he had her pinned as well.

"I'm not going to try to sell it," she insisted. "That's not why I kept it."

Omaron thrust the medallion away from the cliff with his rod. The loud scrapping sound across the rocks caused Inesca to wince.

"The reason is unimportant. You were not supposed to keep it at all. It does not belong to you. What if it had fallen at someone else's feet?"

"What if it had?" Inesca demanded as she dismounted. "You won't tell me anything. How can you expect me to understand if you keep silent about it?"

She strode forward to pick up the medallion, but Omaron swung his rod at her outstretched arm, knocking it back. "Leave it," he said. "If they find you with it, they will accuse you of being a thief."

Inesca returned his gaze with a glare of her own as she rubbed her arm. "You told me that the rider it belonged to was dead. How can I be a thief if I happened to find a dead man's medallion?"

Inesca pushed his rod aside forcefully and scooped up the medallion. She rubbed the dust from it gingerly with her skirt.

Omaron shook his head in disapproval. "Since it belongs to a dead man, stop treating it like a good luck charm. That medallion should be cast aside."

She waited for him to explain as she weighed the medallion in her hand, but

Omaron turned and began walking back down the path. Inesca's hand closed over one of the pieces of her inheritance from her father. Omaron had to know what it was that drove her father from his life in the Six Realms to the East Province, but he also seemed determined not to tell her. Perhaps he was right about keeping the medallion in a bundle on her saddle. She opened her hands to look at it again before she resolved to hide it with her father's other possessions.

Chapter 10

Kestorn wiped the sweat from his brow as the sun poured down its heat from a cloudless sky. The sack of oats in his arms felt heavier by the second, and he hoped none of the other riders were watching. Doing some hard work to train and care for Lord Edgerr's horses had never bothered him, but fetching supplies from town like a slave was embarrassing.

As he drew near to Lord Edgerr's camp, Halon called to him from the post where he was tied.

"When are you not hungry?" Kestorn asked the stallion with a smile as he set the sack down and took out his knife to open it.

"Who gave you permission to feed that stallion?"

The annoying pitch of the voice told Kestorn immediately who it was, and as he looked up, he could tell by the satisfied smirk on Trestan's face that the jackal had been watching him. Kestorn ignored him and cut open the sack.

"That stallion's been causing trouble again, so he's not to be fed until tomorrow. That will teach him to obey his masters," Trestan insisted.

Kestorn released a scornful laugh. "You don't starve a racehorse before a race," he said.

Still smiling, Trestan stepped into his path and positioned himself just inches from Kestorn's face. "Lord Edgerr demands it. And I shall decide how the horse that I'm going to ride is to be treated."

Trestan's foot kicked the sack of oats at Kestorn's feet and knocked it over, spilling half the oats across the grass.

"Looks like you have more work to do," he said and laughed as he walked away.

Kestorn stood as stiff as a statue with a scarlet face, and he clenched his fists. "If the other riders don't get him, I will," he said quietly.

Halon pulled at his rope impatiently as he eyed the oats on the ground. Kestorn sighed and sat down, pulling at some weeds in the grass. A shadow passed over his shoulder, and he tensed again.

"Why do I always find you in the middle of a mess?" a soft voice asked.

Kestorn's head turned quickly as he stumbled to his feet. A fair-skinned young woman with strawberry-blonde hair and silvery blue eyes stood watching him. Kestorn felt his heart beat faster as he caught sight of her familiar sweet smile and beautiful face.

"Laisi, you're here. I mean … I didn't think I'd get to see you until the race in Monterr."

"Father had some trading to do in Sassot, but I might have asked him to come during the time of the race. He'll find better business with all the travelers anyway."

Kestorn sighed. "If you're here to see me race, then I'm afraid you've come for nothing. I've been replaced."

"I came to see you whether you're racing or not," she said. "And since you're not racing, would you care to watch it with me? Father has offered to buy us seats."

"That's the best thing I've heard all day," Kestorn said with a smile. "I don't think Derreth will mind. We were going to watch together."

"Oh, I didn't mean without your brother. He's invited too. Father likes you both, and I didn't want to leave him out."

"Well, if Derreth can't be in a race, his next choice is to be watching one from the stands, so I know he'll say yes."

Laisi looked down at the grass and the oats. "So, what happened here?"

Kestorn's face turned slightly red again, and he hesitated to answer. "I was going to feed Halon, but now I've been told not to even though he needs to be well-fed for the race."

Laisi scooped up some oats from the ground and looked around before walking over to Halon and letting him eat out of her hand. Kestorn checked again to see if anyone was watching.

"No one said I couldn't feed him," she said after brushing off her hands and then running her fingers through the stallion's mane.

Kestorn watched her for several seconds before he realized he was staring and then leaned over to pick up the sack of oats and scoop what he could inside of it. Derreth had accused him of attracting too many girls in the past, but Kestorn had always known it was Laisi he wanted since he'd first met her over a year ago.

"He's going to miss having you on his back in the race," Laisi said as she looked from Halon to Kestorn.

Kestorn walked toward the stallion and scratched his neck and back. "I'm going to miss riding him."

Laisi reached over and placed her hand on his. Halon turned his head to look at them and seemed to nod, causing them to laugh. Kestorn put his other hand around hers and kissed it as he lifted it up.

As his eyes caught sight of movement several feet behind her, he noticed Trestan standing beside the tents. His face was green with an envious glare. Laisi turned and followed his gaze. Then she guided Kestorn's eyes back to her with a light touch of her hand against his face.

"You'll ride Halon again soon," she insisted.

"That's what Derreth tells me."

"That's because you have a clever brother."

"And what about me?"

"Well, you have a handsome face," she said, smiling with a light in her eyes. "And I am fortunate that I can have you by my side during a race for a change."

Laisi squeezed his hand gently before she let go and walked back toward town. Looking back at Trestan, Kestorn shot him a warning glare and then grabbed the sack of oats and carried it to the supply tent.

After taking her evening meal, Inesca received a summons to Lord Beristo's tent. She moved swiftly to answer it. As she entered, Inesca couldn't help but notice the impatience on Lord Beristo's flushed face and Sirryn's frown. She wondered if she had done something else to displease them after the incident in Cerdost.

"You wished to see me, my lord?" she said as she bowed.

Lord Beristo turned around and walked closer as he motioned for her to rise. "Yes," he said. "I wanted to see how my rider is doing. Stand up, and let me have a look at you."

As she straightened, his gaze swept over her face and her limbs as he walked around her.

"I never can persuade Omaron to tell me what I want to know about your training. I wouldn't trade him for anything, but he has a tendency to be overly silent at times. The only information I could get from him was that the gray stallion was in good condition, but nothing about you."

"I don't understand," Inesca replied hesitantly. "What is it that you want to know, my lord?"

"Tell me how you feel about the race tomorrow."

Inesca glanced at Sirryn, searching for the right answer, but he only watched Lord Beristo with a furrowed brow. She had many feelings about the race, but she couldn't comprehend why they mattered to Lord Beristo.

"Well, say something, girl. Are you anxious? Excited? Confident?"

The impatience in his tone prompted Inesca to provide some kind of answer.

"I am ... uncertain, my lord."

Lord Beristo stared back at her as his expression twisted into a frown.

"Uncertain?" he repeated. "Of all the things you could be, that sounds like one of the worst. How can you be uncertain? You have been trained for this race, have you not?"

Looking back at Sirryn again, Inesca now saw that he looked angry but still remained silent.

"I have been trained, my lord," she finally answered.

"Then why are you uncertain?"

"I have never ridden in this race or any like it before. Neither have I ever ridden alongside any of these riders. I know my own skills, and I know the abilities of my horse, my lord, but how can I be certain of anything in this race without first having been tested?"

Lord Beristo huffed and turned away but did not question her again. Sirryn's gaze finally turned to her and gave a slight nod of approval.

"I hope that this is one test you find yourself equal to," Lord Beristo said as he returned to the table where several pieces of parchment lay. "Sirryn disagrees, but I think you ought to know why this race is important to me."

Inesca waited in silence as Lord Beristo stood looking over the table and then closed his eyes.

"Several years ago, it was decided among the lords that the pride of winning a race was not enough of a reward. It has become customary for each lord to surrender gold or silver or a possession of value to the lord whose rider wins the race. Unfortunately, this custom has resulted in making some lords quite wealthy, while others have lost nearly all their wealth. The lords who have more wealth can afford to buy the best horses and tempt the best riders into their service. This often allows them to continue winning more races."

Although he never said it, Inesca knew well enough that Lord Beristo belonged to the group of lords lacking their former wealth. She had overheard enough about his financial troubles while on his estate, and the weariness in his expression was a confirmation of all that she had heard.

"I did not need a fortune to get you or your horse, but I still believe you are capable of winning races even when you are challenged by the best riders the Six Realms has to offer." He looked back at her once more and then waved his hand. "You may go."

Inesca started to back away, but then she paused. "There is one thing that I am certain of," she said softly. "I will pour all that I have into tomorrow's race, and I will not forget what you have done for me."

Chapter 11

On the morning of the race in Sassot, the riders were led to the crest of a green hill a short distance from the main camp. Those who were going to view only the end of the race had left the camp two hours before to begin their leisurely journey toward a green valley, where the victor of the race would be determined. Their route was shorter than that of the riders, but the lords wanted to arrive early enough to begin their financial dealings that had to be made before the race's conclusion.

The race itself was held over rolling hills and some wooded plains. Omaron had shown Inesca a map of the course and explained some of what she should expect. *Rough storms shook this land before we arrived. You must be prepared for a few additional obstacles along the way.* Still, the prospect of riding across these hills and forests was encouraging to Inesca because they reminded her of the land around her home in the East Province. The main difference was the size of the trees that she had seen in Sassot. Most of them had trunks almost as wide as a man's height, and they towered above the plains. The trees around her homeland were smaller and far more twisted than the stiff giants that resided here.

The time allotted for the race was six hours, but Inesca knew her time would have to be less than that if she was going to win. Over such a time span, she would frequently have to decrease Nycor's pace to a lope or a walk, but Omaron had told her to remain behind the main group of riders and take her cues from them. Not until the trumpet sounded to signal the final miles of the race was she to attempt passing them.

"Beware of riding close to any of them," he had warned. "Remember that they are armed just as you are, and their need to win is as great as yours. Give them no reason to challenge you until you must."

He had also insisted that she wear her hair tied and bound tightly in a bun behind her head. If she wore it in her usual long braid, another rider might catch her by the hair and pull her out of the saddle. *"If you fall out of the saddle or are wounded, know that the laws of the race say that each rider must finish on his own. No one is allowed to help you. If you cannot get up or get back on your horse, then you will be left there,"* he had explained.

Inesca dared a quick glance at the riders around her. Two of Lord Felond's men escorted them, and they wore the same color of indigo that marked the rider Destrod and Lord Felond's mare. Despite that he had a reputation as a perpetual loser in the races, Destrod carried his head high with a cold gleam in his eyes.

Lord Atregar's rider had lighter hair, almost a golden brown. Inesca decided that he might be about four or five years older than she was, but still younger than Destrod. He wore a greenish-blue tunic marked by a white fish. When Inesca had asked about the name of this rider, Omaron had insisted that his name was unimportant until he had proven himself in a race.

The fourth and final rider, Trestan, wore the familiar blue and silver colors of Lord Edgerr. He might have been the tallest of them all, for his limbs certainly seemed the longest. Inesca thought the red stallion appeared unsettled beneath him, but surely, he had devoted enough time to train with the horse. After all, he and Destrod were the only riders with some experience in the races.

Inesca looked down at her own clothes. Lord Beristo had granted her request and provided her with a pair of breeches to wear while riding in the race. Her tunic, like the other riders, was designed to bear the insignia of her lord and was green with a gold hound.

When they reached the starting point, Inesca lined up alongside Lord Atregar's rider and turned to watch Lord Felond's man as he pulled out an indigo flag to signal the start of the race. She listened to the rustling of the wind through the trees and the restless noises of the horses. The riders traded wary glances but did not speak to each other.

The flag was raised in the air and swung from side to side twice before being flung downward. Inesca felt Nycor tremble under her with excitement as the horses beside them rushed into a sudden gallop. The race had begun.

⁓

Crowds poured into the Hashir Valley down a narrow slope and toward the large wooden structures standing against the side of the hills. Tiered benches made from the great trees of Sassot created places for guests of lords and the wealthy to sit. A fee had to be paid to enter the tall wooden gate to the seats. Those who could not pay were pushed further down into the standing area where it was more difficult to watch the race.

Derreth followed Gorben, a merchant and friend, along with his brother and Laisi, the merchant's daughter. Gorben had been generous enough to pay for them to watch from a bench where he and his daughter would be seated.

Although he respected the merchant, Derreth had accepted only on Kestorn's account. His brother was fortunate to have the attention of a young woman like Laisi and even more so to have the approval of her father. Although there was no way for them to marry until Lord Edgerr released Kestorn from his service, Derreth hoped that someday, his brother would win his freedom and settle into a house of his own.

As he took his seat, Derreth looked down at the ground where men were packed together in the standing area. Without Gorben's generosity, he and his brother would have been stuck among that crowd today. Lord Edgerr never paid for his other riders to have seats, but that was common with most of the lords.

A large wooden structure with a roof rose above and behind the seating area. Several guards stood on each side of the long box, and inside, the lords gathered to take their seats. An indigo banner with white trim hung from the roof of the box.

"They'll start haggling now over their prize offerings," Gorben said as he followed Derreth's gaze to the lords' box. "The ones who believe they have the greatest chance of winning will offer the most as a show of their confidence and also as a means of prompting the others to give more."

"Lord Edgerr will offer more than he should," Derreth said quietly as he looked away.

"Oh, you don't believe Trestan will win this race, then?" Gorben asked in a low tone as he watched Derreth's face.

"I believe that there could be a more capable rider out there."

Derreth stared at the edge of the valley where the riders would eventually appear. "Do you know anything about the new riders?" he asked.

"Not enough." Gorben sighed. "Lord Atregar's rider is rumored to have been a thief. Some say that he was given the choice of riding for Lord Atregar or facing imprisonment for his crimes."

"And what about Lord Beristo's rider?" Derreth asked with a smile. "There must be some stories about her."

"People have said many things, but none of them know anything except that she's a girl and an Easterner, though I heard one man say she was a half-breed. But I don't understand why Lord Beristo chose her. She cannot be any older than my daughter, and when I see girls in the races, I think about what it would feel like to have Laisi caught in such a competition."

Derreth looked around Gorben at Kestorn and Laisi, who were having their own conversation. Even though Kestorn was angry about being replaced by

Trestan, Derreth couldn't help but feel some relief that he didn't have to watch his brother race today.

"I do not think they should allow female riders in the races," Gorben continued. "Or at least not ones so young. I have seen them killed in such events before, and it is terrible."

Derreth nodded. "I agree, but there must be a reason why Lord Beristo chose this rider."

"Well, perhaps when she loses this race, he will not have her race again."

Gorben turned to engage his daughter and Kestorn in a conversation. Derreth looked around to see if he knew anyone else here. Down in the standing area, he saw the tall, dark shape of Lord Beristo's trainer, Omaron. He stood near the front with his iron rod dug into the ground and leaned against it, but his eyes stared ahead as if he was watching intently for the riders.

Although Derreth had never met this trainer, he knew a little about the man's past and that he had once been a rider himself. Not just any rider either, but one who had won several important races. He was a master with weapons and horses, but the loss of his leg had ruined him. If Lord Beristo's new rider had been training diligently under him, then she might be more of a competitor than Gorben or his brother gave her credit for.

The crowd around and behind Omaron continued to move, and Derreth noticed the flicker of sunlight on coins. There were always men who made bets at the races, but in races like this one, Derreth thought it was foolish to bet for or against riders that these men surely knew nothing about.

Two tall, wooden beams wrapped with layers of purple and white cloth stood several yards beyond the wall that marked the boundary of the standing area. These beams, called the dassdir poles, marked the end of the race. The first horse and rider to come between them would be the winner.

Suddenly, shouts arose from the crowd as a white pigeon flew down into the valley. Scouts posted along the route sent messages with these birds to give the lords some idea of what was happening. The bird flew toward the lords' box, and one of the pigeon keepers hurried out to meet it.

After untying the message from its leg, he carried it back into the lords' box and bowed as he held it out to Lord Felond. Everyone was silent now as they waited for the news. It was quietly read to one of the servants in the box, and the servant grabbed the blue and silver flag in front of Lord Edgerr and raised it high.

Some of the men in the crowd cheered, but others were silent. Derreth glanced over at Kestorn, who was glaring at the blue flag. Trestan was in the lead.

༄

The sun had risen high in the blue sky above the rolling hills, and now it had started to sink again. Inesca kept Nycor moving at a lope as she knew that they must be getting close to the final stretch of the race. It was still too far to ask him to start galloping, and none of the other horses, though moving briskly, were galloping yet.

Not long ago, she had stopped at a brook to let Nycor drink before giving him some oats and letting him rest for a brief time. Inesca kept a close watch on the other riders as they also took this short reprieve. So far, following them had been easy work. She had Nycor gallop when they galloped, and trot or walk when they slowed down. At times, Nycor tossed his head, wanting to keep moving faster, but he held back as she asked him to.

When they neared the last part of the race, some of the riders were yards apart from each other, and Inesca was at least ten yards from Destrod, who, like her, was riding toward the back. At the end of the race, Omaron had told her that the valley would narrow, and they would be pushed closer together.

Thus far, most of the riders had paid her very little attention, except for Destrod. Inesca noticed that he would often glance back at her with a suspicious expression. She had decided that with his pointed nose and small eyes, he reminded her of a large rat. The mare he rode looked like a beautiful horse, but beauty was all she appeared to possess. There was no ambition, no speed, and certainly no spirit in that horse. Yet Inesca did not feel comfortable trying to ride ahead of Destrod just yet. With Omaron's warning in her thoughts, she decided that his presence, behind her and with a blade, would be a mistake.

Lord Atregar's rider remained in front of Destrod, but he looked tense and uncertain. His gaze often turned to the other riders as if he was constantly changing his mind about how fast he should be riding and where he needed to be. Inesca wondered how much training he had received before this race and if he truly wanted to be here.

Meanwhile, Trestan had been in front since the beginning. Inesca would occasionally see Lord Atregar's rider gallop after him, but Trestan always remained ahead. Inesca was impressed at the stamina of the red stallion. He reminded her of Nycor in the way that he grew impatient to run.

Still, she knew her own horse well enough to know that she believed she could catch up with him at this distance. The problem would be getting past the other riders. As they neared the top of another hill, Inesca saw a large boulder that looked like a sleeping bear with outstretched front paws. Omaron had told her to watch for this, so she would know when to start moving closer to the other riders.

Inesca noted that Destrod increased his speed a little at this point as well, but it didn't take long before she was riding across from him on the left. He glanced at her and kept riding. Ahead of her, Trestan urged his horse into a gallop and left Lord Atregar's rider farther behind him.

A trumpet sounded, signaling that they had reached the final mile, and all at once, every horse was galloping at the request of its rider. Inesca felt the wind rush past her face, and a sudden thrill filled her chest as the blast of the trumpet echoed in her ears. In a matter of minutes, she and Destrod were galloping upon Lord Atregar's rider. As they drew closer, Inesca saw that she had already made a mistake. Trestan was riding far ahead to the right of them, and she needed to be on that side, but Destrod was pushing her farther to the left. Lord Atregar's rider was closing the gap between Destrod and Trestan on the right, and all of the riders were now entering the valley as they rode down the hill, which was growing narrower by the second.

If I can't get past Destrod, I'll be stuck in the back for the rest of the race, Inesca realized.

She guided Nycor into a faster gallop and dared to ride closer to Destrod, hoping his mare might back off a little. He saw what she was doing at once though and drew his sword. Inesca drew her own and deflected his blade, but he still blocked her path. Instead of trying to attack her again though, he waited for her to move closer in her attempt to ride past him and then slash at her arm or her neck.

Inesca tried again and then again to fight her way past him, but he was stronger than she was and able to deflect her attempts to strike at him. As she tried to find a path to get around him, his blade sliced through her upper arm, and he guided his horse back in front of Nycor. Inesca grabbed her arm as it bled, and Nycor raised his head as he was blocked.

Not to win the race would be bad enough, but to finish in last place would be far worse. I must get through! she thought. Inesca released her arm and inclined her position forward over the saddle.

As the hill began to level out into the valley, Inesca suddenly caught sight of something ahead of them. They were all riding toward a grove of trees, and a damaged tree lay across the ground. Inesca watched as Trestan, still ahead of them, turned to ride around the tree, and the other riders followed. The direct path to the finish was ahead of the tree, though, and the detour was taking them out of their way.

The massive fallen giant was a formidable obstacle, but back in the East Province, Inesca had trained with Nycor when he jumped fences that were higher than this.

"This is our chance," she said, spurring him into an even faster run.

The gray stallion charged over the grass with no hesitation as he galloped toward the tree. Inesca didn't bother to turn her head to see what the other riders were doing but kept all her attention on the obstacle ahead.

As they rushed upon it, Inesca squeezed her legs around Nycor and adjusted her hold on the reins. Nycor's ears pricked forward, and his front hooves soared into the air. In the half a second that he was in the air, Inesca could see that the jump was perfect. He landed smoothly and raced forward just as he always did.

As the gray stallion galloped away from the shadow of the trees, Inesca saw the red stallion and Trestan just a few yards in front of them. The other riders had fallen behind. Nycor didn't need any further urging to chase after the other horse, and Inesca let him go as he raced over the grass. Trestan turned around and noticed them with a shocked expression.

"You don't mind some competition, do you?" Inesca asked, unable to hide a smile.

He started to draw his sword, but Inesca moved Nycor farther to the left side as the gray stallion continued to gain speed. As the two horses raced across the grass, Inesca caught sight of a stream crossing the valley ahead of them. It was more than just a shallow brook, though, and with the additional power of the recent storms, it seemed to have cut a steep ditch in front of them that was filled with water.

The shortest path to the finish was across one of the wider sections of the bank, and after jumping the huge tree trunk, Inesca knew Nycor could jump this. But before they reached it, Inesca had to draw her sword and block Trestan's blade as he swung it at her twice. He was not as strong as Destrod and was even a little clumsy with his strokes.

"You're *not* winning this race, so get out of my way or be cut out," he growled.

Inesca locked blades with him again.

"I hope you didn't bet against me," she said. Tipping her blade down suddenly, she scratched his hand before drawing her sword away from his.

Trestan cried out as though he had received a mortal wound and dropped his sword as he seized his hand. Suddenly, he realized they were almost upon the embankment, and Inesca watched in amazement as he tried to slow the red stallion down as if to stop it.

She turned forward again to focus on the stream, and Nycor jumped it with ease. As he landed on the other side and continued running, Inesca looked back to see the red stallion fighting Trestan and finally rearing, which threw the lanky rider into the water. The other riders soon jumped over the water as their horses kicked mud onto him.

When Inesca turned back, Nycor had almost reached the two wooden poles, and she urged him into his last burst of speed. She could hear the crowd cheering and shouting. The valley closed in around them, and Inesca finally felt Nycor and her slip through the dassdir poles as the cheers grew louder.

Only when they reached the circle just inside the poles did she gradually slow Nycor. Inesca looked up and saw Lord Beristo's green and gold standard being waved back and forth in victory, and she felt her heart leap amid the noise of the crowd.

The wound on her arm was forgotten, and she raised her hand and waved to those cheering. The cheers grew louder, and Inesca's attention on the crowd caused her to ignore all that lay behind her.

Lord Atregar's rider finished the race in second place behind Inesca, and his expression reflected the dismay he felt at his loss, but surprise accompanied disappointment as he stared at the young woman ahead of him. He dismounted from his horse and cast an uneasy gaze at the crowd, letting his eyes drift up to the box where the lords were seated.

From his place amid the audience, Omaron stood silently near the front where he had observed the end of the race. And when Destrod and Trestan passed the dassdir poles, Omaron noted their narrowed eyes, mouths twisted into frowns, and a fire fueled by humiliation and anger burning in their expressions. Even as they rode out of sight, the trainer watched them warily.

Chapter 12

After the excitement of the crowd had passed, Inesca dismounted from Nycor and searched for a familiar face. No one had told her what to do after the race was over. Where should she go?

She held firmly to her stallion's reins as she tried to move closer to the stream of people leaving the valley.

"Inesca! Here!"

Sirryn appeared out of the masses as he waved to her and motioned for her to come to him. Leading Nycor behind her, Inesca hurried to join him.

"Sirryn, where is Lord Beristo?"

"He's already traveling with the other lords on a separate boat. There'll be another one that will take us back to our camp downriver. Your horse will need rest now that the race is over, and we don't want him to have to travel far."

"What about Omaron?" Inesca asked. "Is he not here?"

"He was here, but he makes his own travel arrangements. He may already be getting on a boat as we speak."

At his urging, Inesca joined Lord Beristo's men who had been left behind to escort them back to camp. Once they were safely aboard the boat and Inesca saw to it that Nycor was comfortable, she joined Sirryn at the bow.

"That was quite impressive," he said as he turned to her. Then he noticed her arm. "You should have told me you were wounded. What happened?"

Inesca suddenly remembered her arm and glanced down at the wound. "Destrod caught my arm with his sword, but I don't think it's very deep," she said.

"Lord Beristo arranged for a physician to be on board in case he was needed. I'll bring him to you."

Sirryn left and returned only seconds later with an older man who cleaned and bandaged her arm.

"Did you see Lord Beristo after the race?" Inesca asked Sirryn.

"No. I'm not allowed in the lords' box, so I never see him unless it is at camp. But as soon as we arrive, I suspect that he'll be there and want to talk to you."

He asked her about the race, but he didn't seem as excited by her success as she had thought he would be. When they reached the camp after about an hour of being on the river, Sirryn insisted that she go to Lord Beristo's tent.

"I'll see to it that your horse is cared for and gets his rest," he assured her.

Inesca patted Nycor's neck as she led him toward Sirryn and handed him the reins.

"Thank you. I'll come back and check on him later."

The sun hung low in the sky as Inesca moved quickly toward the green and gold tents. She caught sight of a tall figure moving slowly past one of the smaller tents, and Inesca hurried to catch up with him.

"Are you glad that you decided to train me now?" she asked Omaron, but her smile faded when she saw his grim expression. "Omaron?"

His gaze hardened. "You disobeyed my instructions," he said.

"Disobeyed? I won the race. Isn't that enough?"

Omaron thrust his rod down into the ground with such force that it drove a hole through a tree root at his feet. "I told you to stay in the back and wait for a chance to get through."

"I tried!" Inesca insisted. "I'm not strong enough yet to fight my way past the other riders. But I can jump and ride better than any of them."

"And now they know it."

The tone of Omaron's voice silenced her. He'd never sounded so angry with her before.

"They know you now," he continued. "And they will tell the others. Next time, they will *not* give you the chance to do it again."

He took a step closer, and Inesca felt all her excitement vanish as his words hung over her.

"The fighting in this race was only playacting, strangers testing the strength of their competitors. But in the next race, the other riders will strike for blood, and they will come after yours. Not because you won this race, but because you flaunted skills that made everyone stand up and take notice."

It was the closest he had ever come to complimenting her, but Inesca felt only the weight of his warning. And yet there was nothing she could do to change what had happened. As her thoughts turned back to the race, Inesca felt her confidence return to her in a rush of heated obstinacy.

"You didn't train me to lose, and I won't hide what kind of rider I am. They were going to find out sooner or later."

His silence was enough to prompt her to move on toward Lord Beristo's tent, but each step felt heavier now. Her confidence waned again, and she felt the disappointment of his disapproval. If this was what it felt like to win, she wondered what it would have felt like to have lost.

Two guards stood outside the entrance to their lord's tent, but they moved to let her pass. Inesca took a deep breath as she walked forward and pushed aside the curtain.

Warm lantern light greeted her as it flickered off the green and gold pattern of the tent. Lord Beristo stood in front of a table with a pitcher and goblets. In his hand, he held a magnificent golden necklace of green gems.

"Inesca! Come in. Come closer, my girl!"

He almost sounded as though he was laughing behind his broad smile, but Inesca could only manage to offer him the faintest hint of a smile in return.

"What is wrong, my dear? You should be celebrating! You're not ill, are you?"

"No, my lord."

"Nothing wrong with our stallion?"

"No, nothing, my lord," she reassured him. "It's just that I'm tired."

"Of course you are, but I'll let you sleep all day ... all week if you wish! What a race! It's been too long since I've had a day like this, but I knew the moment I saw you riding out in that eastern wilderness ... I knew I would never get another rider like you!"

"It is an honor to have won for you, my lord."

"But you don't even know what you've won for me," he laughed. "Look at this!"

He raised the necklace and held it close to her face.

"It's beautiful, my lord."

"It was my mother's, may her soul be at peace," he said as he drew it back. "And I lost it to Edgerr years ago. It was Jirro's doing. He was a decent rider when he wasn't drunk, but he spoiled an important race, and I was forced to give up this necklace. I have you to thank for getting it back."

Inesca bowed her head humbly.

"And I'll have it known that I reward my riders when they honor me with their success. Tell me what it is that you want, Inesca, and if it's in my power, I'll give it to you."

His eyes watched her eagerly as he waited for her answer, but Inesca felt her voice stolen away by his offer. She had never expected something like this. What could she ask for? What did she want?

"Say something, girl. Do you want gold? Or another horse? Or perhaps there's someone who you left behind in the East Province?"

Inesca looked down at his mother's necklace in his hand, and suddenly, she knew what she wanted.

"Everyone my heart ever cared for is beyond this world. Only God could bring them back, but there is something you can do to help me."

"And that is?"

"My lord, my only request is that you send word to Coltar of Monterr and ask him to come so that I may speak with him."

"You wish to speak to a knight? Is this still about your father? I have told you that it is foolish to think someone in his position would know a horse trader from the East Province."

"This is my only request, my lord. Is not one letter of invitation easier to grant than gold or a horse?"

"The letter is easy enough, but knights often travel far across the Six Realms. I may invite him, but it may be a long time before he is found or chooses to arrive."

"All I ask is that you send the letter, my lord, and tell him that the daughter of Koldoth wishes to speak to him about the oath that he swore twenty years ago. After that, you will have done enough."

"Very well, but you do ask for strange rewards, girl. And do not hope for too much. Most people do not like to be reminded of old oaths."

He poured wine from the pitcher into the goblets on the table and gestured for her to take one.

"Thank you, my lord," Inesca said as some of her old smile returned. She lifted the goblet to him. "I shall strive to honor you in the next races."

Lord Beristo picked up his own goblet and drank from it before remembering something else.

"Oh, and you have won a prize from Felond's stables for winning the race in his realm. What would you like, a new bridle? A saddle? I fear that Felond's stables do not offer much, but still, you should have something."

"Omaron told me to ask for a saddle if I ever won a race," Inesca said. "He said I could always sell it if I didn't need a spare and that saddles would be worth more than other things."

"Omaron knows what he's talking about. If you keep listening to him, you'll do well, Inesca."

Inesca's thoughts returned to her encounter with Omaron only moments ago. Lord Beristo might be pleased with her performance in the race, but Omaron certainly was not.

"The races that follow this one are more difficult," Lord Beristo continued.

"But I look forward to seeing you have the opportunity to defeat Lord Edgerr's other riders. He has two brothers who are quite good."

"Yes. Omaron told me about them."

Inesca remembered running into one of them in the crowded streets of Cerdost. Racing against them would probably be just as unpleasant.

"It's not fair that he has both of them," Lord Beristo continued with a sigh. "They're the sons of Arryn, and they've shown it in the races too."

The goblet in Inesca's hands slipped from her fingers and landed on the rug, rolling to the side and leaving a trail of wine in its path.

Lord Beristo had his back turned to Inesca, or he would have seen the expression of surprise on her face.

"The sons of …," she said in barely a whisper.

"Arryn won many races before your time. He was an impressive rider, and I would have been celebrating more often if he had ridden for me."

Inesca reached out and put her hand on the edge of the table, and then she noticed the wine spilt on the rug. Kneeling, she took off her cloak and began trying to soak up what she could. Lord Beristo turned and saw what she was doing.

"You truly are tired, aren't you? Can't even hold a cup of wine. Here, leave that alone. I'll call the servants. This is an old rug and not worth the trouble."

"I am sorry, my lord," she said, keeping her head down. "I will go now if I may."

He nodded. "You may, but be certain to get some rest."

Inesca bowed and walked quickly out into the night air with her cloak still in her hands. She stumbled over a fallen branch on her way to her tent, but tried to keep going before someone could see her. Lord Beristo's words would not leave her mind.

The sons of Arryn. Brothers. Are they my brothers too? Are they my father's sons? she wondered.

As she thrust her way into her tent, she thought about the wooden knight with her father's possessions. Had it belonged to one of them? A sudden urge to see it again filled her, and she threw the blankets on her mat aside, searching for her father's pouch. Her fingers were greeted only by the rough fabric covering her straw mattress. As her heart beat faster, Inesca turned over the pallet and tossed the blankets up in the air. After a moment, she stumbled out of the tent and into the fresh air with wide eyes and a pounding heart.

The sound of logs being tossed onto a fire drew her attention to the center of Lord Beristo's camp. Jirro's form appeared dark against the light of small, flickering flames. Walking toward him, Inesca saw that his back was turned toward her, but he lifted his head at the sound of her footsteps.

"Proud of yourself, aren't you, girl?" he said. He turned his head slightly with a smirk barely visible at the corner of his mouth. "Do you think it will always be so easy?"

As Inesca approached, she could make out a worn leather pouch in his hands.

"Jirro, please …"

"Oh, looking for this, were you?" He held the pouch out toward the light of the fire so that she could clearly recognize it. "What is it?"

"It was my father's. Give it back to me."

He tilted it in his hands. "But it's so worn and old. Hardly a treasure," he said.

Inesca reached out for it, but he pulled it away and held it over the flames.

"Tell me why it's worth so much to you and what you might give me in return for it."

"I don't have any silver to pay for your mead. Now give it back to me."

"Well, if you're not willing to share …"

He suddenly released it, and Inesca dove forward to catch it, but Jirro seized her and held her back with a laugh. With a cry of rage, Inesca drove her head back into the side of his face and shoved him away from her.

The leather pouch had fallen between two smoldering pieces of firewood, and she used a large branch beside the fire to drag it out. Once she had knocked it onto the grass and smothered the traces of fire clinging to it, she saw that the pouch had been burned beyond repair. It crumbled into charred pieces, its mysterious insignia lost. Underneath the remains of the pouch, she found the wooden knight, blackened but intact.

Turning to Jirro, who groaned as he held his hand to his head, she swung the branch into his back and knocked him to the ground. Rummaging through his pockets, she found the ring and the medallion. After picking up the wooden knight, Inesca paused as she stood over him.

"If you dare to touch my possessions again or set foot in my tent, I will strike you down with a sword instead of a branch."

Returning swiftly to her tent, Inesca glanced back to make sure that he remained on the ground. Sweeping back the flap, she climbed inside and kneeled beside her pallet.

Inesca inspected the little knight again and finally placed him within a small drawstring purse that she often wore at her belt. Turning to the other items, she noted that the ribbon had been torn from her father's medallion, but at least she had regained it and the ring.

No doubt, Jirro hoped to exchange them for ale. She tucked the medallion in with the knight but not the ring. Stepping back outside the tent, Inesca saw Jirro stumbling away, and she knelt at one of the stakes to which a corner of her tent was tied. Leather cords had been used to secure the fabric of the tent to each stake, but one had a long piece extending from it.

Inesca cut the bit of extra cord, took it back inside the tent, and slipped the ring onto it before tying it around her neck. Tucking it between her tunic and undershirt, Inesca pressed it close to her heart. If it was true that the rider Arryn was also her father, then these small treasures might be her only hope of learning his past and whether she had any family left in this world.

Chapter 13

Morning light danced upon the river at the edge of Lord Edgerr's camp as Kestorn brushed Halon's coat and hummed softly.

"Your expression hasn't changed once since the end of the race yesterday," Derreth said. "You even smiled like that in your sleep last night."

After a few more strokes with the brush, Kestorn finally turned and glanced at his brother.

"Do you know who was here this morning, still trying to get the mud off of his clothes?"

"Someone who regrets entangling himself with this firebrand," Derreth said, patting Halon's neck. The red stallion turned his head away and snorted as he flattened his ears against his head.

Kestorn laughed. "He never takes losing well, even when it's for his own good."

"If he hadn't spent so much of his energy fighting Trestan, he wouldn't have lost."

Kestorn shook his head. "Trestan lost his chance at winning when he tried to hold Halon back. It's not Halon's fault he was paired with the wrong rider."

"I wonder if Lord Edgerr will see it that way. I doubt he'll be satisfied that the only rider who can manage this stallion is you, Kes."

"Why should he care if I'm the only one who can ride Halon well?"

"Because it means that Halon was never fully broken. And Lord Edgerr's pride will not suffer him to accept that you have more control over Halon than he does."

With more forceful strokes, Kestorn brushed Halon's flank as his brow furrowed.

"What do you suggest that I do?" he asked.

"Just be careful. Don't do anything that would offend him. Respect his authority, and find a way to be humble for a change. If you manage to regain his favor, he might overlook Halon's stubborn refusal to work with other riders."

Kestorn lowered the brush and tossed it to Derreth. "Regaining his favor is a lot to ask when I don't understand how I lost it in the first place," he said.

"Try to please him, Kes. That would be a first for you, and it might at least catch him off guard if it does nothing else."

"I win races for him. Isn't that enough?"

"Lord Edgerr's ego extends beyond the races. To stay in his good graces, we must accept his authority in our training and in everyday affairs. And although you do what he tells you, there's always a clear expression of resentment on your face."

"Have it your way then, Derreth. Next time I'm called before his lordship, I'll wear a mask."

Kestorn picked up a ragged cloth that he had used to wash Halon's flank. It had holes in it, and Kestorn held it up so that it covered all of his face except his eyes. Derreth seized the cloth and pulled it down so that it covered Kestorn's vision before using his boot to nudge his younger brother back into the river behind him.

Kestorn stumbled and fell but managed to seize Derreth's arm and pull him into the water as well. They fell in with a splash, and Halon shied away from the water with a snort.

As the two brothers wrestled in the water, their laughter carried over to a figure standing behind a lone tree several yards away from the riverbank. Brushing some strands of dark hair from her face, Inesca leaned farther around the tree to watch them.

She recognized the younger one as the fair-headed rider with flashing blue eyes and a cocky smile who had insulted her on the day of her arrival to Cerdost. But here, he seemed less disagreeable. Inesca wondered about the age of his brother. He looked a few years older, but she guessed he could not be thirty based on his appearance.

The older brother shoved the younger down into the water again, and Inesca strained for a better view of him. He looked both taller and stronger than his brother, and as he turned, Inesca caught a better look at his face before moving back behind the tree.

She waited a moment and then dared another glance. There was her father's face, only far younger in appearance. His hair was a similar shade of brown to what she remembered seeing mixed with gray in her father's hair. And his smile was the same as the one she treasured in her memory. A sudden pain pierced her heart as she watched him pull his brother from the water and start to lead him back toward camp with the red stallion.

Wisps of cloud drifted in front of the setting sun, and their edges caught fire and turned to gold in the last light of the day. Nycor stood with his head lowered into a large basket of oats, only pausing long enough from his meal to check his surroundings occasionally. Beside the basket, Inesca sat in the grass, leaning her back against a post. Her eyes stared off into the distance as her hands twisted a tough weed that she had pulled from the ground.

Nycor raised his head and whinnied as a dark figure walked into view from behind some of the tents. Standing up suddenly, Inesca shook her wandering thoughts from her mind as the figure came closer. She thought it might be Lord Beristo for a moment, but when he approached, she saw that it was Sirryn.

"I didn't mean to startle you, Inesca. It's a cool evening with that wind from the north bearing down on us. Wouldn't you be more comfortable inside your tent?"

Inesca shook her head. "I wanted some cold air for a change, and Nycor needed some more oats," she explained.

Sirryn glanced down at the half-empty basket. "More indeed. I knew racehorses ate a lot, but this horse always seems to think he's starving."

Patting Nycor's neck with her hand, Inesca smiled and said, "My father once said that my stallion had a fire burning inside of him that would consume every blade of grass in the East Province if we let it. But then he also said it was this fire that would fuel Nycor to run faster than the wind. That's what his name means: wind-chaser. It comes from the old language that was once spoken in the East Province before the common tongue of Rynar was accepted."

"How did your father find the money to purchase a horse like this?"

"My father didn't buy Nycor," Inesca said, running her hand through the stallion's black mane. "He bred him."

"Ah, yes. I'd forgotten that Lord Beristo said your father was a breeder. The sire and dam must have been magnificent animals."

"They were, but Nycor could not have come from anything normal. Even my father's methods with his horses were unconventional. He tried buying horses and raising them in the usual manner in the beginning, but Roegur and his hateful men would steal them. My father learned, though, that they were only adept at catching tame horses. There were wild horses in the forests beyond our home that Roegur never succeeded in capturing. But my father was not afraid to ride after the wild horses."

"He caught some of them, then?"

"Not right away. At first, he wanted only to get a better look at them, and then he waited. One day, he was able to win two beautiful mares in a race against some of the other men from the East Province."

"You hold races in the East Province?"

"They're not as long as the races here, but racing is popular there, just as it is here. My father had one horse that he had managed to keep from being stolen, and even though he had owned better horses, this one was good enough to win him the race."

"And what happened to the mares he won?"

"Well, Roegur boasted to my father that soon the mares would belong to him, but he was to be disappointed. As soon as my father returned home, he rode out into the forest with them. Later, he returned only with the horse he had ridden in the race."

"He let them go with the wild horses," Sirryn said.

"Yes. But it was the stallion running with the wild horses that he wanted. It was a great white beast with a black mane and strong legs that seemed at once to be made of iron and wind, or at least that's how my father described him. I only saw him once, but months later, my father returned from the forest with those same two mares, and both were soon to have foals."

"One of the foals was Nycor?"

Inesca nodded.

"And I have no doubts about who his sire was."

"What about the other foal?"

"She was a pretty thing, white with a silver mane, and she was graceful, but not a racehorse, I think. But she also didn't get much of a chance. Roegur managed to steal her later."

"Didn't he try to take Nycor?"

Inesca smiled. "Nycor was too wild. He would only come to my father or to me. And none of Roegur's men could catch him, although a few pressed close enough to get hurt. However, to make sure Nycor stayed safe, my father and I would let him run into the forest at night. He was faithful enough to return to us during the day."

"Still, was that not a great risk to take with a horse that your father worked so hard to obtain?"

"It would have been better to know that we lost Nycor because he chose to stay with the wild horses than to believe that we gave Roegur and his men another chance to steal him."

"Lord Beristo was told that your father had other horses before he died."

"He did. Nycor would occasionally bring horses from the forest with him.

And for a time, Roegur left to serve his duties as a sheriff in the north. While he was gone, my father was able to keep the horses on our land and train them. People began to come to him to get excellent horses, and our lives were better for a while. When Roegur returned, he and his men caught my father in town. They had heard about his success and demanded that he give them the horses."

"He refused?"

She nodded. "My father was poor, but he was not a coward. I think they hated him because he was one of the few people who would stand up to them. He was badly beaten and sent home draped over his horse. I tried to help him, but he did not recover. Before he lost consciousness, he told me that Nycor was mine and that I should take him and leave."

"Then Lord Beristo and I found you."

"Your timing could not have been better," Inesca said softly.

"But where would you have gone if we had not shown up?"

"I don't know. I barely knew anything about the rest of the world. Before he died, my father refused to let me leave our land unless it was with him, or I was riding through the forest on Nycor. Even then, he was not far away on a horse of his own."

"Considering how much was taken from him, it is understandable that he would want to keep you close."

Inesca's thoughts drifted to Derreth and Kestorn. It seemed that her father had lost more than she realized.

"I believe I understand that better now," she said. "But where have you come from? Lord Beristo walked by and asked about you over an hour ago. I think he's having his dinner now."

"Then I won't disturb him yet. I told him that I would go and see my brother today."

"How is he?"

"Doing well. His wife was ill earlier this year, but she is better now. They have a son in Valmontes training to become a knight, and their daughter is married, soon to have her first child."

"What about your wife? What does she do while you are traveling with Lord Beristo?"

"She stays with her family while I'm away, and she's happier there than she would be traveling across the Six Realms. I will be glad to return to her when the racing season is over, but unlike her, I enjoy seeing what is beyond Ettidor. And it is the only way for me to see my brother."

Inesca's thoughts turned to Derreth and Kestorn. They were strangers to her, and yet she now felt more closely connected to them than anyone else who was alive.

"How do you know what to say to your brother after being separated for such a long time?"

"I like to hear about his family, and I tell him the news from Ettidor. Sometimes we talk about old memories from when we were children."

"Anything else?"

"Well, we talk about the races. He was interested to know more about you. May I ask why you are so interested in my conversations with my brother?"

"It's not something I can easily explain."

He turned to leave, but then she stood up and caught up with him.

"If there ever was a war between Lord Felond and Lord Beristo and your brother was in trouble, would you help him?"

"What kind of a question is that?" Sirryn laughed. "There's never been a war between any of the lords, and there never will be."

"But if there was, what would you do?"

"I will always serve Lord Beristo as his loyal council member and friend, but I would never forget my brother. God gives us our families for a reason. Those gifts are never to be thrown away lightly."

"What if you are not on good terms with your family? What if they despise you?"

Sirryn shot her a strange look. "And what prompts you to ask these questions?"

"I have just been thinking about the past lately and wondering if things could have turned out differently."

After studying her expression, Sirryn spoke again. "In my experience, it is better to try to heal a broken family than to leave it broken. There are some things that cannot be fixed or changed, but the bond that exists within a family is the bond that holds a nation together. That's why members of families are spread out between the Six Realms by the Royal Council. As long as we remember that we are all one nation, not six separate kingdoms, we will have peace. For that reason, it is good for me to be loyal to my lord and to remember that my brother is here in Sassot. My loyalty must be to all of Rynar and not merely to one part of it."

"Is that also true for someone like me?"

"Not all of it. Although, I wish it could be," Sirryn sighed. "I warned you about coming here, Inesca. As someone from the East Province, you do not have the same rights as those who were born here. And riders are bound to their lords more than councilmen are. You do not have the same freedom that you once did."

"Even in the East Province, I did not have much freedom. Not with Roegur lurking about. But I had the freedom to love my father. I did not realize it at first, but that's all I want here. You are right. The bond between a family is strong, and the only freedom I want is to be able to stay true to that bond."

"Then it seems you are in the right place," Sirryn said. "Your father would be proud of what you've accomplished here."

Inesca thanked him and let him walk on to Lord Beristo's tent as she returned to Nycor.

"But Father didn't give me those pieces from his past to win races," Inesca said softly as she laid her hand on the gray stallion's back. "And even if they are Lord Edgerr's riders, he would not want me to forget that they are my brothers."

Chapter 14

Since the humbling of Trestan, life in Lord Edgerr's camp had grown easier. However, the time drew near when Derreth and Kestorn would have to help pack up the tents and travel to Monterr, where the next race would be held. Lord Edgerr had not spoken one word to them since the race, but on their last day in the camp, they received an order to come to his tent.

Derreth noticed that Kestorn looked tense as they entered, so he spoke first. "You called for us, my lord?"

Lord Edgerr rose from his chair as he stared at their faces. For a moment, he said nothing as he looked from one to the other. Finally, he said, "Before we leave to travel to the realm of Monterr, I must choose a rider for the next race. As you both know, Trestan was given a chance to prove himself, but he failed. Even Lord Felond mocked his loss."

Derreth lowered his gaze to his boots. Lord Edgerr would not say it, but it was he who felt mocked. There was nothing worse than to be a laughingstock to the lord who never won races. That Lord Felond could say his rider performed better than Trestan was a true embarrassment.

"I need a different rider for the race in Monterr, and I have made my decision."

Derreth and Kestorn briefly glanced at each other. *It won't be me*, Derreth thought. *Not after his suspicions about the Raegond.*

"I've also grown tired of the trouble from the red stallion," Lord Edgerr continued. Then he stopped and looked at Kestorn. "Will there ever be a time when he can be ridden by someone other than you?"

Kestorn turned his gaze away from Lord Edgerr as the hardness that Derreth had often seen as a result of Kestorn's temper started to fill his gaze, but after a second, he turned back and looked Lord Edgerr in the eyes. "It would be my pleasure to train him for you and for any rider, my lord," he said.

Lord Edgerr turned away from him and walked back to his chair.

"Accomplish that, and you'll have earned the right to ride him again in a race. But as for the race in Monterr, Derreth will ride Celestro."

Kestorn lifted his chin but said nothing. Derreth watched Lord Edgerr with surprise.

"My lord, why not allow my brother to prove himself to you in the next race? He is—"

"*He is* silent, as you should be. And do not forget that I expect the best from you in the upcoming race. If it turns out that I have three incompetent riders in my service, I'll dismiss all of you and start anew, no matter how much it costs me."

Derreth closed his mouth.

"I have not forgotten the notion of selling you to Lord Tolem as slaves for the mines of Monterr. Don't tempt me to act upon it."

Only days before the next of the Great Races remained as hundreds traveled the western roads from Sassot to Monterr. Inesca was grateful that the two realms were near each other, but she marveled at how different they seemed. The green hills of Sassot marked by gigantic trees slipped behind them as mountains stretched toward the sky. Instead of grass and wildflowers, rocks the color of the red sand from the beaches of Farcost rose from the ground.

"You stare as if you've never seen mountains before," Sirryn said as he watched her wandering gaze.

"Never ones this color."

"A layer of red rock runs beneath much of the realm. It makes the land unsuitable for farming, but Lord Tolem's ancestors were able to establish several successful mines in the mountains. They never lacked wealth, and neither has Lord Tolem. Anything his realm does not produce, he can find a way to purchase."

"Where will the race be held?"

"In the midst of those mountains and cliffs to the west. Most of the race will make use of a gorge that was cut by the Siccre River centuries ago, but the river has since been trapped behind a dam."

Inesca glanced at the sparse brush that sprung up between crevices in the rocks.

"This seems like a harsh land for a race," she said. "Nycor and I are more accustomed to galloping across fields and through forests."

"There is little green to be enjoyed here, but you will find that all of the races will be different from the one in Sassot. The other lords often make use of more difficult terrain, but Lord Felond cannot afford to risk anything more dangerous than sloping meadows. His riders have enough trouble winning races as it is."

"Where is the race held in Ettidor? Lord Beristo never showed me the place he used when he hosts races."

"You passed it when we rode out of the East Province and into Ettidor, but we did not direct your attention to the region because it was flooded."

"Flooded?"

"Lord Beristo and his ancestors used the west bank of the Etta River for the races, but this year the river rose above its banks. We are fortunate that we do not have to host a race this year, but it has made Lord Beristo question whether he might not have to find a new location for the future races."

As they rode deeper into a valley between the mountains, Inesca caught sight of the town before them and, beyond it, a road leading to a castle that rose above a cliff.

"Is that the castle of Lord Tolem?"

"No. The lords do not live in castles. Such dwelling places suggest the need for military defense, but the lords are not to be at war with each other, so they live in manor houses on estates. That is an old castle from the time when Rynar was ruled by a king and nobles, but I believe it is now the home of Sir Coltar of Monterr."

Inesca's gaze swung back to the castle.

"Are you certain?"

"Why? Do you want to pay him a visit?" Sirryn laughed.

Her face flushed.

"I've heard of him."

"Well, you would be better off not taking an interest in him. Knights never have much time to spare for anyone but the Royal Council and the lords."

Inesca drew Nycor to a halt to study the castle for a moment longer. Then she turned to follow the wagon carrying Lord Beristo's supplies down the road that led west and away from the town.

"Hold on a minute," Sirryn said as he rode in front of her. "Did you not hear Lord Beristo say that the servants and Omaron would set up camp for us, while we spend the night in the town of Lasnell?"

"That town?" Inesca asked as she gestured toward the one below the castle.

"Would you prefer to travel farther to find another?"

"No," she said quickly. "This one is fine."

"Then come along. Lord Beristo expects us to purchase the best rooms for his stay tonight, and that will not be easy since many who are coming for the race will be seeking lodging here."

Inesca turned Nycor around and followed Sirryn toward the main road leading them farther into the valley. Her attention strayed to the castle again. Sirryn continued to talk without noticing her distracted gaze.

"I advised our lord not to bring Jirro with us this year, but he said that he must. The fool has been nothing but a nuisance thus far. I suppose you heard that he went missing last night. That is why Lord Beristo stayed behind with his guards to find him. I would have remained with him, but Lord Beristo knew that someone would have to go on ahead and make arrangements for lodging."

"Not that I am complaining, but why does Lord Beristo not stay at the camp as he did in Sassot?" she asked.

"He will, but it has become a tradition for the lords to stay in Lasnell two days before the race in Monterr. And Lord Beristo would find it degrading to stay in a tent if the other lords were eating and residing in town. He would be here with us now if not for Jirro."

As they approached the gate in the stone wall surrounding the town, Sirryn untied a small green and gold flag from his saddle and waved it for the guards to see. A few seconds later, the gates opened, and they were allowed inside.

The road continued down the middle of the town, and on either side, inns and taverns of different sizes rose to greet them. As they passed a stable, a couple of men came out and eyed their horses.

"They know business is coming," Sirryn said. "This town rarely has visitors except when races are held nearby. Even when there is not a Great Race, Lord Tolem hosts other competitions in the area. The people here depend on such events."

"Is that why I do not see many houses here?"

"Inns are what they need, not houses. You'll also not see a market here. If you want to buy something, you have to go to the shop owners and their exorbitant prices. We're fortunate, though. It looks like we've arrived before the crowd has."

"Where will Lord Beristo want to stay?"

"At one of the inns that is grand enough but not too expensive. Not all of the lords bring their riders into town with them, but Lord Beristo likes to keep his riders close. Although, that's difficult to do with Jirro unless you chain him to the wall."

"You said that Lord Beristo felt that he *must* bring Jirro. Why?"

"For the same reason he won't lock him up or have him whipped for drinking. Jirro's father is a wealthy knight in Ettidor. Lord Beristo has had to rely on his support several times in the past, and when this knight asked Lord Beristo to allow his son to become a rider, Lord Beristo agreed. At the time, he had no idea that Jirro would be so difficult to manage."

"And he cannot tell this knight how awful his son is?"

"He has told him, more than once. But the knight said that if Lord Beristo wanted to continue to have his support, he must allow Jirro to remain one of his riders, in name at least, and treat him well."

"Won't this knight be angry that I am competing in the races instead of his son?"

"He can hardly make any demands about that after Jirro injured himself by falling off a horse in a drunken stupor during the last racing season. I believe he understands that Jirro is less of an embarrassment to him when he doesn't compete. But Jirro still believes he can get anything he wants or do anything he wants under his father's protection."

"If he loses that protection, life will come as a great shock to him," Inesca said.

"Yes," Sirryn said with a smile. "It might do him some good, but meanwhile, we must endure him."

When another road finally intersected the first, Sirryn turned and led Inesca around a corner to a large inn with a sign that read *The Silver Hoof*.

"I'll go in and get our rooms. You can take the horses to the stable just across the way. It's owned by the blacksmith and his family."

After dismounting, Sirryn counted out some coins for her. Inesca climbed down from Nycor's back and accepted the coins from him along with his horse's reins.

"If that's not enough, tell them Lord Beristo can pay more when he arrives."

Inesca watched him step inside the inn before she led the horses across the road to the stable. A blacksmith's shop and forge were set up near the stable, and a tall, bearded man walked out to greet her, wiping the soot from his hands with a rag.

"I'm Urron, and this is my stable. What can I offer your horses?"

"These horses belong to Lord Beristo. How much will it cost to stable them for the night and give them fresh oats and water?"

"Eight darorrs."

Inesca kept her hand tightly closed over the silver coins that Sirryn had given her.

"I believe my lord was expecting to pay six. Perhaps I should go to another stable and see if they will offer less."

"Do as you wish," the man said as he started to move back to his forge.

Just then, a boy about nine or ten years old ran out from the stable and stopped in front of Inesca, staring at Nycor.

"Is that the gray horse that won the race in Sassot for Lord Beristo?"

Inesca glanced from the boy to the blacksmith and saw enough of a resemblance to convince her that this was his son.

"Yes, it is," she said with a smile.

"Can I touch him?"

Inesca led Nycor forward, spoke to him softly, and nodded. The gray stallion let the boy pet his neck, and then he leaned down and sniffed the boy's pouch at his waist.

"You must be carrying some food on you," Inesca said, watching them.

The boy took a carrot out of his pouch and offered it to Nycor, who accepted it eagerly.

"What about seven darorrs?" Inesca asked the blacksmith.

"Seven is a good price," he agreed.

Inesca handed the reins of the horses to the boy and paid the blacksmith, keeping one coin hidden in her hand as she turned to walk back to the inn.

Chapter 15

After arriving at the camp in Monterr with the horses, Trestan, Derreth, and Kestorn were responsible for setting up the tents with the servants. During most of the ride into Monterr, Kestorn had remained quiet about the race and Lord Edgerr's decision to choose Derreth. His brother's silence was beginning to bother Derreth, but at the moment, he was just trying to focus on driving a stake into the ground for one of the last tents.

"I think I could work faster if we weren't being watched," Kestorn said, joining his brother after putting up his own tent.

Derreth looked up and followed his brother's gaze to two of Lord Edgerr's guards, who were watching them from underneath the shade of one of the tents.

"They're just doing their job, Kes."

"Watching us work?"

"Making sure the work is not neglected."

"Sounds like the same thing."

Derreth wiped the sweat from his face as he surveyed the rest of the camp. The guards finally walked on and passed Trestan, who was lying down. One of them kicked him, and he jumped up and quickly walked over to help the servants with the tent they were working on.

"At least they're making Trestan work," Derreth said.

"Well, are you almost finished here?" Kestorn asked.

Looking back at the tent that he had been helping with, Derreth saw some of the servants come to finish the task of putting it up.

"I think they can manage the rest of it. What did you want?"

Kestorn glanced back at the horses and then at his brother. "I think it's time to train Halon to accept a different rider."

"Who?"

Kestorn's gaze swept to Derreth's face. After hesitating for a moment, Derreth said, "If that's what you want, Kes."

"Well, it can't be Trestan. And there's no one else that I trust to treat him well, but don't get any ideas about keeping him."

Derreth smiled. It wasn't as though Halon could ever belong to him or to Kestorn, but now was not the time to argue that point.

"Understood."

Kestorn led him over to the horses and untied Halon, who was already saddled and bridled. Rubbing Halon's forehead and then scratching his neck around his mane, Kestorn led him to an enclosure surrounded by a fence at the camp. Once Halon was inside, Kestorn let him go. Derreth sighed as he watched the red stallion lope around the area and stretch his legs.

"You're going to make me work for this, aren't you?"

"If he won't come to you, then he won't let you ride him," Kestorn said, but there was a hint of a smile in his expression.

Derreth walked out into the middle of the enclosure and called out to Halon with his hand outstretched. The red stallion lifted his head and his ears perked forward, but then he turned his head and continued loping around the enclosure. Derreth cast a glance at Kestorn, who stood outside the fence now, watching them.

Reaching inside a pouch at his belt, Derreth pulled out some berries that he had been saving for Celestro. Whistling, he held out the berries to Halon.

"That's cheating, Derreth," Kestorn called from the fence.

"And you've never used this technique?" Derreth said, lifting one eyebrow.

Kestorn smiled and continued to watch them. Halon turned his head toward Derreth and eventually came toward him. He didn't hesitate to eat out of Derreth's hand.

"You know me," Derreth said softly as he patted Halon's neck and scratched his head between his ears. "We don't have to make this difficult, right?"

When Halon seemed relaxed, Derreth moved slowly to the stallion's side and drew himself up into the saddle. He felt Halon tense beneath him, and he tried talking to him again.

"Whoa, easy Halon. It's just me."

Derreth saw Halon's ears flatten against his head, and that was his warning before the stallion bolted forward and bucked. Derreth managed to keep his seat since this was not the first time he'd ridden a stubborn horse, but he wondered how long he would be able to keep it up.

Halon continued to fight him, but then Kestorn walked out into the enclosure and whistled. Halon slowed and turned his head toward him.

"It's not the same as having me on your back, is it?" Kestorn said as he gently approached Halon and finally took the reins from Derreth. "But you can handle it, Halon."

Kestorn slowly started to lead Halon around the enclosure with Derreth on his back.

"You're making him nervous," Kestorn said, looking up at Derreth.

"I'm making him nervous?" Derreth said. "This horse loves nothing more than to fight anyone he comes across."

"You have to be just as stubborn as he is if you want to be able to ride him."

"It's easy to see why he likes you then," Derreth said with a cautious laugh.

As evening fell, the town of Lasnell grew busier as travelers filled the roads. Inesca remained in her small room at the end of the upper hall of the Silver Hoof. The room was comfortable but clearly designed to be humble enough for a servant accompanying a far more important guest. She had one window that faced north and provided her with a clear view of the castle above the town.

Her eyes kept turning back to that view as she finished the meal sent to her room. After a few moments, she looked out and saw Sirryn and Lord Beristo with a few of his guards traveling toward the large guildhall in the center of the town. Sirryn had told her that he and Lord Beristo would be joining the other lords there for dinner.

It was strange that the castle above the town seemed so forgotten. Why did the lords not demand a place there to stay the night? But perhaps it was better that they did not pay any attention to it.

Taking her cloak from the bed, Inesca opened her door and stepped out into the hall. She threw the cloak around her shoulders, softly closed the door, and started down the stairs along the wall.

"Going out?"

Inesca stiffened, turned, and noticed Jirro watching her from the doorway of his room which was only a few doors away from hers.

"It's not your business if I am," Inesca said as she started to walk on.

"Doesn't matter. I already know you're not going to set foot outside of this inn."

With an impatient sigh, Inesca turned around to face him. "And why is that?" she asked.

"Lord Beristo posted some guards downstairs to make sure I couldn't enjoy my time here. All they'll let me have is bread and water."

"What does that have to do with me?"

"You don't really expect them to let you leave, do you? Lord Beristo's precious rider who won him the last race. After the hours they had to spend tracking me down, they're not about to lose you."

Inesca felt the heat rush into her face as Jirro smiled unpleasantly while watching her frustration, but she knew he was right. Sirryn had all but told her to stay in her room earlier when he'd encouraged her to get some rest and enjoy sleeping in a real bed for a change.

"I commend you then," she said as she moved up the stairs and opened the door to her room. "You've ruined the evening for both of us."

Shutting the door forcefully behind her, Inesca disappeared back into her room, and Jirro stood there for a moment as his smile faded. He walked back into his room and then moved to the window. After a few moments, he saw a shadow move along the outside wall of the inn, and Jirro smiled again.

"Not yet, I haven't," he said.

He strode quickly out of his room and made his way down the hall. At the opposite end, he hesitated before knocking on the last door. At first there was no answer, but then the door opened slowly.

"I noticed that Lord Beristo wasn't the only lord to take rooms here," Jirro said. "I hope you don't mind my intrusion."

Destrod, Lord Felond's rider from the previous race, scowled back at him from the other side of the door.

"I do if you've come to gloat about the last race. But it makes no difference, as I've no time for talk. I'm to go down and see to his lordship's horses at the stable," Destrod said.

"If you think I take pride in anything that little fool does, you are mistaken," Jirro said. He stepped aside and let Destrod walk out into the hall. "But since you are on your way to the stables, would you greet her for me while you are out?"

"She's outside the inn alone?"

Jirro gestured back toward Destrod's room. "If you don't believe me, look out the window," he said.

Destrod turned and walked to the window on his back wall. Inesca's small frame was visible on a ledge just five feet from the ground. She climbed to the corner of the inn and jumped down in the shadows between the inn and the shop beside it.

"She must be desperate to go somewhere tonight," he said, watching her from the window.

Jirro stepped inside the room impatiently. "Well," he said, "what are you going to do with such an opportunity?"

Chapter 16

Hurin, the blacksmith's son, brushed the gray stallion as he hummed a soothing tune. It still thrilled him that he was caring for a horse that had won one of the Great Races. Glancing at the horse's water trough, he noticed that it was already empty.

"The long ride here must have made you thirsty," Hurin said, patting the stallion's neck.

Stepping down from the stool that he had been standing on, Hurin grabbed a bucket and headed for the well that was not far from the stable. As he drew near to it, he saw the same young woman who had come to the stable to deliver the horses. She recognized him and came closer.

"I need your help again," she told him. "I have a task that requires a horse, but I don't want to use any of my lord's horses. They need their rest tonight. Do you have any that you could spare for a quick ride?"

"My father and I have one mare," Hurin said. "But you'll have to ask him if you can use her."

She nodded and followed him to the blacksmith who was working at his forge. Hurin explained her request.

"Why do you need the horse?" his father asked.

"I have a message to deliver to someone on the other side of town," Inesca said as she held out the silver coin that she had kept earlier. "I'll pay you for the use of her."

The blacksmith eyed the coin but hesitated.

"Is it not enough?" she asked.

"No, it's too much. No one pays in silver to borrow a horse for such a short distance."

"I could have paid you more for the care of Lord Beristo's two horses," she said. "Consider this part of the payment for that service."

After another moment of hesitation, he took the coin.

"Go get Beiru ready," he told his son.

"Thank you. I'll bring her back after I have delivered my message," she promised.

"Well, if you don't, then you will owe me more of these," the blacksmith said with a smile, holding up the coin.

As she passed through the stable, the young woman greeted Nycor and patted his neck. Hurin brought a black mare to her already saddled and fitted with a bridle.

"Beiru is a good horse, but not as fast as yours," he said.

"I am sure she will be good enough," Inesca said.

※

Nearly half an hour after getting a horse from the stable, Inesca neared the castle that towered above the town of Lasnell. Its walls were built into the side of the mountain, and their stones looked to be cut from the same kind of red rock that lent the mountains their hue. A round tower rose up on the southern wall, overlooking the town in the valley below. Just as Inesca started to reach the end of the road, a man on horseback cut in front of her.

"Sir Coltar is not expecting guests during his absence. What is your business here?"

"Absence?" Inesca repeated. "Does he not remain near Lasnell at the time of the race in Monterr?"

"He has many duties as a knight, and of late, he shows little interest in the races. Now, why are you here?"

"I have a message for him, but I was to deliver it in person."

"That will prove difficult. Sir Coltar is traveling across the Six Realms serving the Royal Council."

"Do you know where he is now?"

"Only those traveling with him know that. We are left here to guard his castle until his return."

"When will he return?"

The man shrugged. "When it pleases him," he said.

Inesca sighed and stared at the castle.

"What was your message?" the guard asked. "I am Captain Pyron, his second-in-command. I will try to give it to him when he returns."

"Tell Sir Coltar that a rider in the service of Lord Beristo was here to ask him about an oath that he swore twenty years ago. Ask him if it still means anything to him."

She turned the mare and guided her down the road as a heaviness settled on her heart. With the help of Sir Coltar, she might have been able to learn the truth about her father. She had even dared to hope that he might help her meet Derreth and Kestorn and find a way for her to avoid racing against them. But now it seemed that she might never get to meet this wandering knight whom her father had spoken of.

Upon reentering Lasnell, Inesca noticed the guildhall in the distance, a grand hall decorated with crimson and silver, the colors of the realm of Monterr. A wooden bull with silver-tipped horns, its head lowered as if to gore any unwelcome guests, stood near the door. As Inesca passed the guildhall, the door opened, and several well-dressed guests walked out of its warm light into the night. Lord Beristo moved among them, and Inesca ducked her head as she urged Beiru into a faster pace.

Cutting around the side of another building to avoid being seen, Inesca reminded herself that she could still beat him back to The Silver Hoof if she rode quickly. But as she dared to ride back toward one of the main roads that would lead her to the inn and the stable, Inesca suddenly noticed a figure riding toward her from the opposite direction. His horse was gaining speed, and he was coming right for her.

Inesca directed the mare to her right and led her behind a row of inns, hoping to still be able to find a way to get back to The Silver Hoof. But before they could get far, the other rider appeared from around the corner of a building and began chasing them. Inesca could not see his face in the darkness, but she was certain it was a man.

She urged the mare into a gallop as they raced through the shadows of the town in the moonlight. Suddenly, Inesca noticed an abandoned cart with two missing wheels lying at an angle in front of them. She tried to urge the mare into a jump, but instead, the mare drew to a sudden halt, reared, and turned away from the cart. Now forced to face the oncoming rider, Inesca grabbed the wooden shaft of a spear that leaned against the side of the cart, but when she raised it, she saw that the spear was missing its tip, leaving her with a mere wooden pole.

The other rider slowed his horse but drew a dagger from his belt and raised it as he approached her. Inesca swung the pole clumsily in her left hand and knocked his arm aside, but not before the tip of the blade slashed her wrist and forearm.

Drawing her arm to her side, Inesca stifled a cry of pain and seized the pole with her other hand.

"Is it still wonderful to be a winner?" the rider asked as he lowered the dagger for a moment.

Inesca lifted her gaze to his face and recognized it.

"Destrod? Why are you doing this?"

"To teach you to stay out of the races. The only reason you won last time is because of your horse. An Easterner like you shouldn't be allowed on a horse like that."

"That horse was born and bred in my land. And I raised him."

"Well, you're not riding him now," Destrod said, raising the dagger again.

Inesca swung the pole at his head, causing him to shy away enough for Beiru to get past his horse. Riding into a gallop, Inesca glanced back and saw him following her. He grasped the dagger by the tip as if to throw it at her, but Inesca steered Beiru between two buildings and the dagger flew past her head and landed in the wall of an inn.

On the edge of Lasnell, the door of the guildhall remained opened, and light streamed out onto the dark road. One of the men standing in the doorway was a tall, robust man with dark gray hair cut short enough to draw attention to the sharpness of his features. He wore a crimson cloak fastened with the crest of a silver bull.

Lord Beristo stood next to this man with a thick green cloak drawn over his own shoulders. There was a smile on his face that even the cold night wind could not chase away.

"I will stand by my wager, Tolem. She won the race in Sassot, and she can win this one," Lord Beristo said.

"You cannot seriously expect your little Easterner to succeed here in my race," Lord Tolem scoffed with a hint of amusement. "If I were you, I would not even bet on her ability to survive, let alone her ability to win."

"I'll bet on her ability to surprise you," Lord Beristo said confidently.

"Come, Beristo, we've had enough wagers for one night," a dark-haired lord with a long black cloak said as he joined them. His hair was thick and black, and a well-trimmed beard marked his face. The light from the torches on the outer wall of the guildhall was reflected in his warm gaze, and a golden crest engraved with the symbol of a dragon gleamed from where it hung around his neck. He clapped his hand on Lord Beristo's shoulder.

"The carriages should be arriving soon, and I am ready for sleep after such a long day of travel."

"Salistom, you should have been at the race in Sassot," Beristo said, turning to him. "The journey from there to this race is easy enough to make."

As he spoke, the other lords and their attendants gathered outside the guildhall. Sirryn followed behind them before moving to Lord Beristo's side.

"It seems that your rider is the only one from the race in Sassot who will also be competing here," Lord Atregar said.

"What happened to your rider from the last race?" Lord Beristo asked.

"He was a thief that had shown some skill with horses. I decided to give him a chance in the races, but he failed me."

"You should have had your men cut him down the moment he crossed the dassdir poles behind the others," Tolem sneered.

"I was going to settle for arresting him, but he escaped. Now I think he might be faster on foot than he was on a horse," Atregar explained with an amused tone.

"And what about your rider, Felond?" Tolem asked. "Why are you not entering your favorite?"

"He requires rest and more training," Lord Felond answered defensively. "I've had to choose one of my lesser riders."

"Lesser riders?" Tolem scoffed. "How much worse could they be?"

"They are still better than Edgerr's rider. I've never seen a more humiliating failure," Lord Felond said.

Lord Edgerr's expression hardened, but he said nothing.

"At least you have another rider to choose from," Lord Beristo noted as a carriage approached for him and Sirryn.

"You still have that drunk, don't you?" Lord Tolem asked with a grin.

Sirryn opened the door for Lord Beristo, who turned to them and said, "He's of no use to me. Fortunately, with my new rider, I don't need anyone else."

They watched his carriage disappear into the night in silence until Lord Salistom spoke. "He's very confident. Isn't he?"

"It wouldn't be the first time his confidence was misplaced," Lord Tolem said.

The sound of galloping hooves reached their ears, and as they turned, they saw two riders racing down the road behind them. The second rider rode closer to the lights of a nearby inn.

"Isn't that your rider, Felond?" Lord Salistom asked as he pointed at the figure.

"What is he doing with my horse?" Lord Felond asked in surprise.

He began shouting at two of his guards who rode up alongside a carriage that was coming toward him.

"Stop that rider, and see that my mare isn't damaged!"

The pain in her wrist spread through her arm, but Inesca was only thinking that Destrod had managed to drive her away from where she needed to be. She might not be able to make it back to the inn before Lord Beristo if she did not hurry. What if he found her missing?

She looked down at the wooden pole in her hand and suddenly remembered part of her training with Omaron. Racing to the end of a narrow road, she turned and began rushing back toward Destrod with the wooden shaft firmly grasped in her right hand. She kept it low at her side, and Destrod continued riding toward her even though he had lost his dagger a while ago. As he neared, he leaped toward her as if to knock her from her horse. Inesca raised the wooden shaft and drove the blunt end toward his shoulder. The collision with the shaft knocked him back against the wall of the nearest building, and he fell to the ground unconscious. Inesca looked back and paused for a moment.

Voices and the sound of other riders drew nearer, and Inesca spurred Beiru into a gallop to avoid being seen. She and the mare disappeared into the shadows as Lord Felond's guards surrounded his mare and Destrod.

"My lord, are you certain that you do not wish to change your wager?" Sirryn asked as he entered The Silver Hoof behind Lord Beristo. "When I spoke to him, Omaron did not sound confident about this race."

"Nor did he about the last race, but I will hear no more about it, Sirryn. I could not have wagered less after winning in Sassot. It is expected."

Sirryn waited until they climbed the stairs to the second level of the inn before he spoke. Then he said, "That does not mean it is wise, my lord."

Lord Beristo turned to him with a fierce expression, but after a moment, it faded.

"I have heard your warning, but enough, you can say nothing to change my mind."

Sirryn suddenly shifted his gaze from Lord Beristo to someone behind him, and turning around, Lord Beristo saw Jirro standing outside his room.

"You would do well to hide in your room until called for," Lord Beristo said indignation burned in his gaze again. "After the inconvenience you cost me today, I was ready to break your neck and blame it on a riding accident. And trust me, I could get your father to believe such a story."

The smug look on Jirro's face faded, but then he quickly regained his composure. "I would not trouble you again, my lord, but I thought you should know that your precious rider ran away tonight. I am convinced she stole your new horse as well."

"Oh, Jirro, would you add lying to your other faults?" Sirryn sighed.

Lord Beristo's face reddened.

"Been drinking again, haven't you, you insolent fool?"

"No. For once, I am sober, my lord. And I know the girl betrayed you."

"Do you? Well, we stopped by the stables on our way back to the inn," Lord Beristo said. "And all of my horses—including the gray stallion—are resting for the night."

Jirro stared at him in surprise. Then he said, "Well, the girl is gone. If you don't believe me, check her room."

Lord Beristo walked to Inesca's door and knocked twice.

"This is a waste of time, my lord," Sirryn said. "Inesca would not run away. And she would never leave that horse behind."

"You are right, Sirryn," Lord Beristo agreed, and yet his hand reached out and grasped the handle of her door. "But I still wish to teach this fool not to tell me lies." Pulling the door to Inesca's room open, Lord Beristo stepped inside and glanced around.

"Oh, my lord. I was not expecting you," Inesca said. She stood beside the window with her arms stretched behind her back. Lord Beristo smiled as Sirryn and Jirro moved to the door to look inside.

"I did not wish to disturb you, dear girl, but Jirro was worried about you."

"How considerate of him." Inesca said as her eyes narrowed, catching sight of Jirro.

"Are you all right?" Lord Beristo asked, looking at her again.

"A noise outside of the inn startled me."

"Well, we'll let you get your rest."

Lord Beristo grabbed Jirro's arm on his way out and pulled him down the hall. Sirryn hesitated a moment longer and stepped inside Inesca's room.

"You'll have to be careful of Jirro. It seems he's decided to be your enemy, though perhaps not a very effective one."

Inesca looked down at the floor and did not answer him. Then a breeze streamed into the room and drew Sirryn's attention to the cloak thrown on the table as its corner fluttered in the breeze. Sirryn moved closer and saw that the window was still slightly open.

"Inesca ..."

He noticed the strange expression on her face and that she was still holding her arms behind her in an unnatural pose. After a moment, she finally withdrew them and held out her left hand and arm, which were bleeding. Sirryn's eyes widened.

"What have you done?"

"I'm sorry," she said softly. "I borrowed a horse from the stables for a quick ride. I never meant to risk anything."

Sirryn lifted her arm and studied the wound.

"You have risked everything," he said in a harsh whisper. "Do you want to become a prisoner like Jirro? A rider who loses the trust of his lord is little better than a slave. Remember that you pledged your service and loyalty to Lord Beristo! You cannot take that back now."

"I wasn't trying to."

"Weren't you? Because you went out there tonight, look at what has happened! What if you had been killed? What if this injury hinders you in the race? Lord Beristo is depending on you."

Inesca took a deep breath as Sirryn turned back to inspecting her wound.

"You are right. I'll tell him the truth," she said. She moved toward the door, but Sirryn held her back.

"No, not tonight. I'll sneak a doctor in here later to tend to your arm. Fortunately, it doesn't look too serious. And it's too late to convince Lord Beristo to change his wager for the race, even with something like this. But we will discuss this matter again."

"How much did he wager on me?" Inesca asked.

"That's not for you to worry about," Sirryn said as he tore a piece of cloth from the blanket on the bed and wrapped it around her arm and wrist. "But you must remember that you have a duty to serve him faithfully. And you must never do something like this again."

"I understand. And thank you, Sirryn."

"You know that I want to help you, Inesca," Sirryn said as he went to the door. "Try not to make it any more difficult than it already is."

Chapter 17

A veil of clouds hid the sun on the day of the race in Monterr. Six riders gathered on a level plain that would lead into a gorge that stretched the length of most of the race. Inesca joined the other riders and then glanced back at Sirryn, who had accompanied her to the starting point. Since the incident in Lasnell, Sirryn had hardly let Inesca out of his sight, and even Omaron had shot her a few disapproving looks yesterday at the camp. She felt sure he knew what she had done. If she had been able to speak with Sir Coltar, it might have been worth all the trouble, but as things were, she hated having let them down.

Nycor moved eagerly toward the other horses, and Inesca patted his neck. At least today she would be riding him and not a strange horse that she borrowed from a stable. Finding her place with the riders, Inesca recognized Lord Felond's blue roan mare among the others. The rider was not Destrod, but he turned and cast a glance down at her left wrist, which was still bandaged. Raising his gaze to her face, he shot her a smug expression. Inesca turned her head quickly and looked away.

Derreth rode a golden stallion with a white mane and tail into position between Lord Atregar's new rider and Lord Felond's rider. Inesca dared a few quick glances in his direction, but he never seemed to notice her. When she turned around again, Sirryn was gone, and it was nearly time for the race to begin.

***

Kestorn pushed his way through gamblers exchanging bets on the race until he reached the fence that marked the edge of the viewing area. Before him stretched a flat plain of rock that dipped down into a gorge in the distance. The river had carved this racetrack for Lord Tolem, and once the water had been trapped behind a dam, the layers of rock served as a suitable, yet difficult course.

Although he had to face the prospect of watching the race with the crowd instead of from the back of a horse, Kestorn knew that his brother and Celestro would be in their element on this course. The golden stallion was born here in the mountainous realm of Monterr and could cross steep inclines without faltering.

His body and legs were not as long as Halon's, but this only added to his strength in managing such terrain. After Trestan's failure in the last race, Lord Edgerr was clearly not willing to take any chances this time.

A heavy weight struck the layer of rock under Kestorn's boots, and he turned to see the towering figure of Lord Beristo's trainer, Omaron, approaching with the aid of his iron staff. Derreth had spoken about this one-time rider with reverence unlike anything Kestorn had known his brother to express, and there were few men whom his brother truly respected. Although Derreth might deny it, even his respect for Lord Edgerr was feigned. This grudging acknowledgment of authority was a mere survival tactic, so that they could have a living as riders and not as slaves.

No room for orphans in the Six Realms, Kestorn thought. Only those with fathers or some other supportive guardian could train to become warriors, councilmen, tradesmen, or merchantmen. At a young age, he and Derreth had been threatened with a life of slavery, only to be saved by Lord Edgerr's decision to take them in as future riders because their father had been a rider. At least his reputation had bought them this chance even if he hadn't been able to do anything else for them.

Omaron settled himself at the front of the crowd on Kestorn's left. He turned his head and regarded Kestorn, who found himself staring, and then looked away. Coins jingled behind them as bets were made, but the dark trainer and the fair-headed rider stared into the distance.

A white pigeon flew toward the crowd, and several voices cheered at the sight of the lone bird. It was the sign that the race had begun, and the lords would receive their first report of how their riders were faring at the beginning of the race.

༺❀༻

The clatter of horses' hooves against bare rock echoed in Inesca's ears. Nycor pulled at the reins impatiently as the other horses galloped ahead of them. It was too soon and too dangerous to attempt riding among the other five riders before her. Omaron's warning echoed in her thoughts. *Those who win races are marked by other riders for pain and death. They will seek to put you in your place or put you in your grave. Do not give them that chance.*

Keeping Nycor at a slower gallop, Inesca surveyed the other riders who, for the moment, seemed to be ignoring her. They were all strangers to her, except for Derreth. Inesca was conscious of how often her eyes had strayed toward him

The Legacy of the Lost Rider

before the race began, but he took no notice of her at all. She wondered if he would strike at her if she attempted to pass him, but why should he not? Why should he treat her differently than any other rider?

Omaron had warned her that all the riders in this race were more experienced than she was. *"This is not a race that I think you can win,"* he had said. *"There are others where strategy can be employed to make up for the strength that you lack. But racing through the narrow gorge where the horses will be pressed close together, you will have to fight multiple enemies before you can move ahead. And none of the other riders will hesitate to attack you."*

After asking him what she should do, Omaron had said, *"Ride cautiously, and put your health and welfare above the goal of winning. Even should you finish last, Lord Beristo will allow you to race again. But if you are injured or killed, you will lose everything."*

Although she had not given up the hope of winning, Inesca considered Nycor as she rode behind the others. She did not wish to see him injured, and the danger was as great to him as it was to her. Ahead of her, she could see the large black stallion of Lord Tolem, the lord of the realm hosting this race. Tymo charged ahead with powerful strides and cut a striking figure against the red rocks of the gorge. Near him was Razur, the swift white stallion of Lord Salistom and another serious contender for the race. Omaron had said that these were the ones most favored to win.

As the race led them down a hill, Inesca saw the gorge that stretched nearly half the length of the race open up in the distance. The lead riders steered their horses toward its mouth, and Inesca started to follow them, but then she observed Derreth changing course and riding toward the east. Where could he be going? Omaron had not indicated that there was any other way to reach the end of the race other than to ride through the gorge.

The golden stallion beneath Derreth galloped toward a rocky slope that slunk up the side of the gorge. None of the other riders seemed to notice or care that Derreth had changed direction, but he was nearly in the back except for her. Inesca shifted her gaze from the lone figure to the group of riders and then back to Derreth again.

Derreth uses his head, and if you think only speed matters in these races, he'll teach you otherwise. Those were the words Omaron had spoken to her before the race at Sassot. If he was right, then perhaps Derreth had found the strategy Inesca needed to get ahead in this race. Apart from that possibility, however, she had the choice of following strangers or of following her brother. *It's not a choice at all*, Inesca thought as she watched Derreth continue up the path he had chosen.

⁌⁊

An hour after straying from the mouth of the gorge, Derreth could still see and hear signs of the other riders as they passed through it. He was making good time, and Celestro was doing well despite the steep terrain. Everything appeared to be going according to his plan—that is, everything except the bothersome shadow behind him.

He knew Lord Beristo's rider had been trailing at the back of the group ever since the race began. It was not surprising, considering her vulnerability and the fact that she had employed the same tactic in the last race. But why had she followed him? If it was fear that drove her to keep away from the others, she could have avoided them by simply staying in the back. Nor did he understand what would have prompted her to feel safer with him than with the others. Had he been inclined to attack her, it would have been easy to turn, ride back, and strike her down or steal her horse and leave her to walk the rest of the way. It would not be the first time such a thing had happened in a race.

Regardless of her reasons, Derreth knew she had made a mistake. Her horse was not accustomed to the rough slopes of Monterr. He could tell that her stallion was growing more exhausted with every mile. He would never have the strength to muster the speed required for the end of the race. She would be fortunate if the horse made it to the finish without injury. A single fall or misstep could lead to tragedy for both horse and rider, and the weary animal had already stumbled once.

Glancing over his shoulder, Derreth saw her dismount and lead her horse by the reins. This was one of the last steep inclines at the eastern edge of the gorge, but it wasn't even clear that she and her horse would be able to make it over this one. She slipped on one of the rocks as they gave way under her feet and just managed to catch herself.

Derreth turned to face the expanse of sky waiting to greet him at the top of the incline as Celestro pushed forward at a steady pace. From this position, he could see some of the riders reaching the end of the gorge that led them to higher ground. He watched in surprise as they spurred their horses into a rapid pace. The other riders further back in the gorge were moving at a quick pace but seemed to be conserving their horses' energy for the last stretch that was still several miles ahead.

The Legacy of the Lost Rider

Lord Tolem's rider, Molnar, drove his horse to run at an incredible pace and was the first to ride out of the gorge. Several lengths behind him, Lord Salistom's rider, Cidonn, took note of Molnar's haste and urged his white stallion into a gallop to chase after Molnar. Unable to see these two leaders from their position in the gorge, the riders of Lord Felond and Lord Atregar continued at their regular pace.

Derreth glanced back at them, and from his high vantage point, he saw something else approaching from the other end of the gorge.

༒

Inesca tried to step carefully as she moved up the steep slope while grasping Nycor's reins and urging him to follow her. *I was a fool to come this way, to ignore Omaron's advice, but I can't turn back now. But what a poor rider I am to not even need other riders to injure me and my horse. These horrible cliffs and jagged rocks can do enough on their own.*

As she chided herself silently, she felt Nycor stop again behind her. His hooves slipped and struggled to find a place to stand as he moved anxiously from side to side rather than forward. Inesca turned to guide him higher, but as she looked back, her eyes widened. A river rushed into the gorge with devastating speed, and Inesca realized that it would reach them unless they were able to get to higher ground.

"Come on, Nycor!" she said, straining to get him to move. "Please don't quit now."

He shook his head as he sensed the approaching danger, but instead of trying to run, he only tensed and fought her more.

"Leave the horse!"

Inesca's head spun around.

"Get out of there while you can!" Derreth shouted at her.

But rather than seek safety, Inesca moved down the slope until she was closer to Nycor. Bracing herself against his side, she tried to push him forward. Nycor's weight pressed against her, and Inesca knew that if he lost his balance, he would fall on top of her.

"Move, Nycor, move!" she commanded. "You can make it if you run!"

The stallion snorted and his ears flicked back toward the roar of the water, but he still did not charge forward. The thunderous sound of water rushing along the gorge filled her ears, but in the same moment, she felt the pounding of hooves on the rocks under her feet. A hand snatched the reins from her. Inesca turned to see Derreth move his stallion alongside Nycor. With another horse at his side, Nycor finally began to lift his hooves and make the steep climb toward the safety of the ridge that rose higher and higher above the gorge.

Stumbling after them, Inesca didn't stop to look back at the river. She could hear it growing louder. She fell once but scrambled up again until she caught up with the horses on level ground. Glancing back, she saw the river engulf the rocks where Nycor had been trapped only moments before. The current swept on through the gorge, and Inesca could hear the shouts of men and the screams of horses as the water caught up with them before they could escape.

Her legs began to tremble with exhaustion, and she dropped to the ground to rest. Nycor lowered his head to hers as if to gain some reassurance after moments of heightened stress. Inesca stretched out her hand and patted his neck as she forced herself up. Derreth watched the river as it continued along its path, and then he turned away long enough to cast a reproachful look in her direction.

"Your refusal to leave your horse nearly cost you your life."

"He needed me, but thank you for saving us."

His expression grew stern. And Inesca noticed for the first time that his eyes were brown, not blue like her father's. But when the rest of his face reminded her so much of him, this felt like a startling difference.

"Don't waste your gratitude. The only reason I didn't let the river take you is because I don't want to win by sabotage."

"Sabotage?" she said. "How do you know this wasn't an accident?"

"Accidents are rarely so well-timed. At least one of the lead riders knew this was coming and used it to his advantage."

Inesca began to walk closer, but Derreth was already starting to ride away.

"Go back to where you came from," he said without turning around. "There's no room in these races for riders who need rescuing, and next time, I won't stop."

His horse charged across the rocky terrain with an easy gait but began moving faster as it ran toward the main path beyond the gorge. Inesca watched him disappear as she gently laid her head against Nycor's neck and patted the weary stallion.

Chapter 18

As the first horses charged into the final mile, the crowd cheered and waved the colors of their favorite riders. Some stopped cheering when they realized that only the riders for Lord Tolem and Lord Salistom came into view. The massive black stallion, Tymo, was in the lead.

An attendant raised the crimson and silver flag from the corner of the platform from which the lords watched the end of the race, and Lord Tolem admired his colors with a subtle smile.

"It seems that it is again left to Salistom to offer me some competition in this race, but that is not surprising. The rest of you only win the amateur races," Lord Tolem said. He cast a sneer at Lord Beristo, who only continued to watch the race below.

"I understand your young rider is talented even if she is a strange addition to the races. How did you discover her?" Lord Salistom asked.

Lord Beristo smiled faintly. "She came with the horse," he explained.

Salistom laughed. "And what an intriguing pair they make. I look forward to seeing them compete. So many of our horses and riders train for speed, giving no thought to jumping. It is refreshing to hear of something new brought to the competition."

"You would not say such a thing if she had beaten your rider," Lord Edgerr interjected. "That ridiculous performance should not have been allowed."

"And whose rider are you speaking of now?" Beristo asked. "Mine, or yours?"

"That's enough squabbling between you two," Tolem said. "If you'll pay attention, you'll notice that neither of you has anything to boast of this time. You'll have to work harder to find riders suited to the challenges of races like mine."

Suddenly another cheer arose from the crowd and the lords all turned to see a rider in blue and a golden stallion appear.

"I believe you wanted some more competition," Lord Edgerr said as a smile spread over his face.

Derreth spurred Celestro into a faster gallop as he saw that there were two riders ahead of him only a mile from the dassdir poles. To his benefit, they did not realize that he was behind them as Celestro strove to catch up with the other horses. If he had reached this final mile sooner, he might have been able to get far enough ahead of them to make this an easier win. Still, he was not afraid of fighting his way past them.

Reaching Cidonn, the rider of Lord Salistom's white horse, Derreth drew his sword to be certain he was ready for any attack that might come. Cidonn noted the sword in Derreth's hand and gave him a wide berth, having only just seen him. Cidonn's weapon of choice was also a sword, but at the moment, he did not have the blade held ready in his hands and seemed more focused on racing than on fighting.

Charging ahead, Derreth recognized that his toughest opponent would be Lord Tolem's rider, Molnar. A broad-shouldered brute of a man, Molnar was often known for crippling or killing riders in the races. As he rode up alongside him, Derreth had to defend himself immediately as Molnar swung his blade. The heavy swing sent a jolt through Derreth's body, but he still managed to deflect the blow. As they neared the dassdir poles, Molnar's swings came faster in an attempt to force Derreth to back off, but they were too close to the end of the race for Derreth to move Celestro farther away without giving up the chance to win.

After deflecting another blow, Derreth tried to strike out at Molnar for a change, and his sword caught the edge of Molnar's arm, surprising his opponent. Derreth started to pull Celestro ahead, but suddenly a flash of white caught the corner of Derreth's eye. Cidonn had been guiding the swift white stallion, Razur, to take the lead, while Derreth and Molnar were distracted.

The speed of the white stallion's hooves quickly left Celestro behind, and Derreth found himself in second place as he followed Cidonn through the dassdir poles. His heart grew heavy in his chest as he rode Celestro around the ring in front of the crowd before drawing him to a halt.

The crowd pressed around the fence at the edge of the ring as each of the riders finished the race, and one of the men from the crowd called out, "And the others? How far behind are they?"

Molnar turned to face him and said, "There will not be any others. A flood consumed the gorge and swallowed all who were behind us."

The news spread quickly through the crowd, but Derreth ignored their questions and looked for his brother. Molnar rode up beside him with a dark look on his face.

"I did not see you with us when we rode out of the gorge," Molnar said.

Derreth tightened his grip on the sword in his hand before speaking. "There are other ways to complete this race without passing through the gorge. Whoever released the river in the gorge must not have realized that."

"That sounded dangerously close to an accusation."

"An observation," Derreth said. "One that I will not forget."

Molnar smiled suddenly with a dark look in his eyes. "And we won't forget about you either," he said.

As he finally rode away, Derreth could still feel heat coursing through his face, and he had the sudden urge to ride after Molnar to finish what he had started.

"Are you all right?"

Turning around, Derreth saw Kestorn at his side.

"Well enough," Derreth said as he dismounted, but a frown still marked his face. "That other route I took was more costly than I expected. I could have won if I had not been interrupted."

"By the river flooding the gorge?"

"That was part of it."

"It has been getting worse lately, hasn't it?"

"What has?"

"The traps. Last year, there was the fire in the race in Fortur and the bridge that collapsed in the race in Ettidor. It makes you wonder what they will do next time."

"It's hard to guess when we don't know who is behind all of it."

"What about the lords? They could be trying to throw the race in their favor."

"Those two *accidents* you mentioned from last year resulted in the deaths of the riders who were from those realms. I doubt that Lord Salistom and Lord Beristo planned the deaths of their own horses and men."

"And yet, Lord Tolem's rider survived this time."

"That's true. He knew it was going to happen, but the one behind these traps could be anyone that he knows, or it could be more than one person."

Kestorn opened his mouth to speak, but then he closed it as he saw Lord Beristo's trainer coming toward them. Derreth handed Celestro's reins to Kestorn.

"Take him back to camp for me, Kes."

Looking from his brother to the trainer, Kestorn hesitated for a moment before leading Celestro away. Omaron came closer, driving his staff down on the rocks beneath them.

"You don't seem surprised to see me," he said as he watched Derreth's face.

"It was your idea, then? You told her to follow me."

"She never had such advice from me. I want to know the path you took. You arrived at the last mile later than the first two riders, but Molnar said those behind them were killed in the gorge."

Derreth hesitated for a moment. Then he said, "I rode over and down the slopes alongside the gorge. Your rider followed me."

Omaron considered his words for a moment, and then he turned as if to move on.

"If you didn't tell her to follow me, then why did she do it? And how did you know to come to me?" Derreth asked.

Omaron stopped, but only turned his head slightly to say, "Ask her. But I doubt the answer would please you."

◆

An hour after the race had been won, the crowds had disappeared, and clouds darkened the late-afternoon sky. At the two posts marking the end of the race, Omaron stood silently, staring into the distance.

"There will be no justice for the fallen riders," Sirryn said as he walked toward Omaron. "Many believe Lord Tolem is responsible for the breaking of the dam, but none of the lords will take action against him."

"Why should they?" Omaron said without turning away his gaze. "Only a ruling of the Royal Council could force him to pay for the horses and riders lost, but the council will not act without proof."

"Lord Tolem claims it was an unfortunate accident, and the council will accept his word. But certainly, this was no accident."

"And Lord Beristo?"

"He has returned to the camp, but he lost a great deal in wealth in addition to …"

Omaron took a step forward, striking his staff on the rock beneath him.

"We barely had enough to afford a racehorse before this," Sirryn continued. "Lord Beristo was forced to travel to the East Province in search of an animal that he could buy at a more reasonable cost than the ones sold here in the Six Realms. Now, he'll be left with Jirro and horses that were never meant to race. Still, I wish Inesca had never agreed to race for him."

Rain began to fall over them, and Sirryn made no attempt to dry his face. The droplets struck the two men softly at first, but even when the rain grew more intense, Omaron showed no signs of departing. Sirryn let out a heavy breath before he spoke again.

The Legacy of the Lost Rider

"Lord Beristo sent me to find you. He says we're leaving in the morning."

"Not to Farcost?"

"No. Once he pays the forfeiture fee, he will not have the means to race again this year. We're to travel back to Ettidor. The fee is a demanding price, but risking the last race with Jirro would cost him more."

Omaron remained still. "Tell him not to pay it yet," he said.

Sirryn approached Omaron and studied his face.

"You're still waiting for her."

Finally turning his head, Omaron cast a scornful look at Sirryn. "What else would I be doing?" he asked.

"Meditating, praying for the dead ... I don't know."

A deep scoff resonated from Omaron's throat.

"No, perhaps not," Sirryn said. "But if she was alive, she would have finished the race by now."

"It would not be the first time she was late."

"I did not expect you to have so much faith in her abilities."

"It would not be her abilities that saved her this time. From the back of the racers, she would have seen Lord Edgerr's rider stray from the main path through the gorge. It seems that she followed him."

The rain began to fall faster, soaking their clothes.

"But he finished with the lead riders at least an hour ago."

"The gray stallion is not accustomed to crossing over cliffs and steep hills. They will slow him down."

"Well, when do you expect them back?"

Omaron raised his hand and pointed. Sirryn wiped the water from his eyes and followed the trainer's gesture. Through the curtain of rain and darkness, he saw movement beyond the dassdir poles. He raised his hand over his eyes to keep the rain out of them. The shapes of a horse and a small person walking beside it became clearer.

"I don't believe it."

Inesca's hair was still bound behind her head, but a few loose strands were plastered to her wet skin. Her stallion was favoring his left hind leg, but he walked well enough in other respects. As she finally led him through the posts to where they stood, she leaned against one of them. Sirryn moved to steady her as her balance wavered.

"You did not ride through the gorge," Omaron said.

Inesca shook her head. "No. I'm sorry that I failed you."

Omaron took Nycor's reins from her as he spoke. "Failed? I told you to survive. And you did. It seems you finally learned to listen."

Despite her weariness, Inesca managed a faint smile.

"Come on, we must get you out of this," Sirryn said as he helped her walk on. "I won't have you finish this race only to catch your death in the rain."

⁓

Inesca pulled a thick cloak around her as she sat down beside the fire outside her tent. The rain had finally stopped, and for the first time in hours, she felt warm and comfortable. Her hands stretched toward the crackling flames and remained suspended as they soaked up the soothing heat. At the sound of humming, Inesca turned to see Omaron brushing Nycor. He had bandaged the stallion's leg after rubbing a healing salve over it and seemed confident that Nycor had suffered only a minor injury. He patted Nycor's neck after a few more minutes and left him to rest. As he approached the fire, Inesca rose to her feet again.

"Sirryn told me that you believed I had followed Derreth, but he didn't know why."

Omaron picked up a branch and tossed it into the fire, ignoring her question as he spoke. "You should be resting. Lord Tolem has decided to hold a ceremony tomorrow morning to honor the riders who died in the flood. You will be expected to attend."

Inesca frowned as she remembered what Derreth had said. If this wasn't an accident, then a better way to honor those who had died was to catch the person responsible.

"I thought riders who failed to finish races were not considered worthy of remembrance. Why would Lord Tolem care to honor them?"

"It is his way of appeasing Lord Atregar, who blames him for the flood in the gorge."

"And Lord Felond? He also lost a rider."

Omaron scoffed.

"Few regard him or his riders to be of any worth. If it was only his rider who had died, Lord Tolem would not have taken the trouble to call for this ceremony. But Lord Atregar rules the strong realm of Farcost that contains many of the significant ports that Lord Tolem relies on for trade. He is not so easily ignored."

Having finished his explanation, Omaron started to walk to his own tent. Inesca left the fire and followed after him as she said, "I understand now why you would not tell me what I wanted to know about the medallion."

He paused and waited for her to continue.

"That's why you expected me to have followed Derreth when everyone else thought I was lost in the gorge."

Omaron glanced back at her. "I know what you believe about them," he said. "But just because you believe it does not make it true."

"You're right," Inesca said. "But it is true. Belief or denial on my part, theirs, or yours does not change the truth."

Turning all the way around, Omaron struck the ground in front of her with his staff as he stepped toward her. "It would be better for you if it was not true. Do not forget that you agreed to serve Lord Beristo as a rider with absolute loyalty," he said.

"And I have done so."

Omaron seized her left arm, and Inesca winced as he raised it. The wound she had received from her encounter with Destrod was still in the process of healing.

"Fine. I made a mistake," she admitted.

He released her arm.

"There may come a race when you will have to choose between the duty that you owe to your lord and this bond that you feel toward these two riders in the service of Lord Edgerr. What will you do then?"

Inesca stepped back in silent consideration.

"If you wish to be a rider, then there is only one answer. You have foolishly persuaded yourself that you can divide your loyalty among them and Lord Beristo. Did I not tell you in your training that ties to other riders were forbidden?"

"I cannot change what I have learned. I cannot turn my back on who they are."

"Even if they choose to turn their backs on you? You are an outsider like me. Neither of us was born in the Six Realms, and to the thoughts of most, we don't belong here. If you try to reveal yourself to them, not only will they not believe you, but they will despise you for trying to lay claim to their father's name."

"He was my father too," Inesca said quickly. "And he didn't die in a battle. He died in a shack in the wilderness, and I want to know why. I want to know who forced him to leave his home and family in the Six Realms. Something terrible happened or was going to happen to him. My father wouldn't have run from just anything."

Omaron's expression hardened as he watched her. "This path that you are choosing will only lead to more pain and more loss. If your father gave you that horse, then he meant for you to be a rider. Honor his wishes, and do not allow yourself to be distracted anymore."

Chapter 19

The following morning, the lords and their riders traveled to the edge of the flooded gorge to honor those who had died the day before. From a distance, Inesca could see Lord Beristo riding with the other lords with Sirryn not far behind him. The other five lords traveled unaccompanied except for a few servants.

Sirryn had told her that he would be attending the ceremony, and when she asked about the reason, he said, "*Most of these riders do not have families to mourn for them when they fall. Perhaps if they did, we would be better reminded of the value of life and the horror of death, but I will go so that there will be at least one more person present to remember their loss.*"

Inesca wished that more of those traveling to the gorge this morning felt that way. Most of the lords were solemn and quiet, but Lord Tolem appeared bored as he rode with a hint of impatience in his expression. Not far from him, Lord Edgerr yawned with a weary and disinterested gaze.

The riders walked behind the lords and were forced to travel without their horses today to allow them time to rest. Each rider carried a branch of the lugas tree, which was one of the few trees that flourished in Monterr, and each branch was full of oval-shaped leaves with sharp serrated edges. These leaves created a sweet scent when crushed and were often sprinkled over the dead as an offering of respect.

Among the group of riders, Inesca recognized Molnar and Cidonn from yesterday's race, but there were also eighteen others like Kestorn who had not been chosen to ride. Some of the lords had as many as five or six riders, but Lord Beristo only had Jirro and her.

Each rider wore the colors of his lord, and the riders of the same lords walked together in groups. Inesca walked alone wearing a green and gold dress. Jirro had not been fit to attend the ceremony this morning after having shared some wine with some men from Lasnell the previous night. It was unpleasant to walk alone, but drunk or sober, Jirro would have been an unwelcome companion.

The others ignored her for most of their walk, but occasionally Inesca felt their eyes on her back and heard them whispering. She wished that she could have ridden to the ceremony instead of walking among the other riders, most of whom were almost a foot taller than she was in height. If only Omaron was here to walk near her, but like many of the trainers, Omaron had stayed behind to care for his lord's racehorse.

"And here I thought you were one of the riders we were paying our respects to today," a low voice said to her left.

Inesca turned and saw Molnar and some of Lord Tolem's other riders watching her. Molnar had a smug expression on his face.

"Are you a ghost coming back to haunt us?"

Inesca tried to move farther away from them, but she was hemmed in on every side by other groups of riders. Molnar and the others laughed as they pressed in closer.

"Only the guilty are haunted," Inesca said as she faced them. "But perhaps you have a reason to expect visits from evil spirits."

Molnar's smile faded, and he seized her arm. "The time for collecting ghosts isn't over yet," he said. "You could still become one before the day ends."

Tearing the branch from her hand, he tossed it to his companions and shoved her to the ground. Then they walked on, laughing again. Inesca propped herself up in the dirt and slowly got to her feet.

At that moment, Trestan happened to walk by with a satisfied smirk on his face as he watched her brush the dirt from her arms and hands. Inesca tried to suppress the urge to throw a handful of dirt at his face. She saw Kestorn walking a little ahead of him, but he did not seem to have noticed her at all. As she watched them, Inesca noticed that Derreth was missing. Why was he not here with Lord Edgerr's other riders?

A man dressed in ornate purple cloth passed her by, and Inesca suddenly realized that she was at the rear of the procession as Lord Felond's only remaining rider moved in front of her. Destrod cast a disdainful glance in her direction, still clearly holding a grudge, like Trestan, for her victory in Sassot. But like her, he was fortunate to be among the living. His replacement for the race in Monterr had been killed yesterday in the flood on the slow but beautiful mare that Inesca had seen Destrod ride in Sassot.

As she tried to catch up with the group, Inesca found a lugas branch trampled on the ground with only one leaf remaining. It was probably the one she had been carrying earlier. Molnar and Lord Tolem's other riders had no doubt lost interest in it. She scooped it up and walked on quickly.

At the top of a hill, Inesca watched as the lords reached the gorge, which was now filled with water. The bodies of the two riders lay wrapped in black cloth on the rocks at the edge. Each lord who had lost a rider rode forward and cast white flowers into the water as a sign of honor and blessing.

The lords drew back as the riders were instructed to pluck leaves from their branches and cast them over the lifeless figures. Inesca hurried down the hill to join them, but as she neared the edge of the gathering, a figure in a black hood and cloak appeared on a ridge above them.

"Fools! You come to mark your own graves! Death to the lords! And death to their riders! Today, the Raegond take their revenge!"

He raised a horn to his mouth, and at the sound of it, more men in black appeared from behind the rocks. Inesca darted behind a boulder as they pulled out bows and arrows. Shouts erupted from the other riders as they started to run. The thunder of horses' hooves shook the ground, and Inesca saw the lords racing back up the hill with some of their riders chasing after them.

Arrows flew through the air, but the lords disappeared over the hill in a cloud of dust. The riders, following behind on foot, fell victim to the arrows. Inesca turned her eyes away from the horrible scene, but as she looked back toward the gorge, one of the bodies covered by black cloth jumped to its feet and withdrew a sword, slashing at those who tried to escape by running toward the water.

Inesca's hand patted her belt in search of her sword, but then she remembered that the riders had been forbidden to carry weapons today, lest they try to attack each other. As she looked around, a rock larger than the size of her fist caught her eye, and she seized it as the Raegond archers drew swords and jumped down toward the remaining riders.

Two of the Raegond surrounded Cidonn, the victor of the last race. One of them seized his arms from behind, and the other slashed his stomach and then his throat. Inesca covered her mouth with her hand, stifling a gasp.

The desire to find an escape pounded in her chest, and her limbs felt tense with fear. The path that the lords had used to escape was now far too dangerous. Several of the Raegond had positioned themselves to cut down any who tried to leave that way. But running in the other direction, toward the water in the gorge, was also risky. Some of the lords' companions who had their own horses but who had not been able to flee as swiftly as the Evaliscans, rode about the gorge in search of an escape. Desperate riders began to try to claim the horses, but their attackers were swift to strike at all distracted targets.

A figure moved behind the rocks to her right, and Inesca turned, recognizing two men dressed in silver and blue. To reach them, she would have to risk open ground, but after a moment, she decided to chance it.

Darting out from behind the boulder, Inesca suddenly collided with someone heavy, who landed on her arm. When her vision cleared from hitting her head against the ground, she saw Destrod scrambling up to take her hiding place. As his fingers grasped the edge of the boulder, his body was thrown back to the ground with a sudden force. Inesca felt her breath catch in her throat as she scrambled back and stared at the spear protruding from his side.

"Weren't prepared for war, were you?" a deep voice scoffed.

Inesca turned to see the Raegond who had thrown the spear advancing toward her. He drew a dagger from his cloak, and she could see the glint of his eyes from the eyeholes cut in his hood.

A shadow fell across them both as a horse and rider charged toward the Raegond.

"Run, Inesca! Get out of here!" Sirryn yelled from the horse.

The Raegond nimbly dodged away from the horse's hooves, and, turning the dagger in his hands, threw it at Sirryn. Inesca's eyes widened as she watched the dagger sink into Sirryn's back. He slipped from the horse, which panicked and darted away.

The Raegond laughed and started to turn back to Inesca, but the rock in Inesca's hand smashed into his face first. He collapsed, and she hurried to Sirryn's side. His head was bloodied from where it had hit the ground after falling off the horse, and the blade of the dagger was embedded deep in his back.

"No! Sirryn, please," she cried as she searched for some sign that he was alive. "Stay with me."

He remained motionless on the rocks without even the slightest indication that he was breathing. Inesca put her hand to his shoulder as if trying to wake him from sleep and then pulled him closer to her as she leaned over his body. A terrible wave of pain and fear overwhelmed her.

More cries of pain erupted from the struggle going around them, and Inesca opened her eyes long enough to see Kestorn only yards away from her. He watched the enemies who would soon surround his hiding place. Inesca closed her eyes and wrapped her hand around the hilt of the dagger in Sirryn's back. She pulled hard, freeing the blade. Choking back a cry of grief, she slowly released his body and stumbled on down the hill as tears wet her face.

Trestan trembled and moaned as he crouched low to the ground. Kestorn seized his arm, forcing Trestan to face him and motioning for him to be silent. Their chances at survival were slim enough without Trestan's constant whimpering.

Behind them was a wall of rock too steep to climb, and the Raegond were closing in from the other side. Kestorn saw another outcrop of rocks further downhill. It would provide them with more cover and a possible chance at escape if there was a place to hide.

Hitting Trestan on the shoulder, Kestorn raced down the rocky slope and slid behind the rocks while the Raegond were busy with some of Lord Atregar's riders. Trestan scrambled after him but tripped and ended up rolling into the rocks with a groan. Kestorn wasted no time in pulling him out of sight.

Both breathed heavily, but they stayed low to the ground as Kestorn turned to examine their options. As he looked behind them, he saw to his relief a cavern that opened up into the wall. Derreth had once told him that this area was full of caves, but even he had not figured out how to use them to an advantage in the race.

Kestorn tapped Trestan again, and together they crawled into the mouth of the cavern.

"Surely Lord Edgerr will come back for us," Trestan said as he slunk into a corner.

Kestorn turned to silence him again, but a shadow moved in the dark, and Trestan cried out in terror as a cloaked figure slashed at him with a sword. Kestorn leapt forward to tackle the Raegond, but a force grabbed his arm from behind.

A second Raegond tried to seize Kestorn in a stranglehold, but Kestorn managed to knock his attacker off balance by thrusting his elbow into the man's gut. As they wrestled on the floor of the cave, the other Raegond turned from Trestan and walked toward them with his sword. Suddenly, another figure collided with him and raised a dagger over the cloaked figure.

Kestorn finally freed his right arm from his enemy and punched him in the face, knocking his enemy's head against the rocks. Getting up, he saw that the other Raegond had lost his sword and was now struggling with Lord Beristo's small rider for the dagger in her hand. She was losing the contest of strength, and he had managed to get one hand around her throat and was attempting to strangle her.

The abandoned sword caught Kestorn's eye, and he snatched it up as he walked toward the struggling pair. Seizing her belt from behind, Kestorn pulled the girl away from the Raegond while he kicked the assassin's arm away from her neck. Having wrenched the dagger away from her at the last moment, the Raegond came at him with it, but Kestorn lifted the sword that was now in his right hand and thrust it forward.

The man's eyes widened as he fell to the ground. Kestorn pulled the hood from his head, revealing black tattoos on the man's face and his long dark hair.

"Riders never work together …," he said in confusion as he looked from Inesca to Kestorn. "Should have been easy."

He stumbled back and collapsed on the cave floor. Inesca coughed as she struggled to catch her breath but looked up at Kestorn long enough to see him glance at her. He moved toward Trestan, whose limp figure lay against the cave wall.

"Is he … ?" Inesca started to ask.

"Dead," Kestorn answered after a moment.

He closed Trestan's eyes and stepped back. Inesca moved toward the other cloaked figure on the ground. He was still breathing, but unconscious. She removed his hood and saw that he looked a lot like the other, but there were no markings on his face. Instead, it was his arm, now extended out of his cloak, which bore the strange symbols.

Kestorn picked up the dagger and tucked the sword into his belt. Looking back at Inesca, he saw blood on her face and reached out to see if she was wounded. Surprised by his movement toward her, she drew back suddenly.

"Are you injured?" he asked as he lowered his hand.

Inesca reached up and seemed to notice the blood for the first time.

"No, it's not mine," she answered, sounding both dazed and shaken.

Kestorn seized the Raegond's hood from her hand and used it to wipe the blood away.

"Don't stop to think about it now," he said, tossing the hood away. "We're not out of this yet."

He moved to the edge of the cavern and began inspecting a dark opening. He started to climb into it, and Inesca moved to follow him.

"Before you follow me, you should know that I don't know where this leads," he said.

Inesca met his gaze. "Then we'll both find out," she said.

Chapter 20

After close to an hour of climbing through the dark, Kestorn and Inesca could see light at the end of a tunnel that stretched upward. Their journey had been spent in silence, but every once in a while, Inesca thought she saw Kestorn look back to see how she was managing the climb.

Her thoughts often strayed to her last sight of Sirryn and the things she could have done differently that might have prevented his death. If not for Kestorn moving ahead of her and her desire to keep up with him, she might have sat in the darkness a while longer to mourn his death. She had no great desire to hurry back to Lord Beristo. How could he abandon her and Sirryn like that?

Kestorn disappeared into the light as he climbed out of the tunnel, and Inesca hurried after him even though she was blinded by the strong rays of the late afternoon sun. When she was able to see again, she realized that they had come out near the road back to the camp.

"This is where we part ways," Kestorn said. "No one needs to know that we escaped together."

Inesca nodded.

"Before you go, can I ask why your brother wasn't with you today?"

"He wasn't feeling well. Lucky, isn't he?"

"He will be glad to see you," Inesca said with a faint smile.

"So will Lord Edgerr … I hope. I'll have to tell him about Trestan though," Kestorn added more seriously.

Inesca said nothing and looked toward the east where Lord Beristo's camp was.

"Lord Beristo will be pleased that you survived," Kestorn said.

Inesca's frowned as she stared in the direction of her lord's camp.

"Thanks to you … not him. He was no help at all."

"The lords only think of themselves. Don't expect more than that."

Inesca looked back at him, hearing the bitterness in his voice. Pulling the dagger from his belt, Kestorn reached out and handed it to her. "I have to get back before Derreth goes looking for me," he said. "I would stay away from the forests on the edge of the camp if I were you. The Raegond could be waiting for another chance to attack."

"Thank you," Inesca said as she accepted the dagger.

Although he glanced back at her, he said nothing, but at least he didn't sneer at her gratitude. Inesca started down the path, but then Kestorn's voice stopped her.

"It's Inesca, isn't it?"

She stopped and turned. "How do you know my name?" she asked.

"You won a race. People talk about you when that happens. They start taking notice of things like names."

"You must have won races too. People seem to know you, Kestorn."

"I've won a few."

"Only a few?" she asked with a smile. "I expected more from the best rider in Trineth."

His expression lightened with a hint of amusement.

"So you haven't forgotten that?"

"No, I haven't, and I'm still waiting to see if it's true. But I hope we can meet now on better terms than we did that first day."

Kestorn shook his head. "You are a strange girl," he said.

"And why am I strange?"

"You're different than the other riders. Back in the cave, the Raegond were not expecting someone to charge in and try to help me. They had me cornered, and then you showed up and nearly got yourself killed. I wasn't expecting that kind of courage from you, and neither were they."

Inesca glanced over her shoulder to see if anyone was watching them before she took a step toward him.

"My father told me once that God can use the people around us to strengthen our hearts and to give us courage."

Kestorn lifted one brow and asked, "Does it not trouble him to know you compete in these races?"

Inesca's expression fell. "He died not long ago," she said. "It's almost been four months now. That's when Lord Beristo found me."

Everything grew quiet between them for a moment, and Kestorn massaged his neck.

"Derreth's better with this kind of thing than I am. Our father died in the Battle of Tortesra, but I barely knew him."

Inesca's hand brushed the small satchel tied around the belt of her dress. She suddenly looked down and reached inside of it. Her fingers searched it for a minute before withdrawing a small wooden figure wrapped in cloth. Kestorn turned his gaze away from the road when he noticed that she was distracted.

"What is that?"

"I found it," Inesca said cautiously. "Maybe you'll know who it belongs to."

She stretched out her hands and opened them slowly, revealing the charred wooden knight. Kestorn picked it up with the cloth and turned it around.

"Are you sure someone lost this? This looks like something a person would intentionally throw away."

Inesca's shoulders sagged. "So you don't recognize it?" she asked.

"Should I?"

"Well, I still think you should take it."

Kestorn glanced at the wooden figure warily.

"I can't accept a gift from you, even if it's as pathetic as this is."

"But it's not mine," she said quickly. "So it's not a gift. And you'll probably have a better chance of finding the person who lost it than I do."

Before he could say anything else, Inesca turned and walked quickly down the road again. Her shape grew dark against the fading light of the sun as it set in the rocky cliffs beyond the camp.

Kestorn wrapped the small soldier in the green and gold cloth as he strode toward the blue and silver tents on the eastern edge of the camp. As he passed the crimson tents of Lord Tolem, Molnar appeared from behind one of them. There were patches of dirt on his clothes but no traces of blood.

"And just when everyone starts to assume you are dead, you dare to return. You and your brother don't die easily, do you?"

"Careful, Molnar. You're starting to sound concerned that you might lose to one of us. People will think you've lost your confidence."

Kestorn started to walk around him, but Molnar moved directly into his path.

"It's time for the races to be reserved for the elite. You and your brother aren't welcome in them anymore. The next time that you attempt to race against us, I guarantee that you will never reach the end alive," he said.

Kestorn narrowed his gaze as he shot a glare back at Molnar.

"Kestorn?"

A familiar voice interrupted the tension, and Molnar walked back toward his own tent without giving Kestorn another glance. Derreth hurried toward him and seized his shoulder.

"I've been looking for you ever since the first survivors returned. Are you injured?"

"No, not yet," Kestorn said, still staring in the direction of where Molnar had been standing.

Derreth followed his gaze. "What is it?" he asked.

Kestorn turned back to his brother and stared at his face. Derreth's eyes met his gaze with a sharp attentiveness and although flushed, his face appeared to have a healthy amount of color.

"I thought you were sick."

"It turned out to be nothing. But no matter how awful I felt this morning, I should have gone with you. Lord Edgerr forbade me to leave camp when he returned and I heard about the ambush, but I finally slipped past the guards and was on my way to find you."

"It's probably best that you weren't there," Kestorn said, and then hesitated for a moment as he remembered that he was returning to camp alone. "Trestan was killed."

With a sigh, Derreth removed his hand from Kestorn's shoulder and glanced back at Lord Edgerr's tent.

"Come on. You need your rest. I'll tell Lord Edgerr about Trestan."

As she weaved through the tents to Lord Beristo's camp, Inesca fingered the pouch at her belt, which still contained her father's medallion, although it was lighter without the wooden knight. She had carried the knight with her in hopes of finding a chance to give it to Derreth or Kestorn, thinking that they might recognize it. But it had meant nothing to Kestorn. Still, after what had happened today, he felt more like an ally and less like an enemy.

Nearing Lord Beristo's large tent, Inesca slowed her pace. He was probably being served dinner and enjoying a goblet of wine while Sirryn lay dead in a gorge with the bodies of riders abandoned by their lords. And she would be one of them if not for Kestorn.

As her lips tightened into a frown, Inesca strode forward toward the tent with a much faster pace. A hand reached out and caught her shoulder. She turned and saw Omaron at her side.

"What are you doing?" he asked.

"Going to tell Lord Beristo that I've returned," Inesca said coldly.

"I'll tell him. Go back to your tent and let the servants tend to you."

After releasing her, Omaron stood and waited for her to leave, but Inesca remained where she was. "I have other things to tell him," she said.

"Not now," Omaron insisted.

"Why not? Are you worried that I'll interrupt his meal?"

"He will not have any food tonight. Not while he is in mourning."

Inesca looked at him in surprise.

"As soon as he returned to camp, he sent his guards back to find you and Sirryn. When they reported that you were missing, I expected your return, but they found Sirryn and brought his body back here. Sirryn was his friend, and his death will be hard for Lord Beristo to bear."

"His actions were too late to save either of us, and he was quick to leave us behind when the attack began."

"It was foolish for him to comply with Lord Tolem's plan that only the lords and their riders attend the ceremony. A lord should always take his guards with him. But as for the attack, he did what was needed."

"Running away like a coward?"

"You don't understand what his death would lead to."

Inesca remained silent, but her anger was still clear.

"He has no heir. No son, not even a nephew," Omaron continued. "The Royal Council has already chosen a successor to replace him when the time comes. Their judgment has diminished over the years, and they have chosen an arrogant, greedy dog. Lord Beristo is not a hero, but he tries to be good to his people. He may lose money far too easily at times, but he is also generous, and the needs of those in his charge matter to him. For these reasons, his life cannot be risked."

As her frame sunk a little with weariness, Inesca let go of her anger. Omaron's loyalty to his lord was greater than hers, but she knew he was right. If Lord Beristo had stayed with them and been killed, it wouldn't have helped anyone. She lifted her gaze to Lord Beristo's tent and saw a stranger leaving it with his head bowed.

"That is Sirryn's brother," Omaron explained. "He arrived at the camp while the lords and riders were gone. The council in Sassot wished to send a message to Lord Felond, and he volunteered to deliver it for another chance to speak with Sirryn."

The council member from Sassot walked to his horse but halted when he reached the animal. He remained standing beside it with his head hanging low, and Inesca thought she could see his shoulders shake in the dark.

"Maybe it was my fault," Inesca said in a soft and wavering tone. "Sirryn was coming back to help me. If he hadn't, he might have been able to escape."

Omaron leaned forward on his staff and watched her face.

"You dishonor his courage by questioning his sacrifice. Let him rest in honor."

Drawing a deep breath, Inesca turned her gaze from Sirryn's brother back to Omaron.

"How many of the other riders were killed?" she asked.

"Except for Lord Beristo, all of the lords lost at least one rider. Lord Tolem lost three, Lord Salistom lost four, Lord Atregar lost three, Lord Felond lost one, and Lord Edgerr lost two of his riders."

"No, only one. Trestan was killed, but Kestorn has just returned."

Omaron's expression grew stern again as he watched her. "You have not dropped your interest in the Lord Edgerr's riders as I told you to. I have warned you that someday there will be a cost for such foolishness," he said.

As she looked up again, Inesca saw Sirryn's brother mount his horse and ride off slowly with his head still bowed. Without meeting Omaron's gaze, Inesca answered, "Someday, perhaps. But not today."

Chapter 21

The day after the attack in the gorge, the lords remained close to their camps, keeping their guards with them at all times. They made the decision to travel together in a large caravan to the realm of Farcost for the third and final race. Even though Lord Salistom and Lord Atregar argued that it would make them more of a target, the other lords feared traveling in separate groups with less protection.

Kestorn spent most of the next morning tending to and grooming Halon, who had grown restless after remaining tied up at camp for so long. This would have been a good morning to give Derreth some more time in the saddle with him, but Derreth had been acting strangely since the previous night. Sullen and quiet, almost as if he was angry, Derreth's mood seemed anything but patient enough to deal with Halon at the present.

Still enmeshed in his dark mood, Derreth suddenly appeared from around one of the tents. His brow was furrowed, and his brown eyes bore a strange light. Celestro pulled at the rope that tied him to a post and snorted as his ears flattened against his head. This mysterious dark mood was even affecting him.

"If you've brushed that horse enough, we have other chores to tend to this morning," Derreth said, ignoring Celestro.

Kestorn finished a few more strokes with the brush before stopping.

"It's helping me, and it's helping Halon. What are you doing besides upsetting Celestro?"

Derreth glanced at the uneasy golden stallion and slowly reached up to place his hand on Celestro's neck. The stallion calmed down a little.

"Is there something about yesterday you're not telling me?" Kestorn asked as he watched his brother.

"It's better not to discuss evil memories or past regrets. I already told you that I should have been with you, and that's all."

Footsteps followed Derreth's words, and they turned to see Laisi appear from behind the tents. Kestorn moved to greet her, and she wrapped her arms around his neck as she reached him.

"They said you were missing," she said, holding onto him tightly.

"I was just a little late," he said with a slight smile. "Sounds like me, doesn't it?"

Looking up at his face, she shook her head and returned his smile. "Yes, and it's just like you to make a joke after scaring me."

"But you'll forgive me, won't you? I worked so hard to come back unharmed just to please you."

She did not laugh, but the light in her eyes grew soft and warm as she noted how well he looked.

"You must have come back for Derreth's sake too," she said as she caught sight of his older brother. "Are you feeling better today, Derreth?"

"I am," he said civilly.

Laisi appeared a bit surprised by the coolness of his tone, and Kestorn shot him a look.

"It seems Derreth's jealous that he wasn't there," he said before turning back to Laisi. "So how long can you stay?"

"Not long, I fear. My father is waiting for me to rejoin him. We're on our way to Morret, so I'm afraid we won't be in Farcost for the next race. Are you riding in it?"

"I don't know yet."

"Kestorn, please be careful. There's something wrong about all of this. So many riders have been killed lately."

"I know," he said. "This is not how the races used to be. I liked it better when they were actually about racing."

Lord Edgerr's voice suddenly called out, seeking Derreth and Kestorn.

"I'd better go before I get you into trouble," she said.

Laisi kissed him on the cheek before she darted around the side of the tent. Kestorn watched her disappear with a smile, but Derreth seized his shoulder with a firm grip and turned him around as Lord Edgerr walked into view.

"Do you two expect the caravan to wait for us? The rest of the tents are not going to come down by themselves. Go help the servants before we are left behind."

They bowed to him, and as Lord Edgerr turned to walk away, he stopped and faced them again.

"Kestorn, you will ride in the next race."

Derreth shifted uneasily next to his brother, but Kestorn was only watching Lord Edgerr.

"May I ride Halon?" he asked.

"Of course. Don't you think I want you to win the race?"

"Thank you, my lord."

"Don't disappoint me," Lord Edgerr said as he cast a stern gaze at Kestorn and then a disparaging look at Derreth before leaving them.

"Did you know?" Kestorn asked, turning to Derreth.

"I suspected."

Kestorn watched him a moment longer as his expression hardened.

"We've both had our turns when it comes to the races. Don't fall out of sorts because it is finally my turn again. It's my right to race when the chance comes."

Moving to take down one of the nearest tents, Kestorn began to untie the blue and silver cloth from one of the poles. Derreth followed him and began to work on the same tent.

"Your right? You make it sound like a privilege."

Kestorn tossed one of the tent poles down onto the ground. "It's what I've been trained to do," he said. "If I can't compete, then why am I here?"

"Even training doesn't prepare you to ride into constant danger. What if the next race is like this one?" Derreth said.

"I've handled treacherous races before, and I'm not afraid to do it again."

As the brothers moved to start taking down the other tents, Laisi backed up slowly, keeping out of sight behind the tent where she had been hiding. But as she started to turn around, someone collided with her and she fell to the ground. Pushing herself up, she raised her head and saw a young woman about her age lying on the ground opposite her. She had long dark hair, and Laisi suddenly recognized her as Lord Beristo's rider, the girl called Inesca.

"What are you doing back here?" Laisi asked.

Inesca motioned for Laisi to keep her voice down. Her wide eyes searched for anyone else who might be watching them. Then she rose to her feet and quickly moved away from the tents.

Laisi heard Lord Edgerr's voice draw closer as he directed the servants to take down the tent behind which she was sitting. She got to her feet, and hurried in the same direction that she had seen Lord Beristo's rider disappear.

After a moment, she noticed the girl darting behind some rocks at the edge of the camp. Laisi glanced left and right before following. When she reached the outcrop of rocks, she caught up with the stranger and seized her arm.

"I know who you are, and I'm not letting you go until I get an answer," she demanded. "What were you doing in Lord Edgerr's camp?"

The Easterner pulled her arm out of Laisi's grasp with a sudden jerk.

"I was lost. Just forget that you saw me."

"Not after everything that's happened. You could be a spy in another plot to attack the riders who survived the massacre yesterday."

"Me?" Inesca asked with a smile. "Kestorn must not have told you that we escaped the Raegond's attack together."

"Oh?" Laisi said as her gaze hardened. "No, he didn't say anything about that."

"I only wanted to see how he was doing today," Inesca continued as she stared at Laisi with a curious gaze. "Who are you?"

"My name is Laisi, and my father is a merchant from Trineth. Kestorn and I have known each other for more than a year," Laisi said coolly. "We're very close."

As Laisi spoke, the sudden smile and amusement on the girl's face caused a surge of heat to redden Laisi's.

"I think you've misunderstood my interest," Inesca said. "I'm not here to cause any trouble."

"That's difficult to believe. In the past, Kestorn has attracted more than enough attention from other girls. He doesn't always discourage them as he should, but he's not serious about any of them …"

"Except you?"

"Yes," Laisi replied. "So, what is your interest if you're not a spy and you're not attracted to him?"

Inesca searched their surroundings as if she wanted to escape, but there were still many people dismantling the camp who could easily take notice if she tried to dart away.

"I was only grateful for his help the other day. And …," she hesitated. "I am reminded of my brothers when I see Kestorn and his brother. The way they speak and act is similar. I have sometimes watched them from a distance, so in that sense, I suppose I am a spy."

"Your brothers?" Laisi asked doubtfully.

"I lost two brothers several years ago, and now all my family is gone. When I see Derreth and Kestorn, it's like having some of my family back again—but it's nothing that you would ever need to fear."

Laisi relaxed a little, though she still appeared surprised.

"Aside from all of this, they won't want anything to do with me," Inesca continued. "I think Derreth blames me for his loss in the last race, and Kestorn has you."

"And the races," Laisi added.

"Yes. They do seem to be important to him," Inesca agreed.

"I was hoping he would not race again for a while. Not after what happened in Monterr."

Inesca nodded. "This is my first year in the Great Races, but I was told that these things usually do not happen," she said.

"No, but there have been more deaths of late. Last year was bad enough, but I fear this year will be worse."

In the distance, Derreth and Kestorn became visible again as tents collapsed around them.

"I will do what I can to help Kestorn," Inesca said, facing Laisi again.

"But it's forbidden. Riders are never to help each other in the races."

"We should all have a fair chance to win," Inesca insisted. "I should try to see that Kestorn at least gets that chance."

A cloud shifted in the sky, and the sun cast its harsh light toward them. Inesca raised her hand to her eyes as she studied its position.

"I must get back to Lord Beristo's camp. I hope that everything works out for you and Kestorn."

Laisi stretched out her hand to stop Inesca again. "I misjudged you, Inesca," she said. "But now that we have met, I wish you well in the next race."

Inesca smiled and nodded before she hurried back to her own camp.

Chapter 22

The journey to the realm of Farcost required a week of travel through the northern half of Monterr. Once crossing over the border and into the southern portion of Farcost, the lords gathered for a private meeting in the stately manor of Sir Dynur. A large feast was provided in their honor, but the lords took it in silence as they cast quiet and cold glances at one another. Sir Dynur eagerly departed after the meal, leaving them to their own affairs.

Lord Atregar was the first to stand and explain that he had called the meeting for one purpose. "We cannot ignore what happened in Monterr. And someone must pay for our losses," he said. His eyes turned to Lord Tolem.

"Nothing like this happened to us at the race in Sassot," Atregar continued. "It is only right that we demand compensation for these tragedies that never should have occurred."

"That is an outrageous demand, and do not forget that some of my own riders were lost in the attack," Lord Tolem insisted.

"But not your best rider," Lord Atregar said. "He escaped the flood and the ambush unharmed, while many of our most skilled racehorses and riders did not."

"You cannot hold me responsible for either of those events."

"Both of them occurred in your realm," Lord Salistom said.

Tolem turned and cast a glare at him.

"It was the Raegond. No doubt, they were behind the release of the river into the gorge and the attack the next day."

"Yes, we saw them during the attack," Lord Edgerr said. "No one is saying it was your men who attacked us."

"But we are all responsible for the safety of our realms," Salistom continued. "Yours was a death trap. None of us will want to return there soon."

Tolem cast another dark gaze in Salistom's direction, but the Lord of Fortur appeared to be untroubled by it.

"And we will not agree to attend another race in your realm," Lord Edgerr added.

"I will not hear complaints from you, Edgerr," Tolem said, turning his ire on the lord sitting to his left. "We all know that you lost nothing in the ambush except a fool who humiliated you in Sassot. Your only argument with me is that one of your better riders might have won the last race if not for his struggle with mine at the end."

Edgerr frowned but kept his lips sealed.

"And I will hear nothing from you, Beristo. The fact that your poor substitute for a rider has managed to survive these recent tragedies while worthier ones have died is an insult to this gathering."

Lord Beristo rose from his chair before speaking. "I had planned to stay silent, but now you will hear me, Tolem. The fact that my rider has survived is evidence of her resourcefulness. But if you want to know why everyone is inclined to blame you for their losses, it is because you are a snake-eyed rogue with your father's blood on your hands."

The anger on Tolem's expression was replaced with cold scorn. "My father's death was caused by a hunting accident, and there has never been any evidence to the contrary," he said.

"We hardly need evidence. Your hatred of him was always clear," Lord Edgerr scoffed. "There are some things that are simply common knowledge. You can't truly expect us to believe your father's death was an *accident* any more than we believe Felond is his father's son. Everyone at this table knows he is Atregar's half-brother."

Lord Felond's face flushed as he lowered his head while Lord Atregar turned a wrathful gaze on Edgerr.

"If we are going to raise every old grievance that lies between the six of us, we'll have to remain here a month at least," Salistom interjected.

The moment of tension eased as both Beristo and Atregar took their seats.

"You are right, Salistom. Let us return to the matter of our heavy losses in Monterr," Atregar said. "Tolem, will you or will you not offer us compensation for your failure to keep the Raegond out of your realm?"

"Instead of compensation, what about a challenge instead?" Tolem asked. "I'll agree to compensate you, but only if I see proof that all of you have been able to keep the Raegond out of your realms—starting with you, Atregar, since it's your realm where the next and final race of the season is being held. If there are no attacks during our stay here in Farcost, then I'll acknowledge this supposed debt that I owe you for your lost riders and horses."

"What you are asking me to accept is an invitation to have my own realm attacked," Atregar said as he suddenly rose from his chair again.

"Are you suggesting that I control the Raegond?" Tolem asked as he stood on the opposite side of the table.

The other lords looked silently at him and then at one another.

"The Raegond would never serve one of us," Edgerr said after a moment. "Their war is against our rule. It is foolishness to suggest that they would ever help a lord."

"That is true," Felond agreed, speaking up hesitantly. "We should be looking for a way to get rid of them before they kill one of us."

"Tolem could still send mercenaries to attack our realms under the guise of the Raegond," Atregar said. "We cannot trust him."

Tolem stepped away from his chair, sweeping his crimson robe in front of him.

"Without the support of the Royal Council, you are powerless to demand anything from me, including a second more of my time," he said. "I will see you all at the last race."

As he walked out, the other lords began to rise and take their leave.

"I knew this meeting was going to be a waste of time," Edgerr said, sighing as he and the others departed with their private guards. Atregar remained behind with Beristo.

"If only the rest of us could be as confident as Tolem," Lord Beristo said as he gazed at the chair where Tolem had been seated. "Few of us can afford it. I have heard that Tolem sends the Royal Council a fine gift every year. And they are not so impartial as to question it."

"I lost too many good riders in Monterr," Atregar said, staring into the distance. "One of them was my son's dearest friend. The only reason my son did not come with us this season is because he became ill and had to remain behind. Before long, I will see him again, and he will be waiting to welcome his friend. How will I explain what has happened to him? How will I tell him that no one was held responsible or punished for the death of his friend?"

Lord Beristo nodded and said, "I lost the best member of my council during the attack. He was a braver and a wiser man than I am, and he deserves justice. But I don't know how to give it to him. These Raegond appear and disappear like the wind."

"If the others cared more, we might have a better chance of tracking them down, but I doubt Tolem searched for them very long after the attack," Atregar said.

"And how to make the others care, that is another problem."

Atregar nodded as he placed his hand on Beristo's shoulder.

"You are a decent Evaliscan, Beristo. Honor and sound judgment remain in your keeping. I cannot say that is true of all of us. For that reason, I hope you are able to hold onto your rider and horse. I fear another attack is coming, and I dread its presence here in my own realm."

As he disappeared, Lord Beristo left to seek rest in his own chamber. Several corridors away, Lord Tolem entered his own room. All was dark inside except for a few dying candles. Tossing his robe onto the bed, Tolem dipped a cloth into a basin and wiped his face as he took in a deep breath and released it slowly.

A creaking sound behind him caused him to stiffen and turn around in time to see the tapestry on the opposite wall thrust forward as a hidden door opened from behind it. A cloaked figure stepped out of the dark passageway holding a burning candle.

"What are you doing here?" Tolem asked coldly as he glared at the intruder. "And take that thing off. I know who you are."

The newcomer made no attempt to remove the cloak but gestured toward the row of large windows on the wall to his right.

"Your room has too many windows, Tolem. Do you think I want to be seen with you?"

"Well, this is a fine time for you to come to me. What if you were seen skulking about the halls?"

"Unlike you, I have learned how to move and strike unseen. My actions are not as transparent as yours."

"Do not mock me. It is because of your plan that they suspect me. You assured me that I would benefit from this scheme. Instead, I am being threatened and cast under suspicion."

"They can do you no real harm, and you would not have found yourself in this position if you had made certain sacrifices as I told you to."

"That may be how you manage your own affairs, but you will not sacrifice what is mine."

"You forget that such losses can always be replaced. But since you seem to value your rider, Molnar, you will instruct him to observe the replacements carefully. Remind him that only those who serve a purpose will survive."

"Why not attack the remaining riders of the other lords now? Why wait for the next race?"

"And have an attack occur so near the borders of your own realm? That would certainly confirm their suspicions, wouldn't it?"

"Then wait until we have traveled closer to the coast. I do not wish to rely on any more races. The ambush was far more effective than that complicated mess of flooding the gorge at the precise time. Let us end it soon. I am eager to collect the forfeiture fees from the other lords when they are forced to admit that they cannot compete in the races."

"So your impatience has nothing to do with the fact that you are tired of losing races?"

Tolem's gaze burned with anger as he stared at the speaker.

"Do not forget that I only agreed to help you because you assured me that this scheme would prove rewarding for the both of us. If I decide that the reward does not meet my expectations ..."

The cloaked guest laughed. "What will you do, Tolem? Reveal me? For someone who claims to have such a strong self-interest, you have strange ideas about how to protect and advance yourself."

The lord of Monterr's eyes still smoldered with impatience and rage, but he remained silent as the cloaked figure approached him.

"You must trust that I have your best interests in mind. To kill the riders of the other lords now and yet leave you with Molnar would certainly raise questions that you want to avoid. The use of the races allows us the chance to cast suspicion on the other lords and still destroy those whom we choose. And if the time comes to strike at them outside of a race, it must always appear to be under the cause of savage rebellion. The last thing we want them to realize is that these attacks have been orchestrated for another design."

The eyes beneath the shadow of the cloak's hood studied Tolem's expression that slowly began to relinquish the signs of his anger.

"I will speak to Molnar and deliver your message." Tolem sighed. "He seems to relish your instructions more than I do."

"Don't you trust me?"

"No, but then, when have we ever truly trusted each other?"

"Never, but we understand one another. For instance, you understand that if you ever tried to cross me ...," the figure began, crossing over to the windows and opening one. He moved a lit candle to its edge, and as he stepped back, an arrow flew through the window, snuffing out the light from the small flame before embedding itself in a portrait on the wall.

"Then you would share your father's fate," he continued.

Tolem remained silent as he stared at the arrow. The cloaked visitor returned to the secret door and paused beside it. He removed a bloated pouch from his cloak and set it down on a nearby table. A few gold coins slipped out of the top and dropped onto the floor.

"Here is your reward for your service, as promised. This should be enough to put you at ease again."

He opened the door and left the room as Tolem walked quickly to the table and reached his hand into the pouch, immersing it in gold. He withdrew a handful of coins in his fist and weighed them slowly before sitting down in a chair beside the table. The glimmer of candlelight on the gold was reflected in his eyes.

A breeze from the open window swept past his face, and Tolem rose, moving slowly toward the window. He closed it and stepped back before glancing again at the arrow that had punctured a hole in the painting behind him.

The final race was to be held near the western shores of Farcost, which required almost a fortnight of travel through the northwest realm of Rynar. After completing their journey, the travelers established their camps in Farcost only three days before the race. Just a few hours after their arrival, Inesca was called into Omaron's tent where a table was strewn with maps. Moving to the edge of the table, Inesca saw that Omaron was drawing black lines on one of the maps.

"It is time to go over our strategy for this race," he said without looking up at her.

Inesca studied his markings on the map and noticed that he had drawn a line that split into three and then united again at the eastern edge of the map.

"In the last race, there was meant to be only one path for the riders to take. But here in Farcost, the riders will have to decide because there are three choices: the coast, the plains, or the forest. And remember that once a choice is made, the rules say a rider cannot turn back. The only direction you can ride is forward."

Inesca examined the lines on the map. "Is there no way to start down one path and then ride into another?" she asked.

"No, because each lies on a different level. The road on the coast sinks below the plains, and the forest rises above the plains. But all three lead to the final mile. Those who prove successful on their chosen path will meet there in a race for the finish."

"Which should I take?"

Omaron directed her gaze to the forest.

"No one else will take this choice, but it is the right one for you," he said.

"But would not the plains be a straighter and faster course?"

"Are you prepared to fight your way through the other riders to obtain the lead? Or, if you race ahead of them early, to defend yourself when they catch up to you?"

Inesca dropped her gaze.

"Then you must choose a different path and rejoin them when they are not expecting it."

"The last time I tried a different path, it nearly killed me and Nycor."

"It also saved your lives," Omaron said. "And you will not have the same difficulty this time. You learned to ride in the forests of the East Province. Your stallion may not be able to climb mountains, but he has no difficulty racing through trees."

"How do you know they won't expect me to choose the forest or that they won't follow me?"

"No rider has ever chosen the forest before, even though it allows a rider to cross a slightly shorter distance than the other routes. They fear it will put too many obstacles in their path and slow them down. They do not believe anyone can ride through the forest and still win. They will assume that you have already lost the moment you ride toward it."

"Do you think I can win?"

"I have seen you cover more ground in dense woods than I thought was possible in so short a time. Maneuvering through the trees and the undergrowth is nothing to your horse, and you are as much at home in the forest as he is. Maintain the pace that you have demonstrated in your training, and you will reach the final mile with a chance to win."

Inesca looked down at the map. "That sounds better than what you said about the last race. *A chance to win* is enough for me," she said.

"Put the last race behind you. Everything must be different this time. In this race, you must not follow anyone."

"You mean that you don't want me to pay any attention to Kestorn."

Omaron paused and glanced at her.

"How did you know he would be competing?"

"I might have overheard something about it at Lord Edgerr's camp," Inesca said as she rubbed the back of her neck and turned her gaze away from him.

"You are fortunate that no one saw you. The lords and other riders will not hesitate to seize or attack spies."

Inesca decided it might be better not to mention being caught by Laisi, so she kept quiet.

"As for Kestorn, he is reckless and unafraid of a fight. He will not choose the forest. The strength of his horse is in its speed. He will chase the plains where his horse can run without hindrance, but you cannot follow him."

Inesca nodded.

"As I said, this time, you must not follow any of the other riders," Omaron continued. "When the race begins, I want you to let your stallion run. Urge him to use all of his speed."

"But you have always told me to stay behind. Won't I be in more danger from the other riders if I dart in front of them?"

"This time, you will be in danger if you remain in the back. They will expect that of you, and I suspect that some riders will be killed before they ever draw close to the final mile. That is why you must escape them at the beginning. Give them no opportunity to reach you. Your horse is fast enough to carry you out of their reach until you can get to the forest."

"Do you think they're planning to kill more riders like they did in the race in Monterr?"

"It is hard to know what they intend to do, but I have seen strange things this racing season that cannot mean anything good for you or the others."

"Who else will I be racing against this time?"

Omaron rolled up one of the maps and thrust it into her hands.

"If you are going to be a spy, you should at least learn to gather better information. When Molnar and Segiro have entered a race, Kestorn is the least of your worries in terms of competition."

Molnar's name was familiar to Inesca as the savage rider for Lord Tolem, but the second name was strange to her.

"Segiro is not a new rider?" she asked.

"No," Omaron answered firmly. "He used to ride for Lord Tolem until he was injured in a race nearly a year ago, but now Lord Felond in his desperation for a new rider has stumbled across a skilled one. He could have a chance to win this time."

"Then Segiro has recovered from his injury?"

"He has, and he has a new thirst to prove himself. He was not so different than Molnar before his injury, and now he will be even more dangerous."

"Have Lord Atregar and Lord Salistom also found replacements for their riders who were killed in Monterr?"

"Yes, but I doubt that Lord Atregar's rider will give you much trouble. I have seen him race before, and I know that he will be watching Molnar and Segiro. His interest will turn more toward staying alive than attacking you. As for Lord Salistom's new rider, Arnun, he has never ridden in one of these races before. I do not know whether he will prove to be as good of a rider as Cidonn or not, but regardless of his ability, he will have the speed of Lord Salistom's white stallion to help him."

"So what do you suggest that I do if I find myself near these other riders?"

"Do *not* be near them," Omaron said sternly. "Get away from them at the beginning as I have told you to. You should be able to ride through the forest alone."

"And if I encounter them at the end of the race?"

"Ride hard for the dassdir poles. Draw your sword if they advance toward you, but if you ride well and fast, you may not have to raise your weapon once."

Chapter 23

The day before the race, Lord Beristo took his guards and left the camp to ride with Lord Atregar through the region surrounding the race. They wished to search for the Raegond and any other signs of trouble. Omaron was suffering from a pain that occasionally troubled him in the stump of his right leg, and knowing the dark mood that usually accompanied such pain, Inesca chose to spend the day in her own tent, studying the maps that she needed for the race.

A shadow fell across the flap door to her tent, and Toares, one of Lord Beristo's older servants, poked his head inside.

"I must interrupt you, Inesca," he said apologetically.

"What's wrong, Toares?"

"It's Jirro. He untied your stallion and was going to ride him."

Inesca stood up quickly.

"Nycor will never let him stay on for long. Where is he now?"

"Disappeared. Looking for a drink somewhere no doubt, but it's your horse that I came about. He's run off. After he knocked Jirro to the ground, he took off like lightning."

Inesca sighed. "I tried to tell Lord Beristo that he was getting restless. Did you see which direction he went?"

"Northwest, toward the region where the race will be held."

Inesca grabbed her cloak and walked past him out of the tent.

"Shouldn't I send someone else to go and find him?" Toares asked. "It's not safe for you to go alone."

"Nycor will never come to anyone else, and you must stay here with the camp."

"What about Omaron?"

"Where is he now?"

"Asleep in his tent."

"No, let him rest. His leg's been bothering him all day. It has to be me who goes, but I'll try to be back before anyone notices I'm gone."

"If Lord Beristo returns early, I'll try to give you more time," Toares said.

"Thank you, Toares, but there's no reason for you to get into trouble on my account and certainly not on Jirro's. You might as well tell him the truth and say that you tried to stop me."

Without wasting any more time, Inesca hurried through the other tents in Lord Beristo's camp and then paused when she reached the last one. The late afternoon sun slipped lower into the sky, casting shadows through the gathering of tents. Just beyond Lord Beristo's camp lay Lord Felond's purple and white tents.

Inesca's thoughts turned to the memory of the night she had spent in Lasnell being hunted by Destrod. Passing through Lord Felond's camp seemed to be one of the worst possible choices she could make, but Inesca knew that this was the direction she needed to take to find Nycor. Still, she would at least be cautious enough to travel around the edge of the camp rather than boldly walking into it.

Using the trees on the western side of the camp, Inesca moved slowly past the tents a few yards at a time. There were no guards in sight, but at the sudden appearance of movement, she crouched behind a tree, pulling her cloak around her. When she dared to take another look, she saw a servant carrying firewood between two of the tents.

Breathing a bit easier, she started to rise from the ground, but suddenly she heard the crunch of dry grass under approaching footsteps. Stiffening against the rough bark of the wide trunk at her back, Inesca waited to be found, but the newcomers stopped on the other side of the tree.

"What do you want here, Molnar?" a clear and cold voice asked. "Have you come to finish off your old rival?"

"I came to see if it was true. They said you were riding again, but I never thought you would ride for Felond."

"Is it so surprising that I would change colors when Lord Tolem cast me off? He was quick to be rid of me when I was wounded, but I can assure you that I have fully recovered."

Inesca realized that the other speaker must be Segiro as she remained motionless behind the tree.

"Good," Molnar said. "You will need your strength for this race."

"Is that a threat?"

"Not for you. Rumor is there's a reward for riders that cut the loathsome scum out of this race."

Segiro let out a low, scornful laugh.

"Every rider considers the others loathsome. You had better be more specific."

"Just look down at the scars on your arm. Do they bring anyone to mind?"

"All too often, but it's not that simple. He's fast. Catching him in this race will be difficult."

"Only if you try to do it alone," Molnar insisted.

Silence followed his words, and Inesca's thoughts raced over what she had heard. Who were they talking about? Molnar had mentioned Segiro's scars as though this was all about revenge, but Omaron had not told her who was responsible for Segiro's injury.

"What are you proposing?" Segiro asked.

"A pact. One that can only benefit you."

"And what about him? Why is he here?"

"He's after the reward just as we are, and it will take three of us to slow down our target."

Inesca wondered who the third person was that they were talking about, but she didn't dare move in an attempt to catch a glimpse of him.

"What about the other one? The brother?"

"His time will come. I intend to have a message sent to him after it's too late for him to stop us," Molnar answered.

"You're going to give him a warning?"

"Not a warning. An assurance of what's coming for him."

Inesca held her breath as she heard them move again. In a moment, she saw their shadows fall across her as they passed the tree. To her great relief, their backs were to her most of the time, and they were too distracted to notice her small figure huddled against the tree.

The third man was shorter than either Segiro or Molnar, and Inesca decided that he must be Arnun, the new rider for Lord Salistom, based on the black and gold colors of his tunic.

After what seemed like several minutes, they finally disappeared in the direction of Lord Tolem's camp, and Inesca cautiously rose from the ground. She managed to quietly make her way beyond Lord Felond's camp and to a grove of trees some yards beyond it.

Breathing deeply, she leaned against one of the trunks as her thoughts raced over the riders' words. Omaron had been right to suspect that something terrible was going to happen. Not only were Molnar and Segiro planning to make this race one of deliberate violence, but they also appeared to be targeting a specific rider.

Inesca closed her eyes as she slid down to the base of the tree. She feared that their target might be Kestorn, and it seemed as though Molnar had something in mind for Derreth as well. The sound of footsteps startled Inesca from her thoughts, but a familiar whinny relieved her fears, and Nycor appeared from around the other side of the tree and snorted at her in greeting.

"Well, I hope you had a nice romp," Inesca said as she rose to her feet and scratched his neck. "But you forgot to take me with you."

Nycor pulled away from her, lifting his head as his ears pricked forward.

"What is it?"

Inesca followed his gaze and didn't hear anything at first, but then she noticed a faint noise in the distance. She moved to his side and realized she would have to ride bareback to follow the sound, but she saw that Jirro had managed to put a bridle on Nycor.

"You must have run off when he tried to put the saddle on you," Inesca scoffed as she climbed up onto the stallion. "At least we've practiced without saddles before."

Growing quiet again, Inesca guided Nycor downhill toward the direction of the sound. But just as they passed out of the trees toward a clearing, a forceful grip pulled Inesca from Nycor's back and dropped her on the ground. She groaned and looked up to see Derreth standing over her.

"It seems that I didn't make myself clear during the race in Monterr, so I'll say it again, I don't care to be followed."

Inesca shot a glare up at him as she rubbed her back.

"I was not following you. A fool untied my horse and let him run loose, and I came out here to find my stallion. After that, I heard a noise and wanted to see who was sneaking around."

Derreth appeared to lose interest and began walking back to his own horse, which was grazing in the clearing. Inesca pushed herself up and stumbled after him.

"What are you doing out here, anyway?"

Derreth drew his sword as she approached him. Inesca backed away and held out her hands for him to see that she wasn't carrying a weapon.

"Derreth, I am not your enemy. We're not even racing against each other tomorrow."

"That doesn't make us friends. What do you want?"

"Well, first I want to know what you're doing out here," Inesca persisted. "I thought no one was allowed in this region before the race, according to Lord Atregar."

"My brother is racing tomorrow. I was checking for signs of sabotage, but it's not been easy avoiding Lord Atregar's scouts or searching miles of ground."

Inesca glanced behind him and noticed a vast plain stretching below the trees.

"Maybe it's good that I found you, then," she said. "I overheard Molnar and Segiro talking outside Lord Felond's camp. They've agreed to work together during the race tomorrow, and they're in league with Arnun, the new rider taking Cidonn's place."

Derreth turned away as if disinterested. "You misheard them," he said with his back to her. "Unless all of them can win the race, they would never help each other."

"I saw them make a pact," Inesca insisted. "They're planning to kill someone. They never said a name, but I'm certain they were talking about Kestorn."

"How do you know they weren't talking about you?"

"Because they were describing a man, one that's known for riding a horse well at great speed."

Derreth faced her again and kept his sword lowered, but he did not answer her.

"They also spoke of someone who injured Segiro the last time he raced. Was Kestorn involved in that?"

Derreth finally nodded.

"About a year ago, Segiro and Kestorn were engaged in a fight during a race. Kestorn held off Segiro's attacks as they were riding up this hill, and he managed to reach the high ground where it was level and flat. Instead of slowing his horse, Segiro drove the animal onto the steep ground alongside Kestorn, but his horse lost its footing and fell. It ended up with a broken leg, and Segiro tore up his right arm on the rocks of the hillside. He managed to get up and walk the rest of the way to the dassdir poles."

"With bitter thoughts about Kestorn driving him all the way, it seems," Inesca said. "You see? It is Kestorn they're plotting against. And I heard them mention you as well."

"Why are you telling me this?"

She dropped her gaze, clasping and unclasping her hands. *Do I dare tell him?*

"In the last race, you helped me because you said that you didn't want to win by sabotage. I thought you should know that it doesn't sound like they intend for the race to be fair tomorrow."

"That doesn't explain why you're always trailing after me or Kestorn. I spoke with Laisi again before she left for Morret with her father, and she told me that you and Kestorn escaped the Raegond together during the ambush."

"What else did she tell you?"

"That you said we remind you of your brothers," he said scornfully as though he believed she had merely used that as an excuse to fool Laisi. "I have seen people who remind me of those that I once cared about, but I've never been compelled to become their shadow."

Inesca met his gaze again. "If the resemblance is strong enough, you might," she said.

Although he put his sword back in its sheath, Derreth continued to watch her with a cautious gaze.

"I don't know what you're up to, but you're not helping yourself by taking an interest in us."

"I'm not so sure. If I hadn't followed you in the last race, I would have drowned with the other riders, and Kestorn helped me escape the Raegond. But this time, I'm trying to help you."

"That's not how things are done. Riders don't make alliances."

"Not everyone follows the rules. My trainer may have taught them to me, but I'm learning they are broken all the time," Inesca said impatiently. "Molnar, Segiro, and Arnun are making up their own. And I haven't forgotten that you broke a rule by turning around to help me during the race in Monterr."

Derreth did not answer her and started to lead his horse away. Inesca reached inside her cloak and drew out a small bundle.

"Derreth, wait," she said as she caught up with him. "It's not easy for me to give this up, but you probably have more of a right to it than I do."

As she unwrapped the cloth, Derreth paused and waited for her to hand it to him. She held it out to him, and he took it, raising the medallion to a thin beam of sunlight coming through the trees.

His hand dropped suddenly, and he looked from it to Inesca.

"I was a child the last time I held this. Where did you find it?"

"It was given to me ... by my father."

Derreth's eyes widened, and he opened his mouth to speak. Then he closed it, and his lips pressed together into a frown. He weighed the medallion in his clenched hand.

"I don't know how you came by this, but my father died twenty years ago in the war. I see now what you think, but it's not true."

He turned to leave, but Inesca blocked his path.

"I know that I'm not someone you'd want to claim," she said. "But I could never doubt who you are to me. Not when you have his face."

Derreth stiffened. He paused for a moment and then pushed past her.

"I meant what I said about not wanting to be followed," he said.

Climbing onto his horse, he kicked the golden stallion into a lope, and Inesca watched as he left her behind. Nycor walked to her side and snorted softly. She remained still for several seconds as a heavy ache settled in her heart.

"Omaron warned me," she said quietly.

The rest of their journey back to Lord Beristo's camp remained a blur to Inesca. Fortunately, no one noticed her or Nycor because they would have made easy targets. Her thoughts were far from worries about enemies in or near Lord Felond's camp.

As she approached Lord Beristo's camp, Inesca saw Omaron waiting for them. She guessed by the disapproval in his expression that he had spoken with Toares. Inesca released a heavy breath as she dismounted from Nycor and led the stallion closer.

"Has Lord Beristo returned?"

"Not yet," Omaron said coldly. "But I have been too tolerant with your reckless wandering. You will not leave again without permission."

Inesca kept her gaze lowered.

"You offer no protest," Omaron noted. "What happened?"

Inesca glanced up briefly. "I saw Derreth not long after I found Nycor," she said.

"You gave him the medallion?" Omaron prompted, and his tone suggested he already knew the answer.

Without meeting his gaze, Inesca nodded. The heavy iron rod moved forward as Omaron approached her and put a hand on her shoulder. Inesca looked up at him in surprise.

"There is not much time before we must leave for the race. Care for your horse, and do not dwell on it."

⁂

The sun had long set by the time Derreth reached Lord Edgerr's camp. Despite his distracted thoughts, he had continued to ride far over the territory for the race, but his task had taken him longer than he intended after his conversation with Lord Beristo's rider. As he returned, one of Lord Edgerr's guards met him with a somber expression.

"Your return was expected hours ago."

"It was a lot of ground to cover, but I am ready to give my report to Lord Edgerr."

"It is too late. Some of the lords decided to gather their riders and horses early to take them to the starting point for the race. They left two hours ago."

Derreth dismounted and handed the reins of the horse to the guard.

"I'll take a new mount and ride after them."

But the man halted him.

"You're to stay here. We'll leave in the morning to join the crowd observing the final mile."

"My report cannot wait," Derreth said, knocking aside his hand.

"It will have to," the guard scoffed. "You won't catch them, and no one else is allowed near the starting point."

Derreth stepped back as he realized the truth of that statement. He would not reach Kestorn or Lord Edgerr in time if they had left hours ago. Without anywhere else to go, Derreth slowly withdrew to the tent he shared with Kestorn. When he stepped inside, the emptiness of it struck him, and Derreth lit a candle to chase away some of the darkness. Yet he still felt troubled, knowing it was too late to warn his brother about Molnar and Segiro.

Staring down at his brother's empty mat, Derreth noticed a bit of bright-colored cloth sticking out from under the blankets. He bent down and pulled it out. A lump wrapped in green and gold cloth greeted his fingers. *What was Kestorn doing with Lord Beristo's colors?*

Unwrapping the edges, Derreth pulled the cloth aside until a wooden knight blackened by ash fell into his palm. His eyes widened as he recognized it, and he drew in a sharp breath.

Chapter 24

With the rising sun behind them, the riders assembled behind the raised flags of the realm of Farcost. The strong breeze sweeping in from the ocean whipped the turquoise flags back and forth, making it seem as if the white fish on each one might really be jumping into the air.

Inesca patted Nycor's neck as she moved him into the line between the rider for Lord Atregar and Kestorn. The red stallion, Halon, thrust back his ears and raised his head with a shrill call as his hooves stamped the ground. Nycor snorted and began to stamp his own hooves. Kestorn steadied Halon with the reins and stroked his neck as Inesca tried to calm Nycor. She saw Kestorn glance at her once, but he quickly turned away as the other riders took their positions.

Since their first meeting in Cerdost, Inesca's feelings toward Kestorn had greatly changed, but their stallions still hated each other. *Too much alike in temperament*, Inesca thought. Nycor had always been the unrivaled stallion among her father's horses. Halon's aggressive personality only provoked them both into what Inesca believed would become a fight if she and Kestorn were not present.

Turning her gaze away from Halon and Kestorn, Inesca saw Molnar and Segiro at the other end of the line of riders. They appeared strangely at ease with an arrogant air of confidence hovering about them. Not far from them, Arnun waited atop the white horse, Razur. As she watched him, his gaze suddenly turned to her, and the cold malice in it caused a twinge of fear to seize her heart.

As the moment for the race to begin drew near, restless energy elicited nervous or impatient behavior from the other horses and their riders. One of the attendants was dressed to match Lord Atregar's banner in his turquoise and white tunic. He stepped forward and waved the flag to the left and then to right and then … down.

Inesca urged Nycor into a rapid gallop just as Omaron had told her. With relief, she felt the other horses slip behind them as Nycor charged into the open field. Air swept past her face, and Inesca dared to look behind her. Some of the riders were watching them, but others were focused on their own pace.

Arnun had not taken his attention from her and seemed to ride after her with a murderous look in his eyes, but Kestorn had spurred Halon into a faster pace and perhaps unintentionally blocked Arnun's path to Inesca. Arnun could not drop back and go behind Kestorn without sacrificing the speed needed to catch up to Inesca, so he drew his sword and came at Kestorn as if to scare him out of his way. Kestorn was not so easily startled and drew his own sword to meet Arnun's challenge with a fearless expression. Inesca watched with relief as Arnun finally turned his horse away, realizing that he was unlikely to defeat Kestorn in a direct duel.

Directing Nycor toward the east, Inesca guided him toward the forest that would eventually rise above the plains. The other riders behind her began to split into smaller groups. Kestorn led the race toward the plains with Lord Atregar's rider behind him, but the other riders turned toward the coast. She realized Omaron had made a good choice in sending her to the forest as the distance between her and the others grew rapidly wider.

At least Kestorn is not riding anywhere near Molnar, Inesca thought as she turned around again. But why had Molnar, Segiro, and Arnun not chosen the plains? A sick feeling stirred in her stomach as Inesca glanced back at Kestorn again, and she offered up a prayer for him as their paths separated.

Nycor pulled at the reins as they neared the forest, but his stride did not slacken. Omaron had been right to believe that Nycor would race into the forest without hesitation.

"That's right, my friend," Inesca said as she leaned closer to his ears. "It will be just like back home."

A few hours into the race, Kestorn found himself crossing the plains with only Lord Atregar's rider in sight. He stopped at a brook to let Halon drink before urging the stallion to continue on at a lope. He wanted to be able to reach the final mile before the other riders, who had chosen the coast.

Turning his gaze toward the northeast, he saw the forest standing on the ridge above him. He still wondered why Inesca had chosen that route. It was a shame that they wouldn't get a chance to test her horse's speed against Halon. Ever since Kestorn had seen her race in Sassot, it had been something he had wanted to do.

The final mile and the point where the riders from the coast would rejoin the main path drew near. Kestorn glanced over at Lord Atregar's rider, who seemed to be watching him closely. Having never met or raced against this rider before,

Kestorn was uncertain of what to expect from him. Lord Atregar's usual riders had either been killed in the flood or the Raegond attack in Monterr.

As the horses continued forward through the field of grass, Kestorn suddenly noticed a strange smell rising in the air. He stopped Halon for a moment and leapt down. The smell grew stronger, and Kestorn plucked some of the grass from the ground and raised it to his nose. It was covered in ceraf oil, which was used to ignite torches faster and to cause them to burn longer.

Kestorn looked at the grass surrounding him and Halon in dismay and quickly mounted again as he spurred Halon into a gallop. Lord Atregar's rider noticed and started riding hard after him. *If we could just reach the road beyond the fields that stretches the length of the final mile, we'll be clear of whatever trap was laid here*, Kestorn thought.

After a few more minutes, the barren dirt road appeared in the distance, and Kestorn urged Halon toward it. Movement to the right caught Kestorn's eye, and he turned in time to see two men appear over the ridge that led down to the coast. One of them tossed a flaming torch into the grass, and then they grabbed a rope and disappeared back over the edge of the ridge.

The fire licked through the grass like lightning and quickly caught up with Lord Atregar's rider and horse. The flames found the traces of the oil on the horse's legs, and the animal reared in pain, tossing the rider to the ground to be seized by the fire. His cries filled the air.

Kestorn turned away and saw that the fire would catch Halon before he could make it to the road, but to the left there was a nearby stream and some rocks that offered a chance to escape if they were fast enough.

"We'll have to take a detour, Halon. Come on!"

The smell of smoke was carried to them by the wind as sweat slipped from Kestorn's face. Halon's hooves flew through the air as he raced for the stream. The fire consumed the southern side of the field and quickly surged across the section where Kestorn had originally intended to cross to reach the road.

As they approached the stream, Kestorn turned to see the fire racing through the grass just behind Halon's hooves. Only a leap over the water saved them from the flames, and Kestorn quickly urged Halon onto the rocks beyond the stream until it was clear that the fire would not follow them any farther.

Jumping down from Halon's back, Kestorn approached the stream and gathered some water, which he used to wash the oil from Halon's legs.

"Faster than fire, aren't you?" he said as he patted Halon's flank.

Halon tossed his mane and snorted as his eyes watched the fire still burning on the field.

"We won't be so far ahead anymore." Kestorn sighed. "The other riders have a chance to beat us to the final hill now."

He took the reins and led Halon down the rocks to solid ground, but Kestorn could see that they would have to ride around the fire to reach the main road. From their position, he could also see that only part of the field was burning, no doubt the part strategically covered in oil. But surely this was not Lord Atregar's doing. Kestorn looked back for any sign of the other rider and Lord Atregar's horse, but the flames and the smoke were too thick to see them.

Mounting Halon again, Kestorn urged him forward in hopes of reaching the road before the other riders gained more ground.

Derreth stood among the crowd that had gathered to watch the end of the race. He glanced up at the lords seated on a stage where they would have a clear view of the incoming horses and riders. Their flags were positioned near the attendant charged with waving the colors of the lead rider, but in this race, the crowd would not need any help to see who was winning. The final mile was stretched down a barren hillside, and nearly everyone would be able to see who was approaching the dassdir poles.

Feeling a tug on his tunic, Derreth turned to see a messenger boy at his side. The boy held up a piece of parchment to him. *Strange, who would pay to send something to me?* Derreth thought. Still, he accepted the note, and the boy started to leave.

"Wait," Derreth said, catching him by the arm. "Who sent this? And what if I need you to take a message back to them?"

"Someone gave it to my master and said for one of us to deliver it to you during the race. I don't know who it was. I don't think they cared about a reply."

With that, the boy wriggled free and ran off to deliver another message. Derreth unfolded the note and read a message scrawled roughly as if in haste, but the words were still clear.

You'll be next. Even survivors don't last forever.

Shouts from the crowd erupted around Derreth as his hand tightened around the note. Looking up, he saw people pointing at the sky in the distance. Derreth followed their gaze and saw thick smoke coming from the direction of the plains.

Halon breathed heavily as he finally reached the road that dipped down over the gentle slope leading to the dassdir poles. Kestorn had not seen any of the other riders yet, but the place where the coast stretched up the hill was just beyond them. That was where they would appear when they had crossed the length of the coast.

As if summoned by his thoughts, dust arose from the other side of the hill, and the other riders and their horses came into view. Kestorn heard them shout, and he knew that they had seen him, but he continued to focus on guiding Halon down the hill. The crowd and the lords appeared below, waiting for them in the distance.

But the other riders drove their horses right into his path, and against his will, Kestorn found himself surrounded by them. On his left, Molnar laughed as he drew his sword and swung it at Kestorn's neck. Weaving Halon to the right, Kestorn managed to avoid the blade, but Segiro swung a flanged mace that slammed into his shoulder.

Pain swept through his arm before Kestorn felt it grow limp, but he clasped his sword with his other hand and slashed Segiro's leg with it. Cursing him, Segiro pulled his horse back a little, but Arnun had already taken the lead and was blocking Kestorn's escape. He had come from behind and was attempting to win, just as Cidonn had done.

But instead of trying to stop Arnun from winning, Molnar raised his sword and fixed Kestorn with a malicious gaze. Wincing from the pain in his shoulder, Kestorn spurred Halon toward Lord Salistom's white stallion, Razur. If he couldn't get past them and race ahead, Molnar would cut him down.

Arnun saw Kestorn trying to pass him and turned around suddenly, trying to stab Halon with a short-handled spear. Kestorn leapt forward and seized the spear with his good hand. A sudden jolt in the road cost Arnun his control of the weapon, and Kestorn was able to thrust the spear head into Razur's flank instead of allowing it to penetrate Halon's neck.

Not willing to wait any longer, Molnar charged toward them and forced Kestorn away from the lead. Each swing of the sword was closer than the last, and Segiro was riding up from behind, seeking another opportunity to use his mace.

―――

The relief that Derreth had felt in seeing his brother and Halon appear over the hill had been cut short by the sight of the other riders surrounding him. Each one was taking his turn at trying to kill him, and every second seemed to be driving Kestorn closer to death as his hope of escape diminished.

Derreth was at the edge of the crowd as he watched what was happening. He'd never be able to reach Kestorn in time, but still his feet felt as though they might break into a run in an attempt to save his brother.

Gasps from the crowd arose, and Derreth heard the people next to him say something about another rider. Suddenly from the stage, Lord Beristo stood up, grabbed his own flag, and shouted, "Go, Inesca, go!"

Derreth turned and saw a rider on a gray horse appear from the direction of the forest. It was Inesca, all alone, and she was suddenly some distance in front of all of the other riders. The forest had emptied her out onto the last mile ahead of them despite everyone's expectations regarding the obstacles it contained.

Back on the hill, Kestorn was still being attacked by the other riders. Only Arnun noticed that Inesca was ahead of them, and he started to chase after her. But to Derreth's dismay, Molnar and Segiro didn't even seem to care. Kestorn was still their primary target.

༄

Inesca heard some of the crowd cheering for her as Nycor made impressive strides toward the dassdir poles, and it looked like Lord Beristo was waving her on with his own flag. The thrill of winning filled her heart with excitement, and Nycor must have sensed it because he ran with an energy that seemed to match hers.

With a smile on her face, Inesca looked back to see if there was any danger from other riders who might be behind her. A cluster of riders several yards away from her met her gaze, and she recognized Kestorn between them. Molnar raised his sword and slashed at Kestorn's side.

Her breath caught in her throat as Inesca saw them ruthlessly trying to cut Kestorn off his horse. Even from a distance, she observed the pain in his face. Her hands slackened on the reins for a moment as she felt her limbs grow unsteady. Then, a sudden rush of heat and anger coursed through her. Inesca gripped the reins and guided Nycor to a halt before turning him around. With a loud cry, she spurred him up the hill, drawing her short sword from its sheath. She vaguely noticed Arnun riding toward her on the left, but he was too far away to concern her. Her gaze focused on Kestorn and then on Molnar and his sword.

The group of riders began to descend the slope, and Inesca expected Molnar to spot her at any moment. But as Nycor charged toward them, he remained so absorbed in his attack on Kestorn that he failed to see the danger racing toward him. Only in the last second did Molnar turn his head and notice her, but it was not soon enough to deflect Inesca's sword as she plunged it into the left side of his abdomen. The force of Nycor's uphill stride drove her thrust, and the blade sunk deep before she released it. A shocked expression flickered across Molnar's face, and his sword slipped from his hands. Inesca seized it, instead of attempting to withdraw her own blade.

Riding around Halon's flank, she spurred Nycor toward Segiro. Kestorn, although hunched over in the saddle, was still trying to use his sword to block Segiro's mace from slamming into his head. Inesca rode around to the other side of Kestorn's attacker, but Segiro saw her coming and grasped the mace in his other hand before swinging it toward her instead. But his aim was too high, and Inesca ducked as the heavy metal end swept easily over her head.

Kestorn used his sword to strike Segiro in the side when he was distracted, and Inesca used the hilt of Molnar's sword to hit Segiro on the head, knocking him unconscious. Lord Felond's rider slipped from his horse as Inesca rode closer to Kestorn, but she soon realized that Halon was slowing down and Kestorn's face had grown very pale. She moved Nycor alongside Halon, and the red stallion's eyes widened as he recognized this familiar rival.

Urging Nycor back into a gallop, Inesca saw that Halon followed them with a competitive charge. The red stallion even opened his mouth as if he wished to bite Nycor, but Inesca managed to keep her horse away from his teeth.

"Come on, Halon! Come on!" Inesca shouted at the red stallion.

Kestorn still kept his balance on Halon's back, but he seemed to be growing weaker each second. Inesca could only think about what Omaron had told her regarding the rule that all riders had to finish the race or be left to die. If Kestorn couldn't make it past the dassdir poles on his horse or on foot, then he would die of his wounds.

Kestorn's eyes started to close, and he leaned farther forward on his horse.

"No, Kestorn! You must finish the race!" Inesca shouted. "Stay awake! Please, stay awake!"

Inesca turned her gaze away long enough to see that Arnun was still ahead of them, but his horse had been injured. The white stallion had a wound on his flank, and he was favoring his hind leg. If not for his wound, he surely would have finished already. But when Arnun saw them, his face twisted into rage, and he held a bloody short-handled spear ready in his hand.

"Run, Halon! Run!" Inesca shouted again, praying that the red stallion would know what to do. He focused on the dassdir poles now instead of Nycor, as though remembering his training from previous races.

She deviated from Kestorn's side and drove Nycor toward Arnun with Molnar's sword in her hand. Arnun threw the spear at her, but Inesca had pulled herself from the stallion's back and was hanging onto Nycor's saddle and his neck, allowing her to duck down and dodge it. As Nycor charged toward the white stallion with his nostrils flared, Inesca jumped up and flung herself onto Arnun, knocking him from his saddle.

She landed on top of him and recovered faster from the fall, but Arnun quickly seized her sword hand to prevent her from stabbing him. Meanwhile, the wounded white horse shied away from Nycor's challenge as the gray stallion came at him with his hooves and teeth. Arnun twisted the blade from Inesca's hands and shoved her to the side. But as he raised up to use the sword against her, Nycor reared and brought his hooves down on Arnun's head.

Inesca pushed herself up and leapt onto Nycor's back before turning him toward the dassdir poles. She looked up just in time to see Halon run through the poles, but as he did, Kestorn slipped from his back and landed on the ground just beyond them.

Inesca urged Nycor onward as she watched for some sign of movement from Kestorn's bloodied form. But just as she started to reach him, hands jerked her down from Nycor's back and held her still. Nycor turned in confusion and started toward her, but someone seized his reins. Inesca looked back and saw strangers gripping her arms. Someone took Molnar's sword from her and cast it aside.

"Hold her!" Lord Tolem demanded from the stage. "That Eastern wench has broken the rules of the Great Races. She is under arrest."

Inesca looked toward Lord Beristo, but his face was turned away from her.

"Lord Beristo, do you deny that your rider has broken our laws?" Lord Tolem asked. "And has no doubt shamed you by throwing away the victory that would have been yours?"

"But now it's mine," Lord Edgerr demanded as he stepped forward. "My rider finished the race first. So, I've won."

"Only because of this rebel," Lord Tolem said angrily.

"But my rider did nothing to break the rules. Of course, the girl is at fault and should be arrested, but that doesn't change the fact that my rider won."

"He's right," Lord Salistom said calmly. "Lord Edgerr's rider was ... fortunate, but he did not break the rules. Congratulations on your victory."

Lord Edgerr nodded with a smile, but Inesca turned back to Kestorn and observed Derreth kneeling at his brother's side. Derreth turned him over and smoothed the hair back from Kestorn's face. He reached down and lifted Kestorn's hand in his own. Inesca saw Kestorn's fingers move, and a small sense of relief filled her heart.

Derreth leaned down and picked up Kestorn in his arms, even though Kestorn was nearly as big as he was. One of Lord Edgerr's servants came forward to help him, but Derreth would not allow anyone else to touch him. They disappeared into the crowd, and Inesca started to go limp in the arms of her captors.

"Have her taken away," Lord Tolem ordered.

"Wait," a deep voice called from the crowd.

Omaron pushed through to the front with a piece of paper in his hands.

"Do you still keep this one-legged relic in your service, Beristo?" Lord Tolem asked.

"The rules of the Great Races state that a rider may disregard the other rules under one condition," Omaron said.

"Only if that rider has been threatened by one of the others. But you would need proof of such a threat," Lord Tolem insisted.

Omaron held up a note toward the stage. Lord Tolem started to take it, but Omaron snatched it back.

"It is for my lord," he said.

Lord Beristo walked over to Omaron and took the note. Then he showed it to the others. The hastily scrawled words read *You'll be next. Even survivors don't last forever.*

"My trainer is right. She was threatened."

"It was not a threat that made her decide to turn around," Lord Tolem said. "She went back to help Lord Edgerr's rider. We all saw it!"

"This threat filled her with rage and fear," Omaron said. "I tried to help her control it, but the attack at the end of the race caused her to lose control of her actions. She did not know what she was doing."

The lords glanced at each other in silence.

"According to our own laws, she is pardoned because of this," Lord Beristo said as he motioned for the men to release her.

"And you do not wish to punish her for allowing someone else to win?" Lord Tolem asked.

"That is my affair," Lord Beristo said. "I will deal with her. The rest of you have your own riders and horses to tend to or bury."

Omaron grabbed Inesca's arm and led her away as they followed Lord Beristo.

Chapter 25

After water had washed the blood from Kestorn's face and chest, he still looked pale. His right shoulder was broken, and the servants had stitched up two gashes on his chest from Molnar's sword. His face and body were bruised, but he was alive.

Derreth sat beside his brother's bed, holding the green and gold cloth wrapped around the small wooden knight. His thoughts continually drifted back to the race. He had never seen other riders work together to ambush another, especially at the risk of giving up the chance to win. On the other hand, he had never seen another rider turn around and ride back to help another with all the lords and the crowd watching. The penalty was too great, and why should a rider care if one of the others was killed?

Drawing the cloth back, Derreth ran his thumb over the helmet covering the knight's face. *He was killed in battle. One of the survivors saw it and testified to his courage. Everyone said my father had died a hero. Now a foreigner claims it's all a lie, but she must be mistaken. And yet she must believe it, or she never would have ridden back to help Kestorn.*

Kestorn groaned, and Derreth lifted his gaze to his brother. He leaned closer as Kestorn's eyes opened and his mouth twisted downward with an expression of pain.

"Why am I not dead?" he asked.

Derreth smiled a bit at Kestorn's surprise.

"Halon carried you through the dassdir poles. How do you feel?"

"Awful. My shoulder …"

"The bones are broken. And it didn't help when you landed on it after you fell off Halon."

"It feels like I fell on my head."

"You might have done that too. But I have some good news for you. You won."

"What?"

"You won the race, Kes."

"No, I didn't," Kestorn scoffed.

"I don't think you're the one who gets to decide that."

"But I couldn't have won. I don't even remember anything except Molnar and Segiro trying to kill me. And that other rider ... Arnun."

"So, you didn't see her?"

"See who?"

"Inesca. She, well ... she helped you. Once you were away from the other riders, Halon did the rest."

"Is she all right?"

Derreth paused for a minute. "She will be," he finally said.

"And what about Halon?"

"Barely a scratch on him. He'll be fine. Here, drink this. It will help you sleep and not think about the pain."

Derreth helped Kestorn lift his head enough to drink the contents of a wooden cup. The physician had left some snibir herbs that Derreth could crush and mix with wine to help Kestorn rest while his shoulder started to heal. After draining the liquid, Kestorn lay down and closed his eyes again, suddenly looking very tired. Derreth drew a blanket over him.

"Get some rest. I'll check on Halon for you."

"And about Inesca," Kestorn said, opening his eyes again. "Are you certain she'll be fine? She could get in trouble for helping me if the lords saw it."

Everyone saw it, Derreth thought to himself.

"You don't need to worry about her, Kestorn."

Kestorn started to close his eyes again.

"You should have seen what she gave me, Derreth. Some odd gift ... not sure it was much of a good luck charm."

Derreth tightened his grip on the wooden knight.

"Did she tell you where she found it?"

"No. She said I might find someone it belonged to. Strange, huh?"

Kestorn drifted off into sleep before he could receive an answer, and Derreth continued to study the wooden knight with its faded paint and singed condition.

"More than you know," he said under his breath as he left his brother to rest.

Inesca sat on the ground outside Lord Beristo's tent with guards standing nearby. In addition to making sure she didn't try to leave, they seemed to be waiting to see what would happen to her. Nycor leaned down and nudged her shoulder.

"For your sake, I'm sorry I had to ask you to do more than race today," she said as she reached up and stroked his neck. "But you were very brave, my friend. Thank you for your help."

Nycor blew air onto her face and let her hold onto his nose. A tear slipped down her face as Inesca could not ignore the warning of what was coming. Omaron had been inside Lord Beristo's tent for what felt like hours. She wasn't sure what they were saying, but it was unlikely that either of them would be able to trust her to race as they wanted her to after this.

Suddenly, light spilled onto the grass as the tent flap opened, and Omaron appeared. He motioned for her to enter, and Inesca pushed herself up off the ground. Taking a deep breath, she walked inside and stood before Lord Beristo, who was leaning with his hand on the table.

"I want to hear it from your own mouth," he said. "I want to hear why you ruined our chances of winning this race."

"I couldn't let them kill him, my lord."

"Why not? He's not the only rider ever to have been attacked in a race."

Inesca glanced at Omaron, but he was staring straight ahead.

"But he was the only rider in this race who was my brother."

Lord Beristo looked from Inesca to Omaron.

"That's not possible."

"I must disagree, my lord. I don't understand all of it, but the man that you spoke of, the rider, Arryn of Fortur. He was my father too."

Lord Beristo ran his hand through his hair.

"Did you know about this?" he asked turning to Omaron.

"I knew."

"And you just let her continue to think that she could treat him like her brother?"

"He told me what would happen, my lord. It was my choice," Inesca said.

Lord Beristo was silent for a few minutes as he walked through his tent.

"And this is my choice. You will leave my service at once, but your horse shall remain with me. Our deal was that you could keep him only as long as you rode for me. Today, you stopped riding for me, and you rode for someone else."

Inesca felt a heavy weight settle over her chest.

"I did not wish to fail you."

Lord Beristo motioned for Omaron to open the tent.

"Get her out of here."

Inesca found herself thrust out into the cool night air. Two of the guards were already leading Nycor away, but he was nervous and struggling. Inesca started to go to him, but Omaron held her back.

"Just let me have another minute to say goodbye."

"It's too late for that now."

He pulled her in the other direction until they came to the road that the supply wagons used when traveling through the camp.

"You are the most ungrateful rider I have ever trained, but this time you must obey me without breaking my trust."

A wagon appeared in the night. It slowed as it approached them.

"Climb into the back. This trader is going to the realm of Trineth. He will take you to a woman named Joviann, and she will give you shelter for a time."

Inesca studied the wagon with an uncertain gaze.

"Did you regain a weapon after the race?" he asked.

She shook her head, and Omaron seized her hand and placed something hard and cold into it. Inesca looked down and saw a dagger lying in her palm.

"You are not out of danger yet," Omaron said, pulling her attention back to his face. "Do not go looking for Derreth or for Kestorn. You must stay away from us and stay away from them. This is the final command I give as your trainer."

Omaron looked away as if he had heard something, and then he thrust her toward the wagon.

"Hide yourself."

Inesca climbed behind some barrels, and Omaron pulled a large cloth over the back of the wagon. The wagon jolted as it began to move, and from under the edge of the cloth, Inesca caught a glimpse of Omaron moving away with the aid of his staff.

A hundred miles away from the western coast of Lord Atregar's realm, a few riders in black rode into a grove of trees. A sliver of the moon cut into the night sky like the edge of a curved blade, and a cloaked figure moved under the trees as the riders approached.

"Why have I been called to Farcost?" the cloaked figure asked as the two riders dismounted.

One of them drew out a letter and handed it to him. It bore a round seal, but the mark was plain and signified nothing except that its author had no wish to identify himself.

"Here is a message from the master. Two riders are dead, and another is wounded after the last race."

"Was that not the plan all along? Though, if I had been given more time …"

"The riders who died were meant to live, and the ones who lived were intended for death," the other rider said.

"How?"

"An Eastern girl. Lord Beristo's rider."

The cloaked man listened in silence.

"For three days, we have hunted for her. Her horse remains with Lord Beristo, but there has been no sign of her."

"And you believe she is heading east toward Trineth? I see. Then I will look for her on my way there."

The cloaked man turned and began to leave them, but one of the others mounted his horse and rode in front of him.

"She must not interfere again."

"Is there a reason why you expect her to do so?"

"No one knows how she became involved in the first place. Who is to say she won't appear again?"

"Well, if she does, I will take care of this nuisance."

Looking at each other in silence, the two men in black turned their horses around and rode back to the west.

Chapter 26

The smell of bread wafted through the air, waking Inesca from her sleep. The thin straw mattress rustled beneath her as she sat up and stretched her sore back. The small wooden room was cloaked in darkness without a single window to let her know that it was morning.

It's not much, but people who are just grateful to be alive usually don't care how big a room is. And you must be in some trouble, or they wouldn't have sent you here. Joviann's words came back to Inesca's mind in the dark. *You can have the room and meals for two weeks. After that, you'll have to go.*

But go where? It had taken her three weeks to reach the town of Bartrir and Joviann's inn. And now, a week and a half had passed. Still, Inesca didn't know what she would do when she ran out of time. Not that hiding here in a room by herself had been wonderful, but Inesca had been trying to sort through her options. She could try to get back to the East Province. But the town of Bartrir was hundreds of miles away from the border, and if she was caught by anyone on the way, then she risked slavery, imprisonment, or death. Yet even if she did reach the East Province, what would she have there? A chance to go to the mill again?

Trying to stay in the Six Realms didn't offer better opportunities. She might end up a slave here. And she couldn't expect Derreth or Kestorn, if he was even alive, to help her. She knew she couldn't go to them. But she had thought of one person she might turn to, if she could find him. Sir Coltar of Monterr was still out there, and that's who her father had wanted her to go to. *If only I knew how to get to him.*

Her stomach rumbled in hunger, and Inesca rose from the floor in search of Joviann and her breakfast. Outside her room was a small ladder that led to a hallway on the second level of Joviann's inn. She climbed down and made her way to the end of the hall where a railing stood a set of stairs. Inesca leaned over the wooden rail and saw men dressed in fine clothes gathered around the tables below, shouting orders for food and drinks at Joviann's four sons.

Suddenly, a hand seized her arm, and Inesca turned quickly as she pulled her arm away.

"Now's a fine time for you to be coming down from the loft," Joviann huffed as she looked Inesca up and down. "If one of those men was to look up here and see a lone girl hanging over the rail, they'd get the wrong idea about the type of inn I run."

Inesca frowned, but she pushed past the comment.

"Could I go down to the kitchen?"

"Not that again. I'll never get my work done if you create another mess by trying to help with the cooking."

"I just need to get out of that room for a while."

"You can step outside through the back door. My youngest is out there with the goat. Just don't distract him too much from his work. And don't try to help!"

Joviann disappeared down the hallway, and Inesca slipped down the steps and hurried through the back door before anyone noticed her. The light hurt her eyes for a moment as she walked toward Eimon, a ten-year-old boy with dark eyes and a quiet personality. He sat on a wooden stool, milking the goat without acknowledging her.

"Good morning, Eimon," Inesca said hesitantly. "The inn is very busy for this time of day."

He said nothing to her as he continued to focus on his work.

"Could you tell me who the guests are?"

"A few knights and their men. Nothing but more work for me today. I must go to the stable later this morning and help tend to their horses."

Inesca remembered Joviann telling her that Eimon also worked for the owner of the stable to help earn some additional money for his family.

"What would you rather be doing?"

After a moment, he paused and pulled a piece of paper from his tunic. Inesca unfolded it and saw a skilled sketch of a Naldorr buck.

"This is very good. Where did you see this buck?"

"There's a forest not far outside of town. Since Trineth is so near the Naldorr Forest north of the Six Realms, bucks like this often roam through our land. When I am older, I'm going to hunt one just like the buck in my sketch."

"Perhaps these guests will leave soon, and then you'll have more time for sketching."

"They will. All the knights are going to Morret. I heard one of them talking about a summons from the Royal Council, demanding that the knights meet with a representative from the Council. Something about trouble from the Raegond."

"Where is Morret?" Inesca asked eagerly.

"Why do you want to know?"

"It sounds like I will need to go there to find someone I am looking for."

"It's not far. Two days journey south of here."

Inesca thanked him and slipped back inside the inn. Hurrying up the stairs and back to her room, she forgot about breakfast, but immediately started making plans for her departure.

The city of Morret was a bustling center of trade for merchants within the realm of Trineth. It had grown in size ever since the lavish knight known as Sir Bercorr had made his home within its walls. Having been rewarded for his past services to the Royal Council, Bercorr had a fortune that he used to buy the rarest and most beautiful wares that merchants could offer him.

All the knights had been invited to his manor at the northern edge of the city for their gathering. With their arrivals, merchants had also flocked to Morret, knowing that knights often carried money to spare, more so than most lords.

Among these was Gorben of Trineth, returning to the realm of his birth and of his family. His wife, Salell, and daughter, Laisi, remained near his booth to help him with his business. They were kept busy by the large crowds in the street, seeking the best goods that the competing merchants had to offer.

But suddenly through the chattering of the crowd, a loud voice began calling out as one of Sir Bercorr's men, a large brute named Durokos, pushed his way through the street.

"Stop that slave! She's a runaway!"

Inesca darted through the throngs of customers around the carts and booths of merchants. Surrounded by strangers, she paused only long enough to determine which direction she should take. A rough grip seized her shoulder as a man caught her trying to run past him.

"Here, I've got her for you."

Reaching into her belt, Inesca pulled her dagger from its sheath. A shallow cut to the hand was all it took for the man to release her with a cry of surprise. Stumbling through more people, Inesca tripped over someone's foot and landed on top of a basket containing fine cloth from the realm of Fortur. The fabric spilled onto the ground with Inesca, and she saw the shocked and angry face of the merchant to whom it belonged.

"Not in the dirt!" he said as his hands tried to seize it from underneath her.

Inesca moved to get up, but the fabric was wrapped around her legs.

"Father, what's wrong?"

A young woman appeared to help him but stopped when she recognized a familiar face.

"Inesca?" Laisi said.

Opening her mouth to speak, Inesca tried to think of how she could explain, but a hand seized her cloak and pulled her off the ground.

"There you are! You must be new as you do not know what Sir Bercorr does with his troublesome slaves."

"I'm not his slave!"

"You're his. Or else you'd have some other master to claim you, but you'll wish you weren't his slave when he's done."

He started to pull her away, but Gorben stepped in front of him.

"I'll have to speak with your master about this cloth that his slave has ruined. He'll have to pay for my losses."

"Sir Bercorr doesn't have time for your muddy rags. If you had stopped this troublemaker sooner, she might not have trampled your goods."

Inesca tried to pull herself from his grasp as the merchant argued for compensation, and then another figure pushed himself into the fray.

"Wait! That's not Sir Bercorr's slave."

Inesca turned her gaze to the new speaker and saw a most familiar face beside the merchant and his daughter. Kestorn looked well-recovered from his injuries, but he was wearing a blue cloak trimmed with Naldorr wolf fur, a piece of fashion far too expensive for any rider. But as she glanced down, Inesca noticed the old boots and plain breeches that Kestorn was wearing.

"How do you know this isn't his slave?" Durokos asked impatiently.

Kestorn continued to stare at Durokos with an unwavering gaze.

"Because she is mine. Shouldn't I know my own slave?"

Turning to the merchant, Kestorn placed his hand on the man's shoulder.

"I will settle the cost of the fabric." Then he looked back at Durokos. "But first, you must release my slave."

"Not until I get some clear answers. Who are you? And if this is your slave, what was she doing in Sir Bercorr's home?"

"I am a friend to the representative of the Royal Council. I traveled here with him, and the reason my slave was in your master's home is because I sent her to deliver a message to him."

Durokos's skepticism seemed to fade as he released Inesca, and she quickly moved to Kestorn's side.

"Then you have my apology for the trouble, but I wish your slave had said as much instead of taking off like a bolt of lightning."

"I tried …," Inesca started to protest, but Kestorn elbowed her.

"She's new and still requires some training."

"I can see that," Durokos said gruffly.

Suddenly the crowd began to part as travelers on horseback rode toward the city's gate on their way out of Morret. A carriage with gold trim followed them.

"There is your friend, the representative, now," Durokos said. "I will let them know that you are here."

As he left them to get the attention of the travelers, Kestorn pulled off the robe and tossed it onto a cart behind him. He grabbed Inesca's arm and dashed through the crowd. Those who had overheard the exchange between him and Durokos laughed as Kestorn made his escape. Durokos heard the laughter and turned to see that the fair-headed young man and the Eastern girl were gone.

Inesca heard his shouts in the distance, but Kestorn pulled her through an open shop, down another street, and behind a stable until they were a safe distance away. Once she had caught her breath, Inesca smiled and let out a short, scornful laugh.

"I told you not to call me a slave again. And why did you assume that would work?" she said.

"There are no Easterners this far west in the Six Realms unless they have lost their freedom. I had to give him some kind of excuse, or he would have dragged you back to become a slave in Bercorr's manor."

Inesca felt the color rush into her face as she stopped to consider what had nearly happened.

"Fine, I'll say thank you if that's what you want to hear. I am grateful for your help, but what are you doing here?"

"I've been traveling with Laisi and her father for over a week now. And what about you? Still causing trouble?"

Inesca sighed. "I don't ask for it," she said.

"Well, wandering from Lord Beristo's side is an odd way of avoiding it."

"Wandering?"

"Why aren't you with him at the camp near Bartrir?" Kestorn asked.

"Bartrir?" Inesca repeated. "The lords are here in this realm?"

Kestorn shot her a strange look with one eyebrow raised.

"At the end of the racing season, one lord must host the others in his realm. The lords come to be entertained, and they bring their riders and horses to compete in small contests. This year, it was Lord Edgerr's turn to bring them to Trineth."

"Then why are you not there?" Inesca asked.

Raised voices from the nearby street caused Kestorn to pause. He motioned for her to quietly follow him. They crept around the edge of the stable and stopped. Inesca saw a man being thrown out of a shop as some of the armed men of Morret surrounded him. Strange black statues were thrown on the ground near him.

"What is going on?" Inesca asked softly.

"I have not seen anything like this since I was a boy," Kestorn said as he stared at the statues. "Those are idols of the Calavi, a cult that began in Evalisca and was carried to Rynar by some of the Evaliscans that followed the original six lords here. But anything related to the cult is forbidden in Rynar. The last king demanded that it never be tolerated here."

"I've never heard of them."

"Well, they're not supposed to exist anymore, and it's not hard to see why the king forbade their presence in Rynar if you've heard the rumors about them."

"What do the rumors say?"

"That they worshipped evil spirits who crave blood spilled in dark deeds like murder and treachery. They had all sorts of dark rituals. That's why they were even hunted down in Evalisca and supposedly destroyed. But the king of Rynar feared the survivors might try to come here. Fortunately, it seems he prevented that, but sometimes their books and idols are sold as items of interest—but only by those who are willing to defy the laws of the Royal Council."

"What will happen to him?" Inesca asked as she watched the man being led away after his merchandise had been thrown into a sack.

"The punishment for selling or owning anything connected with the Calavi is death. That's how much the last king of Rynar despised it."

"Why would anyone risk death to sell statues? And who would buy them?"

Kestorn shrugged.

"In most cases, I would say he was after the money. But as you said, who would buy them?"

Leading her out into the street, Kestorn took her to a house where a servant opened the door for them and let them inside. Kestorn led her up to a room on the second floor where they could talk privately.

"This is the home of Laisi's father. We'll be safe here."

"I still don't understand why you are not with Lord Edgerr," Inesca said.

Kestorn leaned against the nearest wall and stared out a window to his right.

"I'm not a rider anymore."

"What happened? Are you still hurt?"

"My shoulder is not yet fully healed, but I can still ride. I wasn't given a choice about the races, though. Derreth convinced Lord Edgerr that too many of the other lords and riders would want me dead after what happened, so he gave me permission to leave his service."

"Then you are free now?"

"Yes, I'm free," Kestorn said as his brows furrowed. "If that's what you want to call it."

Inesca glanced out the window and saw Laisi walking toward the house with her father and mother.

"But you have Laisi," Inesca said. "That means something to you, doesn't it?"

Kestorn's expression softened.

"It does, but I realize now that I never wanted to stop being a rider. I always hoped that Lord Edgerr would give me more freedom and yet continue to allow me to race for him."

Inesca's gaze studied his eyes and the lines on his face. He didn't seem as young as he had before. After a few seconds, he caught her staring, and she looked away.

Kestorn rubbed the back of his neck.

"I suppose I should thank you for what you did at the race."

Inesca shrugged. "Well, we're even now," she said.

"Maybe so, but you haven't said why you helped me, why you risked your own life in challenging Molnar, Segiro, and Arnun and in almost being arrested. I don't remember much about the end of the race, but Derreth told me what happened."

"What else did he tell you?" Inesca asked.

Kestorn paused.

"What else am I supposed to know?"

The sound of the door being opened below them drew their attention to the stairs leading down to the main floor.

"Look, I'm here because I will soon ask for Laisi's hand in marriage," Kestorn told her. "So, if you had any idea that we ..."

Inesca groaned as she realized what he was going to say.

"No, it was never anything like that."

Kestorn stared back at her with some confusion. "You are certain?" he asked.

"I am."

He frowned as he noticed her lack of hesitation.

"You don't have to say it like that," he huffed. "I only asked because it's common enough for girls to take an interest in me."

Inesca failed to hide the curt laugh that escaped her mouth before she forced a cough. "Can't we drop the subject?" she asked.

Kestorn still appeared dissatisfied.

"So, in the race in Farcost, you risked everything to turn around and help someone who meant nothing to you?"

Inesca shifted restlessly before him. *Why couldn't Derreth have told him?* she wondered.

"Isn't it possible for someone to care about you without those kinds of feelings?"

"You mean as a friend?"

"Yes," she said quickly, seizing upon his response. "As a friend."

"You have an odd way of choosing friends," he said. "We were supposed to be rivals. And I still don't understand how you confused those two things."

Inesca lifted her chin.

"I didn't confuse them, but I made the right choice."

Kestorn relented with an amused smile and a chuckle.

"Well, I'll never understand where this sense of confidence you have in me comes from, but it's flattering."

Maybe someday you will, Inesca thought. *If I ever find the right time to tell you.* At that moment, Laisi appeared with her father, who looked none too pleased with Inesca.

"Start explaining what happened down there," he said, looking from Inesca to Kestorn.

Laisi cut in first. I tried to tell you, Father. This is Lord Beristo's rider. We saw her race in Sassot, remember? And she helped Kestorn in Farcost."

"Then you're not a slave?"

"No, sir," Inesca said. "I'm sorry about your cloth. I don't have any money to pay for it, but if there's something else …"

"Don't concern yourself with it. It's not as ruined as I made it out to be, but it seemed like a good chance to make a profit."

"And you were very helpful as a distraction, Father," Laisi said with a smile.

"Well, I can play a part when I have to. But if you're not a slave, then why did Durokos believe you were?"

"I slipped into Bercorr's manor and tried to pass as one of his slaves to find someone, but he wasn't there. And then when I tried to leave, well, they weren't ready to let me go."

"Who were you looking for?" Kestorn asked.

"I've been seeking Sir Coltar of Monterr, but every attempt I make to find him has turned out worse than the last. I'm beginning to doubt that he is anything but a phantom."

"Why would you be looking for him? You should be with Lord Beristo. I can't see him being pleased with his rider chasing after a knight from another realm," Kestorn said.

"It doesn't really matter anymore." Inesca sighed. "Like you, I am no longer a rider."

"What happened?" Laisi asked.

Inesca dared to glance at Kestorn, and she saw that he already understood.

"You were dismissed, weren't you? Because you rode back to help me."

Inesca nodded.

"You should not have interfered. You could have been arrested for breaking the rules of the race."

"It was my choice, and I do not regret it," she said.

"But why were you looking for Sir Coltar of Monterr?" Gorben asked.

Inesca hesitated and looked away, twisting a loose thread from her left sleeve in her fingers.

"I-I think he knew my father. I hoped to ask him some questions."

"Who was your father?" Gorben asked.

Inesca coughed and cleared her throat. "Could I trouble you for some water?" she asked. "I haven't had any all day."

Laisi put her hand on Inesca's shoulder.

"No more questions, Father. She looks exhausted, and we can at least offer her something to drink and eat and a chance to rest."

Inesca shot Laisi a grateful look even though she doubted Laisi knew the real reason for her discomfort.

"I'll send word to Derreth to let him know you're here," Kestorn said as he started to leave them. "He'll want to know."

The mention of Derreth's name sent another wave of uneasiness through Inesca. They had not spoken since before the race in Farcost, and he had been furious with her then. She hoped that her actions had since changed his mind.

Chapter 27

After receiving permission from Lord Edgerr to travel to see his brother, Derreth borrowed a spare horse and rode to Morret. The city was no longer as crowded as it had been only a week before. The knights had finished their meeting and dispersed across the Six Realms to search for the Raegond, which the Royal Council had deemed a threat that needed to be extinguished.

When he arrived at the house near the edge of the city, Derreth knocked at the door and stepped back. Glancing up at one of the windows on the second level, he caught a glimpse of a small figure with long hair who then seemed to vanish. But the color of the hair wasn't right for Laisi. Maybe it was one of the servants.

"Derreth," Gorben said as he opened the door with a warm smile. "We hoped to see you before long."

"Thank you for allowing my brother to stay with your family," Derreth said as he entered.

Shutting the door behind him, Gorben clapped him on the shoulder.

"We've enjoyed having him."

"Are you sure?"

Gorben laughed. "Yes," he said, "and now that you are here, it will be even better."

"Regretfully, I can't stay long."

At that moment, Kestorn and Laisi walked into the room. Derreth stepped closer to take a better look at Kestorn.

"You look good, Kes. How's your shoulder?"

"Still hurts, but I can move my arm more than I used to. We were planning to come to Bartrir and watch the festivities."

"I feared as much, so I came to stop you. It won't be safe for you to come and see me until after the other lords have returned to their realms. You still have enemies in their camps."

"But you don't?"

Derreth's brow furrowed, but his frown faded as he turned to Laisi.

"Forgive my manners, Laisi. I hope my brother has not been too much trouble for you and your father."

Laisi smiled warmly as she glanced at Kestorn.

"I think my father is enjoying his help … as am I, but we gained another pair of hands when Inesca joined us about a week ago."

"Inesca?"

Derreth's gaze swept back to his brother with a wary gleam in his eyes, and yet nothing in Kestorn's expression or behavior indicated that Inesca had told him anything.

"I sent you a message. Didn't you get it?" Kestorn asked.

"No. I must have left before it arrived," Derreth said as his tone grew more solemn.

"She's resting upstairs," Laisi said. "Father says she works harder than any of his hired men."

"But not harder than me," Kestorn said with a grin.

"Kestorn, everyone works harder than you, even when you're not injured," Laisi said with a smile.

Derreth stepped around them as Kestorn started to protest. His eyes turned to the stairs, and as he started to climb them, a combination of hesitation and impatience caused his boots to move at an uneven pace.

On the second level, he saw that there was only one room with the door slightly closed. Carefully, he pushed it open with his hand until he could see Inesca sitting beside the window. She wore a plain white shirt and a brown skirt, no longer the bright and fine garments of a rider.

Daring to get closer, Derreth opened the door far enough for him to step inside the room. The door creaked as it swung wide, and Inesca turned around.

"Derreth?"

He tensed at the hopeful tone in her voice.

"Laisi told me you were resting. I should not have bothered you."

As he moved to leave, she stood up and walked after him.

"Bother me as much as you want. I'd prefer that over being ignored."

Derreth stopped though the reluctance in his expression was clear.

"Is the racing season finished?" Inesca asked.

"The races are, but the lords are still gathered near Bartrir. They plan to hold some more competitions next week. They're not finished making bets and winning prizes."

"Kestorn mentioned the competitions too, but I don't understand. These aren't races?"

"No. They're more like jousts."

"Do you joust?" Inesca asked.

"Some," Derreth answered shortly.

A moment of silence passed between them as Derreth seemed to waver between leaving the room and staying a bit longer.

"What are you doing here?" he asked.

Inesca frowned at the slight accusatory edge to his voice.

"I was traveling through the city on my own business. Meeting Kestorn again was not something I had planned, but after he learned that I had been dismissed, he insisted that I stay here for a while."

"Morret is a little out of the way for someone returning to the East Province, isn't it?"

"I'm not going back east," Inesca said.

A short, scornful huff indicated Derreth's surprise and disapproval.

"You can't stay in Rynar. If any of the other lords or riders find you, they will not spare you. And as for those who don't recognize you, they will treat you like a slave."

"I know that well enough. But if it's my stay in this house that bothers you, then don't let it concern you. I can depart in a few days if you wish."

Shaking his head, Derreth moved away from the door and took a step closer to her.

"I did not come up here to chase you away. I will always be grateful for what you did for Kestorn. You should know that much."

"Well, you turned back for me," Inesca said.

"That's not why you went back for Kestorn though."

"No, I suppose it's not."

Inesca dared to lift her blue eyes to search his face.

"Do you believe me now? I mean about our …"

"Don't say it," Derreth said quickly.

She winced at his sharp tone.

"The way you speak of this man makes it sound as if he is dead. Is he?" Derreth asked.

Lowering her gaze, Inesca felt the pain of her father's loss renewed in her heart.

"He is, but his death is still too near for me. Just four months ago."

She glanced at Derreth again and saw that his expression had not softened.

"Death is always too near. You may say otherwise, but my father died twenty years ago, and the pain of it still lingers in me."

"And you do not wish to add to your pain the shame that I would bring to your family," Inesca said as she watched him.

"It is not because you are an Easterner that I refuse to believe you. It is what you are asking me to accept."

"And what is that?"

"If your father was also mine, then he didn't die in the war. He crept off like a coward, leaving Kestorn and me to starve without anyone to help us. I once thought my father's death in battle was hard enough to bear, but the thought of a father who abandoned us is far worse."

"I don't believe he stayed in the East Province because he wanted to," Inesca said. "I saw him stand up to a cruel sheriff and his men countless times. He wasn't a coward, and he wouldn't have left the Six Realms unless he thought he was protecting you."

"If that's true, he still failed. I've spent my life trying to protect Kestorn, and now every rider in the Six Realms is being hunted down and massacred. We wouldn't even be riders if he had been here for us."

The resentment in his tone silenced Inesca for a moment. She hadn't realized being a rider troubled Derreth so much.

"What would you have been?" she asked.

"Maybe a knight. But young men are never accepted by the Royal Council to receive training or an education without a father or a guardian to support them."

"I find it impossible to believe that my father would leave you without a guardian. He would have wanted to know that his sons had someone to rely on."

"Well, that is not what happened," Derreth said coldly. "And how do you know that you haven't made a mistake? Perhaps your father was not who you think he is. He could have been a different man from Rynar."

"One who looks like you?" Inesca asked. "Or perhaps you have other relatives wandering through the East Province?"

Derreth's eyes narrowed as he turned and walked out of the room. Inesca chided herself inwardly for her harsh remark.

"I shouldn't have said that. I'm sorry," she said as she followed him toward the stairs.

"Don't say anything to Kestorn. Whether I choose to tell him about your wild theory or not is my affair. Agreed?"

"It's not a theory. It's the truth, but I won't say anything about it to him. At least not until I understand what happened to my father here."

"And what if you find out that he's not who you think he is? What if he was a criminal? Or what if he's not connected to us? You may have given up everything you had for a couple of strangers."

"I couldn't regret helping Kestorn even if what you say is the truth. But it's not."

Derreth paused, though his gaze did not turn to look at her. After a moment, his feet began to carry him down the stairs.

"Wait," Inesca said as she moved to his side. "For so long, I have wanted to ask about your mother. Will you tell me who she was? And what happened to her?"

He paused again.

"Her name was Elacia. I was seven when she died, but I remember that she used to sing to me and my brother when we were children. And her hair was the same color as Kestorn's, but her eyes were brown like mine."

Inesca thought of her father and how he had tried to sing to her as a child. His singing had always been rough and unsteady, but still it had calmed her whenever she was afraid. She wondered if he had heard his first wife sing those same songs to his sons, but it had been so long that Inesca couldn't remember any of them.

"She died a year before the Battle of Tortesra when a plague swept through Trineth," Derreth continued. "It was very difficult for my father to bear. No doubt I was naïve as a child, but I felt certain that my father would never marry another woman and that he would always remember her."

The edge of accusation in his tone caused Inesca to take a step back. Her hand touched the cord around her neck from which the ring hung under her tunic, but if she revealed it to him now, would Derreth not be even angrier to find her with the ring that probably belonged to his mother?

"I do not believe that he forgot her ... or you and your brother."

"But he never came back, did he? And if you are right about my father, I guess he found a way to avoid being lonely."

Derreth pressed on down the steps before she could speak again, and Inesca felt a mix of anger and doubt well up in her heart. It pained her to hear her father and mother being spoken of in such a way, but Derreth's doubts made sense. If she had been in his place, would she not have felt the same? A heavy weight settled on her emotions as questions about her father's reasons stirred in her thoughts.

A few days after Derreth's departure, life in the home of Gorben and his family seemed to return to normal. The uneasiness Inesca felt in being near Derreth faded, and in his absence, she grew more at ease around Kestorn. Laisi and her family graciously treated her as a worthy friend, and she liked helping them in any way that she could.

With some time to spare one morning, Inesca wandered down to the stable after completing a few chores. She enjoyed being around the horses, but it also caused her to miss Nycor. Laisi's father owned only mares and geldings, all with temperaments that were well suited for a merchant, but none of them were spirited and bold like Inesca's gray stallion.

As she entered the stable, Inesca grabbed a couple handfuls of oats and put them in a bag before offering it to Poleg, a sweet gelding, who was often overlooked because he was quieter than the other horses. Nickering softly, Poleg moved closer and accepted her gift.

"I wouldn't have thought he was your type."

Inesca turned and saw Kestorn watching her from one of the other stalls with a brush in his hand.

"And here I thought I was alone," Inesca said with a smile. "You're not usually quiet enough to surprise me like that."

"Oh, so you're telling me to leave," Kestorn teased as he walked out of the stall and set the brush on a shelf.

"Do what you want. I only came here to be around the horses." Poleg finished his treat, and Inesca smiled as she drew the feed bag away. "I guess this is what I'm used to."

"But it's not the same, is it?"

Inesca glanced at his face and saw that he was serious now.

"No, it's not the same. None of these are my horse."

Taking the pitchfork, Kestorn started moving fresh hay into one of the empty stalls that had been cleaned out.

"It's probably hard for you not to think of Halon, isn't it?" Inesca asked.

"It is, but what's even harder is having spent your life training for something that you can no longer do. I worked hard to become a great rider and to train Halon. None of that matters now."

Poleg nickered again, and Inesca scratched the base of his neck.

"I would like to have raced Halon against your stallion," Kestorn said as he paused and looked back at her. "No weapons, no tricks. Just racing."

Inesca nodded as she stepped away from the gelding. "I would have enjoyed that."

She thought of what Nycor might be enduring without her. Were they trying to force him to accept Jirro as a rider? And how was he being treated?

"My stallion, Nycor, was born to be a racehorse, but he deserved someone more dedicated and more skilled than me."

"I heard that you and that stallion came to Lord Beristo together. That's unusual for most riders and their horses."

"Nycor was my father's horse, and my father meant for him to be mine. But that's not how the rest of the world saw it."

Kestorn stopped pitching hay and put the pitchfork back against the wall.

"Do you ever think of going back to the East Province?"

"No. I don't have anything to go back to, but what about you? What will you do?"

"Stay and work for Laisi's father. I think he plans for me to take over for him someday. Can you see me as a merchant?"

Inesca smiled faintly, but the truth was that she couldn't.

"Maybe someday you'll become wealthy enough to buy some horses. You could become a trainer or a breeder. I can imagine you selling horses, but perhaps not satin and spices."

Kestorn patted the neck of one of the mares as he glanced at the other horses in the stable.

"I hadn't thought about becoming a trainer. What made you think of it?"

"My father bred, raised, and even trained horses. He loved working with them, and I've always thought that you should do something you love if you can."

"So, what will you do now that you're not a rider anymore?"

"I still think I ought to try to speak to Sir Coltar of Monterr."

"You don't give up easily, do you? Are you sure he's worth the trouble it would take you to get to him?"

"Why? Do you know him?"

"No, but knights only socialize with other knights or with lords. What makes you think that he would talk to you?"

"I have to try. It's been kind of Laisi and her father to let me stay here, but I can't expect them to let me live with them forever. And after everything that has happened, this Sir Coltar is all that I have left."

"Then I hope he is able to help you. If you ever need a place to stay again, come back to us."

"Thank you, Kestorn. I'm glad to have you as a friend."

"You didn't give me much choice in the matter," he said with a smile. "Aren't you obligated to be someone's friend after that person saves your life?"

Inesca tossed some oats at him, but he managed to dodge most of them with a triumphant laugh. Then Kestorn flung some hay in her direction.

At that moment, Laisi appeared in the doorway to the stable. Kestorn straightened up, and Inesca brushed the hay from her clothes as best she could. Laisi did not smile as she entered and saw bits of hay in Inesca's hair.

"I just came to tell you that Hairum has been delayed in his errand for father, and he won't be able to deliver your letter to Derreth."

"I'll have to deliver it, then," Kestorn said as he started to accept the letter in her hand, but then Laisi quickly pulled it away.

"But Derreth doesn't want you to go near that camp while the lords are there. You could be attacked by one of their men."

"Laisi, that letter contains important news from the other realms from a trader that Derreth asked me to talk to before he left. I promised that I would send it to him."

"But not to deliver it yourself. It's too dangerous, Kestorn."

Inesca cleared her throat. "I'll take it to him" she said.

They turned to look at her, and Laisi appeared relieved for a moment. However, Kestorn spoke up quickly. "It would be just as dangerous for you."

"So, you are admitting that it is dangerous and that Laisi has a reason to not want you to go?" Inesca asked.

Kestorn sighed. "It's my message. I should be the one to take it to him."

"But you already promised Laisi and her father that you would help them on their journey to Nantos," Inesca reminded him. "They need you here. And no one is expecting me to be there, so they won't be looking for me."

"If you're certain that you want to do it," Laisi said as she held out the letter.

Inesca took the letter before Kestorn could protest.

"I am more than certain. It'll be a way for me to repay all of you. Can I borrow one of your horses though for the journey?"

Laisi nodded.

"I'll leave tomorrow morning, then," Inesca said as she walked out of the stable.

Kestorn frowned as he watched her go. "I do not think this is a good idea, Laisi," he said.

"She was right when she said that no one near the camp would be looking for her. The last time he was here, Derreth said everyone knows Lord Beristo dismissed her."

"That doesn't mean that they won't see her, though."

Laisi stared up at his face.

"Are you concerned about her because she saved your life or for another reason?"

"What do you mean?"

"Lately you've been in poor spirits. I've barely gotten you to smile in the past few days, but I heard you laugh just now when you were with her."

Kestorn looked surprised at first, but then he smiled.

"Well, now I know how to make you jealous," he teased, but Laisi shot him a glare. "Come, forgive me, Laisi. Would you believe me if I told you that you don't have anything to worry about?"

Laisi's expression softened. "But I am worried about you," she said. "I'm happy Inesca has been able to stay with us, but you do not seem like yourself."

Kestorn sighed and smiled ruefully.

"I am not pleased with your father's plan for me to become a merchant. It's not for me, but I don't want to disappoint him. After all, I still hope to ask for his permission to marry you."

Her eyes brightened, and she smiled warmly.

"You're serious about asking him?"

"I've wanted to ask him for years now, but I couldn't when I was a rider. I wouldn't have been free to marry you. And Inesca helped me see that maybe I could go back to working with horses as a trainer or a breeder, but I don't mind working with your father until I'm able to do that."

"Why couldn't you have told me sooner that all of this was about being a merchant? I never wanted you to feel like you had to be one, and Father will get over the disappointment."

"I hope you are right. He often sounds so pleased over the prospect. But as for Inesca, there is nothing between us," Kestorn said with a laugh. "She's more like a sister to me than anything else."

Chapter 28

Rain poured down over Bartrir as a night wind drove the water through the air at a high rate of speed. Derreth drew his cloak tighter around him as he stood beneath the shelter of the overhanging roof from the blacksmith's shop. The blacksmith had gone to bed hours ago and would never know that his shop had another purpose to serve tonight.

"It seems that I chose our meeting place well," a low voice said.

Derreth watched as another man in a cloak appeared from out of the rain.

"You took your time getting here, Ruesord," Derreth said as he tried to shake the water from his own cloak.

"I had to search the area to be sure no one followed you."

"Do you think I want to be followed? If Lord Edgerr discovered me so far from camp, he'd have me whipped."

"I know, but we must be careful with all that has happened. There can be no doubt now that a spy has infiltrated the Raegond."

Derreth searched the darkness around them warily.

"I never had doubts that we were being watched. But why did you send for me to meet you here?"

"Another council has been called by our leaders."

"We agreed there should be no more council meetings until the spy was caught."

"All of the efforts made to find the spy have failed. Nothing is being accomplished, and nothing will be accomplished until we, the Raegond, are able to hold council together."

Derreth shook his head.

"We cannot risk another attack."

"What are you worried about? Your brother is far away from this place. He will not be at risk this time."

"He never should have been at risk," Derreth said, trying hard to keep his voice low.

"They said you would resist the idea of another council meeting, but I am to remind you of the oath you swore to the Raegond. Your presence and service are required. And you cannot break from us now."

"It was never my intention to break the oath that I swore," Derreth said. "When is the meeting to be held?"

"In two days. Come at the usual time. You know where to find the old ruins of the castle of Sir Nalhoth?"

"Yes. Tell them that I will come."

Moving away, Derreth walked back into the night as he pulled his cloak over his head to shield himself from the rain. The messenger, Ruesord, turned and disappeared in the opposite direction. The rain continued to pour down upon the blacksmith's shop. In a room at the back of the building, the blacksmith snored in his bed, and his cat slowly rose to stretch. It turned in a circle and lay back down upon a rug as the man continued to breathe heavily. A few drops of water leaked through his roof, but still the night was peaceful for him.

Outside, near the place where Derreth and Ruesord had spoken, there were two large barrels beside the blacksmith's bench and his tools. A shadow moved behind the crack between the two barrels, and a figure stood up from behind them. With wide eyes and an expression of horror on her face, Inesca stared off in the direction that she had seen Derreth leave.

When Derreth returned to Lord Edgerr's camp, he found that all except for a few guards were still asleep. And the guards who remained awake had gathered under a tent to keep dry rather than to keep a good watch. The rain had worked to his advantage tonight.

Earlier in the day, wooden shelters and platforms had been built by servants and workers to help keep the rain from soaking through the tents. Lord Edgerr had threatened to have them beaten if even a drop of rain entered his tent. Although it had meant more work for them, Derreth was grateful for the chance to find someplace dry to change his clothes and rest.

When he entered his tent, he stopped and gazed at all of the empty space around his pallet. In the past, he would have shared a tent with Kestorn and sometimes Trestan, but now it was only him. As he removed his wet clothes and changed into a dry tunic and breeches, Derreth noticed a letter lying on the blanket over his pallet.

As he opened it, he recognized Kestorn's handwriting. He knew that Kestorn had intended to send this to him, but it seemed strange for it to arrive at night, especially on a night as wet as this. And why would the deliverer leave it on his bed like this? Normally, servants or messengers waited to deliver letters in person and perhaps earn a few coins for their service.

His eyes started to grow heavy as he sat down to read the letter, and Derreth decided that he could ask Kestorn about the letter and its deliverer the next time he saw him. It wasn't worth losing sleep over tonight.

* * *

Joviann yawned as she shuffled between the tables, picking up the last dishes of the night. All the guests were finally in their beds, and she hoped to be asleep in her own in a few minutes. As she started toward the kitchen, a sudden knock at the door nearly caused her to drop the dishes she was carrying. The knock came again, and Joviann mumbled under her breath as she walked toward it.

"We're not taking any more guests at this hour!" she said as she opened the door.

The rain was pouring down on the street, and a wet figure with dark hair stood on the other side of the door, looking miserable.

"Joviann, may I just sit inside, even if I can't have a bed?" Inesca asked.

Joviann's expression changed to one of surprise.

"I didn't think I'd see you again, but come inside and try not to bring all of the rain in with you."

Inesca hurried past her and then stood shivering as Joviann shut the door.

"I can pay you this time," Inesca said, still shaking. "I have some money with me."

"Oh, never mind that. Come to the kitchen, and we'll get those wet clothes off of you while you sit near a fire. I think I have some blankets you can use."

"I thought I wasn't allowed in the kitchen anymore," Inesca said with a faint smile.

"Well, I can make one exception tonight."

Joviann led her into the kitchen and, in a matter of minutes, had Inesca dried off and wrapped in a warm blanket near a fire. She took the wet clothes and put them on chairs in the other room to dry. She found one of her old work dresses for Inesca to wear, and although it was a bit big, it would be comfortable enough to sleep in. She also gave Inesca something to drink and eat.

"Now, what are you doing here? Did you walk all night in the rain?"

"No, I rode a horse through it. I know it was foolish, but when it started to rain, I thought it would be good weather for me to travel in. Not many others would be out to see me."

"Well, not many want to catch pneumonia."

"I left the horse at a stable in town," Inesca continued. "I would have gone back to where I came from tonight, but I finally decided that I was getting too wet, and I needed time to think. I realized your inn was not too far away, so I came here. But I can pay you."

"If you were staying in a room, I might charge you, but all the rooms are taken. I won't charge you for sitting in the kitchen."

"And the last time I was here? Don't I owe you something for that?"

"It was all paid for," Joviann said as she left to find another blanket. "And seeing as you left before the two weeks were over, I suppose I owe you a bit in return."

Omaron must have paid for my stay, Inesca decided. *He was the one who sent me here after all.*

"Here we are," Joviann said as she brought another blanket. "It's not much, but you can stay here tonight."

"Thank you. It's far better than being outside in the rain."

"Well, don't ride through a storm next time."

Joviann picked up one of the extra candles and headed toward her room. Inesca curled up in the blankets as she sat and watched the fire crackling in the fireplace. She needed to let Kestorn know that she had delivered his letter, but how could she face him after what she had seen tonight?

How can Derreth be one of the Raegond? she wondered. *They've killed so many people, including Sirryn. I saw them attack Kestorn and kill Trestan. And now I know why Derreth wasn't there or didn't seem to be there. He was with the other Raegond in the attack, but how could he be part of that? What would my father think of one of his sons being a member of a secret band of murderers?*

The conversation between Derreth and the other Raegond started to replay itself in her mind. *"It was never my intention to break the oath that I swore."* Derreth had admitted that he was loyal to the Raegond, but they had also talked of a traitor, a spy. Was there any chance that Derreth was that spy? Was he only pretending to be one of the Raegond in an attempt to stop them?

Inesca leaned her head back against the wall, and she began to wish she had not agreed to deliver Kestorn's letter or that she had delivered the letter to Derreth in person. Instead, she had grown afraid to confront him again after their last conversation.

Upon arriving at Lord Edgerr's camp, she had seen Derreth leave his tent to check on the horses. She decided to leave the letter on his bed, and when she left, she started toward town to find a way to get out of the rain. Her horse had already been stabled in town because she thought she might be spotted riding on horseback through the encampments.

As she passed the blacksmith's shop, Inesca had turned and seen someone walking in her direction. At first, she thought that the stranger had seen her and was following her, but then she realized that his head was down with a cloak pulled over it to shield him from the rain. She decided to hide behind some barrels until he passed her, but he didn't pass the blacksmith's shop. Instead, he walked to it and stopped a few feet from her hiding place.

When he removed the cloak from his head, Inesca realized it was Derreth. She had thought about standing up and speaking to him, but then she saw that he was waiting for someone. And after getting a strong feeling that she was not supposed to be there, Inesca decided to stay hidden and see what would happen. And then she had witnessed that horrible conversation.

What should I do now? she asked herself. *I can't tell anyone. Derreth would be killed if they found out. And what if he isn't really one of them? If he's the spy, then it is even more important for me to keep his secret.*

Inesca thought back to what the messenger had said about the meeting that was coming in just two days. *Dare I follow him to it? I've made quite a habit out of following my brothers around, but this time I'm not sure if I want to. Then again, it's almost as if I was handed this information. I can't just ignore it.*

※

Two days after meeting with the messenger under the blacksmith's roof, Derreth entered Lord Edgerr's tent hoping that his next excuse would satisfy his lord.

"I saw you riding Halon the other day," Lord Edgerr said as he motioned for Derreth to come closer. "You do seem to know how to manage him, but you're not as fast as your brother, are you?"

"Kestorn had his own set of skills, but I have won races for you before, my lord. And I will again, but at the moment, Halon needs to be fitted with some new horseshoes."

"I'll have one of the servants do it."

"With your permission, my lord, I would like to take him to town. We need to purchase more, and when it comes to shoeing Halon, you know how unruly he can be. I should be there to manage him."

Lord Edgerr glanced at Derreth's face for a brief moment, but then he turned away.

"Go then, and see that nothing happens," he said.

Derreth bowed and walked quickly out of the tent as he went to collect Halon. Together, they traveled into town, but instead of going to the blacksmith's shop to purchase the horseshoes, Derreth took him to the stable where he knew the lad who worked there. It was still early, so there weren't many people around, and Derreth hoped no one would see him bringing Halon into town. The stable boy, Eimon, greeted them at the door.

"I thought you'd be out at the camp getting ready for the competitions. I wish I could go to see you joust next week."

"I'd be pleased to have you there cheering me on, but today I need you to take care of this horse for me. I'll return for him later, but keep him in the back where he's not easily seen. I don't want other people to know there's a prize stallion here."

"Don't worry about that. I won't let people bother the horses while they're resting. Anything I need to know about this one?"

"Just that he can be bad-tempered, so keep him in the stall. And if you give him some sugar, he should behave for you."

Derreth handed the reins over to Eimon, and Halon shook his head a little, but Eimon pulled out some sugar and suddenly Halon was eager to follow him. Derreth surveyed the stable and noticed that there weren't many horses here. Then he caught sight of a bay mare in one of the stalls with a blaze on her forehead.

"Anything wrong?" Eimon asked after he had put Halon away.

"No, it's just that I know someone who owns a horse like that one."

"You know Inesca?"

"Inesca?" Derreth repeated, and as he glanced back at the bay mare, he realized that Gorben must have lent the horse to her. "Is she here?"

"She arrived back in Bartrir a few days ago, soaking wet from the rain. It took me a long time to get the mare dry."

Derreth took out some coins and paid him.

"Eimon, I need you to tell her to stay at your mother's inn until I come to see her."

The boy looked at the coins in his hand.

"But you've given me too much."

"The extra is for your help."

As he walked out of the stable, Derreth began to move faster. The sooner he got away from town, the smaller the chance was of him being seen. He doubted that anyone here would report his movements to Lord Edgerr, but he didn't want to take any risks.

The knowledge that Inesca was here caused him to wonder why she had not tried to meet with him. It seemed likely that she had delivered the letter to his tent, but why stay hidden? Did she mean to stay to watch the jousts? It wasn't safe for her to be here.

As he reached the forest within which he would find his destination, Derreth looked behind him to see if he was being followed before continuing on.

Chapter 29

Inesca watched from behind a tree on the edge of town as Derreth stole away to the forest. It wouldn't be easy to follow him in there, but something else was weighing more heavily on her mind. To her left, Inesca had seen a man standing on the other side of the building that was next to the stable. He had watched Derreth come out of the stable and walk toward the forest.

Inesca had intended to follow Derreth more closely, but with this stranger observing him, she didn't dare move from her hiding place. He had not noticed her yet, and she hoped to keep it that way. After a moment, Inesca saw him disappear behind the building, and seconds later, a white pigeon, one like those used to send messages in the races, flew toward the sky.

If only I had a bow and arrow, Inesca thought as she helplessly watched the bird fly away. It could not mean anything good for Derreth.

At last, the man reappeared and began walking in the same direction that Derreth had traveled. Inesca waited until he entered the forest before she dared to follow him across the field. Fortunately, it never occurred to the man that someone might be following him, so he didn't look back.

Inesca walked as quickly as she could so that she would not be too far behind him, and when she reached the edge of the forest, she was able to find him among the trees. He moved again, seemingly watching Derreth ahead of him.

I feel ridiculous, Inesca thought to herself. *I thought I'd be following Derreth, not trailing after someone else following him. I could alert him to the person following him, but I don't know who this person is. I'm not even sure I know who Derreth is anymore.*

For almost an hour, Inesca continued to quietly shadow the man following Derreth. She noted that this man didn't appear to be carrying a weapon, so she doubted he was an assassin. But she watched him carefully just in case.

He wasn't much taller than she was, but that proved to be to his advantage as it made it easier for him to hide. Some red hair poked out from under the brown hat he wore. The rest of his face was clean-shaven, but he looked kind of dirty, as if he had been sleeping outside all night. Inesca touched her own face and thought she might not look very clean either. She had spent a lot of time waiting and hiding outside this morning to see when Derreth would leave.

After some time of trailing the man ahead of her, Inesca saw the ruins of a castle appear amid the trees. The man before her stopped to watch Derreth disappear behind one of the stone walls. Inesca waited until he finally crept forward before she ventured closer. On the other side of the wall, she watched him descend down some old stone stairs, but then he hesitated and climbed back up again. She darted behind the wall and waited for his footsteps to grow fainter.

When she dared to look again, she saw that he had moved to another section of the ruins and then he seemed to disappear into the ground. She moved closer and found a place where the ground opened up into the lower level of what used to be the castle. A rope tied to the remains of a pillar had been left behind.

Inesca glanced at the steps and then back at the rope. Either way, she didn't know what she would find down there, but she needed to know who this man was and what he was up to. Grasping the rope, she climbed down into the darkness and hoped that he wasn't waiting for her at the bottom.

Derreth followed the hallway from the steps to a large underground room where a table and several chairs had been recently added to the old chamber. Torches lit the bare walls, providing a dim light. Within the chamber, he saw several of the Raegond leaders waiting for him. The need to seek Lord Edgerr's permission had made him late, but at least he was here.

"It is good to see that you were able to make it," Tyrus said as he rose to greet Derreth.

The silver-haired leader of the Raegond seemed to have aged a year each time Derreth had seen him lately, but his figure was still tall and muscular, reflecting the life he had once had in Valmontes, training young men to become knights.

Derreth bowed his head respectfully to Tyrus, but his expression remained stern. "I managed to satisfy Lord Edgerr with my excuse, but I still say this meeting is not a good idea," he said. "There could be an attack going on right now, and we would not know about it."

"The risk will be worth it if we can uncover the traitor," said Cartul, another high-ranking member of the Raegond. He was broader than Tyrus, and his expression was usually marked by a fierce and untrusting gaze.

"We don't yet know that there is a traitor," Tyrus insisted. "If someone has found a way to spy on us …"

The Legacy of the Lost Rider

"If there was a spy, then our identities would have been revealed, and we would all have been executed by now."

"If the purpose of this meeting was to argue, then I see no reason in staying and taking further risk as to what may be happening out there," Derreth said, refusing to sit down.

"It would be unwise of you to try to leave now," Tyrus said as he caught Derreth's arm.

Derreth looked at him and then at the others.

"You think I'm the traitor?"

"Some of us do," Cartul said. "You are the newest member of the Raegond, and we've never had these troubles before."

"I have always fully supported our cause, and I'm not afraid to answer your questions or face your accusations."

"Then let us sit down and begin. I am confident that you will prove innocent of these charges," Tyrus said.

The part of the castle that Inesca had climbed into had grown pitch black as she moved farther away from the entrance. At any moment, she might run into the man she had been following. Or she might lose her way in this tunnel and become trapped down here.

She stretched out her hand and felt her way along the stone wall as her heart pounded in her chest. Then she heard a soft noise and froze against the wall. For a few seconds, nothing happened, and she wondered if she had imagined it.

A sudden glow of light appeared ahead of her, and a man walked past the end of the tunnel with a torch. He didn't stop or bother to look down the tunnel where she hid, but for a few brief seconds, the light illuminated the darkness. Inesca looked at the wall across from her and felt her heart jump as she saw the man she had been following. And he saw her.

A look of surprise shot across his face but was quickly replaced by a menacing gaze. Inesca felt sure he meant to murder her as darkness started to consume them again.

When the light vanished, Inesca dropped to the floor and heard him rush forward, but he tripped over her foot and landed somewhere behind her. Feeling trapped in the complete darkness, Inesca scrambled forward toward the end of the tunnel. She didn't care if the Raegond were there. She wanted light and the ability to see her attacker.

As she neared the end of the tunnel and saw a faint glow of light beyond, a sudden force threw her to the ground. Wrestling with the stranger, Inesca tried to knock him back, but his hands quickly found her throat and seized it with a crushing grip. She pulled a dagger from her belt, but he knocked that from her hand before she could use it.

Unable to draw breath, Inesca felt the darkness growing even thicker around her, but then her outstretched hand found a small, loose piece of stone. While her right hand was caught in his grasp, his knee had pinned her left arm to the floor, preventing her from lifting it any higher. But using her left hand, she seized the small stone at her fingertips and knocked it against the other stones on the floor.

She felt her attacker's grip loosen as he tried to search for her hand to stop her. Inesca struggled but could not break free of him, so she tapped the stone again and again. He finally let go of her neck altogether in desperation.

The light began to return to the tunnel. Inesca kicked the man away from her, but he seized her foot and held on. Their struggle continued until a voice shouted something from the edge of the tunnel. The man released Inesca's foot and began to run, but another figure with a torch raced after him and tackled him to the ground.

A rough grip seized Inesca's arms and dragged her out of the tunnel. Another figure appeared dragging the man who had attacked her. Their captors pulled them down a corridor and through a doorway. As she looked around, Inesca realized the man holding onto her arms was Ruesord, the messenger who had spoken with Derreth outside of the blacksmith's shop.

After being forcibly led into a room lit with torches, Inesca was thrust down onto the floor in front of several men. The man who had followed Derreth was pushed down beside her.

"Well, we may have found some spies after all," one of the men said.

As more gathered around them, Inesca saw Derreth with them. His eyes widened, but she kept quiet, wondering if it would be wise to ask for his help in front of the rest of the Raegond.

"Separate them and question each," one of the Raegond ordered.

The others nodded, and the guards pulled them up and led them toward opposite tunnels. Inesca cast one more glance at Derreth as she was forced from the room.

Once the guards had gone and the leaders of the Raegond had separated their prisoners, Derreth turned to Tyrus and drew him aside.

"I knew you were one of us, Derreth," the older man said as he appeared relieved.

"And I hope that the man we have caught is our spy, but I know the girl," Derreth said. "She may have followed me here, but she's not a spy."

The relief on Tyrus's face faded.

"You know our penalty for trespassers. We cannot make exceptions even if she isn't a spy. And if you speak up for her, the others may return to their doubts about you. Cartul will argue that you led her here."

Derreth paused and turned away from Tyrus as he stared down the hall where Inesca had been taken.

"Let me go with you to question her."

Tyrus hesitated as he searched Derreth's gaze.

"It is your right as one of our own to be present during questioning, but do not fool yourself. You cannot save her."

Chapter 30

When they reached the place where Inesca was being held, Derreth saw that her wrists had been bound together and that she was surrounded by Cartul and the others. One of them used the back of his hand to hit her when she did not answer a question, knocking her against the wall. Derreth froze behind Tyrus and stiffened as if he too had been struck.

Inesca turned back to them, and her gaze drifted to Derreth's eyes. The side of her face where the guard had struck her was bleeding.

"She claims that she followed the other man here. And that she was not working with him," Cartul said as he faced Tyrus and Derreth. "But she won't say any more. Sounds like a poor story to me."

"How were they found?" Derreth asked as he stepped closer.

The others turned to face Ruesord, who stood off to the side.

"She and the man were engaged in some kind of struggle," he reported. "When we saw them, the man ran, while the girl remained motionless. She gave up rather easily."

"Hardly the mark of the guilty," Derreth said.

"You're not trying to argue that she's innocent, are you?" Cartul asked suspiciously.

"I still need to hear her account," Tyrus cut in as he moved closer to Inesca and pushed past Cartul. "What else do you have to say, girl?"

Inesca leaned against the wall, but she lifted her gaze when he spoke to her.

"I followed the other man here. He used a rope to climb down into the tunnel, and I went down after him. Eventually, the tunnel that we passed through trapped us in darkness. When one of your men walked by the other end with a torch, he noticed me for the first time, and he tried to kill me. I couldn't overpower him, so I tried to make noise—anything to stop him from strangling me in the dark. That's when your guards found us."

"And who are you?"

"My name is Inesca. I was a rider for Lord Beristo."

"And now?"

Inesca paused, realizing that she didn't quite know how to answer such a question.

"I'm not really anything else at the moment. I was just passing through Bartrir."

"Why did you follow the other man? Do you know his name? Or do you know if he is working for someone?"

"I've never seen that man before in my life." Inesca sighed. "He just looked suspicious."

"Suspicious," Cartul muttered.

Inesca held her tongue, but her face was tense with anger. Her thoughts seemed to distract her for a moment, and after a pause, she spoke again.

"I can tell you that I saw him send off a white pigeon before he came down here."

The mention of the pigeon caused a sudden reaction as their expressions quickly changed and their eyes widened. Derreth glanced behind them as if expecting to see an enemy storming the ruins in search of them. If a pigeon had been sent, then the location of their meeting had surely been reported.

"We must leave at once," Tyrus said. "Bring her with us, but cover her eyes and gag her."

Derreth watched as Cartul helped the others blindfold and gag Inesca. There was little he could do to help her now except stay close.

Tyrus pulled Ruesord to his side and said, "Take the other prisoner to another location and question him carefully. Come and find us when you have finished."

Ruesord nodded before disappearing down the hall. Tyrus sent a few others to clear away any signs that they had been meeting in the ruins before he was ready to depart with Cartul. Derreth followed them hesitantly, still watching Inesca.

It was only minutes later when Inesca felt the blindfold being pulled from her eyes. She squinted and blinked as strong sunlight beamed down upon her. When her eyes adjusted, she saw that they were in the forest. One of the men pushed her closer to the trunk of a tree and tied her to it.

Derreth stood off to one side, watching and listening for any sounds of the men that he kept expecting to come after them. Surely their enemies were not far off after having received the whereabouts of the Raegond. Inesca's warning might have saved their lives, but he still couldn't understand what she had been thinking. He supposed that the only reason she would follow the spy was because the man had been following him, but she appeared reluctant to admit it.

Feeling trapped in a different sense, Derreth knew that his current position among the Raegond was a dangerous one. If he said too much in her favor or admitted that it was his fault the spy had found them, then his life could also be at risk. But he also could not allow them to kill her.

"This isn't good enough, Tyrus," Cartul insisted as he glanced around at the trees. "We can't question her properly out here. If she screams, someone will hear it."

Derreth spun around and locked gazes with Tyrus.

"We haven't time to take her somewhere else," Tyrus insisted wearily. "And we will not resort to such barbaric means of questioning."

"Why are you two suddenly so soft about this one?" Cartul asked, looking from Derreth to Tyrus. "There's more to this than her just being a girl, isn't there? Why are you so keen to protect her?"

"Without her, we wouldn't even know that one of our meetings had been discovered," Derreth protested. "That's at least one reason to hesitate before you do anything unnecessary, Cartul."

"Enough," Tyrus demanded. "We must finish this and be gone from this place."

He led them back to Inesca and untied the cloth gag from around her mouth.

"If you answer us softly and do not raise your voice, then this will go easier for you," he said.

"I've told you everything that I know," Inesca said, keeping her voice low but firm.

"Doubtful," Cartul insisted. "Why would you follow a man you had never seen before? Hope to become a spy one day yourself, do you?"

Inesca's gaze flitted to Derreth, and Tyrus noticed it. He watched Derreth for a moment, and then turned back to Inesca with a look of regret. After another long pause, he turned to Derreth.

"Go find Ruesord, and see if he is having any more success with the other prisoner. He will have gone to the cave at the other edge of the forest."

"No," Derreth said firmly. "I won't be *sent* anywhere."

"Derreth, it's no good."

"She's not a spy."

"Perhaps not, but she is a trespasser. The penalty is the same."

Cartul drew his sword from its sheath and started toward Inesca, who shrunk back against the tree. Shoving his way past the others, Derreth seized Cartul's arm and held him back.

"I know this girl, and she knows me. She must have been curious about my actions and decided to follow me. I did not lead her here on purpose, but I can assure you that she's no spy."

"Spy or no spy, we still have to kill her," Cartul said. "You should have been more careful and made sure you came alone."

"I can't let you kill her."

"You know our laws, Derreth," Tyrus said. "Come away, and I'll see that it's quick."

Derreth moved in front of Inesca protectively and drew his own sword.

"It won't be quick, because you'll have to go through me first."

"We'll see about that, boy. I can still get around you, but you'll get a few hard blows first," Cartul said as he tightened the grip on his own blade.

Though he was disappointed that his resolution did not seem to faze Cartul, Derreth stood firm and waited for the broad-shouldered man to advance.

"Stop!" Inesca said from behind Derreth as she strained at the ropes binding her. "If you're going to kill me, then you needn't waste your time with this man. I don't know him."

"No one is going to believe that, Inesca," Derreth said without turning around to look at her.

"But I don't know you. I thought I did, but now that I know you're one of these murderers, I want nothing to do with you. And I certainly don't want your help."

Her tone echoed with anger aimed at him more than at the rest of her captors. Derreth stepped to one side to catch a glimpse of her face.

"Murderers?"

"All of those riders and Sirryn, Lord Beristo's gentle councilman," Inesca said as she turned her gaze on the other Raegond. "What did they ever do to you that you had to slaughter them?"

The men before her turned and looked at each other with strange expressions.

"She means the ambush in Monterr," Derreth explained. "She believes we are responsible, just like everyone else. But that's not surprising when you are threatening to kill her now."

"Protecting our secret and killing just to turn a river red are not the same," Cartul said, but he lowered the blade a bit. "We only deal death to traitors ... and trespassers."

"And am I a traitor because I served a lord?" Inesca asked, glaring at him.

"Do you hate the lords so much that you see all their loyal servants as traitors? Traitors to what?"

"You must ask the hooded ones that," Tyrus said. "They are the ones who claim that the riders must be destroyed and that the lords must be overthrown. We never wanted such things."

Inesca stared at him with a suspicious gaze.

"Are you not the Raegond? The men in black hoods are yours."

"No. They have nothing to do with us," Derreth said in a firm tone. "Do you think I would ever serve with any who tried to kill my brother?"

"Then if you weren't involved, why were you gone the day of the ambush? And don't say you were sick."

"I was called to a meeting with the real Raegond, so I lied about being sick to avoid questions from Kestorn and Lord Edgerr. The hooded strangers waited to strike until we gathered together, so that they could blame us for their crimes. I did not understand how they knew when our meetings were being held, but you've helped us discover their spy, which is another reason why your life should be spared."

He turned back to the others as he spoke, but Inesca only watched Derreth.

"Then who are these men who call themselves the Raegond?"

"We would very much like to know," Tyrus said. "But they seem to disappear as quickly as they appear."

"Enough of this," Cartul said as he raised the blade again. "We know what has to be done."

Derreth moved back in front of Inesca.

"There has to be some other way," he said, looking at Tyrus who remained quiet.

"Not when she's seen our faces," Cartul said. "Even if she wanted to keep our secret, our enemies could find a way to force it from her. And if you're suggesting we keep her prisoner, you know we move around too much to be bothered with a captive."

"Then cut us both down if you feel certain you have no choice. I've made mine," Derreth said.

Tyrus seized Cartul's arm. "Wait," he said. "Let us try to find another way to resolve this."

"He agreed to our laws when he swore to serve us. If he stands in opposition to our judgment, then he has broken his oath."

"When it comes to Derreth, we are bound by a debt greater than our laws. That debt must surely buy him some additional consideration."

Cartul scowled but stepped back, allowing Tyrus to move closer to Derreth.

"Derreth, I've told you before that I knew your father, but I may not have explained that he was one of my closest friends and allies. That is why I intend to see your life spared regardless of this mess and your obstinacy. But I cannot save her."

Derreth's expression changed to one of surprise.

"If that's enough to save me, then it's enough to save her," he said and stopped before taking a deep breath. "She is my sister."

Their gazes turned from him to Inesca, who stared at Derreth in amazement.

"You expect us to believe that this Easterner is your sister?" Cartul asked.

"Half-sister," Derreth conceded. "But she is of my father's blood."

"How old are you?" Tyrus asked Inesca.

Her answer caught in her throat for a moment as Inesca looked from Derreth to the other men. She could hardly believe that he was claiming her as his sister.

"Eighteen," she said after finding her voice again.

"And you are certain?" Tyrus asked, turning to Derreth.

"I wanted to deny it at first, but she had his medallion, and the way she describes him fits what I remember about him. And she says that my face resembles his."

"It does," Tyrus agreed. "I have always thought that you bore his likeness." He turned back to Inesca. "Is Arryn still alive?" he asked her.

Cartul put his hand on Tyrus's shoulder.

"It's a clever story, but what proof does she have? Derreth may well be saying all of this to save her life. I am not convinced."

"It is possible," Tyrus protested. "He could have had a child in the East Province, and she is the proper age."

"I demand more evidence than that," Cartul said coldly. "We have never spared an intruder before, and I will not do so lightly."

"And my word isn't good enough for you?" Derreth asked.

"No man's word, except your father's, has ever been good enough for me."

Inesca looked down at her chest and again struggled to pull her hands free, but they were bound tight.

"Derreth," she pleaded. "There's a cord around my neck. Lift it up for me."

He turned and used one hand to pull the cord over her head. When he held it up, he found that a silver ring with a red-jeweled flower hung from it.

"This was among my father's possessions that he sent me to collect after he died," Inesca said as she stared at it. "I think it belonged to Derreth's mother."

Derreth stared at it intently, but Cartul reached forward and seized it impatiently. He raised it to his eyes and studied it closely.

"That is Elacia's ring," Tyrus said. "Arryn had it made for her. Red kylainis blooms are common in the realm of Trineth where she grew up. It served as a reminder of the promise that he made to her when they married."

"What promise?" Derreth asked.

"Your father planned to bring your mother back to this realm to live and raise their children. But she became ill and died before he could afford to buy the land."

Cartul lowered the ring reluctantly.

"Are you satisfied?" Tyrus asked impatiently.

"I never am, but let the girl keep her life," Cartul said, tossing the ring to Derreth, who caught it and held it tightly.

"Is Arryn still alive?" Tyrus asked Inesca again.

Inesca's expression shifted to reflect weariness and pain.

"No, he died about four months ago. I would not have left him if he was still alive. But I did not know about this life that he had here. He had always been called Koldoth in the East Province and refused to speak of his past."

"Arryn knew how to keep a secret. Too well at times, I'm afraid," Tyrus sighed. "I feared that I would never see him again."

"But you knew he didn't die in the war?" Derreth asked as his brows furrowed. "You've known all this time, and you never told me?"

"Several of us knew," Cartul said. "But what would you have done if we had told you?"

Gripping his sword tighter as a sudden rush of anger filled his heart, Derreth said, "I would have gone to find him."

"And run away from Lord Edgerr? You would not have gotten ten miles without being arrested for deserting your lord."

"Derreth, we had hoped to tell you, but we never expected you and your brother to be placed in Lord Edgerr's service. Once you were bound to him, we knew it would only make things worse for you if you knew the truth," Tyrus said.

"Why did he leave?"

"We don't know all the details, but I'll explain what I remember … only not now. I have the other prisoner to attend to, but you and your sister may rest easy. We must spare her life now. But are you certain you do not know the man we caught?" he asked Inesca.

"Yes. I had never seen him before this morning. When I saw him following Derreth, I decided to follow him to see what he was up to."

"Well, he'd better not start claiming to be a son of Arryn, or I'll come back for you," Cartul threatened.

Tyrus led him away, and soon Inesca was alone with Derreth, who leaned back against another tree with a heavy sigh. He put the leather cord around his neck so that the ring slipped down behind his tunic. As she watched him, Inesca felt some displeasure when the last item from her father was not returned to her, but she knew that it belonged to Derreth more than it belonged to her.

"What were you thinking?" Derreth asked her as he massaged his forehead. "You nearly got us both killed."

"I'm sorry. But if you hadn't kept this a secret …"

"A secret?" Derreth repeated as he opened his eyes. "Do you expect the members of the Raegond to announce their identities to the world?"

Inesca's gaze hardened.

"And why is it so important that they stay a secret? What are you plotting in those tunnels with those men?"

Derreth pulled out the dagger that the spy had knocked from her hand and cut the rope binding her to the tree. Inesca rubbed her numb wrists and arms.

He led her to a sack that had been carried out of the ruins when the Raegond fled out of fear of discovery. Pulling out a roll of cloth, Derreth set it in her hands.

"Open it."

Inesca lifted the bundle and unrolled its edges. As the light hit its surface, she saw that it was a standard made from deep blue cloth. It bore a golden lion rearing on its hind legs with a crown near its forepaws, but it was not a crown with six points like the one always seen on the standards of the lords. This crown was mostly a gold circlet with one raised point. Beside it was a long gold scepter with a white piece of cloth sewn at its tip.

"That represents a rare gem called a zalist that is only carried by the king of Rynar. The scepter and its jewel were buried with King Eisron. There was another zalist sealed in a pendant that was always worn by the king's son, but it was lost when he died," Derreth said. "This is the standard of the house of King Eisron, which faded from renown when he left this world without an heir."

"Why do the Raegond keep it?"

"Because he charged their families long ago with its safekeeping and with the protection of Rynar. He asked his most trusted knight, Sir Oreloc, to create this secret guard of Rynar. The Raegond were formed to help protect the Six Realms, not to destroy them."

"Isn't that the job of the Royal Council?"

"The king knew that the council would eventually fail and become blind to the weaknesses of the Six Realms. And it has happened. They stay in their island city, and they do not see what is truly happening within the realms. Knights and lords may become corrupt or seek too much power, and the council accepts gifts from them without question. But the Raegond can move between the realms, observing the actions of those who pose a threat to the security of Rynar."

Derreth took the standard from her and gazed at it as he said, "Let no tyrant rise to take my throne. Let no war tear apart your own. The laws of God and king to keep, my right-hand guard, Rynar, while I sleep."

"And this is your purpose?" Inesca asked.

"Yes, it's the creed that was given to Sir Oreloc by King Eisron himself. It's the reason why we exist and the reason why it's dangerous to walk into one of our secret meetings. We've made enemies over the years, and if they discover our secrets, we'll be destroyed. Then who will protect the Six Realms from ambitious lords and cruel knights?"

"What do you do when you find one who is trying to steal too much power?"

Derreth took out a dagger and held it out to her as he met Inesca's gaze.

"Oh, I see why some of them might be afraid of you," she said as she took it from him.

"Usually it doesn't go that far," Derreth explained as he rolled the standard up again. "A warning or a setback in their plans is often enough to put them in their place, but we will do what is necessary if they are destroying the lives of the people."

As he set the rolled cloth down again, he motioned for her to come with him.

"You and I should return to Bartrir. There may have been another attack if that spy was able to send word to those whom he was working for."

Derreth started to walk on through the trees, but he stopped when he saw Inesca hesitate.

"You can follow me this time. You have my permission for a change."

"It's not that. I wanted to know if you meant what you said."

Derreth shot her a strange look.

"Did you mean it when you said I was your sister? Or were you just saying that to save my life?"

"Only a fool would lie to the Raegond. Some of those men may not be as young as I am, but they are powerful."

"I thought you didn't want to believe that my fath ... our father didn't die in the war."

"I can't argue against it anymore. You heard what Tyrus said."

"Yes, but if you don't want to accept me, I'll go. I only followed you this time because I didn't want to believe that you were really a part of the attacks. I thought you might have been the spy."

"You nearly caused me to be killed like one."

Inesca noted the disapproval in his tone and started to walk off on her own. Derreth caught up to her and put his hand on her shoulder.

"But I believe I can forgive you for that," he said, turning her around with a gentle grip. "If you can forgive me for everything I've put you through."

Inesca paused for a moment. Lifting her gaze to his face, Inesca thought she saw a trace of affection in his expression.

"And since you are my sister, we should stay together," Derreth continued.

Inesca crossed her arms and lifted her chin.

"Don't say that because you feel responsible for me. I can manage on my own."

His curt, scornful laugh answered her. "I have yet to be convinced," he said. "Every time we cross paths, I find you in some kind of trouble. You are worse than Kestorn."

Inesca sighed as if in annoyance, but she remained quiet when she found that she was unable to deny the truth of his statement.

"But I would have you come with me," Derreth said with a warm smile. "We'll start anew as brother and sister."

With a nod and a smile, Inesca turned and began to walk at his side.

Chapter 31

Back in Bartrir, Eimon shoveled hay in the stable while the owner tended to some business for the lords at their camp. Halon moved restlessly in his stall, and Eimon paused for a moment to check on him.

"We both probably wish we were somewhere else right now," he said. "At least they don't give you chores to do."

Halon's ears flattened against his head, and Eimon walked closer as he noticed how nervous the red stallion suddenly seemed.

All at once, the wide doors at the end of the stable were flung open and several men in black hoods rode inside. They carried burning torches, which one of them threw onto a pile of hay. Eimon rushed forward with his pitchfork to stop him, but one of the men grabbed him by the arm and flung him against the wall. The boy's head struck the wooden beams, and he fell onto the ground.

Tossing ropes around Halon's neck, the raiders pulled the lines tight as Halon kicked and struggled in his stall. The other horses began to panic as the fire burned higher. One of the raiders opened the gate of Halon's stall, but as his companions pulled Halon from it, the stallion's hooves knocked the man to the ground and trampled him. The others surrounded Halon and used the ropes to pull him from the stable.

Inesca and Derreth were crossing the field when they saw the hooded riders leaving the stable and smoke rising from it. They ran toward the stable and hurried inside to find it full of thick smoke and hot flames.

"Find the boy and get him out of here!" Derreth said before he ran toward the sounds of the horses.

Inesca crouched down and searched for Eimon until she found his limp form on the ground. She dragged him out through the doors and then lifted him in her arms until she was able to reach Joviann, who had come running the moment she saw the smoke.

Coughing, Inesca turned back and returned to the stable in search of Derreth. Several horses burst from the smoke just as she reached the door, nearly colliding with her. When no more appeared, Inesca dared to walk back inside.

"Derreth!"

The crack of a beam overhead caused Inesca to tense as she looked above her. Suddenly, another horse came galloping out of the smoke with Derreth on its back. He seized her by the arm and pulled her onto the horse as it ran toward the open doors. A flaming beam crashed behind them as Derreth guided the horse out of the smoke and into the sunlight.

When they were safely away, Derreth drew the horse to a halt and dismounted. Inesca pushed herself off the horse's back as she and Derreth collapsed on the ground, coughing and gasping for air. Joviann hurried toward them with a bucket of water.

"You two make a fine pair taking on a monstrous fire without a drop of sense or water between you," she said as she used a wet cloth to wipe the ash from their faces.

"How's your son?" Inesca asked when she found her voice.

"Bruised, but not burned. His brothers have taken him back to the inn. You have my thanks. He's waking up now. Said the Raegond attacked the stable, though I can't see why."

Derreth cast a glance at Inesca. Joviann offered them some water, and they both accepted some before Derreth said, "Go and tend to Eimon. We're fine now."

"Well, I'll leave the water," Joviann said as she turned and headed back to her inn.

Inesca glanced up at the horse beside them and saw that it was the bay mare she had borrowed from Laisi's father.

"Halon was not in the stable when I freed the other horses," Derreth said. "They must have taken him."

"Are you certain your friends are not involved with this?" Inesca asked. "They could have sent men to do this during your meeting."

"You still don't understand who the Raegond are. They're not interested in killing riders or stealing horses. They were never a group of rebels trying to overthrow the rule of the Evaliscan lords. That would mean disaster for the Six Realms."

"Sometimes it sounds like you are still the enemy of the lords."

"Only the ones who step out of place. Otherwise, we are loyal to them and seek to protect them. That is why I try to serve Lord Edgerr faithfully even if I don't always tell him everything. The Raegond are strict, but we don't want to be cruel or unjust."

"Execution for trespassing is a bit more than strict in my mind," Inesca said. "And Sirryn, one of Lord Beristo's council members, told me that his daughter and her husband were killed by the Raegond. Were their deaths truly necessary?"

"That could not have been our doing. I knew of Sirryn. He was a good man. For a time, there were many attacks on families of high-ranking members of the councils that only made the Raegond even more hated. I began to search for them after a friend of mine from Lord Edgerr's household was killed. When I found the true Raegond, they spared my life and tried to convince me that they were not behind the attacks. I was as suspicious as you were, but the longer I was with them, the more I saw that it was not their desire or goal to harm the people of Rynar."

"And what about the Battle of Tortesra between the knights and the Raegond and some of the raids before that? That sounds like more than just putting a lord back in his place."

"Those rebels fighting against the lords in that battle were not of the Raegond. They called themselves the Raegond to make their revolt seem greater than a band of disgruntled peasants, but they were led by an outlaw called Slotair who never had any ties to the Raegond. He had a grudge against Lord Edgerr and decided that all the lords should pay for the crimes of one. The real Raegond, including Tyrus and Cartul, fought on the side of the Evaliscan lords."

"But if Slotair and his men were only peasants, then how did they manage to gather enough weapons and supplies to wage a war against the lords?" Inesca asked.

"We're not sure. Cartul told me that was always part of the mystery. But now someone, perhaps the same person who helped Slotair, is trying to use the name of the Raegond to commit horrible acts of violence throughout the Six Realms."

The roof of the stable collapsed as the flames engulfed the building. A crowd had gathered to make sure the fire did not spread, but the look on their faces was one of anger and confusion.

"If anyone ever finds out who you are, Derreth, they'll hold you accountable for these attacks."

"I think someone already knows," Derreth said grimly. "How else would that spy have known to follow me?"

The cries of birds in the distance drew their attention to the camp that lay just beyond the town. Smoke had begun to rise from it as well.

"Come on," Derreth said as he helped her up. "It seems they haven't finished yet."

The smell of smoke wafted through the tents on a warm breeze. Nycor pulled at his rope as his eyes widened. Omaron moved toward him and stroked his neck as he searched the sky. Shouts echoed from beyond the circle of tents.

"What's going on?" Lord Beristo asked as he exited his tent with Jirro.

"Summon your guards, my lord," Omaron said. "Something is wrong in the camp. It may be another attack."

"The Raegond would not dare openly attack us here. We've our guards and the protection of Sir Bercorr's men."

"Sir Bercorr and his men were called away due to a rumored attack in Ettidor," Jirro said. "They will not be here to help defend."

"How do you know?" Omaron asked as his eyes narrowed.

Lord Beristo turned to Jirro with a questioning gaze, but Jirro pulled a dagger from his belt and raised it as he approached Lord Beristo.

"You are one of the Raegond?" Lord Beristo said in surprise.

"No, but I am one of many," Jirro said with a cruel grin. "And we have decided that you must die."

"Guards!" Lord Beristo called.

"If any are still alive, they are too busy to help you now."

Omaron moved closer.

"You made an error in revealing yourself, Jirro. Not a drunk after all, but a traitor," he said.

Jirro laughed, and his arm tensed as he prepared to strike Lord Beristo. But with quick movements, Omaron twisted the top of his staff, and his right hand detached a spear tipped with an iron point from inside the rod. He grasped the post that Nycor was tied to with one hand, and with the other, he threw the spear at Jirro.

The traitor saw the danger too late, and Jirro was thrown to the ground with the spear point through his middle. Lord Beristo stepped away to steady Omaron as he leaned on the post, but Omaron held up his hand.

"I will slow you down, my lord. If you can find any of your guards, you must go now."

The sounds of battle echoed around them.

"I fear the time to escape has passed," Lord Beristo said. "I must have at least one man by my side, or I am no lord. I am glad that you are the one that remains."

Lord Beristo fetched a sword for both of them from his tent and returned to Omaron, who turned to cut Nycor loose.

"They should not get this horse," he said.

As if having heard his words, several riders in black hoods appeared and rode toward them. Leaving Nycor tied, Omaron turned to face their enemies with the sword. But at that moment, two other riders on horseback appeared from behind the tents and moved to intercept the attackers.

Derreth cut down two of the riders with his sword, and from behind Derreth, Inesca jumped onto a third, knocking him from his horse. More of the black-hooded attackers arrived on foot, and the one still on horseback, knocked Derreth from his mount. Omaron dealt heavy strokes with his blade to all of those around him, and Inesca used her dagger to strike after evading the swings of her enemy's sword.

After what seemed like several minutes, the attackers fell back, giving the four defenders a chance to breathe until a new wave of mounted attackers rode in and cut the rope that bound Nycor. They herded him out of the camp with their horses.

"No!" Inesca shouted as she tried to chase after them, but Derreth seized her arms and held her back.

"We can't stop them like this."

"Is that what all of this has been about?" Lord Beristo said as he watched the disappearing riders. "Stealing racehorses?"

"No, it's more than that, your lordship," Derreth said. "Killing riders and taking the horses ... it's as though someone wants to stop the races."

Inesca turned back to Omaron and Lord Beristo. And then she saw Jirro lying a few feet away.

"He was my replacement?" she asked.

"I was going to return to Ettidor, but the day after we sent you away, Jirro's manner improved," Lord Beristo said. "He asked for a second chance, and I chose to give it to him. I was going to let him compete in the jousts. But it was a trap to get me to come to Trineth and this camp. As it turns out, Jirro was one of our enemies."

Omaron stretched out his hand to Derreth, and the young man aided him in moving closer to Jirro. Then Omaron pulled his spear from Jirror's abdomen.

"It's a pity he died so quickly. We might have been able to get more information from him."

Inesca turned her gaze away from Jirro's corpse, but then she looked back at his arm sprawled above his head. The sleeve had slipped above his elbow, and she could see black tattoos on his arm.

"These are the same marks I saw on the men who attacked us in Monterr. Do you know what they mean?"

Derreth walked closer to get a better look.

"Those symbols are unlike anything I've seen before in the Six Realms."

"That is because they are not from the Six Realms," Omaron assured them. "I cannot tell you what they mean, but I have seen them once before. One of the men who came to my people's island to take slaves bore them on a silver band around his arm. He took some of my people back to his land, to Evalisca."

"Not here to Rynar?" Lord Beristo asked.

"I was taken on the ship here. But his ship sailed in the opposite direction."

"Then there are Evaliscans in the Six Realms who are not of the lords' houses?" Inesca asked. "Is that supposed to happen?"

Lord Beristo narrowed his gaze as he stared down at Jirro. "No," he said. "And who knows how long they've been here."

"But Jirro's father is a knight from Ettidor, isn't he?" she asked.

"Jirro might have joined with the enemy after they arrived, or perhaps this knight in Ettidor is not what he seems to be," Derreth suggested.

"Either way, he will answer for this man's treachery," Lord Beristo said as his face reddened. "It was he, after all, who insisted I take Jirro in."

Having drawn closer to inspect the tattoos on Jirro's arm, Lord Beristo suddenly pulled the dead man's limb up and pointed to one of the symbols.

"Although the others are unknown to me, I recognize this mark. It is one used by those cursed murderers, the Calavi."

Omaron inspected it, while Derreth and Inesca looked on in surprise.

"How do you know this, your lordship?" Derreth asked.

Beristo scoffed as he promptly dropped Jirro's arm once Omaron finished studying the mark.

"Those wretched dogs are forbidden from coming to Rynar, but there have often been scattered traces of their presence. In my youth, I was taught their emblems so that I might recognize the fiends when they appeared. But I never looked for one among my own riders."

Omaron cast a cold gaze down at Jirro.

"He played the fool well, pretending to be a useless drunk to avoid suspicion. But this explains why I saw those marks on an Evaliscan in my past, for that is where the Calavi have come from. But instead of wearing their marks on ornaments, they now use tattoos."

"Kestorn told me they were destroyed," Inesca said, looking from Omaron to Derreth. "Even in Evalisca, I thought they were slain."

Lord Beristo snatched up a spare cloth and wiped his hands as he stepped away from Jirro.

"No doubt, that was what the people of Evalisca wished to believe, but the

Calavi know how to hide themselves until they become a most unwelcome surprise."

Omaron turned to Inesca with a stern gaze. "And what are you doing here?" he asked.

Inesca cleared her throat, remembering Omaron's last command to her, and then glanced at Derreth before turning back to Omaron.

"Would you believe that I tried to stay away?"

Omaron said nothing, but Lord Beristo walked over to her and clapped a hand on her shoulder with a smile. "Well, I, at least, am glad to see you, Inesca," he told her.

"But you cast me from your service, my lord."

"Not willingly, but you made yourself such a target after the last race. Omaron insisted it was necessary. We spent hours arguing about it in my tent before I agreed to send you away."

Lord Beristo looked to Omaron and waited for him to explain.

"You would not have lasted long had you remained with us," Omaron said. "And Derreth had provided a place for you to go."

Inesca turned to Derreth. "You paid for my lodging and food at Joviann's inn?" she asked.

"Derreth also gave me the note that saved you from arrest," Omaron added.

Derreth sighed as he met Inesca's gaze. "I wanted to repay you for helping Kestorn," he explained.

"Why didn't you tell me?"

"You might have misunderstood my actions. I was ready to help you, but ..."

"Not to accept me," Inesca finished.

Lord Beristo looked at them. "So, you really are brother and sister?" he asked.

Inesca and Derreth looked at each other, but it was Omaron who answered. "They are."

At Derreth's expression of surprise, Inesca said, "He's known longer than I have."

"I raced against your father more than once," Omaron said before turning to Inesca. "You have his riding style because he trained you. Your brothers had to learn without him, so their style is different. When you showed me your father's medallion, my suspicions were confirmed."

Derreth lifted one brow. "What do you mean by his riding style?" he asked.

Omaron met his gaze. "An attentive trainer notices slight habits or preferences, and there were things they shared," he said. "But then, there was also the obvious. Your father was clever and strategic about races like you, and he successfully rode fast and willful horses like your brother. Yet what everyone remembers is that he jumped obstacles in races."

Inesca listened with interest, but she could not be surprised.

"Yes, I saw him make many impressive jumps while training horses in the East Province. And I asked him to teach me." And her eyes widened as she remembered the race she had won. "Is that why you were angry with me when I made the jump in Sassot?"

Omaron looked at her with furrowed brow and said, "As I said, you showed your skills too early. But you also reminded people of Arryn, and that seemed unwise."

Inesca's gaze drifted to his staff.

"Did you race against my father the day you lost your leg?"

Omaron righted an overturned stool and sat down upon it. One of his hands moved to the stump of his leg.

"Another rider wounded me in the leg and knocked me to the ground several miles from the end of the race. It was your father who laid me across my horse, so that I could reach the dassdir poles alive."

"He broke the rules of the race?"

"More discreetly than you did," Omaron said with a hint of a smile.

"But everyone believes he died in the battle. How did you know that he could have had a daughter?" Derreth asked.

"When I was taken from my home as a slave, I believed that I had lost everything that mattered. But when I showed skill with horses, Lord Edgerr made me one of his riders. I did well in the races until I was attacked, and my leg was wounded beyond use. Lord Edgerr was ready to cast me out, but Lord Beristo offered to buy me while I was still weak. My leg had to be removed, but he still wanted me to train his riders. And instead of treating me as a slave, he has paid me for my service and trusted my judgment. For that reason, he will always have my loyalty. I also wanted to repay your father for the help that he gave me during my last race, but when I found him again, I discovered his secret, and I sought to join the cause he supported. It took some effort, but he managed to convince the others to accept an outsider."

"You are ...," Inesca began, but Omaron interrupted her.

"Once. Not anymore, but I have served Lord Beristo in many ways. Some of which I cannot speak of."

Lord Beristo started to question the interruption, but then he dismissed it with a wave of his hand.

"As you wish, Omaron, keep your secrets, but it is hard to know that I had the daughter of the famed rider Arryn of Fortur in my service and that I was forced to give you up, Inesca."

Inesca smiled ruefully.

"I should thank you for letting me go, but I did not wish to leave, my lord."

Derreth said nothing as he turned and walked to the horse they had ridden into the camp. He led it closer and held out the reins to Inesca.

"I need to return to Lord Edgerr and see if he is among the survivors," Derreth said, drawing Inesca's attention back to him. "You must not stay here. Go back to Joviann, and wait until you hear from me."

"But Kestorn will be worried about you when he hears of this," Inesca said.

"He will receive word from us soon enough. You are not to wander alone and risk someone attacking you."

As she hesitantly took the reins from him, Derreth moved closer and put his hand on her arm.

"Inesca, I don't want to see you harmed. Be careful, and go quickly before someone sees you."

At the concern in his voice, Inesca mounted the mare and spared one more glance for Lord Beristo and Omaron.

"I would take you back if I thought you would be safe with us," Lord Beristo sighed. "But I cannot be certain of anything today. Go on, my girl."

Omaron nodded, and Inesca said farewell to them as she rode back toward the town. Derreth watched her ride away in silence, and then he bowed to Lord Beristo.

"Keeping her out of trouble will not be an easy task," Omaron said when Derreth's gaze turned to him. "But watch over her nonetheless."

Derreth nodded before setting off through the camp. It took time passing through and around the various tents. He saw the devastation caused by the attack, but he noted with surprise that many of the lords, if not all, had survived. However, most of the remaining riders had not.

When he found Lord Edgerr's blue and silver tents, many of them were scorched, but Lord Edgerr was standing outside of them with a few of his guards. His clothes looked singed, but otherwise, he appeared unharmed.

"Where is my stallion?" Lord Edgerr demanded the moment he caught sight of Derreth on foot.

"Taken, my lord. I failed you."

As his expression darkened, Lord Edgerr seized a broken spear and struck Derreth across the face with the wooden handle. Despite the pain he felt, Derreth remained quiet.

"How much longer do you expect me to be patient with you? I cannot account for your whereabouts during attacks, and now you return without my horse. And don't tell me you were getting shoes put on the stallion, because the blacksmith never saw you. I sent someone to find you when the attack began."

"It is true. I did not go to him," Derreth admitted. "I put Halon in the stable, believing that I had time to speak with a friend first. But the stable was attacked and set on fire. I ran inside to free the horses and save Halon, but he was not there. The men who set fire to it had taken him."

"And why should I believe this story?" Lord Edgerr asked.

"At least a dozen people saw me come out of the stable. One of them I know by name. She runs an inn in Bartrir. You can ask her if you don't believe me."

Lord Edgerr backed away though he continued to watch Derreth with a suspicious gaze. "The golden stallion is gone too," he said after a moment. "It seems the Raegond were after racehorses today."

Derreth wiped some blood from his face. "What can I do for you, my lord?" he asked.

Lord Edgerr turned away long enough to look at the smoking tents.

"Nothing," he replied. "You're not a rider without a horse."

"Would you give me leave to go after the men who did this?"

"You mean, would I let you leave my service?" Lord Edgerr scoffed.

"No," Derreth said. "I will not forget that I am bound in service to you, but I feel that the best means of serving you now is to find these enemies and retrieve your horses."

"The knights should be handling that."

"But they're not. And even if they do catch these men, they may keep the horses for themselves."

Lord Edgerr remained silent.

"I have not always accomplished all that you wished of me, but I have served you faithfully," Derreth said. "I came back to prove that to you today."

"And if I let you go, when would you return?"

"I do not know, but I will return."

"Go then," Lord Edgerr finally said. "As it turns out, the payment for slaves for the mines is lower than I thought. It wouldn't even be enough to buy a new horse, so I suppose it's not worth trying to sell you."

After bowing, Derreth turned quickly and walked out of the camp before Lord Edgerr could change his mind.

Chapter 32

Under the shelter of a scarlet and silver tent, Lord Tolem strode around a table with restless impatience.

"My lord ...," a servant said, pulling aside the cloth over the entrance.

"I gave orders not to be disturbed!" Tolem said, turning around and thrusting his scarlet cloak behind him.

"But my lord, you asked for news about which of your guards survived the attack," the servant persisted nervously.

"Not now, you fool! Get out, and send everyone away."

"Send them away? But where, my lord? Some of your guards are wounded."

Tolem drew his sword and raised the tip to the servant's face. "Send them far enough away that, should I exit my tent, I will not find them within the reach of my blade," he said.

Turning in haste, the servant stumbled over his own feet as he scrambled out. Hurried footsteps echoed from outside as several others moved out of the reach of Tolem's anger. Sheathing his sword, Tolem turned away with a sigh.

Several minutes passed as the daylight outside the tent slowly faded into the darkening shades of evening. Tolem remained standing, occasionally moving from one side of the tent to the other, and when the tent began to grow too dark, he lit a few candles.

At last, the flap to the entrance of the tent moved again, but this time a cloaked figure entered.

"I sent for you hours ago," Tolem snapped as he turned to face the visitor.

"Your pardon, Lord Tolem. My master sent me in his place."

Tolem clenched his fist. "Does he think he can ignore me?" he asked.

The figure bowed and then he drew out a heavy purse of coins, which he set on a table. As he did so, the gleam of a bracer on one arm shone in the candlelight.

"Here is compensation for the stallion that you lost in the raid."

Tolem's brow furrowed.

"Tell your master that I still demand to meet with him. I never sanctioned this attack, and I will have my best horse returned."

The cloaked figure responded with a low laugh.

"Don't you think that would look rather suspicious? All the other lords have lost their finest horses, but you manage to reclaim yours?"

Tolem drew his sword and held it toward the cloaked figure. "I will not be spoken to with such insolence by a negligent knight," he said.

The cloaked figure grew quiet, but he gestured beyond the tent before speaking. "My lord, if I do not leave this tent alive, then neither do you. I trust you remember your last meeting with my master?"

Tolem slowly lowered the sword, but he still appeared angered.

"Remind your master that I know all. I could tell the others."

The visitor laughed, but in such a dark, self-confident manner that Lord Tolem paled. His threat had not gained him the response he had hoped for.

"And what would that accomplish?" the voice from behind the cloak asked. "It is not my master they distrust. It is you."

Though he was still pale, Tolem's dismay faded into rage.

"If he planned from the beginning to accuse me, why wait so long to do it?"

"It was never my master's intention to accuse anyone," the cloaked figure answered coolly. "However, it will go badly for you if you attempt to betray him."

Tolem backed away and sheathed his sword as the veracity of those words crawled over him, but he still cast a resentful gaze at the figure standing opposite to him.

"Your master is very careful in managing his secrets, isn't he? But even he could not control what happened in the last race."

The cloaked figure no longer seemed amused.

"Yes, I heard about it. But I was also told revenge might have been taken on the girl if your fool of a rider had been able to control his urge to gloat and not sent a threat to Derreth."

"What threat?"

"The note, my lord. Did you not recognize Molnar's rough handwriting when you saw it? My master said Molnar had no reason to send it to the girl. He believes Derreth passed it off to Beristo's trainer at the end of the race."

"If your master knew as much, why did he not say so? We could have denounced their story about the threat and arrested the girl."

The cloaked figure took a step closer.

"By doing so, my master would reveal he knew your rider well enough to recognize his handwriting and know his plans. That would appear rather curious, would it not?"

Tolem scowled.

"No more so than you serving another lord."

The cloaked figure drew back and bowed. "I serve both of you," he said. "And in spirit of that service, let me urge you to forget your anger. You will gain nothing from attempting to reveal my master. Take the profits you gain from your business with him, and be content."

Tolem's scowl lessened though he still looked displeased, and the cloaked visitor departed without offering more.

As he traveled on foot, darkness covered the town before Derreth reached Joviann's inn. When he knocked, she opened the door cautiously, but Joviann smiled upon recognizing him and quickly let him enter. As she returned to the kitchen, Inesca appeared from one of the rooms upstairs and hurried down to greet him.

Derreth felt relief sweep through him when he saw that she had arrived safely, but Inesca's smile faded the moment she caught sight of him.

"What happened to your face?"

Derreth touched his lip. "Not all lords are like Beristo," he explained. "Lord Edgerr blamed me for the loss of Halon."

Inesca poured some water on a cloth and moved to clean his face, but then she hesitated. Derreth started to take the rag from her, but he stopped as he noticed her expression. He drew a chair closer, sat down in front of her, and waited.

Inesca smiled and wiped the blood from his nose and lip. Derreth winced when she began a bit too eagerly, and Inesca drew her hand back with an apologetic smile.

"Sorry. I've never been great at this sort of thing. Father always said I was too impatient …"

She suddenly halted, and Derreth studied her in silence. It was still difficult for him to think of his father living another life in the East Province after the war, but now he considered that Inesca would have looked after him if he was injured or sick. For a moment, Derreth sat in silence before he said, "There is no reason for you to stop unless you wish to."

Inesca slowly lifted the rag and began to clean his face again. As she finished, Derreth caught her arm gently to prevent her from leaving.

"How did he die?"

Inesca met his gaze, and he saw tears in her eyes.

"He refused to bow to the whims of a sheriff in the East Province until one day, he was attacked. He made it home to me, but I couldn't …"

She started to turn away, but Derreth drew her closer and embraced her as she tried to hold back her grief. Amid his own confusion, Derreth felt his father's loss anew, and he could hardly restrain a few tears falling from his own eyes.

But after a short time, Inesca steadied herself and stepped back.

"How long can you stay before you must return to Lord Edgerr?" she asked, wiping her eyes with her hand.

Derreth breathed out slowly as he took a seat again.

"He has given me leave to search for the horses. I must return to him eventually, but for a little while, I may travel freely."

Inesca nodded as she sat down next to him.

"We'll search together then."

Derreth shook his head. "No, Inesca," he said. "I will escort you back to Kestorn. Then I will seek the horses."

She opened her mouth to protest, but he put his hand on her arm.

"You were the one who said that Kestorn should be told we survived the attack, and I will not risk chasing after these hooded men with you beside me. It places you in too much danger."

"But if you find Nycor, I must be there."

Derreth smiled.

"If he will not come with me, then I will set him free. We may go to look for him together if I am forced to do that, but you cannot come with me to seek these enemies."

Inesca frowned.

"And you should not go alone."

Derreth offered her a faint smile.

"Perhaps I will have some of my friends with me, but I want you and Kestorn to stay together while I am away."

Inesca looked at him with some surprise. "Are you going to tell him?" she asked.

Derreth smiled encouragingly and nodded as Joviann and Eimon arrived with some food for them. Joviann began to talk with them, but the meal was brief as both of her guests grew weary.

Chapter 33

The journey to Morret required two days of travel by the main roads, but it was the morning of the third day of travel before Derreth and Inesca neared Gorben's house on the outer edge of the city. Their pace was slow as the bay mare had to carry them both when they did not walk alongside the horse, and Derrreth chose paths that diverged from the main roads to avoid anyone catching sight of Inesca.

Now, as they approached the last miles to the merchant's home, Inesca walked at Derreth's side as he led the mare with a gentle, yet firm hold on the reins. Since he still felt like a stranger at times, Inesca had moments of uncertainty in his presence. Yet, she reflected with a smile upon the days and nights they had spent together on the road.

Once he claimed her as his sister, Derreth refused to step back from being a protective older brother, but he also possessed a warm sense of humor and a deep sense of compassion that Inesca had managed to glimpse a few times when he lowered his guard. It both pained and comforted her when she noticed aspects of Derreth that reminded her of their father. But often, she kept these thoughts to herself.

Despite his doubts about his father, Derreth had been willing to speak to her about some of what he remembered. He tried to brush aside his bitterness, but Inesca could see he felt abandoned. In such moments during their conversations, she desperately wished she had the answers to reassure him and justify their father's actions, but she did not know how to do so. And what would Kestorn think when Derreth told him that she was their sister?

"You are unusually quiet this morning," Derreth said, disrupting her thoughts.

Inesca met his gaze, and she suddenly felt more at ease as she noted his smile.

"I had a question in my mind last night before I fell asleep. I've heard that our father was both a rider and a knight. Sirryn called him Sir Arryn of Fortur, so does that mean he rode for Lord Salistom in the races?"

Derreth shook his head.

"Riders may be slaves or free men, but either way, they usually have no choice with regard to the lord that they ride for. Our father rode for Lord Tolem's father until his death, and then he rode only one year for Lord Tolem," he explained.

"Tolem?" Inesca asked with a disgusted expression.

Derreth huffed.

"I believe we can guess why he quit to become a knight instead. No doubt, Lord Tolem's style of racing did not meet his approval. He was born a free Rynarian and could choose to change his life. Even if he could not race for a different lord, he was able to choose another path."

Inesca's brow furrowed.

"He meant for you and Kestorn to be free as well. I wish we could have spoken to …" and she halted as she almost mentioned the Raegond. "To those who knew more of him. They must have some answers."

Derreth turned his gaze to the forest ahead of them.

"After I have seen them again, I will tell you what they shared with me."

Inesca grew quiet, but then Derreth reached into a leather bag he had placed over the saddle. When he withdrew his hand, she recognized the green and gold cloth in which she had placed the knight. He held it out to her, and she took it with some surprise and unwrapped the knight.

"I found it among Kestorn's things, and I recognized it at once. Father carved it for me when I was a boy."

Inesca traced it with her fingers, thinking the blackened wood had seen better days.

"Jirro stole my things one night and tried to burn them," she said. "That's how it ended up like this. But after the attack in Monterr, I gave it to Kestorn, hoping he might recognize it."

Derreth shook his head. "He was too young to remember it, but this was important to me as a boy. And when our father had to leave for the war, I asked him to keep it close. He tried to refuse me, but I felt certain he needed it. I'm not sure of the reasons now, but perhaps I thought it would lead him back to me. I never expected to see it again after others said he died."

Inesca gazed down at the knight before holding it out to Derreth.

"He kept it safe, so he could return it to you. I found it with the ring and the medallion when he told me where to look."

Derreth took the knight back, before drawing the ring and cord out from under his tunic.

"I know these became important to you, Inesca," he said, glancing her way and tucking the ring and cord away again. "But let me hold onto them for now."

Inesca nodded. "Such tokens of his old life are hardly mine to claim, but I think he would be glad to know they allowed us to meet," she said.

Derreth grew quiet and thoughtful as they walked on together for several minutes, but at last he said, "Although I wish I could have been trained as a knight, there were days I loved being a rider. And yet, I would have traded every horse and every race for one more day with him."

Inesca listened in silence. *Until this year, I had my father every day of my life. But his days with our father are only distant memories,* she thought. Her steps lagged, and Derreth slowed his own pace as he shot her a questioning look.

"When I first spoke of him to you ..." Inesca took a breath and paused for a moment. "It was thoughtless of me. I can only guess how painful this is for you, Derreth."

He put his hand on her shoulder as they walked on together.

"I have more to ask forgiveness for than you, Inesca." He smiled faintly. "Are you certain you wish to claim us as your brothers?"

The warmth in his tone lifted her mood, and Inesca's eyes brightened.

"It is too late to retract such a claim, and you know it."

Derreth chuckled as he drew his hand back, and Inesca's expression fell again. "How do you think he will take the news?" she asked.

The horse halted beside them as Derreth stopped again. Inesca felt suddenly uncomfortable as she observed the familiar hills around Morret. Soon they would be standing in front of Gorben's house.

"I do not think you have anything to fear," Derreth said. "Kestorn was so young when our father ... well, when he disappeared. It has always been different for him."

Inesca listened quietly as she considered how her presence had affected Derreth's understanding of the past. *So much of it must seem distorted and confusing to him now,* she considered.

Derreth forced a smile. "But I suspect he will be angry with me," he said. "So let us get this over with."

Despite her fears, Inesca managed a smile, but then Derreth halted her again as his expression grew serious.

"We discussed this last night, but remember that you should not tell Kestorn about my involvement with those whom you met outside Bartrir. Someday I will reveal it to him, but at present, the others would be displeased if I told him."

Inesca nodded as she walked on with him, and they entered Morret and began to approach the house. She clasped his arm as her steps grew hesitant again, but Derreth shot her a comforting look.

Before he could speak again, Laisi found them as she was returning to the house with one of her father's servants.

"What a relief it is to see both of you," she said with surprise. "We received word of the attack in Bartrir yesterday, and Kestorn swore he would leave tomorrow morning to find you if we did not hear of you soon."

Derreth smiled. "I know I have you to thank for delaying him, Laisi. We are both well, but I must speak with my brother before I go to your father," he said.

"Of course. Kestorn was just in the stable."

Derreth thanked her and began to lead the mare away, and Laisi asked the servant to assist him as she remained with Inesca.

"I should ask your pardon for sending you with the letter to Derreth," Laisi said with concern as she faced Inesca. "Kestorn was right. It was too dangerous."

Inesca smiled. "I am glad I went. It was right for Kestorn to stay here with you."

But as her gaze turned back to follow Derreth, she saw Kestorn emerge from the stable and embrace his brother. Inesca felt her throat tighten as she watched Derreth greet him and then step back to speak to Kestorn. The servant took the mare into the stable, and Derreth drew Kestorn aside. He turned to notice her as they moved away from the stable, and he smiled, appearing pleased to see her return safely. But as Derreth began to speak, Kestorn turned back toward him again.

"Inesca! It is wonderful to see you have returned unharmed," a warm voice said. Inesca tensed and turned around.

Gorben walked to his daughter's side, and Inesca realized that Laisi had been watching her with a curious gaze.

"Thank you, sir," Inesca said with a distracted reply. She shot him a brief smile and then turned back to observe Derreth and Kestorn.

"Has Derreth returned too? We will be a merry house tonight," Gorben said happily. "I should go and welcome him."

But Laisi held him back, and Inesca shifted uncomfortably beside them.

"Derreth had an important matter to discuss with Kestorn. And we should consider tonight's meal now that we know we have guests," Laisi said.

The rest of their conversation faded away as Laisi walked with her father into the house. Inesca's heart beat loudly in her ears as she watched the two brothers but could not hear what was said.

Derreth kept one hand on Kestorn's shoulder as he spoke, and Kestorn shook his head. Then he retreated a few steps, but when he turned and saw Inesca, he stopped. She recognized the confusion in his eyes and felt frozen until Derreth beckoned to her. With slow steps, she approached them.

"Kes, it is as I told you. Our father didn't die in the war. And the reason I know this is because of Inesca." Derreth drew closer to her and put his hand on her back. "She is our sister."

Kestorn looked from Derreth to her without speaking. Inesca felt that she could hardly breathe each time his gaze swung to her, but eventually, she dared to take a step toward him. Only when Kestorn's gaze softened with affection and he suddenly leaned closer, swiftly embracing her, did Inesca feel the tension leave her.

"You believe it," she said with some relief as she returned his embrace.

"How could I doubt that you are my sister?" Kestorn asked with a smile as he drew back and faced her. But then his expression fell as some thought occurred to him. "You said your father died months ago."

Tears came to Inesca's eyes, bright blue eyes like her father's and like Kestorn's. And she saw her pain reflected in his eyes.

"Yes, I wish we could have all met before that time."

Derreth stepped forward. "I know you have questions, Kestorn, so we will talk more, but Inesca did not know who we were until after the race in Sassot. Since that time, she has been trying to find a way to tell us," he said.

Kestorn's eyes widened as he faced his brother. "And how long have you known?" he asked.

Derreth's expression did not change.

"She told me not long before the race in Farcost, but I had my doubts until this week. I wanted to wait to tell you until I knew it was the truth."

Kestorn took a step back, though he cast a cold glare at his brother. "Even if you had doubts, I had a right to know. And you forbade her from telling me, did you not?" he said.

Derreth nodded. "I did. Blame me, not her for the secrecy."

Kestorn turned away, but Inesca darted in front of him.

"Please don't let this day end like this, Kestorn. You must have the same questions that Derreth has. I wish I could tell you why our father went to the East Province and why he didn't try to return to you sooner. Derreth wanted to give you those answers, but we don't have them yet."

Kestorn listened and then he faced Derreth again. "What has changed?" he asked. "Why do you no longer have any doubts?"

"I learned that a few others knew our father did not die in the Battle of Tortesra, and I hope to gain more answers soon."

Kestorn frowned. "But you do not intend for me to join you," he said.

"You are needed here," Derreth said gesturing back to Gorben's house. "Or at least, wherever Laisi and her family go, that is where you should be. And I want Inesca to stay with you."

Inesca listened quietly, but she turned and glanced at Kestorn to see how he would respond. He sighed and moved restlessly for a moment before saying, "So be it, as long as you return and share what you learn."

Derreth smiled faintly. "I will," he said. "But today, Inesca and I have other things to discuss with you. And we will neglect the hospitality of Gorben and his family if we remain out here any longer."

Chapter 34

After only one day of rest and answering Kestorn's questions, Derreth received a note from a messenger and insisted that it was time for him to leave. Inesca suspected that he had received word from the Raegond to meet them, especially since he grew stern whenever she asked him to change his mind and let her accompany him.

Kestorn also appeared unsettled by his departure, but he accepted it on the condition that Derreth return to them within the month and bring them news of what he had learned. He also demanded to know where Derreth was headed.

"See that you tell no one else, but I am going to the Nafgil River." Derreth sighed. "You will not remember, but we spent time with our father and mother there before you were three years old. I will meet a friend of our father's there as he knows the place as well," Derreth explained.

And then he was gone, and however glad Inesca was for Kestorn to know the truth, she still felt uneasy watching Derreth leave. But there was not much time to dwell upon her discontent. Gorben's intention to travel to Nantos and buy new goods had been delayed by rain and warnings of attacks by the Raegond on the roads. As the weather changed, his mind turned to business again.

Kestorn agreed to ride to the outer road and inquire about conditions from passing travelers, but once he left the city behind, he noticed someone following him and rode back to confront his shadow.

"You know it isn't safe out here. I asked you to remain behind," Kestorn said as he shot a look of annoyance into the trees near the road.

Inesca led one of Gorben's horses out of the forest, and she held up a bow with a determined expression.

"You could have enemies out here. I'll stay out of sight, but I'm not going back," she said.

Kestorn sighed as he noticed the quiver of arrows on her back and gestured to them. "I hope you know how to shoot."

Inesca smiled. "I won't waste an arrow here, but remind me to show you when we return to Gorben's home," she said.

Kestorn huffed, but he smiled faintly before he started to continue along the road.

"Keep to the trees, and don't draw attention to yourself."

⁂

After a few hours riding along the road and speaking with travelers, Kestorn began to think he had enough news. All the reports had sounded promising, and Kestorn started to begin the ride back to Morret when he heard the approach of men and horses.

Armed men in red tunics and gray cloaks guided their horses toward Morret until Kestorn rode out into their path. The leader halted his company and cast a glaring reproach at him.

"I am Captain Pyron. These men and I have important business in Morret. Who are you to delay us?"

Kestorn scoffed at the man's tone.

"It is only a short delay, captain. I have no wish to linger here talking to you, either, but for the sake of a friend, I want to know the state of the roads to Nantos."

Captain Pyron scowled and drew his sword.

"Move out of the way, fool."

Kestorn cast a cold look at him, but he began to move aside. One of Pyron's men grew impatient and moved to strike him anyway, but then another horse and rider burst onto the road and moved between them.

Inesca drew an arrow and held it near her bow, but she did not draw it back and prepare to fire. She turned her gaze turned to the leader as she said, "Captain Pyron, we met in Monterr. I still wish to find Sir Coltar to seek his help, but I cannot allow you to attack this man. He meant no harm to you or your companions."

A look of recognition appeared on Pyron's face, and he commanded his men to leave the strangers alone.

"I remember you, but I have not yet been able to deliver your message to Sir Coltar. Yet I know his latest duties often keep in him in the forests near Pilun. If you wish to find him, that is where you should go."

Inesca lowered the bow and arrow as she smiled, but Kestorn frowned and pressed closer.

"Those are strange lands. How generous of you to send my friend into danger to seek a knight who may or may not be found."

Captain Pyron rode around them, casting a cold gaze at Kestorn.

"Sir Coltar must tend to the defense of Rynar in many distant regions of the Six Realms. But I will not be delayed longer, and I have no more words for impudent peasants."

He commanded his men to ride on to Morret, and Kestorn watched them disappear before turning to Inesca.

"Do not think of riding out there," Kestorn said. "You are not going after this knight."

Inesca looked at him in surprise. "Our father told me to find him. Don't you see? Sir Coltar might have the answers we've been waiting for," she explained.

Kestorn's brow furrowed. "But you have us now. You don't need Coltar," he said. He took her hand in his and clasped it firmly. "Let Derreth chase after the answers to our questions. My sister belongs here with me."

Inesca grew quiet, and after a moment, she put her other hand over his. "All right, Kestorn. Let's go back. It's starting to grow dark."

He smiled and let go of her hand as they rode along the road together.

Chapter 35

The ride to the Nafgil River brought memories to Derreth's mind that he had believed lost before this day. For so long, his concerns had been only about the present: his brother, the races, the attacks, and attempts to frame the Raegond. He had forgotten what it was like to let his mind wander over the past and to remember things like the sound of his father's laugh, the smile on his mother's face, and Kestorn's unsteady attempts at walking as a toddler.

As he neared a place where the branches of a large tree had grown so long that they rested against a rising slope of rocks, Derreth halted his mount in the shade. Another figure rode out of the shadows, and Derreth urged his horse closer.

"No more secrets about my father, Tyrus."

The leader of the Raegond nodded.

"I know this conversation is long overdue. But first, I will give you this," Tyrus said. He handed Derreth a folded letter as he guided his horse closer. Opening it, Derreth recognized his father's handwriting.

Tyrus,

What I have uncovered will take everything from me. Despite the price I have paid for the truth, it is still difficult to believe that Slotair is being supported by one whom he wishes to overthrow. He doesn't realize that he's being used by one of the lords. My service to the Raegond was discovered before I could learn which one it was. And now I know only that my enemies are coming for me.

As long as I remain alive, my sons are in danger. But if I die, then they may be left alone to grow up in peace. Seeing now what this path I have chosen is going to cost me, I here confess that I regret the oath I swore to aid you as a friend to the Raegond. It is one thing to risk your life in the midst of battle, but it is another to see everything you have ripped from your hands and perhaps lose it for all time.

There is only one friend I can trust. He is childless and never seems to be in want. It is to his hands that I will entrust my sons' futures. You will forgive me when I tell you to stay away from them, Tyrus. In serving the Raegond, my sons would someday share my fate. And I know my enemies will be watching them closely.

If the plan of my friend succeeds, I may still live to return and see my sons again even though soon I will be dead to all I have known. Do not try to help me or my sons. That is all you can do to repay me.

May God protect the Six Realms of Rynar while they stand.
Arryn

"Why did you never tell me that our enemy was one of the lords?" Derreth asked as he faced Tyrus again.

Tyrus urged his horse on toward the river. "Come, your note mentioned a place your father might have left a message for you. We will talk on the way."

Derreth spurred his mount to follow Tyrus's horse, but then he glanced behind them. "Can we be certain that I have not been followed?" he asked.

Tyrus did not look back.

"If anyone has tried to do so, they will regret it. We have our own watching this forest." But with a glance at him, Tyrus offered a faint smile and said, "I hope you left your sister somewhere safe this time."

Derreth let out a weary breath as he nodded. "Yes. She's with Kestorn, but she wanted to come."

Tyrus turned away. "It is good you kept her away," he said. "We will protect her, but she is not one of us. I still wish she had not seen our faces."

Derreth's expression grew stern. "She will keep our secrets, but you have kept enough from me," he said. "Why did you not tell me about this information from my father sooner?"

"You are in the service of a lord," Tyrus said. "If you saw him engage in anything suspicious, I knew you would report it to us. And I believed telling you would only endanger your life."

Derreth rode in silence for a moment as he glanced at the letter in his hand.

"It sounds as though this enemy used Slotair and his rebels to weaken the strength of the other lords, but his plans must have extended farther than that. What else did my father uncover that forced him to leave?"

"Your father gave us the information that was used to win the war with the rebels. He found out where the enemy was going to be and told us that Slotair was a mere puppet being used by a far more powerful enemy."

"Why have you not discovered which of the lords was behind the plot?"

"As your father says in the letter, our enemy realized how close your father was getting to the truth. He abandoned the scheme he had been attempting to work through Slotair and the rebels. By the time the war was over, we had lost any hope we had of identifying him. And your father had disappeared to protect you."

"He was right about this enemy watching me," Derreth said as he glanced around at their surroundings again. "The reason the Raegond never had any trouble until I joined them is because I was the only one this enemy knew to follow. Whoever he is, he is surely the one behind the recent attacks."

"I suspected that as well, and I failed your father by not keeping you out of this," Tyrus said. "I hoped that after you became one of us, we could protect you and try to repay your father. I did not believe you were still being watched after all these years."

"But who is the friend he mentions in the letter?" Derreth asked. "No one cared for me or Kestorn after we were told our father died in the war. And he cannot mean Lord Edgerr because he has two sons, both of whom were born before my father disappeared."

"I wish I knew. But as you can see, your father wanted me to stay away from you and your brother. There were some secrets he refused to share with me. You see, he was not a true member of the Raegond, only a friend to our cause."

"It sounds like he didn't fully trust you," Derreth said.

"You never trusted us when it came to your brother," Tyrus reminded him. "You always wanted him to be left out of things and yet still protected. I'm not sure if you can have it both ways."

Derreth guided them the rest of the way until they reached the top of a hill overlooking the Nafgil River.

"My father and I used to fish along this bank," Derreth said as he stared down at the rocks and brush below. Everything appeared the same even though he had not been here in over twenty years.

After dismounting and walking closer to the water, Derreth turned to his left and weaved through some trees before finding the cave that he and his father had explored. Tyrus followed him to the entrance.

"This place is well hidden. I never would have known it was here from the hill," Tyrus said.

Derreth inspected the mouth of the cave.

"It is smaller than I remember, but I was a boy when last I played here. I can still fit inside, and if my father had planned to leave anything behind for me to find, he would have known to leave it here."

Tyrus nodded. "I will wait with the horses. You will know best what to look for in this place," he said.

Derreth stepped into the cool darkness of the cave. After a minute, he came to a portion of the cave that was extremely narrow. Derreth found that he could squeeze through the gap. Pushing on ahead, he drew himself into the hollow chamber on the other side.

Light streamed through a crevice high upon the cave wall, allowing Derreth to inspect the chamber without straining his eyes or requesting a candle from Tyrus. Turning slowly around the room, Derreth searched the rock formations for anything that his father might have left for him. Yet after moments of searching, he found nothing.

"It was a small hope," Derreth said aloud. He sighed to himself as he leaned against the rocks behind him.

His hand reached out and found a wide, yet flat rock near his side. Looking down, Derreth remembered how as a boy, he had thought the rock looked like a low table and the smaller ones beside it could have been chairs. A memory suddenly returned to him, one of sitting here with his father. Kneeling, he stretched his hand under the overhanging ledge and felt along the cave floor. In moments, his fingers found the edge of a wooden box.

After seizing it and pulling it out into the light, Derreth used the tip of a hunting knife to pry the lid open. A single roll of parchment lay inside, and it contained the following message.

My son,

In hopes that you might come back here to remember better times, I have left this message to provide some form of explanation to you. I trust your new guardian to pass the truth on to you when you are old enough, but I feel that I owe you some words of my own. This was not how I wanted our lives to turn out, and I hope that someday you will forgive me.

As a reward for my service to the lords of the Six Realms, I will be entitled to land in the northeast edge of Trineth. Your guardian will possess it until you come of age.

Watch over your brother, and know that it was never my wish for us to be separated. I know that we have both struggled since the death of your mother. For a time, I believed that I had found my purpose again by chasing a quest that took me away from the thoughts of her death. But in doing so, I have failed you as a father. I should have stayed close to you and your brother, for now I may have lost you forever.

I can offer you nothing else except to tell you that I shall carry the memories of my sons with me to my last breath. I will trust God to provide for you when I cannot, and I pray that you will not turn away from Him as a result of my failings.

You may wonder why I did not take you and your brother with me, and these past days, I have entertained every hope that might allow me to do so. But I know you are being watched. If I go to you, we will all be slain. If I leave, you will be spared.

Someday, if I learn it is safe for me to return, I will come back to find you. Look after your brother until that time, and take care, my son. You have enemies in the Six Realms who may still be watching you.

    Derreth read the letter several times as he held his father's final words to him. If he had found this letter a year ago, its message would not have made sense to him and might have stirred up feelings of resentment and anger. But now, he sensed the brokenness of his father's tone. And it only pained him to think that they had not been able to meet again before his father died.

    Carrying the letter with him, Derreth pressed himself back through the narrow passage and walked out of the cave until he found Tyrus.

    "Did you find something?" Tyrus asked.

"A note of farewell. But it does not provide answers except to confirm that my father intended for a guardian to give me and Kestorn a better life than the one we have had."

Derreth handed Tyrus the letter so he could read it.

"This part here is strange," Tyrus said, pointing to the beginning of the letter. "Your father says he is going to be given land in return for his service. He must mean for his supposed death in battle."

"Why would the lords give land to someone who was dead?"

"There have been times where they give land to a knight's family in his name. It is a means of providing for those who have lost fathers in war if a guardian is ready to claim them. But although your father was honored by name after the battle, nothing was said about giving him land."

"That does not mean that this so-called guardian did not get it," Derreth said. "In the other letter, my father mentioned a friend. Someone who helped him fake his death so his enemies would stop looking for him. This same friend was supposed to act as a guardian for me and my brother."

"And you believe this friend may not have followed through with your father's wishes?" Tyrus asked. "Perhaps he was killed in the battle, and thus, he was unable to help you."

"But someone brought back the news of my father's death. His body was never found, but the story of his death in battle was well-known. It had to start somewhere. Do you remember where the story came from?"

"It was a long time ago, Derreth."

Derreth shot him a determined look, and Tyrus drew back as he searched his memories.

"Cartul shared it with me. He had been traveling with some of the knights returning from the East Province after the Battle of Tortesra. One of them said he observed your father chasing after Slotair, but in the struggle that followed, Slotair pushed your father from his horse and over the Tartori Cliffs. Your father managed to catch hold of Slotair, and they both fell to their deaths. Slotair's mangled corpse was found and destroyed, but your father's body was not recovered. Of course, having read your father's letter, I knew the story was false. And it was a pitiful excuse for a lie. Your father had never been knocked from a horse by another man, and that weasel Slotair was hardly strong enough to do it."

"But who told the story?"

"It was one of the other knights. Cartul never told me which one it was. But that land your father refers to here, I know who owns the territory. It is Sir Coltar."

The Legacy of the Lost Rider

Derreth listened quietly. He might have heard the name before from Lord Edgerr, but he couldn't remember for certain.

"He's had it for at least seventeen years or more now," Tyrus continued. "I know, because he keeps the border guarded and doesn't like to have people cut across his land."

Derreth took the letter back from Tyrus and folded it before sticking it in his cloak. Then he walked quickly back to his horse.

"Derreth, where are you going? The lords cannot know about this letter. You'll never be able to convince them that the land belongs to you and your brother without telling them the truth about your father, and you know you can't risk that."

"I'm not going to the lords," Derreth insisted. "I'm going after a knight."

Tyrus grabbed his arm. "You believe Coltar is the friend your father mentioned?" he asked.

Derreth drew his arm out of Tyrus's grasp and said, "I doubt that he is anyone's friend."

"And what if he turns out to be what you suspect? Coltar will have armed men riding with him after all these attacks. If you accuse him of stealing land from your father, he could have you killed. And if he is connected with your father's enemies, he may try to kill you on sight."

Derreth mounted his horse. "Can you lend me a sword?" he asked.

Tyrus remained standing in front of the horse, ignoring the question. "We must face this together, Derreth," he said. "I will gather the rest of the Raegond."

Derreth gave no sign of dismounting.

"Gather them, and send Ruesord to guard Kestorn and Inesca. I left them in Morret, but with all these attacks, someone might still seek to harm them. I shall ride on to seek this knight. If you and the others come soon, I will delay confronting him until you arrive, but I will not linger here while he enjoys one more moment of his treachery."

Tyrus studied him and then walked to his horse and drew out a spare sword. As he returned and handed it up to Derreth, he said, "Be careful. We do not know what may be waiting for you."

With only a sliver of moonlight in the sky, Inesca quietly led a horse into the hills beyond Morret. Gorben's gelding, Poleg, readily followed the gentle hands that had been feeding him extra oats and sugar since her arrival in his master's home. Inesca patted his neck in gratitude for his silence. With such a calm and easy-going horse, she had no trouble slipping quietly from the stable without waking anyone.

Some regret slowed her steps as she thought of the note left behind in her room. She hoped only that Kestorn would not try to come after her, but she feared he would. Perhaps Laisi could convince him to remain and wait for her return. Poleg nudged her arm as if curious about her hesitation, and Inesca climbed into the saddle.

As her thoughts turned to Gorben and her additional regret in borrowing one of his horses, Inesca remembered the conversation she had shared with him two days earlier.

She had been helping the merchant sort through some recent acquisitions, when Gorben had said, *"I'm delighted to discover that when Laisi marries Kestorn, I'll not only claim Derreth as a son, but you shall also become a daughter to us, Inesca."*

Inesca smiled.

"I hadn't thought of it that way. Is it typical for families in Rynar to adopt the sisters and brothers of the ones their children marry?"

Gorben patted her on the shoulder.

"It depends on the families, but as you and Derreth have no one else, my wife and I wish you to consider yourselves part of our house." But then Gorben's expression turned grim. *"But I fear there is little I can do for Derreth. His service to Lord Edgerr will often keep him far from us."*

Inesca frowned. *"But Lord Edgerr might release him yet,"* she said.

"Ah, if only it could be so, my dear. But I do not believe that will ever come to pass. This reprieve is only temporary."

Inesca lifted one brow. *"But he released Kestorn. Why couldn't he release Derreth too?"*

Gorben shook his head.

"You know Kestorn is like a son to me, and he has a gift with horses. As do you." Gorben chuckled. *"It must be passed down from your father, I suppose."*

Inesca smiled, but she wondered where this was headed when Gorben's face sobered again, and he continued. *"From a lord's perspective, Kestorn is a gamble. Sometimes it pays off, and sometimes the risk is greater than the reward."*

"Is it not that way with Derreth as well?" Inesca asked.

Gorben walked over to some bundles of cloth and unwrapped the outer layer for her to see what rested under the protective covering.

"Which of these catches your eye?"

Inesca walked closer and surveyed two kinds of cloth. Turning away from the ivory linen, she pointed to the silk turquoise fabric that caught the light.

"And so it is with all my customers," Gorben noted. "But there are times when the traders who deal in silk cannot sell me as much as I might wish to buy. This is never the case when I buy linen. And then there are times when I have bought too much silk, but because it is more expensive, I may encounter customers who are unable to buy it."

"And the linen is something your customers can afford, even if they are not lords, knights, or councilmen," Inesca considered.

Gorben nodded. "As a merchant, I can rely on this," he said, raising the linen in his hand. "Thus, I will never cease to buy and sell it."

Inesca's expression fell. Then she asked, "Has Derreth truly proven so valuable to Lord Edgerr?"

Gorben sighed as he wrapped up the cloth again.

"He has. In my memory, no other rider has won as many races for Lord Edgerr. I was surprised that Derreth did not win the last race he entered, but Kestorn told me the flood delayed him."

Inesca's eyes widened.

"No, it wasn't the flood. It was another rider who slowed him down," she said softly. "But from what Derreth has said, I did not think he had Lord Edgerr's favor."

Gorben huffed. "Lord Edgerr is proud. He looks for ways to humble those who offend him, but it doesn't mean he has any intention of letting Derreth go."

Inesca's gaze swept over Gorben's other wares, and she noticed a scarlet fabric.

"Could someone else convince him to release Derreth?" she asked.

Gorben looked at her with surprise.

"Someone else? Who did you have in mind?"

"A knight, for example."

Gorben considered her words. "I can't see why a knight would make it his business to interfere, but some are tasked with finding and sending other men to train as knights in Valmontes," he explained. "With the races being in such disarray, a knight could perhaps persuade Lord Edgerr to release Derreth." As if changing his mind, Gorben shook his head. "It is a wishful thought, but not likely to happen, my dear."

Yet this thought had remained with her as she continually remembered Captain Pyron's message. Inspecting a few maps had shown her that she could reach the forests near the town of Pilun without having to leave Trineth. With just a few days of traveling north, she could reach this place.

Even if he will not assist Derreth, Sir Coltar will be able to explain these *mysteries about my father,* she thought. Inesca urged Poleg into a gallop as they passed beyond the hills, and she grew eager to cover a fair distance while the night lasted. In this moment, she wished Nycor was with her, and she hoped he had escaped his captors. But as her thoughts turned to her father, Inesca took comfort in the knowledge that she would at last find the man he had spoken of before he died.

Epilogue

As night fell over the realm of Trineth, a cloaked figure slipped silently to a lone wooden hall that rested a mile beyond the nearest town. As he entered and climbed the stairs to the second level, the warmth of candlelight greeted him but failed to disturb much of the darkness lingering in the corners of the hall. At the far end, a figure seated in a chair was barely visible. The newcomer drew closer and bowed.

"Have you spoken with Tolem?"

"As you commanded, master. He has grown compliant again."

The one seated in the chair rose and faced him.

"Never assume a fool will not act upon his impulses. Tolem may yet try to betray me, but if he does, I am prepared. Can you say the same of the fools in your keeping, Sir Coltar?"

The knight removed the hood of his cloak as he faced his master.

"I am close, my lord. I know you wish the sons of Arryn dead, but there is still a use …"

A cold, scornful laugh interrupted him.

"That is what you told me of Arryn. And he was nearly the end of my endeavors."

Sir Coltar fell silent as his master walked closer to the smoldering ashes in the hearth.

"I was willing to indulge this absurd plan of yours while they were merely boys condemned to short lives in the races. But now, they survive when they should not. And the Raegond eludes me still. Did you not tell me that your spy should have uncovered them at their latest meeting?"

Sir Coltar bowed again. "I will have them soon, my lord," he said. "But that is why I need Derreth alive. Once I have the Raegond, Derreth will die."

His master grabbed a thin iron rod with a pointed end and placed the tip among the warm embers in the hearth.

"And what of your last failure?"

Sir Coltar smiled. "Arryn is dead. Your will has been carried out, my lord. I told you I would dispose of him once he was no longer needed."

His master turned and raised the hot iron to Sir Coltar's neck, hovering just above it.

"I will not accept mistakes this time, Coltar. You are certain it is at an end?"

"I am," the knight said firmly.

The hot metal remained close to his skin.

"And this Eastern girl. Who is she?"

Sir Coltar appeared surprised, but then he frowned. "There is no connection, my lord. But if it pleases you, I will find where she is hiding," he said.

His master scoffed as he lowered the iron rod and placed it back on the hearth.

"You were not present at the last race to observe what I witnessed. Look for a connection, and then pull this weed out by its roots. She has caused enough trouble."

As his master moved toward a table in the room, Sir Coltar observed him quietly before adding, "I must meet with your other servants at Pilun to finish some business there. The Calavi are restless but are still eager to serve you. And soon, my lord, you will have the Raegond in your hands. These remaining riders will be only the first to fall."

His master turned, and the glow of candlelight illuminated his face. The gleam of relentless ambition flickered in the amber eyes of the dark figure of Lord Salistom. A gold crest, one marked with the symbol of a dragon rising above a six-point crown, sealed a black cloak around his shoulders.

"No, not the first. Many have fallen, and more remnants of Rynar's past must perish. Loyal knights, foolish lords, and the greatest offense of all, the Royal Council. All of it can burn. The death of the races was just the kindling to set it ablaze."

"Your rule of Rynar is at hand, master," Sir Coltar said with a bow. "Long live the king."

Glossary

Long vowels in pronunciations are indicated by capital letters.

The Lords of the Six Realms of Rynar (rI-nar)

    Atregar (at-tra-gar)—Lord of Farcost (far-cost), colors: turquoise and white.
    Beristo (bear-is-tO)—Lord of Ettidor (et-ti-dor), colors: green and gold.
    Edgerr (ed-ger)—Lord of Trineth (trI-neth), colors: blue and silver.
    Felond (fell-ond)—Lord of Sassot (sas-sot), colors: indigo and white.
    Salistom (sal-is-tom)—Lord of Fortur (for-tur), colors: black and gold.
    Tolem (toll-em)—Lord of Monterr (mon-tear), colors: crimson and silver.
    Mastren (mas-tren)—one of the original lords.
    Glenmir (glen-mir)—one of the original lords; the ancestor of Lord Beristo.

Riders

    Arryn (air-in)—a former rider and knight of the Six Realms.
    Arnun (ar-nun)—a rider for Lord Salistom (realm of Fortur).
    Cidonn (sid-don) a rider for Lord Salistom (realm of Fortur).
    Derreth (dare-reth)—a rider for Lord Edgerr (realm of Trineth).
    Destrod (des-trod)—a rider for Lord Felond (realm of Sassot).
    Inesca (in-es-ca)—a rider for Lord Beristo (realm of Ettidor).
    Jirro (jeer-rO)—a rider for Lord Beristo (realm of Ettidor).
    Kestorn (kes-torn)—a rider for Lord Edgerr (realm of Trineth).
    Molnar (mol-nar)—a rider for Lord Tolem (realm of Monterr).
    Segiro (sa-gir-O)—a rider for Lord Felond (realm of Sassot).
    Trestan (tres-ton)—a rider for Lord Edgerr (realm of Trineth).

Horses

    Beiru (bA-rU)—a mare in Lasnell.
    Celestro (cell-les-trO)—Lord Edgerr's golden-colored stallion often ridden by Derreth.
    Halon (hAl-on)—Lord Edgerr's red stallion often ridden by Kestorn

Nycor (nI-cor)—Inesca's dapple gray stallion with a black mane and tail.
Poleg (pol-ig)—one of Gorben's geldings.
Razur (rA-zer)—Lord Salistom's white stallion ridden by Cidonn and Arnun.
Tymo (tI-mO)—Lord Tolem's black stallion often ridden by Molnar.

Other Characters

Bercorr (bear-cor)—a knight of the Six Realms.
Cartul (car-tull)—a member of the Raegond.
Coltar (coal-tar)—a knight of the Six Realms.
Durokos (dur-O-kus)—one of Sir Bercorr's men.
Dynur (dI-nur)—a knight of the Six Realms.
Eimon (I-mon)—one of Joviann's sons.
Eisron (Is-ron)—the last king of Rynar.
Gorben (gor-ben)—a merchant from Trineth.
Hurin (hurr-in)—the son of the blacksmith, Urron, in Lasnell.
Joviann (jO-vE-ann)—a woman who runs an inn in Bartrir.
Laisi (lAy-sE)—Gorben's daughter.
Lerom (lEr-om)—a captain of Lord Edgerr's guards.
Koldoth (kOl-doth)—the father of Inesca.
Omaron (O-mar-on)—the trainer for Lord Beristo's riders.
Oreloc (or-lock)—a knight in the service of King Eisron.
Pyron (pI-ron)—the captain in the service of Sir Coltar.
Roegur (rO-gur)—a sheriff in the East Province.
Ruesord (rU-sord)—a member of the Raegond.
Salell (sal-ell)—Gorben's wife.
Sirryn (seer-rin)—a member of Lord Beristo's council.
Slotair (slO-tair)—the leader of the rebels in the Battle of Tortesra.
Teyres (tA-ress)—a king of Evalisca (the father of the original six lords).
Toares (tO-ress)—a servant of Lord Beristo.
Tyrus (tI-rus)—a member of the Raegond.

People Groups

Calavi (cal-uh-vI)—a cult forbidden in the Six Realms by King Eisron.
Evaliscans (ev-al-less-kins)—people from Evalisca (ev-al-less-ca).
the Raegond (rAy-gand)—a secret society in the Six Realms.
Rynarians (rI-nar-E-ans)—people who were born in Rynar.

Geography

Bartrir (bar-trir)—a town in the realm of Trineth.
Cerdost (ser-dost)—a town in the realm of Sassot.
Etta (et-ta)—a river that separates the East Province from Rynar and the Six Realms.
Lasnell (las-nell)—a city in the realm of Monterr.
Morret (mor-et)—a city in the realm of Trineth.
Nafgil (naf-gil)—a river in the realm of Trineth.
Naldorr (nal-door)—a forest in the north beyond the Six Realms.
Nantos (nan-tOs)—a city in the realm of Trineth.
Petrigor (pet-ri-gor)—large island nation that has been the enemy of Rynar.
Pilun (pil-oon)—a town in the realm of Trineth.
Selgoa (sel-gO-a)—an ocean south of the Six Realms.
Septamar (sep-ta-mar)—a river that runs through Rynar from north to south.
Siccre (sE-crA)—the river in Monterr that was held back by a dam.
Tortesra (tor-tes-ra)—plains in the East Province where a significant battle once took place.